Enchantment

JoAnn Durgin

ISBN: 978-0-9864076-2-8

Cover Design: DINO PICCININI (Original Design)
LYNNETTE BONNER/INDIE COVER DESIGN (Design Modifications)

Author's Note

~~♥~~

Dear Readers,

Of the twelve total novels planned for The Lewis Legacy Series (including **Prelude**, the prequel to The Lewis Legacy Series), **Enchantment** is the one installment where I strongly advise you first read at least one (and preferably more) of the preceding books in the series. While this book *can* be read on its own, each previously featured TeamWork couple, the TeamWork kids, the single volunteers, and one new recurring character, all make appearances in **Enchantment.**

As such, an awareness and familiarity with the characters, events, and earlier stories will greatly benefit the reader's enjoyment. On the following pages, you'll find a listing of all the currently published and upcoming novels in The Lewis Legacy Series. You'll also find a list of the TeamWork crew (including the book in which their love story is featured or in which they were introduced) to help refresh your memory.

In essence, this is a "bridge" book in the middle of the series. **Enchantment** is a love letter to my readers, if you will, and an opportunity to revisit with old friends, meet new ones, and fall in love all over again. Rest assured, my signature humor, romance, drama, and adventure await you within the pages of this novel.

Please note the events in this book take place in early October 2005, only a few weeks after the TeamWork men's trip to New Orleans in the aftermath of Hurricane Katrina (at the end of **Moonbeams**, Book 5). I felt it was important for the crew to get back to the basics of TeamWork Missions in serving alongside one another as they strive to live their faith by example. One romance hinted at in previous books blossoms in **Enchantment,** and two other romances begin to bloom during their two-week mission in Albuquerque, New Mexico.

Special thanks to Elaine Holt and author Norma Gail for providing information relative to the Albuquerque, New Mexico, area; Randy Myklebust, Pilot Coordinator for the Albuquerque International Balloon Fiesta; Beverly Lytle and Karen Richardson for their medical expertise; Muriel Hernando for French translation assistance; and Marina Neubauer-Perkins (with Dawn Steadham), and Kevin O'Teter (with Cammi O'Teter) for German translation assistance. To all of you—your kindness and generosity in answering my questions is sincerely appreciated.

With all that said, this book is dedicated to you, my faithful readers. You have helped to make my writing journey a true joy and blessing. It's my prayer that you will enjoy *Enchantment* as much as I love bringing this important installment of the series to you!

Blessings,
JoAnn Durgin
Matthew 5:16

Books currently available in The Lewis Legacy Series:

Prelude (Prequel)
Awakening
Second Time Around
Twin Hearts
Daydreams
Moonbeams
Enchantment

More adventures to come!

Abide
Pursuit
Roundabout
Underground
Assurance

Enchantment
Book Description
~~♥~~

Sam and Lexa Lewis and their TeamWork Missions volunteers are together again! A two-week mission brings them to New Mexico—the Land of Enchantment—as they work on a church building alongside their new friends in the One Nation under God congregation of Native American Christians. Outside forces, both unseen and overt, impede and threaten their efforts. But with faith to guide them, and the strong bonds of friendship to sustain them, the crew faces the challenges together as they persevere for the Lord's glory.

Eliot Marchand hopes the mission in Albuquerque will finally give him the opportunity to pursue a relationship with the beautiful Marta Holcomb. With his dangerous assignments around the globe, and little time to spend with her, is a relationship worth the risk to both their hearts?

Successful business owner Dean Costas wants to get to know the lovely Sheila Morris better, but his court-appointed charge, Felipe Hernandez, might cause trouble after he takes a liking to Sheila's pretty 14-year-old daughter, Angelina. Will Dean have time to romance the shy widow or will they need to focus their energies on chaperoning the teenagers?

Bringing together every couple and familiar characters from the previous books in The Lewis Legacy Series—including the TeamWork children—*Enchantment* will sweep you away! Love is in the air, so join the fun with the crew for Albuquerque's International Hot Air Balloon Fiesta, a one-of-a-kind TeamWork Talent Show, revelations and updates in the lives of the close-knit crew, the introduction of one new TeamWork volunteer, and even a surprise visit from two beloved characters.

Enchantment. Visit with old friends, make new ones, and fall in love all over again!

Enchantment
The TeamWork Crew in New Mexico
~~♥~~

Samuel J. Lewis, Jr. ("Sam") and Alexis Clarke Lewis ("Lexa")
City of Residence: Houston, Texas
Children: Joseph ("Joe"), twins Hannah and Leah
Sam—Domestic Missions Director for TeamWork Missions, a worldwide Christian missions organization; Author of Christian marriage and family life books
Lexa—Co-Founder and Partner of Doyle-Clarke Catering
♥ *Love story featured in Awakening, Book 1*

Sheila Morris, Widowed, Social Worker
City of Residence: San Antonio, Texas
Daughter: Angelina Morris
♥ *Introduced in Awakening, Book 1*

Marcus A. Thompson ("Marc") and Natalie Combs Thompson
City of Residence: Wellesley, Massachusetts
Children: Grace ("Gracie")
Natalie is expecting their second child
Marc—Founder and CEO of Thompson Sports Advertising (Boston)
Natalie—Kindergarten Teacher
♥ *Love story featured in Second Time Around, Book 2*

Dean Costas, Single, Founder and Owner of Leather, a chain of retail stores in Texas and Louisiana; Court-appointed guardian of Felipe Hernandez (introduced in this book)
City of Residence: Leon Valley, Texas
♥ *Introduced in Second Time Around, Book 2*

Eliot Marchand, Single, Profession: Classified
State of Residence: Texas
♥ *Introduced in Second Time Around, Book 2*

Joshua A. Grant ("Josh") and Winifred Doyle Grant ("Winnie")
City of Residence: Houston, Texas
Children: Chloe, Lucas ("Luke"), Emily
Josh—Attorney and General Counsel for TeamWork Missions (twin of Rebekah Moore)
Winnie—Co-Founder and Partner of Doyle-Clarke Catering
♥ *Love story featured in Twin Hearts, Book 3*

Kevin C. Moore and Rebekah Grant Moore ("Beck")
City of Residence: Houston, Texas
Kevin—Co-Owner and Manager of Moore Lumber, Houston, Texas
Rebekah—School Operations Director, TeamWork Missions (twin of Josh Grant)
♥ *Love story featured in Twin Hearts, Book 3*

Gayle Ferrari, Single, Employed by Doyle-Clarke Catering
City of Residence: Houston, Texas
♥ *Introduced in Twin Hearts, Book 3*

Marta Holcomb, Single, Employed by Doyle-Clarke Catering
City of Residence: Houston, Texas
♥ *Introduced in Twin Hearts, Book 3*

Landon C. J. Warnick and Amelia Jacobsen Warnick ("Amy")
City of Residence: New York City, New York
Landon—Publisher and Senior Editor, LCJW Publishing
Amy—Acquisitions Editor, LCJW Publishing; Editor at *Habits* Magazine (younger sister of Mitch Jacobsen)
♥ *Love story featured in Daydreams, Book 4*

Mitchell A. Jacobsen ("Mitch") and Cassandra Thorenson Jacobsen ("Cassie")
City of Residence: New York City, New York
Mitch—Independent Stockbroker and Financial Analyst (older brother of Amy Warnick)
Cassie—Enrolled as a Full-Time Student (upon return to New York)
♥ *Love story featured in Moonbeams, Book 5*

♥ *Plus two special surprise guests join the crew in New Mexico!*

Theme Scripture Verses
in Enchantment
~~♥~~

2 Samuel 22:31
As for God, His way is blameless;
The word of the Lord is tested;
He is a shield to all who take refuge in Him.

Psalm 28:7
The Lord is my strength and my shield;
My heart trusts in Him, and I am helped;
Therefore my heart exults,
And with my song I shall thank Him.

Psalm 91:5-10
You will not be afraid of the terror by night,
Or of the arrow that flies by day;
Of the pestilence that stalks in darkness,
Or of the destruction that lays waste at noon.
A thousand may fall at your side
And ten thousand at your right hand,
But it shall not approach you.
You will only look on with your eyes
And see the recompense of the wicked.
For you have made the Lord my refuge,
Even the Most High, your dwelling place.
No evil will befall you,
Nor will any plague come near your tent.

Proverbs 29:25
The fear of man brings a snare, but he who trusts
in the Lord will be exalted.

I Corinthians 12:12
For even as the body is one and yet has many members,
and all the members of the body, though they are many,
are one body, so also is Christ.

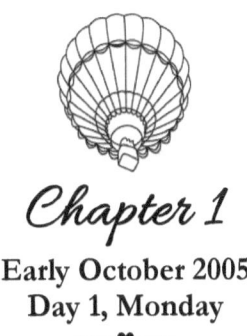

Chapter 1

Early October 2005
Day 1, Monday
~~♥~~

Together again.

Dragging fresh air into his lungs, Sam Lewis lifted his gaze to the Sandia Mountains and then to the cloudless blue sky. "Bring it on, Lord. Remind us why we're here and what you want us to do."

"I'm sure He will." Beside him, Lexa scooted closer and nudged his arm. "It's so beautiful here. After your tough mission with the guys in New Orleans last month, it'll be great to reconnect in a more relaxed, fun atmosphere."

"Agreed." Taking her cue, Sam draped his arm around his petite wife and tucked her close to his side. Surveying the expanse of open field before him, his heart was full. Soon this space would be filled with vehicles bringing his faithful TeamWork Missions volunteers to the campsite in the outer reaches of Albuquerque, New Mexico. Two weeks in *Tierra del Encanto*, The Land of Enchantment, named for its scenic beauty and rich history. A time to work alongside their new friends in the One Nation under God congregation of Native American believers to help finish their new church building.

"Excited to see Sheila and Angelina?"

"Sure am." Sam could hear the excitement in Lexa's voice. "I'm glad Dean's bringing Felipe, too."

Ah yes, Felipe, the 15-year-old juvenile delinquent, as Dean referred to his charge.

Kissing the top of Lexa's blonde head, Sam gently tugged on the long braid that reached halfway down her back. "Want a little history lesson while we wait?"

"Always. It'll help pass the time."

"*Sandia* means watermelon in Spanish, and it's a reference to the reddish color of the mountains at sunset." Sam pointed to the mountain range in the near distance. "We're seeing the range from the east, but on the west side—the steeper, rugged side—there's a long ridge with a thin layer of green conifers near the top that supposedly suggests the rind of a watermelon. Then, you have the other story. According to the Sandia Indians, the Spaniards got it all wrong and it was actually squash growing on the mountains, not watermelon."

Lexa smiled. "However they got their name, the mountains are beautiful."

"That they are." Stubbing the toe of his work boot against the ground, Sam frowned. Hard as a rock after an extended drought. In the early afternoon sun, he was warm in his jeans and T-shirt. Removing his black Stetson, Sam ran the back of his hand over his forehead.

Lexa tugged the hat out of his hand and perched it playfully on her head. In her jeans and white cotton top, she was lovelier now—after seven years of marriage and three children together—than the first time he'd spied her outside the San Antonio bus station. Suitcase in hand, she'd been ready to take on the world. And just like that, she'd fascinated him. Still did. Always would.

"Break it up, you two. I've come to join the welcoming committee. Time to behave yourselves." Marta Holcomb strolled toward them. Brushing aside a shoulder-length blonde curl, she gave them a bright smile.

"We're just keeping things lively for you until Eliot gets here." Reclaiming his hat, Sam tipped the Stetson to Marta before settling it in its proper position.

"Who said I'm here to greet our globe-trotting TeamWork volunteer?" Marta's question sounded much too casual. Surely she knew she wasn't fooling them.

"I think you just did." Lexa squeezed Sam's hand.

Based on past behavior, Eliot wouldn't be adverse to spending time with Marta. Not at all. Likeminded and close in age, they'd been flirting and skirting—Lexa's terminology—around one another for the past couple of years. Until now, Eliot had never stayed in one place long enough for a romance to take root. If they wanted, the next couple of weeks would give his two TeamWork volunteers the opportunity to explore the possibilities.

With her strong, independent spirit, Marta would be a good match for Eliot in terms of the rigors and absences of his job if something were to develop between them. They'd be plenty interesting to watch during this work camp.

Marta crossed her arms. "Well, would you look at that? Mr. Marchand has finally decided to grace us with his presence."

A white Hummer spewed dust and gravel as it made its way toward them. Sam had never seen Eliot in a Hummer, but as the vehicle came to a stop a few hundred yards away, he studied the personalized Texas license plate. WNDRLST. Wanderlust? Yep, that seemed appropriate.

"I suppose that small tank fits Eliot's international man of mystery image," Marta said.

"Landon's bringing his jet. Whatever it takes to get us all here."

Marta laughed under her breath. "Point taken, Mrs. Lewis."

A taxi came into view while they waited for Eliot to climb out of the Hummer. "That must be the San Antonio group." Lexa released his hand and hurried in the direction of the car.

The back driver's side door flew open and Angelina Morris scooted out of the car like she had a rattler nipping at her heels. Now almost 15, the once tiny seven-year-old girl Lexa had befriended on her first TeamWork mission had grown surprisingly tall. While Angelina favored her petite mother's dark, delicate features and slender frame, she'd inherited her height from her late father.

"An-An-Angie, w-w-wait!" Sheila slipped out of the back seat and hurried after her daughter.

Dean stepped outside and closed the front passenger door. Leaning against the taxi, he rapped his knuckles on the roof. The expression on his face said it all as his gaze met Sam's. Although he gave him a nod, Dean's mouth was set in a firm line and the muscles in his cheeks flexed. Normally steady and unflappable, his disgruntlement might have a lot to do with the tall teenager with straight dark hair tied in a ponytail who climbed out of the car next.

From the way he eyed Angelina, this kid might cause trouble if they didn't rein him in quickly. With Lexa beside him, Sam strode forward, his hand outstretched. "You must be Felipe. I'm Sam Lewis, and this is my wife Lexa. Thanks for coming to help us out."

"Hey." Felipe shook his hand and nodded to Lexa before shooting another glance at Angelina. The girl tapped her foot up and down, turned her head, and avoided looking in their direction. But not before Sam caught the spark in Angelina's eyes as her gaze skimmed over Felipe. Wonderful. He wasn't ready for her to be intrigued by boys. He'd already been praying for when his own son and daughters reached the age of dating. Thirty sounded about right.

"This should be interesting," Lexa murmured. No kidding.

"How was the trip?" Sam made sure to keep his tone non-threatening and non-judgmental although he wanted to grill Felipe on whether he'd misbehaved or been disrespectful to Angelina. He must have done something. Said something. She wouldn't be looking at him that way if they'd discussed something as mundane as school or the weather.

"The trip was okay. We made it alive, so that's cool." Raising one hand, Felipe flashed a smile. "I swear I didn't do anything, man. Just tried to talk to her." Ah, yes, a natural charmer with the edge of bad boy in him. Straight white teeth and clear brown eyes. Good-looking kid, muscular and lean in jeans and a red T-shirt strained across his chest.

No wonder Sheila might be worried since she'd once fallen for a similar type in Howard Morris, Angelina's father. A boy who'd gotten Sheila pregnant as a teenager, abused her, and then fallen into a life of crime that eventually got him killed. And now the best thing Howard Morris had ever done was in his mission camp watching a boy who may—or may not—mean trouble.

Teenage hormones in kids raised in Christian homes were hard enough to control at times, so an extra dose of prayer for this young man couldn't hurt. "I'd appreciate your help unloading the suitcases," he said to Felipe, pleased when he readily fell into step beside him.

When they reached the taxi, Dean shook Sam's hand and quickly embraced him. "I hope it wasn't a mistake to bring him here," he said under his breath as Felipe walked to the back of the taxi with the driver. "I feel like I should apologize for his behavior before we even get started."

"No worries," Sam said. "Give him a little time. It'll work out." They needed to give Felipe the benefit of the doubt and follow the *innocent until proven guilty* credo. Get to know him.

As Dean settled the taxi fare with the driver, Felipe worked beside Sam to haul the suitcases and bags from the trunk. After setting them on the ground, Felipe sauntered in Angelina's direction. From where she talked with Lexa, casting frequent glances at the teenage boy, Sheila looked prepared to throttle him.

Dean chuckled under his breath. "I might need you to send Lexa or the TeamWork posse after that kid."

"I don't think that'll be necessary," Sam said. "From what I can see, Sheila's already got a good handle on it."

"Sheila's an amazing woman, Sam. I wish I'd gotten to know her before this trip. Makes me wonder if I've been asleep at the wheel." They both watched as the taxi departed down the narrow gravel path leading back to the main, two-lane road a quarter mile away.

"I'd say it's more like you've been on autopilot and haven't seen the road directly in front of you. You've also been busy growing your business, and that takes a significant chunk of time." Sam angled his head toward Felipe. "Not to mention you've had your hands full. We'll help keep an eye on Felipe if you want to get to know Sheila better while you're here."

"I plan on it, but I hope Sheila feels the same way considering I brought the juvenile delinquent into the equation."

"Maybe you and Sheila can spend time together chaperoning Felipe and Angelina."

Dean cracked a grin at Sam's suggestion. "I like the way you think."

"Every now and then I come up with something inspired."

Both men turned when Felipe's voice rose. Standing in front of Sheila, he raised both hands as if in surrender.

"Mrs. Morris, is it okay if I talk with Angie for a minute? Just talk. I swear I'm not gonna say anything bad to her. Promise I'll be good." He lowered his hands to his sides. "I'll keep my hands to myself. Nothing going on here."

"M-m-make s-s-sure it d-d-doesn't." With a wary expression, Sheila gave him a slight nod.

If Sam wasn't mistaken, there was a hint of puppy love in the way that young man looked at Angelina. Good old-fashioned infatuation. He'd take that any day over the alternative.

Dean grunted. "The ride out here to the camp was forty minutes of Felipe saying every dumb, inappropriate thing he could to try and get a rise out of us."

"He's probably just testing your limits," Sam said. "How was the plane flight?"

"Surprisingly quiet and uneventful. I don't think Felipe's ever been on a plane before so he might have been nervous. He didn't ask for anything to drink or snack on and didn't say much of anything. Mainly hunkered down in his seat and closed his eyes. Then made up for lost time in the taxi."

Sam gave the other man a quick squeeze on one shoulder. "Like I said, give us a few days. I've talked with the guys and they'll be great with Felipe. We'll put him to work and he'll feel a part of the team soon enough."

"I hope you're right." Dean didn't sound hopeful. "I appreciate your efforts to make him feel welcome." His dark eyes met Sam's. "When he says something surly or uncooperative, I have to remind myself where he's coming from. Felipe's had a tough time of it and he's only a kid."

"Any idea how much longer he'll be with you?"

"Indefinitely at this point or until he comes of age to go it alone. I'm fine having him around. The company's nice in some ways."

"Is he still resistant to going to church with you?"

"Yes. Stubborn as can be. I've focused on modeling a moral lifestyle without trying to harp on him. He's had some adjustments in the past six months."

Sam nodded. "So have you, and I'm sure you're more of an influence than you know."

"Not so sure about that based on recent events." Regret surfaced in Dean's expression.

"Keep working with him. How's he doing in school?"

Dean's frown faded, replaced by a smile tinged with what looked like pride. "Believe it or not, the kid's a borderline genius when he applies himself."

"Good to hear. If you want, come with me while I say hello to the ladies." Removing his Stetson, Sam walked to Sheila and wrapped his arms around the woman who was similar in height and size as Lexa. "Great to see you. Welcome."

"W-w-wouldn't m-miss it, P-P-Papa B-Bear." Sheila returned his hug and then motioned to her daughter. "A-An-gie, c-c-come o-over h-h-here and s-say h-hi to S-Sam a-and L-L-Lexa."

With a frown aimed at Felipe, the young girl ran over to them. Her frown eased when Lexa opened her arms wide. To one side, Dean joined Sheila and engaged her in quiet conversation. Based on the light in Dean's eyes when his gaze rested on Sheila, this work camp was growing more interesting by the minute.

6

Gathering Angelina in her embrace, Lexa kissed her cheek. "We're so happy you and your mom are here with us on this mission. Everyone's looking forward to seeing you."

Sam smiled as he watched them together. Leave it to his wife to make everyone feel immediately at ease and welcomed. *Loved.*

"Me, too. I've missed you, Lexa." Angelina's dark-eyed gaze briefly met Sam's over Lexa's shoulder and she gave him a sweet smile. Those eyes held a maturity and wisdom well beyond her tender years. Like Felipe, she'd already experienced more loss and heartache than most people did in a lifetime. These two teenagers might be good for each other during this mission.

Lexa smoothed one hand over Angelina's long, straight black hair. "It seems like only yesterday when you sat on my lap in that schoolroom in San Antonio, staring at my braid." She touched one of the girl's earrings. "You've always liked wearing long, dangly earrings, haven't you?"

"Yeah, and I wear my hair braided a lot. Like you." Coming over to Sam, Angelina leaned her head against his chest for a brief moment and moved her arms around his middle. "Hi, Papa Bear. Love you."

"Love you, too, Angel." This girl held a special place in his heart and always reminded him of God's providence. After returning her hug, Sam lowered his voice. "Felipe giving you any trouble?"

She laughed under her breath. "I can handle him."

"Lexa and I are here for you and your mom. Call on us if you need anything."

"I know. Thanks." Angelina ran over to join the ladies.

Sam moved his focus to Marta. A worry line had surfaced between her brows as she talked with Lexa and Sheila. As he watched, Marta darted another glance in the direction where Eliot had parked his vehicle. She probably wondered if Eliot would ever make his appearance, and Sam figured he must be filing some report or catching up on phone calls or e-mails.

As if on cue, Eliot opened the door of the Hummer.

Chapter 2
~~♥~~

"Well, it's about time," Marta said, half under her breath, as Eliot tossed a duffel bag onto the ground and then jumped down from the vehicle.

Sam darted a glance at Marta. The upturn of her lips belied her sarcasm. If she were one of his kids, she'd be jumping up and down by now.

A few seconds later, Eliot closed the door of the Hummer and then slung the bag over one shoulder as he headed in their direction. A beep sounded as he pushed his keys into the front pocket of his khaki shorts. In work boots and a plain black T-shirt, he wore dark sunglasses and a red, backwards Astros baseball cap. His skin was deeply tanned, his jaw and chin covered with stubble, and his short brown hair was streaked with blonde highlights. That was new, most likely natural from the strong sun where he'd been until the last few days.

Although Sam had encouraged Eliot to take a few days of R&R before joining them, his international volunteer had declined and assured him he'd arrive today. True to form, Eliot was only off by a couple of minutes on his estimated time of arrival. Punctuality meant a lot in Eliot's line of work. Important to the point of meaning the difference between life and death in the most literal sense.

Moving forward, Sam replaced his Stetson and walked to meet him halfway. "Welcome, brother."

"Hey. Great to see you again, Sam. Everything according to His purpose." As was his custom, Eliot bumped fists with him in greeting. "Better circumstances than New Orleans last month, that's for sure." After dropping the duffel bag to the ground, Eliot grabbed his hand and pulled him into a quick, tight hug.

"Hold up, buddy. Don't crush me." Eliot apparently didn't know his own strength. Or maybe he did.

"Sorry about that." Eliot leaned close and lowered his voice. "Lexa's not expecting, is she?"

Sam chuckled. "Not that we're aware of, no."

Eliot turned to Lexa. "Mrs. TeamWork, always a pleasure." In a surprise move, he swept her off the ground, whirling around with her in his arms, spinning in a full circle and making her laugh. Kissing her cheek, he lowered Lexa to the ground before turning to face Marta. A wide grin spread across his face. "Marta, you're looking great as always. And irritated with me. As always. Glad to see you're part of the TeamWork welcoming committee." He lifted his arms to the sky. "Isn't it great we could all be together in the Land of Enchantment?"

Something lit in Marta's eyes. "Wouldn't miss it. Took you long enough to get out of your vehicle. Checking up on your girlfriends around the globe?"

"You know it. Jealous?"

Marta squealed and then laughed when Eliot scooped her up in his arms and spun her around the same as he'd done with Lexa. Her protests faded and she flushed when he planted a noisy smacker on her cheek. Losing her footing when he set her back on the ground, appearing dazed, Marta playfully swatted Eliot when he attempted to steady her. "You've manhandled me enough, sir. I'm fine, thank you."

"Ah, Marta. You love it. You know you do."

"Didn't say I didn't, but were you downing straight caffeine shots on the drive here?"

"Caffeine's my drug of choice." Putting one hand over his mouth, Eliot blew into his palm and then sniffed as if checking his breath. "Is my caffeine breath offensive to you?"

Marta gaped. "You're a nut, you know that?"

Laughing, he bowed before her. "*Oui*. And proud of it."

Tilting her head, she quirked a brow. "I was referring to your hyperactive behavior. And what's with the French?" Her violet-blue eyes widened. "Wait a second. Were you in France on your latest adventure?"

Eliot shrugged. "Relax. It's only a word. Would you prefer another language?"

"Depends. How many languages do you know?"

"A few."

Sam smiled at Marta and Eliot's antics and exchanged a glance with Lexa. Eliot had slipped for a second there but he'd recovered well.

"Whoa. Who's that dude? Is he with the NFL?" Sam looked over at Felipe, unaware the teenager had come to stand beside him.

"That's my friend Eliot Marchand," Dean said, joining them. "He's not a pro athlete, but he could be if he wanted."

"Yeah. He looks fierce." Felipe's gaze moved to Sam. "Is your hand okay, man? He must have a mean grip."

"It's fine, thanks. And yes, he does."

With Marta by his side, Eliot greeted Sheila and Dean. After a few moments of conversation, Eliot hoisted what looked like the heaviest suitcase as if it was featherweight. Grabbing a few more bags with straps, he tugged them over his head. "Where to, Sam? Lead the way."

From the corner of his eye, Sam spied Felipe assisting Sheila and Angelina with their remaining bags. If that was his effort to earn brownie points, it was a good start.

"Hold up a second," Sam called to Eliot as Josh Grant approached and greeted the newcomers. Josh's oldest daughter, Chloe, skipped beside her father, her blonde curls bouncing. The excitement in the air was nearly tangible, especially when Chloe threw her arms around Angelina and hugged her tight. Their kids all loved Angel and she'd be invaluable in helping the ladies on this mission.

"I got a message from Amy," Josh told him. "They've had a smooth flight and they should be here in the next ten minutes. I told her we'd marked the big red X in the field for Landon to put down the bird."

"Excellent," Sam said. "Right on schedule." That big X was far removed from where the other vehicles were parked and they'd followed the FAA's explicit specifications. "Everyone able to make it?" Not that he doubted it, but the fact they'd cleared their schedules for two weeks was a testament of their loyalty to TeamWork and the mission.

"The Warnicks and the Thompsons are all onboard." Josh nodded to Sheila and Angelina. "I know you're happy to have them here with us. Been a long time." His gaze moved to Felipe. "Is that the boy you mentioned earlier?"

"Right," Sam said, lowering his voice. "Felipe Hernandez. His mom's in and out of detox and his dad's in prison. From what I know, there were no other family members willing or qualified to take him. Dean's his court-appointed guardian."

Josh whistled under his breath and ran a hand through his blond hair. "That's rough. You mentioned he had some trouble with the law. What happened?"

"He stole a car with some of his buddies. The judge in San Antonio granted special permission for Dean to bring him here. It was either this or juvenile detention." At the moment, Felipe chatted up Eliot like they were old friends. "I don't think he's a bad kid. He's just in need of some serious adult guidance. We'll keep him busy, put him to work, and show him firsthand how giving back to others is a whole lot more gratifying."

"Manual labor's good for the soul." Josh's green-eyed gaze met his. "This mission's going to be good for all of us, Sam. Back where we belong."

"That's the plan. If you and Chloe can wait here until the plane lands and then go out to welcome the others, I'm going to head back to the camp with this group." He grinned. "When they get here, try not to hassle Marc too much."

Josh laughed. "Come on, buddy. Don't steal my fun. Somebody's got to tease Thompson when you're not around. The guy practically begs for it."

"Tell the gang we'll see them soon."

Josh saluted him. "Will do, boss. We'll meet you back at the camp in a bit."

"Thanks." Sam motioned to the others. "This way, folks. Follow me."

Let the adventure begin.

Chapter 3

~~♥~~

Marta listened as the ladies and Angelina chatted on their way to the camp, their steps stirring up small clouds of brown dust. Not that they excluded her, but she was lost in thought and content not to engage in conversation. Marta caught Lexa's glances directed her way more than once. Besides being her boss, Lexa was her friend. She'd observed her interactions with Eliot enough to understand their wonderful but unusual relationship. If she could even call it a relationship. *Wacky* pretty much described it.

He's here less than half an hour, and I'm already a fool for him.

No other man had ever affected her this way, and she could stand to be a little less obvious. When Eliot was around, her best intentions were often scattered and left in the dust.

Eliot was almost of even height with their six-foot-five TeamWork leader—all lean, solid muscle with wide shoulders and a broad chest that tapered to slim hips. Marta had seen enough male swimmers in her competition years to recognize a man who worked out and took care of his body. Eliot obviously kept himself physically fit, but, unlike a lot of men, he didn't seem overly conscious or arrogant about it. The prospect of spending two uninterrupted weeks in close proximity with him was exciting yet intimidating.

She might be out of practice with flirting, but she couldn't ignore the signs when a man was interested. No doubt about it, Eliot was interested. And she couldn't stop staring at him. Talk about carrying a torch. At the end of this project, they'd either hate each other or be wildly in love…or somewhere in between.

Marta startled when Eliot stopped walking, lingering behind the others. He grinned over one shoulder in her direction, making her pulse jump. How she detested it that she couldn't see his eyes because of those sunglasses.

"Coming, Marta? You're dawdling." Eliot's tone was teasing, playful. He had a very attractive dimple on the right side of his mouth that surfaced when he was amused. However, it was currently camouflaged beneath his facial stubble. Not that she minded the scruff, but she'd grown rather accustomed to that dimple.

"I'm going over some things in my mind," she said. "No need to wait. You go on ahead."

"And leave you out here as fair game for wild beasts and creepy crawlies? I don't think so."

Even though she knew he was teasing, Marta shuddered. "Thanks for the image although I appreciate your protective instincts. Are you offering to be my bodyguard for the duration of this mission?"

"If that's what you'd like." His grin grew wider and the dimple made its welcome appearance. "Are these important things you're pondering on this glorious Monday afternoon?"

"My, someone's awfully cheery. Always a good thing," she assured him. "If you consider helping Lexa and Winnie compile the list of groceries, sure." No way would she give him the satisfaction of admitting her true thoughts.

"Food is critical to our well-being in a camp like this, especially when we'll be doing a lot of manual labor. Got to keep our strength up. So, yeah, I'd say it's important. When did you arrive in New Mexico?" He waited until she was beside him and then paced his steps with hers. She appreciated his consideration since he could so easily outdistance her.

"A few hours ago. Gayle and I drove together from Houston. We started out yesterday and stayed overnight in the Amarillo area."

"Sounds like you were just ahead of me on the highway then."

"Trust me, I would have remembered that white tank if you'd passed us on the highway. Although"—she shot him a wry grin—"a few Texas state troopers flew past us in pursuit of someone in the Dallas-Ft. Worth area."

"Good try. You won't catch me getting any tickets."

"By the way, I'm assuming your personalized license plate stands for Wanderlust?"

He laughed heartily. "Ah, you broke my code."

She mock gasped. "May it never be! You can't tell me you don't push that white tank to its speed limits on the open road. Or maybe you do, but you have connections with law enforcement officials?"

"I'll never admit to a thing."

"I wouldn't expect anything less." What the man said was true. For one thing, she didn't even know where he lived except to assume it was in Texas since his vehicle sported a Lone Star license plate. Maybe he was a guy who lived in a sparsely furnished apartment since he was rarely home and poured most of his money into his Hummer. She'd known a few guys like that. Could be he needed that tank for his personal safety. Or, it could be that her overactive imagination running rampant, which it sometimes tended to do, especially when it concerned the man walking beside her.

"And I didn't necessarily buy the tank—as you call it—for speed."

"Will you let me drive it sometime?" She mock sighed like she imagined a Hummer groupie would do. "I'd like to know what it feels like sitting behind the wheel of such a powerful vehicle."

Eliot chuckled. "I'm sure it can be arranged. At least out here in the wide open spaces, you're not likely to hit anything."

"Except you. Look out since there are lots of trees around the campsite. Tall, thick ones with broad bases. I'm a very safe driver, I'll have you know." Marta gestured to his duffel bag. "Hand over one of those bags, will you? I feel sort of useless here."

"Can I quote you on that?"

She laughed. "Time for a truce."

When she reached for the strap on his bag, Eliot tightened his hold. "I've got it, thanks. You were the best part of the welcoming committee—no offense to Sam or Lexa—so I wouldn't call that useless." She felt his gaze on her as they walked. "Besides, I like keeping company with you. I meant what I said. You really do look great, Marta. Terrific. Better than ever."

"Thanks. And you seem...taller." Although pleased, she was a bit flustered by his compliments. "Did you grow a couple of inches since I last saw you?" He towered over her. Of course, the last time she'd seen him, she'd worn five-inch heels and an evening gown, not athletic shoes, casual shorts, and a TeamWork T-shirt.

"No, I'm not any taller. And before you can ask, I'm not wearing lifts in my boots. No enhancements needed. I've been this same height since I was fifteen. Maybe you're shrinking?"

She scrunched her nose. "Bite your tongue. It took me fourteen years to reach *this* height." At five-foot-seven inches tall, she stood solidly in the middle of the TeamWork women.

"Life's treating you well?"

"I can't complain. Keeping busy with Doyle-Clarke Catering." Since Eliot wouldn't relinquish any of the bags, Marta pushed her hands down into the pockets of her shorts. "How about you?"

"Been hectic. This mission is a refreshing change. Slower paced." A sigh escaped his lips as he lifted his face to the sun. "Right now, that sounds really good. It's peaceful out here. Nothing like the fresh air and being out in the open spaces, is there?"

"It's a bit remote for my liking. For a short-term project, it's a nice change from the city."

"Remote or not, this environment suits you."

Tilting her head, Marta surveyed him as they walked. "You know, Eliot, I'm not sure how to take all these compliments from you."

The corners of his mouth tipped. "*Accept* them, that's how."

"Been a little starved for female companionship lately?" Although they sometimes teased each other mercilessly, she was completely comfortable with Eliot. In a way, they both thrived on it, especially when they started slinging it back and forth. Never put-down insults, but fun, flirty taunts that energized them both.

His deep, throaty chuckle emerged. How she'd missed it.

"No, but digging a little deeper here"—Eliot moved ahead and turned to face her, walking backwards, not missing a step—"no other woman is like you, Marta."

What was that supposed to mean? She was glad when he turned to face the front again. "Have you been away from home a lot in the past few months?"

"You could say that."

They both fell silent as they walked. What could she ask that he could answer? Whatever he did for a living was top secret. Not that the members of their close-knit TeamWork crew hadn't bandied about theories. Some of their ideas had potential but others were preposterous. It had been suggested that he was a member of the CIA, FBI, or some other governmental agency. Or a branch of the military, maybe even special ops. The man didn't drawl and he possessed no readily identifiable accent, not even a hint of a regional dialect. And did he really speak multiple languages? He might not be forthcoming with information—either by necessity or choice—but Eliot had never lied or purposely misled her.

"How long has it been since we last saw each other?"

Eliot's question interrupted Marta's musing. Stealing a glance at him, she marveled how he wasn't in the least bit winded under his heavy load. She pretended to consider her response although the answer was on the tip of her tongue. Not that she'd been counting.

"I believe it was at the TeamWork banquet in Houston when they honored Sam last March."

Eliot nodded. "That was a fun night and a well-deserved honor for Sam."

"Yes, it was. It was great to see everyone dressed in their formal wear for a change. The event got you in a tuxedo, anyway. I wasn't sure it was possible." He'd been debonair and dashing, the most handsome man in the room.

"You must have conveniently forgotten that I was a groomsman in Kevin and Rebekah's wedding."

He's right. "I must be slipping. Score one for your powers of recall."

His lips upturned. "I remember that slinky lavender number you wore at the banquet. That gown earned you a lot of male attention."

Marta gasped. "Excuse me? My gown was not slinky. I don't *do* slinky. It was…shimmery." Wearing that floor-length evening gown—the most expensive, gorgeous dress she'd ever owned—made her feel like a princess, at least for a few hours. Being in Eliot's arms for their one dance together had fueled more than a few daydreams. Who knew Eliot could dance as if it was second nature? The man was a fascinating contradiction in any number of ways.

"Call it what you want but it was appealing, brought out the color of your eyes, and highlighted your femininity." Amusement tinged his words. "Does that sound better?"

"Not sure, but there's a difference between shimmery and slinky. To be clear, I didn't wear it to make men notice me. I wore it to—"

"Make you feel pretty? Like a woman?" Eliot chuckled under his breath. "I can't believe I can make a woman like you blush, and I'm sure it hasn't been all that long since a man complimented you."

He'd be wrong there. It'd been so long she couldn't remember. She wasn't about to ask what he meant with the *woman like you* comment. Hopefully it had more to with confidence than anything else. "You darted off from the ballroom that night without saying good-bye." Let him think what he wanted about that statement. She only hoped she hadn't sounded pouty since she detested that particular quality in other women.

"Sorry about that. It couldn't be helped." His grin faded, his tone no longer teased.

"Well, you're here now and that's the main thing. I hope you don't have to rush off and leave our mission."

"I don't plan on it. I'm on my own time."

Relief rushed through her. "Glad to hear it. Nice of you to take your personal days here instead of on some tropical island beach." If he'd chosen the latter option, she wondered if he'd be alone. No sense in going down that particular rabbit trail.

"The truth, Marta? There's no place I'd rather be for the next two weeks. Serving the Lord with my TeamWork family? It keeps me going. I've been anticipating this mission for a long time."

Since there had been delays in this mission in Albuquerque, she'd been pleasantly surprised he'd been able to make it fit into his schedule.

"I make time for the things, and the people, that are most important in my life," he said.

Could the man read her mind? When she stole a glance his way, Marta glimpsed the set of his jaw. Eliot amazed her with his dedication to TeamWork and his seemingly relentless energy. When *did* he take time off for himself? Let down his guard and completely relax? Did he ever date? Had he ever been involved in a long-term romantic relationship?

And there you go again. Maybe she should embrace her fascination with the man once and for all. The all-too-familiar fear surfaced. She'd already experienced the pain of losing two important men in her life. As great as Eliot was, why risk her heart?

Because Eliot might just be worth it.

A sleek private jet soared overhead. Squinting into the sky, Marta smiled when she recognized the plane, and especially when she spied the landing gear. "Thank you, Lord. That's Landon's new plane, Madelyn II."

"Ah, right." Stopping beside her, Eliot tilted his head upward. "I hear Warnick's increased his flying for TeamWork projects these days."

"That's what I understand. His flying and publishing Sam's marriage and family life books keep him busy." Marta turned to him.

"I think it'd be good to stop and pray for them. Right now." After Landon's crash landing outside Houston the weekend of the mini-TeamWork reunion in February 2004, Marta knew Eliot would understand her spur-of-the-moment prayer request.

"Excellent idea. Let's do it." After lowering the bags to the ground, Eliot clasped her hands in his much larger ones. "Lord, we pray for your guiding hand on Landon and safety as he lands the plane. As we begin this mission, we ask that you continue to bless our efforts. Be with Sam and Lexa as they lead the group, and keep all of us healthy and open to the possibilities you bring our way."

Puzzling over what Eliot meant by *possibilities*, Marta focused on the words of her own prayer. "Heavenly Father, thank you for bringing the members of our TeamWork family to us safely." Pausing a moment, she squeezed his hands when she heard the landing gear squeal. A few tears slipped down her cheeks and she let them go.

"Lord, help us to be a good testimony to the One Nation congregation and also to be witnesses of your love to Felipe. Thank you for Dean's faithfulness in bringing him here. I pray that we can walk away from this mission with our bonds of friendship strengthened and a renewed understanding of how great you are. We ask these things in the name of our precious Savior. Amen."

"Amen." Leaning close, surprising her, Eliot planted a quick kiss on her forehead. "You bless me with your spontaneity." With a quick swipe of his thumb on her cheek, he absorbed the moisture from her tears before she could wipe them away. After gathering the bags again, he offered her one of the smallest ones.

"Thanks." Pulling the strap over her head, Marta positioned it cross-wise over her body. "Eliot, answer something for me. Why do guys call each other by their last names, like when you called Landon by his last name just now? My brothers do it, too. I've always wondered about it but never asked them. Is that some kind of macho guy thing?"

They continued walking. "Don't really know except that it comes naturally. Generic to our gender, I guess. If you prefer, you can call me Marchand and I'll call you Holcomb. Don't want you to feel left out, sweetheart."

Sweetheart? "As long as you're not implying I'm masculine."

He laughed. "Considering our conversation of the past few minutes, I seriously doubt you have cause to question my feelings on that subject."

Warmth flooded Marta's cheeks. At the same time, she caught Eliot's wince as he repositioned his sunglasses. She stopped walking and he followed suit. Turning to face him, she raised one hand but then let it drop to her side.

"What's on your mind?" he said. "We need to get to the camp sometime this afternoon."

"In a minute. Do me a favor and take off your sunglasses."

"Why?" His brows arched behind the upper rim of his shades.

Reaching into the pocket of her shorts, Marta whipped out her sunglasses. She settled them in place along with a dose of defiance as she lifted her chin.

The corners of Eliot's mouth quirked. "Right. First we pray, and now you're *playing* me?" He shook his head.

"Stop being so defensive already." Blowing out a breath, Marta stared into the distance and moved one hand to her hip. What to do with this man? "I'm concerned about you, Eliot. Surely you know that."

His forehead furrowed in a deep frown. After taking another step forward, he then did an abrupt about face before striding back to her. "Since you're curious, why don't you do the honors?" He crossed his arms over that broad chest, enhancing his muscles to the point of distraction. "Have at it."

Relieved when Eliot didn't turn away or step back to avoid her touch, Marta carefully lowered the sunglasses and pulled them away from his face. Unfortunately, her suspicions had been correct. The skin beneath his left eye looked ghastly. She inhaled a quick breath. Based on the rainbow of colors—purple, blue, and yellow—at least his bruised skin appeared to be healing. She'd never seen such a whopper of a shiner and her two older brothers had sported more than their fair share through the years.

"Oh, Eliot." As soon as the words slipped past her lips, Marta knew they were a mistake. He started to position the glasses on his face again, but she stopped him with one hand on his arm. "Does it hurt? Can you at least tell me that much?"

He grunted. "No, it doesn't hurt. It just looks like it does."

"The guy who did this had a solid right hook, and I'm sure it *did* hurt. Once upon a time."

"I don't live in a 'once upon a time' world, Marta." If only this man would let down his guard long enough to allow her emotional access to his life. That was something that he'd been reluctant—or unwilling—to reveal. She preferred to believe it was more a matter of being unable to tell her for whatever reason.

"You know what I mean." Marta gently ran her fingertips over his smooth, tanned skin close to the affected area. "Can you tell me what happened?"

Eliot's deep brown eyes settled on hers. Such *soulful* eyes. Those eyes held a story she hoped to hear one day. He covered her fingers with one large, warm hand. "Doesn't matter much now, does it? All I can tell you is the other guy's nose looks a lot worse than my eye."

If he thought she'd find amusement in that comment, he'd be disappointed. "I didn't expect such a clichéd response from you." With more than a pinch of regret, Marta slipped her hand from his grasp. "I'm sure you're doing what you believe is somehow justified, but how long are you going to keep exposing yourself to danger? Keep playing these games?"

Something in Eliot's eyes hardened at her comment. Great. Her use of the word *games* might have been ill-founded, but how could she know? Seemed she'd already managed to alienate and possibly even anger him, and that was regrettable. Based on his response, he'd interpreted her empathy as pity. Stubborn man.

"I suggest we keep moving," he said. The shades were back in place; it could be that his eye was especially sensitive to the sunlight. Even if he wanted, Eliot couldn't hide that black eye from the rest of the crew for long. Guaranteed, those sunglasses would be off by dinner.

Marta angled her head to the east. "The camp's not much farther. This way." Eliot trudged silently beside her. Holding her tongue around this man did not always come easily. Hopefully he understood it was just as she'd told him—she cared about him. Deeply. More than she probably should.

Good job, Marta. What an inauspicious start to the mission.

Chapter 4

~~♥~~

Eliot deposited Angelina and Sheila's bags in the women's dorm. He tried to ignore the look of hurt on Marta's face as he headed across the camp. Yeah, he hadn't handled that well. He'd speak with her later in the day once he got his head on straight. A few minutes spent in prayer before dinner would be advisable. Jet lag never helped his disposition. Hopefully he could grab some decent shut-eye tonight.

As he entered what he assumed was the men's dorm, based on the map Sam had e-mailed to him last week, the outer screen door slammed behind him. After removing his sunglasses and lowering his duffel bag to the floor, Eliot paused a few seconds for his eyes to adjust to the much dimmer light inside the small building. Hard cement floors and steel walls. Basic and utilitarian conditions but at least it wasn't primitive. He'd seen worse. Lived for weeks in them.

From what he knew, this was an old church camp that hadn't been used much in the past few years, replaced by a newer, updated campsite a few miles away. For their two-week mission, these facilities offered everything they'd need. As always, Sam had scouted out this location to make certain everything was functional and met the safety specifications, especially with the kids in tow.

"Hey, Eliot!" Mitch stood beside a bed in the middle of the room but crossed the room to give him a quick man-hug. "Glad you could make the mission. Looks like you've been someone else's hero since I last saw you."

"Good to see you, too, buddy." After Sam called him in to find Mitch in New Orleans last month, he'd located him easily enough, but the poor guy had been severely dehydrated, near-starved, beaten, and left to waste away in a hole unfit for swine. In spite of the strange circumstances of their meeting, he'd liked and admired Mitch immediately. Not much was more gratifying than returning a missing person to their loved ones, especially a brother in the faith. Normally he'd locate the person and then slip out the door before moving on to the next assignment. Mitch's situation had been unique and Eliot looked forward to getting to know him better.

"How are you healing up?"

"Almost good as new. Cassie still gets after me if I try to lift something heavy or do too much."

"She's a good woman." Eliot had known Cassie since the TeamWork volunteers traveled to Montana a few years ago on a personal mission to help Marc and Natalie Thompson. A pretty girl with long auburn hair and a gracious demeanor, Cassie had a deceptively soft Alabama accent that belied a backbone of steel. From what he knew of Mitch, their personalities would complement one another.

Eliot shot a cursory glance around the room. A long row of twin beds lined the far wall and a couple of desks sat on the opposite side of the room. All of the guys except Sam would be housed in this building. Their TeamWork director and his family had their own quarters with a small attached office on the opposite side of the camp. According to the plan, Winnie and Natalie would share a dorm with their kids, but Josh and Marc would bunk here so they could come and go from the worksite without disturbing their families.

"This should be fun," Eliot said. "Hope snoring doesn't bother anyone."

Mitch laughed. "Are you admitting you snore?"

"Nah. I just know there'll be some sad sap romantics in this bunch who'll be lying awake missing their wives. Do you know where I'm expected to bunk for the duration?"

Mitch pointed to the far corner. "Dean arrived a few minutes ago and picked the bed by the window. The bunk next to it is open."

"Great. Sounds good." Talk about sorry saps. If he didn't get himself under control, he'd be worse than the married guys on this mission. Maybe he could learn a few things from them. Get some advice. Marta had hit too close to home with her jab about him playing games. If only she knew. She *couldn't* know, and therein was the crux of his conflict. Considering the work camp hadn't even started, he was in big trouble when it came to the gorgeous, feisty blonde with incredible eyes.

Retrieving his duffel bag, Eliot tossed it on the bed outfitted with clean sheets and a lightweight blanket. The chocolate candy on the pillow made him smile. He appreciated the unexpected, welcoming touch. Courtesy of Lexa and Winnie, no doubt, since they'd arrived last week with their families in order to clean and set up the camp.

Mitch's forehead furrowed. "Listen, I'm sorry to hit you up with this right off the bat, but—if you haven't already heard—Kevin's mom, Elizabeth Moore, died of a heart attack a few weeks ago. It happened right after Kevin returned from New Orleans. She'd suffered a heart attack a few years ago, but she'd been doing better." Mitch blew out a breath. "So, her death was sudden and unexpected."

"That's tough. Thanks for telling me," Eliot said. "I only met her once. Kind of ironic since it was at the funeral for Josh and Rebekah Grant's dad. She seemed like a nice woman and I know Kevin's tight with his family." Even though he didn't see them often, at least Eliot still *had* both his parents. Landon's father had also passed away in the past year. A sharp twinge reminded him that he hadn't been a good son lately, especially being an only child. While he was at the camp, he should call them. At least they understood his career didn't allow frequent communication and that *he* needed to be the one to make the contact.

Mitch nodded. "I just thought you should know. When Marc and Landon get here in a few minutes, Sam's going to take a group over to the worksite. Are you game?"

"Always. Let me make a pit stop first and then I'm ready. Please tell me there's running water and a toilet nearby."

"The good news is that we have running water," Mitch told him with a grin. "The not so good news is that we're sharing bathroom facilities with the women. There's a building in the middle of the camp."

Eliot groaned, part in jest, part in truth. "Sounds like I'll be taking advantage of the outdoor facilities when I can." Not that he wasn't used to it on occasion. He just didn't want to make a regular habit of roughing it *that* much. Hopefully he'd get a shower every day or else he'd be bathing in the closest stream, pond, lake or whatever body of water New Mexico had to offer.

"I think it's illegal to use the outdoor facilities."

Eliot cocked a brow. "You don't say."

"In all fifty states, from what I know. Welcome back to America, my friend. Assuming you've been—"

"I'll try to refrain from my uncivilized ways." Eliot found it endearing how the TeamWork crew tiptoed around the subject of his travels. He knew they were curious, but they respected his privacy by not asking questions he couldn't answer.

Mitch grinned. "Lexa promised to keep the women on a schedule, and there's some kind of system in place."

"Good to hear." Eliot eyed his new friend. "Must be tough for you and Cassie since you're the newlyweds in this group. That is, unless someone's gotten hitched in the last month that I haven't heard about yet. That's always a possibility with this group."

As long as Marta hadn't gotten hitched or found herself a boyfriend. Her presence at the makeshift parking lot indicated otherwise. She didn't sport a diamond on her ring finger. Marta had a lot to offer the right man. *Right* being the key word. It'd been all he could do not to crush her against him and give her a *great to see you again* kiss. He hadn't kissed a woman for the right reasons in way too long, and he'd definitely wanted to kiss Marta. After telling himself the whole trip to Albuquerque that he couldn't get involved, the mere sight of the woman had turned his thinking upside down. Maybe the warm temperatures were getting to him and messing with his mind. Maybe not. Yeah, he was messed up. And desperately needed sleep.

"Cassie and I will steal time together when we can," Mitch said. "In a way, it'll be fun, like when we were dating. We'll see how creative we can be. I'm sure you're looking forward to spending quality time with Marta."

"Word sure travels fast in this group. Bunch of matchmakers." With a smirk, Eliot tore the wrapper off the chocolate candy. Belgian chocolate, no less. Tossing it in his mouth, he savored the rich, creamy taste. Leave it to Lexa and Winnie not to skimp on cheap chocolate. Balling the wrapper in his hand, he aimed and pitched it into a corner trash can.

Mitch tugged his T-shirt over his head and tossed it on the bed before pulling another shirt from a bag on his bed. "Look out, buddy. You don't stand much of a chance. I've heard about the slow dance between you and Marta. She's a great girl and I wish you two the best if that's what you both want." He shoved his arms through the sleeves of the T-shirt and smoothed down his dark hair. "I've been doing some light repairs around the camp today. It got pretty chilly last night but the afternoon sun can get pretty warm. Best to wear layers."

"Thanks for the tip." Eliot pulled a few things out of his duffel bag, including his tattered brown leather Bible, and laid them on his bed. He'd carried that Bible everywhere he'd traveled in the world. An old man named Juan had given him the Bible at a church in Santiago during one of his earliest assignments. Broken and lost after losing a comrade, he'd fallen on his knees on the cold stone floor and cried like a baby. Juan held him, rocked with him, prayed for him in faltering English mixed with Chilean Spanish, and then introduced him to a man named Jesus. Most pivotal moment in his life. Every time Eliot held his Bible, he felt the power, the strength, of the Lord. Sure, it was only an object, a book, but that Bible represented God's promises. Represented healing, redemption, and hope for his hurting soul.

Eliot's throat clogged with sentimentality, a rare occurrence, and he grunted. "When did you and Cassie arrive?"

"Last night. We rented a car and drove from Manhattan to Houston and then stayed a few days with Kevin and Rebekah before heading to New Mexico. Spent one night on the road."

"Ah, that explains it. You stored up on the way here. Smart thinking."

Mitch laughed. "I highly recommend married life. Sounds like maybe you should consider it sometime."

"I will one of these days. Need to retire first." Oh, he'd considered it plenty, especially in recent months. After a stressful, grueling day, someone to curl up with during the lonely, long nights was the best thing he could imagine. Someone to share meals with, go to a movie, take the dog for a walk, be silly together—all the normal things of life he hadn't been able to enjoy. He'd dated a lot, but except for one relationship back in his university days, he'd never had a long-term girlfriend for longer than a few months. Since then, he'd never stayed in one place long enough. In many ways, his lifestyle suited him. After the last few assignments, he'd awakened to the realization that his wants, as well as his needs, were slowly evolving. Maturing perhaps.

You want a woman, Marchand. You want Marta.

His life had never been normal and there was no end in sight. Why get close to Marta when he had nothing to offer her other than danger and possible heartache? He couldn't do that to someone he cared about, couldn't do that to someone he loved. Not that he loved Marta, but if were honest, he wouldn't need a whole lot of convincing. He was on the verge of falling off that cliff. A ludicrous notion considering he'd never even kissed the woman. Then again, his depth of feelings for Marta without any actual physical contact spoke volumes.

Flirting with her on the path to the campsite hadn't been brilliant in terms of keeping her at arm's length. Part of him wanted to grab Marta and never let her go while another part of him wanted to sprint in the opposite direction as fast as he could run. Where did the happy medium lie? Only the Lord knew, but if he intended to make a move, he needed to do it now before some other guy did. Marta was too great to stay single.

"You know, Eliot, I might not be standing here if it weren't for you."

Mitch's words brought him back to the present. "Just doing my job, man. Following my instincts and where God leads. I'm glad I could be there for you." Although he'd heard similar words of gratitude more times than he could count, they still made him uncomfortable.

"Me, too." Mitch angled his head toward the door. "If you're ready, I'll show you where the facilities are located before the women take over."

"Sounds like a plan. Once the ladies get in there, it'll probably smell all flowery or fruity."

"Trust me, you get used to it," Mitch said. "Sam and Lexa have a tub in their quarters for the kids to use. You might be able to sweet talk Lexa into using it while you're here."

"Yeah, right. Nothing enforces my masculinity more than grabbing my rubber ducky and taking a good long soak in a bubble bath. Let's go."

Mitch grinned as they walked out of the men's dorm together. "You're all right, buddy."

"So are you, Mitch."

Chapter 5

~~♥~~

"Did Eliot get here okay?" Gayle looked up at Marta as she stepped into the kitchen of the dining hall.

"He sure did." Marta jumped as the screen door slapped against her heels. She walked to the steel preparation table and failed miserably at assuming an expression of nonchalance.

"And?" Cassie pulled carrots from the massive refrigerator and then moved over to the double sink. "Is he still as handsome and heroic as ever?"

"Not to mention ever so dreamy and mysterious?" Gayle teased.

"If you mean strong as an ox and as stubborn as a mule, you would be right. And yes, those other descriptions also apply." Now more than ever. "Put me to work, please. I'm currently in need of a distraction."

"You can help me mix the meatloaf." Gayle gestured to the card on the stainless steel preparation table. "Lexa's new recipe. I'm preparing three batches and we need three more to feed this crew."

"Sounds easy enough. Always glad to be a guinea pig for Lexa's dishes. Leave it to an experienced caterer to try out a new recipe on a crowd." Plucking a pair of disposable gloves from the box on the table, Marta pulled them on and flexed her fingers. "Where have Lexa and Winnie gone?"

"They're over in the office finishing the grocery list and going over the menus." Cassie lined up three bowls in front of her.

Marta nodded. "Speaking of which, is there a schedule posted somewhere to tell me what I should be doing in the next two weeks?"

"Lexa's going to give us a schedule after dinner tonight, between the kitchen clean-up and devotional time," Cassie told them.

Gayle smiled. "I'm painting a Noah's Ark mural in the church nursery. The kids are going to help me. Make it a group project."

"That's awesome!" Cassie said. "Winnie told me you're in demand as a portrait painter these days."

"I'll brag on Gayle since she'll never do it." Marta winked at her friend. "She has some high-profile celebrity clients now. You know how it goes with those well-connected, famous types. Once someone with influence starts telling their inner circle, that's all it takes. Doyle-Clarke Catering will be blessed to hold onto Gayle much longer before she's being flown all over the world as a private portrait artist."

"Yeah, right." Gayle waved her hand as if dismissing her comment, but her smile indicated she was pleased.

"Hey, you never know. It could happen." Marta turned her attention to Cassie. With her flushed cheeks, sparkling blue eyes, and lush auburn hair, Cassie was radiant. "And you! You've never looked prettier, my friend. I miss you like crazy now that you're living in New York, but I can see how happy you are. That takes some of the sting out of it and makes me love that husband of yours all the more. Even though he stole you away from us."

"Thanks. I miss you all, too, but married life is great." If possible, the color in Cassie's cheeks bloomed.

"I guess so." Marta measured seasoning into the meatloaf. "If I didn't know all of you personally, I'd think some of our stories are fabricated fairy tales. And don't either one of you well-meaning but misguided souls dare tell me that someday my prince will come"— she raised a spatula—"or else!"

"Oh, I think your prince has already arrived, but he needs to kiss the beautiful princess and wake her up." Cassie backed away when Marta flicked a dishtowel on her arm.

Gayle laughed. "Or maybe it's the handsome prince who needs to wake up."

"Not to change the subject, but I have some exciting news I'm dying to share, but I've been sworn to secrecy for now," Cassie said. "I'm hoping I can share it with everyone while we're here."

"No fair saying something like that and then leaving us dangling." Gayle pushed a strand of her shoulder-length, dark red hair away from her face with the back of her glove-covered hand. "Let me guess. You're pregnant? I think it's in the water with this group."

Marta lifted the bunch of the carrots on the counter beside Cassie. "Speaking of dangling."

"No, no, that's not it. Mitch and I hope to have a baby in another year or two, but I'd like to get some of my schooling out of the way first." After digging around in a utensil drawer, Cassie pulled out a vegetable peeler and went to work with a vengeance. Watching her, Marta marveled how this was the girl Winnie and Lexa used to keep *out* of the kitchen. Now it seemed she'd inherited that unspoken title.

"Seriously, Marta, I hope you'll make it your personal mission here in New Mexico to find out more about Eliot," Gayle said. "I'd hate to see you two waste this opportunity by playing your cat-and-mouse games."

Marta squelched her frown. "That's not what it is, but I'm not sure what to call it." The mere mention of Eliot's name made her pulse thrum in double time. "It will be nice to get to know him better on this mission. If only he'll let me close enough to do that. That might be the difficult part."

"We're all rooting and praying for you," Cassie said. "The few times I've seen you and Eliot together, I've noticed something between you that's very special."

"When you danced together at the TeamWork banquet, I could have sworn someone shot fireworks above your heads." Gayle smiled. "Not that you would have noticed. You and Eliot were totally lost in each other."

"Then after that one dance together, Eliot disappeared from the ballroom and out of our lives for months. As usual. Like the male version of Cinderella. He shows up to charm the girl and then poof! He's gone." Marta smirked. "And again with the fairy tales!"

Cassie set a bowl of finely shredded carrots between them on the preparation table. "Based on what I've seen, one of Eliot's best qualities is his loyalty. I'm sure he had to do some finagling to get time off for this mission. One of these days, he'll reevaluate his priorities, and I'm confident you'll play a large part in that process."

Cassie's words gave her hope, but how much could she cling to the observations of others, close friends or not? Marta stared at the bowl of carrots. "You're already done? Look out, world. Cassie Jacobsen is a maniac with a vegetable peeler."

"Amazing what you can learn once you spend some time in the kitchen. Divide the carrots and stir them into the meatloaf please. It's one of Lexa's secret ingredients. It's on the recipe card," Cassie insisted when Marta raised a brow. "She says it's the best way to get the kids to eat their veggies."

"Lexa would know." Gayle's green-eyed gaze met Marta's before she focused on adding the carrots to the first batch of meatloaf. "Promise me you'll allow this attraction with Eliot to play out, girlfriend. That's the only way to see if a relationship can work out long-term. You owe it to yourself."

"And we're back at that again, are we? Nice to have my life mapped out for me."

Cassie laughed. "Marta, I seem to remember you teasing me about Mitch when I first met him."

"Yes, well," Marta said, "it *was* Valentine's Day weekend, and you two were the cutest couple in the history of the planet. And would you look at how well all that worked out?"

"And now it's your turn." After making that observation, Gayle avoided her gaze.

Marta added carrots to the second and third bowls of meatloaf mixture. As she worked, she spied the men as they walked past the dining hall windows. As if she had some kind of homing device, her gaze settled directly on Eliot where he walked between Dean and Mitch. "Do you know where they're headed now?"

"Sam's taking them over to the worksite." Cassie carried a bowl of green beans from a side table over to the sink.

"Are they going to start working this afternoon?" Gayle said, handing Marta the measuring spoons when she asked for them.

Cassie shook her head. "There's not enough time. Sam wants to show them around the worksite and introduce them to Pastor Chevy and some of the men from the One Nation Church."

"Pastor Chevy?" Marta said. "Is that—"

"That's his nickname," Gayle said. "Cheveyo is his true name. It's Hopi and translated means Spirit Warrior. His wife is Galilah, and she goes by Lila. Winnie said that name is Cherokee, and the name means attractive. The members of the One Nation Church come from a number of tribes although more from the Navajo tribe."

"Hi ladies." Rebekah Moore opened the screen door and joined them at the table. The tallest of the TeamWork women, she wore shorts and a TeamWork T-shirt. Marta thought she looked a little pale. Beck's long blonde hair was loosely piled on top of her head, and small beads of perspiration dotted her forehead.

"Hey, Beck!" Marta's greeting was echoed by Gayle and Cassie.

"Sorry I'm late to help. I was feeling a bit light-headed after lunch and Kevin insisted that I take a short nap."

"That man's a keeper," Marta said. "Are you feeling better now?" She exchanged a glance with Cassie. Goodness. Why did they automatically jump to the conclusion that Beck might be pregnant? Could be because they all knew Beck, and especially Kevin, couldn't wait to become parents.

"A little, thanks." Rebekah's smile didn't quite reach her green eyes. "What can I do to help?"

"You can finish preparing and seasoning the green beans. I'll bring them to you in just a minute." Cassie glanced at the ancient but functioning clock on the wall. "We'll plan on putting the meatloaf in the ovens an hour from now. Then the side dishes will go in half an hour later. This kitchen is old, but at least it has multiple ovens and all the appliances work well."

Marta spied a tall, wooden stool in the corner of the large kitchen. Hauling it across the cement floor to the preparation table, she caught Rebekah's wince at the scraping noise. "Sorry about that." Marta patted the seat. "Here you go. Sit while you work. It'll be more comfortable."

"Thanks, Marta. Has Eliot arrived yet?"

She and Eliot must be a bigger topic of discussion than she'd realized. "Yes, he's here. We'll be announcing our engagement by the end of the mission. I'm teasing," Marta added quickly after Rebekah gave her a wide-eyed look. Sweet as she was, Beck could sometimes be a wee bit gullible.

"We've already discussed Mr. Marchand and encouraged our friend here to go for it," Gayle told Rebekah with a pointed glance in Marta's direction. "Now that they're both in the same place for the next two weeks."

"Kevin and I think the world of you and Eliot," Beck said. "If it's in the Lord's will, it'll work out."

Marta sighed. "That's the voice of reason speaking right there. Marta Marchand sounds too weird, though, don't you think?" *What am I saying?* How silly. She wished she could retract. She might as well climb onto the roof of the dining hall and proclaim to the world that she was falling in love with Eliot. If she wasn't already there.

"Speaking as the woman who went from a long last name ending with s-o-n to one with s-e-n, it doesn't matter," Cassie said with a bright smile. "I wouldn't trade it for anything."

Rebekah gave Marta a wan smile. "Maybe you should practice writing the name in your journal. I think Marta Marchand has a nice ring to it. It's catchy."

Marta frowned. "Yes, Mrs. Moore. Maybe I should write it on the chalkboard a hundred times for good measure."

"Marmar could be your couple name. You know, combining your two names like the celebrities do. Or how about Mariot?" Gayle laughed. "Either of those strike your fancy?"

Marta cleared her throat but the corners of her mouth quirked. "We're not in middle school here, ladies. I can't tell you how thankful I am that none of the guys are around to hear this conversation. Next topic, please."

"Fine, but you're the one who brought up the name game." Gayle shrugged and crossed her eyes when Marta shot her a look.

As she worked, Marta thought about the group of TeamWork volunteers on this mission. Business owners, teachers, caterers, and a publisher, editor, and social worker among them. One of the things Marta most loved about this diverse group was that, as successful and cosmopolitan as some of them were, they were all solid in their faith, humble, and they donated their time, efforts, and financial blessings to TeamWork and other Christian ministries around the globe.

At times, she felt like a peon in the midst of all their success. To be fair, none of her friends had ever made her feel that way, so perhaps it was her own insecurities surfacing. They were all growing up while she remained stagnant, and that wasn't a place where she wanted to live. Earlier in the day, Cassie had casually mentioned going to the Metropolitan Museum of Art as if it was nothing out of the ordinary. Gayle painted world-class portraits of the wealthy and famous. Marta's discontent was caused by something she couldn't define. She loved working for Doyle-Clarke Catering, she adored her church, and her friends. Still, something was missing.

You have your faith and your best friends in the world are here with you now. What more do you need?

As the other ladies worked and talked around her, Marta allowed her thoughts to wander to Eliot once more. Slowly releasing a deep sigh, she forced herself to focus on her task. If she didn't watch it, she might add a secret ingredient even *she* couldn't remember. That wouldn't be good for any of them.

Chapter 6

~~♥~~

Angelina was more than aware of Felipe as he chatted up everyone as they all found seats in the dining hall. Who did he think he was, coming into this group like he owned the place, especially for their first dinner together? The guy could schmooze and charm everyone, even the adults. Probably trying to get in their good graces so he could hit them up for money or favors later on. She'd seen his type before and she didn't like it, didn't trust it. Didn't trust *him*.

Do not judge so that you will not be judged. Funny how the Lord gave her a verse when she needed it although she couldn't always remember the exact reference. Somewhere in the Book of Matthew sounded about right for that one.

I get your point, Lord. She had no right to judge Felipe. Even though he could be annoying, he also fascinated her. Felipe looked and sometimes acted older than most of the boys she knew from school but then he'd open his mouth or do something dumb to completely dispel that idea.

Angelina watched through veiled eyes as Felipe crouched and did the old *pull a quarter from my ear* trick with Gracie Thompson and Chloe Grant. They both laughed and stared at him with adoring eyes. So he was good with kids. Big deal.

"Miss me?" Felipe plopped down next to her a minute later. Her lack of response didn't diminish his enthusiasm. Picking up his fork and knife, he started drumming on the tabletop.

"Nope." Angelina put her fingers over his hand, stopping his actions. "Do you have ADHD?"

"If I do, I don't know it. Just a regular guy doing what guys do." He continued his drumming.

Angelina quirked a brow. "That's not what I heard."

He laid his utensils on the tabletop. "Okay, you can't say something like that and not explain. Speak to me." Felipe *was* cute. Handsome, really, with his thick dark hair and intense eyes. She couldn't let on how she felt about him, though, or he'd puff up with pride and act all arrogant and full of himself. Still, there was something about him that she liked more than she should.

She had to be careful with Felipe since Mama was already suspicious of him because of their trip. Even now, Mama darted frequent glances in their direction. Angelina knew Mama trusted her. She'd never done anything wrong. Some kids called her boring, a goody two shoes. Not that being obedient all the time was fun, but it was safe.

Ask him. "Felipe, did you steal a car? Because I heard Dean tell my mom that you did."

"Technically? Yes. But it's not like it sounds." Felipe frowned. "I'll tell you if you promise to hear me out and not interrupt me until I'm done. Deal?"

She held up one hand. "I promise."

Felipe leaned closer. "Here's the thing. I was hanging out in my neighborhood one night, and a couple of the guys decided to borrow a car. Not steal it, exactly, but just borrow it and have some fun, you know? So, there was this expensive sports car parked on the street. I mean the kind we never see that cost more than most houses. Red, shiny, and a woman magnet. Anyway, the guy who owned the car is dating this totally hot chick down the street. She's—"

"Spare me the details. Please." Angelina rolled her eyes.

"You interrupted, bad girl." He gave her a wink. "The plan was that we'd spin around the city a few times in the car. I swear to you, we were gonna return it. The dude left the engine idling while he went to the front door. Then…"

Angelina couldn't help it. She groaned. "Don't even tell me."

"You asked, but fine. I won't tell you." Picking up his fork, Felipe resumed the drumming.

"Did you get thrown in jail or what?"

"Not gonna tell you." He drummed with more enthusiasm than before. He was actually pretty good and drew curious stares from some of the others at neighboring tables.

"Don't be a jerk, Felipe."

"I'm not being a jerk," he said. "You broke your promise."

He had her there. "You're right. I'm sorry. Forgive me?" Batting her eyelashes, Angelina gave him her best smile.

Felipe stopped drumming. "Okay, Angel, since you're being nice to me now."

Boys could be such pushovers, but why did he have to call her that? Her daddy was the only man who'd ever called her Angel. Then Sam started calling her Angel, but she was okay with it since Sam was a father figure. Hearing the nickname from Felipe was bittersweet. Slowly turning her head, making him wait, Angelina finally lifted her gaze to his.

"Okay, the thing is"—Felipe heaved a sigh—"I was given a choice by a judge. I could come to this camp with Dean and work off my sentence, or I could go to juvenile detention. I figured coming here would be a whole lot more fun than sitting in that he—"

"I get your point." She didn't like bad language and wasn't about to let him to start spouting it around these people. If he did, they'd heap love on Felipe and figure out a way to show him that spewing foul words wasn't in his best interest. She had to give the TeamWork volunteers credit for creativity. "So, you've been in detention before?"

He didn't answer.

"I guess that's my answer." Realizing she'd slumped a bit, Angelina sat up straighter on the bench. "The way I see it, if you were in the car, you were guilty of stealing it."

"Don't tell me you're one of those people who sees everything in black and white with no gray areas." Felipe frowned. "Look, Angel. It's not like I'm gonna be running around stealing stuff and causing trouble. I gave the judge my word. I *keep* my word."

"That was nice of the judge to give you a choice. And it shows maturity that you came here. Don't think you got off easy, though. You're going to work hard while you're here. Trust me."

"Yeah, thanks for the reminder. Slave labor." His grin stretched across his face. "Having you here will make it a whole lot more interesting. As long as you don't get all judgmental on me, we could have some fun, you and me."

Felipe's sentiment made Angelina frown. "Don't get any big ideas."

"Hey, ideas are good. I've never met a girl like you before."

"What do you mean?" Maybe that was a leading question. Angelina returned a wave from Gracie Thompson. With her dark hair and big blue eyes, the little girl was very pretty. From what Chloe told her, Gracie could also be a troublemaker. Angelina stifled a giggle when Gracie glanced around the room and then punched Joe Lewis in the arm. Not hard, but enough to get his attention. It worked.

"Meet me later after the Bible time and I'll tell you."

Angelina's breath caught. Meet him after devotions? Why? She had a feeling he meant without anyone else around. That wouldn't be the smartest idea. Then why did it make her warm all over thinking about it? She avoided Felipe's gaze and focused again on Joe. He'd moved away from Gracie and sat by his little sisters. Smart kid.

Sam rose to his feet and thanked everyone for joining their special mission in New Mexico. Angelina tried to focus as their TeamWork leader told them he hoped they were settled in their quarters and how he was looking forward to what the Lord would do in the next two weeks. Feeling a sudden, inexplicable chill, Angelina ran her hands up and down her bare arms.

"You okay?" Felipe's dark eyes rested on her, making her squirm. For a second there, she thought she detected genuine concern.

She lowered her gaze. "Like you really care." Although she'd mumbled that last part, she knew Felipe heard.

"You might be surprised. It's not all about me, you know. I can be a good listener if you need one. You just have to be willing to give me a chance. Want me to run to the dorm and get my jacket?"

He'd really do that? That was a very sweet offer. If she said yes, he'd probably do it, too. Not that she would test him. The fact that she'd been allowed to sit next to Felipe at one end of the long table, more to themselves, was unbelievable. Angelina thought they'd be stuck with the little kids, but the children sat beside their parents, at least for tonight. Glancing at Lexa, Angelina suspected she might have something to do with her and Felipe being allowed to sit together. She must have talked to Mama and convinced her Felipe wouldn't try any moves on her at the dinner table. As if reading her mind, Lexa glanced her way and winked.

Angelina startled when Felipe nudged her knee beneath the table. Sam was in the middle of a sentence. "...we're thankful Dean brought Felipe to join us for this project. I hope you'll all take the time to get to know him better while we're here."

"That guy's like the most religious person I've ever met," Felipe whispered as those in the dining hall echoed Sam's *amen* at the end of his prayer. "That was still decent of him to introduce me. Is he a priest or something? He sounds like one but he doesn't wear all black or have one of those little white collars."

Angelina kept her voice low. "He's not a priest. Sam and Lexa are awesome people. All the TeamWork members are great."

"Do they go around talking about God all the time? That can get old real fast."

"No, but I'm sure they don't even think about it."

Felipe's skepticism was obvious in his expression. "What's that mean?"

"God's a natural, personal part of their lives. That's how they live. You talk to your friends about things going on in your life, right?" She waited until Felipe nodded and then continued. "That's how it is with the people here in the camp. God's their friend. He's a living, breathing presence in their lives."

Felipe didn't say anything for a long moment. "Hold the fort! This isn't like one of those weird religious cults or anything, is it? You know"—he pretended to drink something and then grabbed his throat with both hands as if he were choking—"where they poison themselves? 'Cause if it is, just tell me now."

Angelina stared at him. "That's an awful thing to say! I hope you'll give them a chance to get to know you. I can guarantee you they'll be praying for your sorry soul tonight."

That made her sound like a snit. In truth, Felipe had been pretty nice to her. Still, it was discouraging that what she'd told him hadn't seemed to sink through his thick skull. She needed to give him time. It's not like she could snap her fingers and he'd immediately start living for Jesus. She needed to be patient and show him by example.

"I'm still trying to get used to Dean."

That comment surprised her although she'd noticed a strain between the two guys on the trip to New Mexico. "If you ask me, you couldn't have a better surrogate parent than Dean Costas."

"Surrogate? I thought that was a woman who has a baby for a couple who can't have kids."

Angelina couldn't help it. She giggled. "It's like a substitute. I mean, Dean didn't have to take you in, but he did, anyway."

Felipe snorted. "From what I know, the judge pretty much ordered him to take me."

Angelina met his gaze. "I don't know that a judge can tell a single man he *has* to take you. But whether or not he did, Dean stepped up and took responsibility. Even though you don't know him well, he's family. Come on, Felipe. You have to admire him for that."

"Yeah, maybe, since no one else wanted me." He'd muttered that statement, half under his breath. Angelina lowered her gaze, consumed with sadness. She couldn't imagine being in his position. All things considered, he'd turned out okay. Maybe Felipe needed someone to believe and trust in him. Wasn't that, deep down, what *everyone* wanted?

"Hi, Angelina." Cassie put a plate of meatloaf slices and a bowl of steaming green beans on the table. She smiled at Felipe. "Hi, Felipe. I'm Cassie Jacobsen. It's nice to meet you. Thanks for helping us out on our mission."

Felipe thanked Cassie and watched as she left their table. "These women around here are fine. Not a dog in the bunch."

"That's so chauvinistic and derogatory," she hissed. Angelina's frown deepened and she shot him a look she hoped conveyed her disgust. "To think I was about to compliment you. For a tiny little second there, I'd started to believe you might have some manners hidden inside that crime-riddled body of yours. Guess I was wrong."

Patience.

Felipe laughed, displaying a great set of teeth framed by a terrific smile. Must be inherited since she doubted a kid with his background would have worn braces or had regular dental care. Oops. Was that stereotyping?

"See, that's why I need you to reform me, Angel. If it makes you feel better, you're the prettiest woman around. But you might as well admit it now." He waved his hand across his chest. "You like this body."

Angelina sputtered and started to rise from the bench. Might as well let Felipe know right now that he couldn't get away with saying things like that to her. She wouldn't tolerate it.

Felipe put one hand on her arm. "I take it back, Angel. Really. I'm sorry. I say dumb things without thinking all the time. I'll try to be better."

She looked at him long and hard and then down at his hand on her arm.

"Go on," he said, withdrawing his hand. "Leave me if you want." Something surfaced in his eyes, but she couldn't begin to figure out what it was. Sadness? Hope? Longing for something he wanted but couldn't have for some reason? Far be it from her to know.

Angelina dropped back down on the bench. "For one thing," she huffed, "I'm not a woman. Yet."

The grin he turned on her was maddening. She needed to watch what she said.

"You think I'm touching that line after you yelled at me?" Felipe shook his head. "No matter how old I get, I swear I'll never understand your species."

"Well, then, I guess that makes us even. And stop swearing about stuff so much." Angelina didn't say another word as they filled their plates and began to eat. Surprisingly, neither did Felipe.

She'd prayed before leaving on this trip that she could be a positive influence on him.

So far, that plan hadn't worked out so well.

Chapter 7

~~♥~~

Eliot knocked on the screen door outside Sam's family's quarters. "Sam, it's Eliot. You in here?"

"I'm back in the office. Come on in."

Closing the door behind him, Eliot stepped inside the small building. He liked the way Lexa managed to make it homey. A nice quilt covered the bed, and lots of throw pillows added a nice personal touch. Cozy, and that was a word he rarely used. Smelled pretty good, too. Seemed even Sam made concessions to femininity. As he walked past the left side of the bed, he caught sight of a Bible nestled between the pillows. He could definitely learn a few things from this couple.

Eliot ducked through the doorway of the small office and nodded at Sam where he sat behind a small desk. The room wasn't much more than four walls, the desk, a bulletin board, and a couple of chairs. Sam's laptop was open and he gestured to the folding chair on the other side of the desk. "Have a seat. Just getting ready for tonight's devotions."

"Sorry to interrupt. Got a few minutes?"

"Not a problem. My door's always open." Leaning back in his chair, Sam crossed his arms behind his head and stretched. "What's on your mind?"

"Marta."

Sam's lips creased in a wide grin. "No fooling. Is there something specific about Marta that you'd like to discuss?"

Might as well get straight to the matter. "I've dated a lot, but I've never had an ongoing relationship other than for a few months at a time in school. The fact of the matter, Sam—and trust me, I feel like the biggest kind of fool for admitting this—is that I don't know how to be a…boyfriend."

Based on Sam's expression, the man was trying not to smile. "Once you get to a certain age, the term 'boyfriend' sounds rather juvenile. As far as being in a relationship, it starts with liking and admiring a woman. Wanting to spend more time with her. From what I've seen, that's not an issue between you and Marta."

"It's not." Eliot shifted on the uncomfortable chair. "Here's the thing. As you know, my lifestyle isn't exactly conducive to dating. Some of my assignments have required that I spend time with women. But since I became a Christian, I've never compromised my vows to the Lord regarding purity."

When Sam nodded, Eliot knew this man understood he'd compromised a whole lot more before giving control of his life to Christ. He'd confessed his transgressions to the Lord and knew he'd been forgiven unconditionally. Now it was time to move forward and not dwell on the things he couldn't change. He only prayed Marta would understand. He wanted a chance for a relationship with her, not the door slammed in his face with finality.

"Care to elaborate on the meaning of *spending time*?" Sam said.

"On occasion, in order to make a situation believable, I've dated a woman here and there. Done some kissing but nothing more than that. And not for purely selfish reasons or for pleasure."

"Have you ever gotten emotionally involved with any of the women?"

"No, not even before I became a Christian. I won't lie and say it's been easy."

Sam nodded slowly. "You're wondering how your job will be affected if you start a relationship with Marta. And vice versa."

"Pretty much, yes. The first thing I thought when I saw Marta standing in that field today was how much I care about her. I'll confess my thoughts weren't exactly pure."

"You don't need to confess anything to me, Eliot. That's between you and the Lord."

"I know, but as my friend and mentor, I want you to know. And yes, I spent a few minutes in prayer before dinner." Shaking his head, Eliot started to rise from his chair. "Forget it. Thanks, but I'll work it out."

"Sit. You're here and it's important. Talking about it will help." Sam motioned for him to take the chair again. "I take it you're hoping to begin a relationship with Marta during this mission?"

"That's pretty much it, yes. With your permission."

Sam's brows lifted and he seemed surprised by that last statement. "You're a hard worker and so is Marta, but I'm no taskmaster. You should have a lot of time to spend with Marta while you're here. I'd encourage you to take full advantage of those opportunities and create more of your own. She wants to work over at the church site, too. I'm sure you can figure out the rest."

Eliot nodded. "I respect Marta. You know that, Sam. But, in some ways, I'm not sure I'm worthy of her."

"I know the standards of morality in your home country can be different. And you didn't become a believer until you were in your early twenties." Sam closed his laptop and drummed his fingers on the case before his blue eyes met Eliot's gaze. "Not to mention your family isn't just any family. As far as your job, you're in a unique position, Eliot. Of course, I don't know any specifics—as it should be—but your assignments have possible far-reaching implications, including the potential to impact national security at times. Am I right?"

"You are."

"I can't begin to imagine what that's like," Sam said.

Eliot raked his hand through his hair. "How can I start something with Marta knowing I'll probably be asked to do the same thing again? That'd be cheating, and I couldn't do that. Not to any woman, but especially not to Marta."

"I admire your sensitivity to the situation from Marta's point of view. The way I see it, you also have an opportunity here in New Mexico that you've never had before. I suggest you take a walk with Marta tonight. Be honest and tell her as much as you can. Open up and share your heart."

"How can I do that without telling her, 'Oh, by the way, sometimes I have to kiss another woman, but it means nothing'? Marta's a strong woman, and I'm not sure she'd be accepting or forgiving of that kind of scenario. She'd probably accuse me of being an escort."

Sam ran one hand over his chin and the corners of his lips lifted. "Not to make light of it, but I'm sure a lot of men would consider your position enviable. Like an actor, you're sometimes required to play a part, but what you do is as real as life gets."

"Actors get to go home at the end of the day and leave it all behind," Eliot said. "I'm in it 24/7." Just thinking about it made him tired. Maybe he should take a vacation. Go somewhere and sleep for a few days. Take his Bible and spend time in prayer. Renew his *soul.*

"I'm sure it's mentally exhausting. That's why I hope you take time off when you can. No man can keep up that kind of pace indefinitely." Sam sat back in his chair. "I also know how things change when you meet that one special woman."

Standing, Eliot crossed his arms and began to pace beside the desk. "There was a time when I considered that aspect of my assignments as a perk of the job. Like I said, I've never become emotionally involved and I've always made it a point to avoid entanglements. Sometimes it took some well-choreographed footwork. After I met Marta a few years ago, I began see things differently. Now it's to the point where I think of Marta all the time. I'm sure she'd find it amusing if she knew that I've prayed for her all over the world. She probably has no clue how much I care about her."

"I'm sure that's true, but I also know Marta would want to know," Sam said. "She's one of the most loyal, open and honest women I've ever known."

"On the level here." Eliot stopped pacing and met Sam's gaze head-on as he planted both hands on the desk. "Do you think I have a chance with her? I'm talking long term, not a two-week romance. If I'm going to pursue this, I'm in it full throttle."

Sam smiled. "Yes, I'd say you definitely have a chance with Marta. May I make another suggestion?"

"Please do. That's why I'm here. I need the benefit of your wisdom." Squaring his shoulders, Eliot rotated his neck to ease out some pesky kinks. A good reminder that he wasn't getting any younger, although he still had a number of years to serve in his current capacity.

"Talk to your superiors and see if you can be given assignments where you won't be put in a position where you feel uncomfortable or that you're compromising your morals and personal convictions. They should be able to read between the lines. You've been with them a number of years now, and I'm sure you're an invaluable part of the team."

"I hope you're right. That also brings up something else." Eliot lowered his voice. "If anything unforeseen comes up on this mission and you need to give anyone information about me, my last name is

Polaris. Stephen. There's an ID in the back pocket of my wallet. Other than that, you know nothing."

Sam's eyes widened. "I hope that won't be necessary, but I know you wouldn't ask without reason." He hesitated. "As I recall, Polaris is the brightest star in the constellation."

"So they say." The muscles in Eliot's jaws flexed. "Then there's the other part of the equation. The overriding factor, perhaps." He swallowed. Hard. "If I start something with Marta, there's always the possibility that—when I say good-bye to her before leaving for an assignment—I might not return. I've only had myself and my parents to think of up until this point, but bringing someone else into the picture? Would that be fair to Marta?"

For the past decade, his assignments had been his lifeblood and passion. No longer could he deny the stirrings for something more. Stirrings that had plagued him in the past few months. While there was something to be said for the routine, the familiar, the safe, he'd pushed aside those thoughts for fear he'd get sloppy. If he became too sloppy, a misstep could get him killed. It wouldn't take much, and a constant female distraction could be the worst thing to happen.

Or the best.

Eliot glimpsed the compassion in Sam's eyes. He sank onto the chair again.

"We all take a risk by loving someone, Eliot. The ultimate example, of course, being how God loved us enough to send His Son to live and walk among us all the while knowing He'd eventually be put to death. Of course, we can't know what our future brings. Granted, your job's dangerous, but I know Marta well enough to know she'd rather take the risk than not. She's a good woman, a strong woman, who loves the Lord and has a heart for reaching the lost the same as you do. In my biased opinion, you two would be great together. As far as when you return to work, I hope you'll keep this verse in mind: 'The fear of man brings a snare, but he who trusts in the Lord will be exalted.'"

After Sam said a short prayer, Eliot almost choked on his words of gratitude. "Thanks, Sam."

Sam rose from his chair and gestured for him to lead the way from the office. A few seconds later, he stepped beside Eliot on the porch. "As I suggested earlier, share your heart with Marta and then take it from there. I think the key is to make the decision together."

"From what I understand, that's the best way to build a strong foundation."

"Works for me," Sam said.

"Keep praying."

Sam gave him a nod. "Always, brother."

Chapter 8

~~♥~~

After helping with the kitchen cleanup, Marta walked the short distance to the devotional circle with Lexa. Glancing at her watch, she noted that at six-thirty, the sun had begun its descent on the horizon. Sam told them they wouldn't be able to build a bonfire during their mission because of the dry conditions. That was a shame; she'd looked forward to making s'mores with the kids and something about a bonfire was special.

As they approached the devotional area, Marta stopped. The circumference of the circle was illuminated by paper bags placed at regular intervals between the log benches. "How beautiful!"

"The bags are called *luminarias*," Lexa said. "It means *lights* or *illuminations* in Spanish. Pastor Chevy's wife, Lila, brought these to us earlier today. There's sand inside each bag to weight it down and a lit candle in the middle. I've asked Angelina and Felipe to bring the older kids out here after dinner each night to set them up."

"I've seen them at Christmas and at cancer relays before," Marta said. "They always lend an atmosphere of warmth and welcome."

"I think so, too. Lila said luminarias are part of a southwestern tradition to commemorate Mary and Joseph's journey to the stable. Then in the early 1800s, people began using luminarias instead of building bonfires."

"Nice tradition. Seems Sam isn't the only one who enjoys history."

Lexa laughed. "Guilty as charged."

Marta found a seat on one of the vacant benches as Lexa crossed the circle to join Sam and their children. Leah ran over to her and planted her little hands on Marta's knees. "Can I sits with you?" The dark-haired tyke gave her the sweet smile that always melted her heart. She'd had a couple of sleepovers in the past year with the twins and Joe to give Sam and Lexa a romantic night away.

"Of course, sweetie." Marta pulled the toddler onto her lap and kissed her cheek. "Have you had a fun day?"

"Uh huh." Squirming on her lap, Leah nodded. "I helped Mommy maked peach cobbler. For Daddy. He saided he loved it."

"You did? Your cobbler was absolutely scrumptious!" Marta balanced Leah between her knees, arms wrapped around her, lightly bouncing her back and forth.

"What's scrumpshis?"

"It means it was so good that I wish I had some right now." Marta's heart warmed when Leah giggled.

"Do you ladies mind if I join you?"

At the sound of Eliot's deep voice, Leah snuggled closer and burrowed her head into Marta's chest. The child didn't know Eliot well and wasn't used to him. As brawny and muscular as he was, Marta imagined he must be rather intimidating. Not to mention his black eye. He'd ditched the sunglasses since his black eye was a moot point by now. Marta couldn't help but wonder how many times he'd sported one. Hazard of his job perhaps? Trying to explain his shiner to the kids had been a challenge. She'd overheard Lexa trying to tell Joe what happened to Mr. Eliot earlier in the dining hall and she hadn't envied Lexa that task.

"This is Mr. Eliot, Leah. He's my special friend." She smoothed hair away from the little girl's eyes as Eliot carefully lowered his large frame onto the log bench beside her as if testing his weight. Considering she was holding Leah, it wouldn't be good to send her flying off the bench.

"Ohhh. He's weally big." Turning her head, Leah peeked up at him. "Are you Goliath?"

Marta swallowed her grin and caught the way Eliot's eyes lit. The tiniest lines at the corners of his eyes crinkled. Since he seemed at a loss to know how to respond, she needed to say something. "Mr. Eliot is tall—just like your daddy—and he's a very gentle giant."

"Did somebody throwed a stone at you?"

"No one threw a stone at me." The corners of Eliot's lips upturned.

Leah leaned closer, peering at the area beneath his eye as if inspecting the wound. "Does your booboo hurt?"

Marta's heart lurched when Eliot's eyes softened. "No, honey. It doesn't hurt."

"Guess what, Leah?" Marta continued to bounce the child on her knees.

"Whats?" Sticking her thumb in her mouth, Leah stared up at Marta as if she had all the answers. The implicit trust youngsters held for adults often stole her breath.

"I saw Mr. Eliot eat two whole bowls of the peach cobbler tonight."

That caught Leah's attention. "You did?" She gave Eliot a bright but shy smile more reminiscent of her quieter twin sister. "Hannah and me helped Mommy maked it. My daddy loves it."

"Did you now?" Eliot rubbed his stomach in an exaggerated way and made smacking sounds with his lips. "It was the bestest peach cobbler in the whole world."

Marta ducked her head to hide her smile, finding it incredibly sweet to see a grown man act silly to please a child. She hadn't observed Eliot around children except on rare occasions. When Hannah called across the circle to her twin sister, Leah slid down from her lap and waved to them. "Bye, Marta. Bye, Gentle Giant."

"Bye, Leah." Eliot chuckled under his breath. "Thanks for defending my honor."

"Always. I think you have another female fan."

"I love kids but haven't had the opportunity to be around many of them. So, how old are Lexa and Sam's twins now?" Eliot dug into the hard ground with the heel of his boot but it wasn't budging.

"They'll be three on Valentine's Day. Before that, Joe turns four in December."

"Hard to believe." If she wasn't mistaken, she detected a *life is passing by me too fast* wistfulness.

Feeling a night chill, Marta zipped her Baylor University hoodie and crossed her arms on her knees. "Listen, Eliot. I'm sorry for prying into your life earlier. I had no right."

He nodded but stared straight ahead. "I understand your curiosity. We're good friends and friends share things like that. My situation is different. And a little strange."

"I understand. Well, sort of." Turning toward him, their knees touched, sending a heightened awareness of him through every part of her. "I heard what you did for Mitch in New Orleans, so I have no reason to criticize anything you do. Cassie and Mitch are so grateful that they can't stop expounding on your virtues. Rightly so, and I mean that in the best possible way. Not being sarcastic in the least. You're a true hero to them. You swooped right in there"—Marta motioned with her hand as if it were a bird before lowering her hand to her lap—"and saved the day. You're apparently very good at what you do. Not that I ever doubted it for a second. I can't begin to imagine how many other people you've probably rescued. Or saved. Or both." Why was she stumbling over her words?

Eliot's gaze moved away from her again. "I'm thankful I found Mitch."

"We all are. How *did* you find him, anyway? Wait." She raised her hands. "Let me guess. You can't answer that one either? See, I can't seem to stop myself."

"No worries. In answer to your question, I asked around in the ward where Mitch had been working. I found out where he was last seen, talked to a few locals. It's amazing what information people will give up when they're offered the things that tempt them the most. It's the ultimate seduction."

Marta sucked in a quick breath. "You're not talking about anything illegal, are you?"

Eliot leaned close, for her ears only. "Yes, but only as an enticement. I'm not talking seduction in the sexual sense. Seduction takes many forms. People can be surprisingly gullible, Marta. A large part of what I do is as much mental as it is physical. I try to read people by analyzing their motivations and end goals. Then I follow through with an effective plan."

"Ah," she said. "So, what you're saying is that—at heart—you're a psychologist?"

"Sure, if that works for you. I need to give credit where it's due. The Lord had a whole lot to do with me finding Mitch."

"How so? I mean, of course He did. But in what way, exactly?"

Eliot didn't immediately respond. "I don't know how to answer that except to say that He's blessed me with intuition, opened the right doors, and pointed me in the direction of the right people. And he's given me the good sense to know when to follow a lead or when to recognize and respect a closed door."

"You're a fascinating man, Eliot Marchand." She stared at him in wonder. "Tell me, is there anything you don't know?"

"Sure. Lots of things."

"Felipe can't stop talking about you," she said to fill the silence when he offered nothing further. "He's got all kinds of theories. Like you're a super spy or a double agent."

"You're starting in on me again, you realize."

"You told me not to feel as though I have to apologize, so I'm not," she said. "However, I *will* say that I think you'd look handsome in tights and a cape."

"Don't get your hopes up. Never going to happen in this lifetime. And that's more what a superhero wears, not a spy or a double agent."

"Hey, don't knock it," she said. "I'm sure you heard about the Renaissance-themed first birthday bash for Leah and Hannah. Sam was the king, complete with crown, tights, and a crown. Didn't hurt his image any. Same for Josh as the king's court jester."

"Good for them. Still not happening." His dimple surfaced. "I'm sure Thompson had a field day with it."

Marta laughed. "He did."

"Of course, Felipe's other theory is that you're an incognito NFL player."

Eliot cocked his head to one side. "Now *that* I'd consider." Leaning back on his palms, he extended his long legs in front of him and crossed them at the ankles. Typical Eliot. He wasn't giving an inch, neither admitting nor denying a thing. What an adventurous life he must lead. At least he'd stayed safe from harm—except for the black eye—in his latest travels. Marta couldn't bear the thought of anything happening to this man.

Across the prayer circle from her, Kevin planted a kiss on Rebekah's forehead. Beck seemed to be feeling better. Next to them, with Gracie on his lap, Marc moved his arm around Natalie. A few months into her pregnancy, Natalie wasn't showing yet. After some initial morning sickness, she now glowed and was the picture of health. And Gracie. With an exquisite china doll face surrounded by a mass of gorgeous dark hair and a perennially mischievous smile, Gracie was already pushing Joe's buttons. They should be fun to watch.

"Want to take a walk together after the devotions?" When she hesitated, Eliot nudged her shoulder. "Come on. You know you want to."

"Why? So we can play twenty questions about your job some more?"

"Not at all. I prefer Lexa's term of 'flirt and skirt' with one another. At least I think that's what I heard."

He *knew* about that? Covering her mouth, Marta muffled her laughter. Eliot's radar must be set on high.

"I don't think I heard your answer."

"Yes, Eliot. The answer is yes."

She moved her gaze around the circle as a convenient distraction or she'd be tempted to stare at the man all night. Winnie and Josh sat next to Cassie and Mitch. Chloe snuggled between Cassie and Winnie, Luke was on Winnie's lap, and Josh bounced Emily on his knee. All three of the Grant kids were fair-haired, green-eyed, and adorable.

Marta suppressed her sigh. The perfect family.

No, Marta. No family is ever perfect.

The Grants had weathered their share of storms, but they'd found their peace. All of the couples sitting around the circle had endured trials of one kind or another. They just made it look easy. With faith, family, and close friends to lean on. That's what it was all about in order to get through the journey. Sometimes she wondered if her journey would ever truly begin.

Sam and Lexa's three kids sat between their parents. Joe, a miniature version of his father, kept a protective eye on his younger twin sisters. The fraternal Lewis twins reminded Marta of Red-Rose and Snow-White, a German fairy tale her grandmother used to read to her. Leah was Red-Rose, dark-haired and outgoing, whereas Hannah was Snow-White, fair-haired, quiet, and shy. The sisters got along well, and Marta admired how Lexa chose not to dress them alike and encouraged their distinct, individual personalities unless they asked to be "twinsies," which they sometimes did.

Dean sat between Felipe and Angelina—that made her smile— while Sheila sat next to Gayle. Sheila darted frequent glances at the teenagers. While Marta understood Sheila's concern, she also worried that her overprotectiveness might have the opposite effect and push Angelina in the opposite direction. She also noted how Dean couldn't take his eyes off Sheila. Interesting.

"Is something going on with Sheila and Dean?" she whispered to Eliot.

"On Dean's part, yes. He's impressed by her, and I'm pretty sure he's hoping for more. As long as he can reassure Sheila that Felipe won't lead her daughter down the road to ruin."

"Felipe's all right. I wasn't a bad kid, but I definitely had my moments of rebellion."

"Didn't we all?" True enough, and Marta wasn't especially surprised to hear it from Eliot.

"I envision you as a scrappy kid. Am I close to the truth?"

Eliot's dimple appeared again. "You could say that."

They both sat up straighter as Sam opened with a short prayer. As Kevin and Cassie led the group in a few hymns and praise choruses, Marta enjoyed listening to Eliot's deep tenor. In some ways, his voice reminded her of Sam's—heartfelt and natural. She preferred to sing quietly since her pitch wasn't exactly perfect. Well, not even close. Her brothers had teased her relentlessly when she'd auditioned for a singing group in high school. Never again.

Sam rose to his feet with his Bible in hand. "Friends, on our first night together, I think it's important to remember our purpose and why we're here. We're not only helping to finish the construction of a church building for the One Nation under God congregation, but we're here to be witnesses of the life-changing love that can only come from the Lord."

Marta glanced around the circle, admiring how Sam commanded everyone's attention and respect. An ordained man, he was bold in proclaiming his faith in Christ and often led them in devotions at their TeamWork gatherings. Their leader and mentor *lived* his faith and consistently modeled a godly lifestyle. And now his ministry extended to a popular book series centering on biblically-based principles for building a successful marriage and family.

"When we think of missionaries," Sam continued, "we often think in terms of overseas countries where a large percentage of the population has never heard the soul-saving message of Jesus Christ. While it's true we're to be witnesses wherever He sends us, we're also called to be missionaries right here in our own country, whether in Texas, in Massachusetts"—Sam nodded to Marc and his family— "New York"—he angled his head toward Amy and Landon, then at Mitch and Cassie—"here in New Mexico, or anywhere else in our great country. Some of the members of the One Nation congregation are new believers who've overcome tremendous odds. A number of them have separated from their families and their old ways at great personal cost in order to follow Jesus. Most of us can't imagine what that's like but, as you know, that's what being a Christ follower is all about, folks. Picking up the cross and being unashamed to share our faith."

Sam slipped on his eyeglasses and then opened his Bible. "The verse I'd like you to meditate on tonight is from Hebrews 13, verse 2. It goes like this, 'Do not neglect to show hospitality to strangers, for by this some have entertained angels without knowing it.' Hospitality works both ways. In part to say thank you for helping to build their church building, our brothers and sisters in the One Nation congregation have graciously offered to cook dinner for us in our dining hall on Wednesday night. They've insisted on serving us, and all they ask in return is that we show up and enjoy the meal with them. I ask that you join us and be prepared to meet some of the best people you'll ever have the honor of knowing."

Sam tucked his glasses back in his shirt pocket. "That, my friends, is practicing the kind of hospitality that God intends. Hospitality that extends beyond our own inner circle. In large part, that's what TeamWork is all about, and it's our calling as ambassadors. When Lexa and I scouted this location, Pastor Chevy and his wife, Lila, treated us with that kind of hospitality when they graciously hosted us in their home."

Closing his Bible, Sam's voice was low and resonant. "The Lord has given each one of you unique and special talents. First Corinthians 12, verse 12, tells us 'For even as the body is one and yet has many members, and all the members of the body, though they are many, are one body, so also is Christ.' Whether a member of TeamWork, or a member of the One Nation Church, we're all called to serve the one true God."

Marta's breath caught as Sam's gaze zeroed in on Felipe. "You are precious to the Lord, and you're important to us." The expression on Felipe's face was difficult to read, but she could tell he listened.

Slowly turning around the circle, Sam's gaze encompassed each of them. "You're here with us in New Mexico for a reason. Never doubt that. The Lord is pleased by your presence here and your willingness to use your talents on His behalf. Our efforts will be blessed."

Clearing his throat, Sam's voice sounded a bit rough as he continued. The deeply held conviction, the *passion* in their TeamWork leader, never ceased to amaze her. Marta moved her gaze to Lexa. The love and pride in her expressive face as Lexa listened to her husband was a beautiful thing to witness.

"In closing, remember that—as always—there's power in numbers. I hope you'll let us help ease your burdens. If there's anything you need us to pray about with you, we're here for each other, friends. If you ever need private counsel, please know that my door is always open." Sam nodded to Josh before sitting beside Lexa.

Eliot squeezed Marta's hand as Josh ended the evening in prayer and then dismissed them. "Get plenty of rest, folks, and be prepared for breakfast in the dining hall at six in the morning." Josh laughed as protests and groans traveled around their circle. "Hey," he said, "don't hate the messenger, people."

Eliot offered his hand to Marta. "May I have the honor of escorting you back to the ladies dorm?"

"That's preferable to escorting me to the men's dorm. That wouldn't be appropriate." When he shook his head, she felt like a fool. She needed to watch the sarcasm. In some ways, it was a nervous reaction.

After tonight, she didn't know how many opportunities they'd have to spend together in the evening. The men planned to head back to the worksite after the prayer circle most nights to get in a couple more hours of work while the ladies and the children remained in the camp.

If she wasn't needed elsewhere, she might ask Sam if she could tag along. No, that wasn't the right word. Above all, she certainly didn't want to appear like a loyal puppy jumping around Eliot's feet. *Like me! Like me!* Goodness, she'd appear desperate.

"Marta?" Eliot arched a brow and waited, still holding out his hand to her. "Ready?"

As she grasped Eliot's hand and he pulled her to her feet, Marta hoped they'd take the long way home.

Chapter 9

~~♥~~

"Come with me, Angel." With his warm hand wrapped around hers, Felipe tugged her beside him as they walked.

"Where are we going?" Angelina didn't bother trying to pull her hand away, but she didn't want to think about the reasons why not.

"Someplace where we can be by ourselves for ten minutes. They're like a bunch of watchdogs around here." Stopping behind the dining hall, Felipe pulled her around to face him. She appreciated that he was gentle, never rough. In the back of her mind, she knew this wasn't a good idea. She should have been strong enough to resist him. Other than a dim light mounted on the outside wall, the only illumination was the moon. A light, chilly breeze softly rustled the leaves of the nearby trees.

When he released her hand, Angelina lowered her gaze. She didn't want Felipe to think that he made her nervous. Not that she was afraid of him. She wasn't. *Intrigued* best described how she felt about him. Catching a whiff of strong men's cologne, she wrinkled her nose. She'd noticed it at the prayer circle. What had he done? Run back to the men's dorm after dinner and sprayed it all over his body? That would have been a foolish thing to do considering all the bugs out here in the boonies.

Felipe planted one hand on the wall beside Angelina and leaned in close. With his breath warm on her cheek, he lifted her chin with his other hand. "Look at me, pretty girl," he coaxed, his voice low and a little husky. "You've never kissed a boy, have you? Never done anything?"

"What do you mean?" Angelina stammered, putting her hands behind her back and leaning against the wall. Thinking better of it, she crossed her arms in front of her. "I talk to boys all the time. I never even used to do that very much." Boys were generally annoying, bothersome, and sometimes downright stupid. She was dying to ask Felipe how many girls he'd kissed, but she didn't dare.

He'd probably give her a rundown of his love life and that wasn't something she wanted to hear.

"I like you. A lot. You do look like an angel, you know." Lifting a section of her long dark hair, Felipe twirled it around one finger. "You're probably the prettiest girl I've ever seen."

"Thanks, I think," she mumbled, trying to keep her voice calm and not doing a very good job of it. He'd probably said that to a lot of girls. And *probably* the prettiest girl? She wasn't sure if she should be flattered or offended. Feeling a tickle, Angelina scrunched her nose but couldn't stop her sneeze. And then a second sneeze.

Felipe frowned. "You got allergies or something?"

"No," she said after sneezing a third time. Mama taught her to pick her battles, and insulting the way he smelled wouldn't be good. Besides, she kind of liked the scent of his cologne. He just needed to learn moderation.

"You're not afraid of me, are you?" Assuming a deep pout, Felipe crossed his arms, mirroring her, and leaned against the building. "I haven't tried anything. Not that I didn't want to. You have to give me some credit, Angel. I've been very respectful."

"I have no reason to be afraid of you, Felipe. And yeah, thanks for not…trying anything."

"Like I said earlier, you're different from the other girls. In a good way."

She swallowed hard and met his gaze again. "How?"

Felipe's eyes softened. "You don't do things the way other girls do. Say things."

Angelina wasn't sure she wanted to know what he meant by that statement but felt it couldn't be flattering to any of the other girls. She stared at him, her eyes wide. "What kinds of girls do you know, anyway?"

"Some of them aren't so nice, if you know what I mean. They try to tempt me by wearing tight skirts or shorts, and their tops are cut down low in the front. They try to show me things and they want me to do stuff. With them. *To—*"

"Stop it already. That's enough out of you." When Felipe started to run his finger down her arm, Angelina swatted him away. Drawing in a quick breath, her heart pounded. "Please don't say things like that to me. I'm not like those other girls. Get that through your thick skull right now."

What Felipe said was shocking and unlike anything any boy had ever said to her. Part of her wanted to run away, but she couldn't move even if she wanted. If only Felipe weren't so good looking, it would be much easier to resist him. What he said was exciting and stirred feelings in her, giving her that all-over warm feeling. This couldn't be good.

"Hey, I'm just telling the truth. I thought chicks liked it when a guy tells them how gorgeous they are."

Time to try a different tact. "Felipe, tell me something."

"Sure. Anything you want. As long as you promise me a kiss."

"Nope. Can't do that." Angelina turned her head to avoid the intensity of his dark eyes.

"Ah, come on, Angel. Never?"

"Um, no. Not anytime soon," she stammered.

"I bet I can change your mind. What's your question?"

Angelina returned her gaze to his. Was his cockiness an act? Mama told her that people boasted when they were insecure about themselves. She'd also told her that if a boy got too close, she could deflect his attention with conversation. Questions worked as a deterrent to other things. Hopefully, that would work now. "Until today, have you ever been on a plane before?"

Felipe's eyes widened and he appeared momentarily stunned. "Why does that matter? Have you?"

"I asked you first. But no, I haven't." Why was he acting so defensive?

"So I've never been on a plane. Big deal." He turned to face her, still leaning against the wall.

"Take roller coasters," she said. "When you're up in the air on a roller coaster, you don't have anything between you and the open air. At least in a plane you have a thick steel casing or whatever around you."

"Yeah, true," he said. "Like a metal cocoon. I guess it's the idea that you're up thousands of feet in the air. And all the stuff you hear on the news about planes crashing—"

"It's okay to admit you were scared, Felipe."

"I wasn't scared, okay?" His tone sounded testy, and Angelina hid her smile.

"Fine. You weren't scared. Concerned. Is that better?"

Felipe frowned. "Do you have a point?"

Angelina lifted her chin. "I'm scared of some things, too. Being on an airplane didn't scare me, but being around boys....well, that kind of scares me. And I'm not saying I'm going to do anything with you. Because I'm not. For a whole bunch of reasons." That came out all wrong and wasn't at all what she'd intended to say.

"Ah, Angel." Felipe moved one hand over his chest, above his heart. "No fair saying something all sweet and sexy like that. You don't have to be scared. I'll show you."

"That's not what I meant!" She pushed against his chest when he drew close with a look in his eyes she knew couldn't be good. "Did you not hear what I just said? I'm not trying to be sexy, you big old ball of hormones! What's up with guys, anyway? I'm only 14 years old!"

He raised a brow. "Almost 15."

She sighed. "I don't even know what I want to be when I grow up. My favorite foods are still chicken fingers and macaroni and cheese, and I've only worn a bra for two years. Give me a break."

Okay, that last comment wasn't appropriate and she should have thought it through before spouting such a thing. Felipe had her emotions all mixed up and she was approaching this situation all wrong. What did she know of these things?

Great job telling Felipe about Jesus, Angelina. Had she learned nothing from her TeamWork friends? No way could she tell Mama about this conversation without her blowing a gasket and making them leave the camp. Mama didn't like Felipe, but more than anything, Angelina didn't want to leave. But she'd never admit the reasons out loud. Never in a million years.

Felipe stared at her for a few seconds before a grin creased his face. "I like macaroni and cheese, too. It's my favorite food and always has been, even when I ate it practically every day. Getting all the food groups wasn't exactly high on my parents' list of priorities. I'm not even sure what they are—the food groups."

"Fruits, vegetables, grains..." Angelina's words faded when Felipe placed two fingers over her lips.

"Stop now or I *will* kiss you. That's a promise." Trailing his fingers across her lower lip, his eyes never left hers. That must be one of the moves Felipe used on girls. She could see why a lot of girls would like this boy. Up until now, she'd wondered if he was all talk. Maybe not. Another reason she needed to be very careful around him.

"I don't need a lesson," he said. "You want the honest truth? I need a friend. Do you think you can be my friend?"

Drawing oxygen into her lungs, Angelina nodded. "Yes, Felipe. I can be your friend."

Moistening his lower lip with his tongue, Felipe gave her a small smile. "Wanna know why I want you as my friend? I mean, more than some girl I could meet at school or in a mall or something?"

What a random question, and sort of insulting. She figured he must meet girls wherever he went. They probably threw themselves at him. "Why's that?"

Felipe's gaze settled on her. "I watched you with Chloe and Gracie tonight. You're like a role model to them and that's kind of awesome. I've never met a girl our age who's so..." He lifted his shoulders. "I don't know. So good. So *pure*. And I'm not just talking physically. I'm talking about in your soul. In here." Fisting his hand over his chest, he thumped it a couple of times. "You care about people and you tell the truth. You don't lie even when you get on me about stuff." The light in his eyes dimmed. "I didn't have parents or anybody to tell me what to do or not do. Dad was in jail a lot, and Mom always went off to do her own thing, and she left me alone half the time."

Angelina snapped her gaze to his. "Even when you were little?"

"Pretty much. Getting their next hit or being with their friends was more important, I guess."

"What about your grandparents?"

"Dead on my dad's side and my mom's parents disowned her or something. All I know is that they live someplace in Ohio and must not care about me."

"Maybe they don't even know about you." Not that she had any grandparents to speak of, either.

"My mom told me that I wasn't planned. And, uh"—he scrubbed his hand over his face—"she didn't know what to do with me." A deep frown furrowed Felipe's brow. "Sometimes I'm surprised she had me in the first place. And that I'm still here. I used to have this dream about hitching a ride to go find my grandparents. I'd show up on their doorstep and say, 'Surprise! You have a grandson. Here I am!'"

Angelina swallowed, touched by his words. At least she'd always known she was wanted and Mama took very good care of her. "I'm sorry you've had to endure all that." She'd tell him about Papa sometime but not now.

"Have you been a Christian a long time?"

That question surprised her, coming from Felipe. Startled, Angelina lifted her gaze to his.

"Of course, you have. Probably since you were a baby, huh?" At least he didn't sound mocking.

"My mom started taking me to church and Sunday school when I was five. It's not a bad thing to be a Christian, Felipe. If you want the honest truth, making the decision to accept Christ into my heart was the bravest, *best* thing I've ever done in my life. I was only six, but I still remember how it gave me such a sense of comfort. I trust God's promises for my life."

With his arms still crossed, Felipe shook his head. "Yeah. Dean's been working on me, but I haven't given in yet. I never really paid a lot of attention to God talk before. I mean, Dean's a good guy and all, but he's a grown-up. Until I met you, I've never met anyone our age who believes in all that cr—"

"It's not about giving into anything," she said. "It's about admitting that you do wrong things and that you need help from someone else. From God. And you accept that Jesus died for you."

"Huh? I mean, sure I've seen all those pictures of Jesus on a cross. My mom used to wear a crucifix, if that counts. It's not that she really believed in any of that stuff or thought that it made her a better person. She never told me about any of it, though." He shrugged. "Religion was never a big thing in my family."

"The point is that Jesus didn't *stay* on the cross, Felipe. God sent Jesus to the earth, and He knew that He'd be put to death. But Jesus died for me, for you, for Mama and Dean, and for anybody who accepts what He did. Then the Holy Spirit—"

"Information overload." Felipe held up one hand. "I can only take so much at a time of this religious talk."

An inner urging kept her going. She wasn't done yet. "You don't know Christ because you've never had anyone *tell* you about Him before."

"Is it your job to tell me?"

"Yeah. It kind of is."

He studied her for another long moment as if pondering her words. "I like what I see in you, Angel. It's in your eyes and everything about you. Are you saying you care about me enough to tell me about Jesus?"

Hope shot through her. "Yes, I care about you, Felipe. Beneath all your big talk, you're okay." Partly from nerves, she couldn't help teasing him. "When you're not full of yourself or trying to flirt, I see the *real* you. The real you isn't so bad, and I want you to go to Heaven when you die."

"Well, I'm hoping that's not gonna be anytime soon." Tilting his head, Felipe studied her as if she were a curiosity. More than when he was blatantly trying to shock her, *this* boy captured her interest. This quieter, more considerate, and caring Felipe was a guy she'd like to get to know better. He moved closer, almost nose-to-nose with her. If he moved his head one way and she the opposite way, and they scooted closer together, their lips would meet. Angelina held her breath, hardly daring to breathe.

For the first time, she wished a boy would kiss her. *This* boy. But no. That would be wrong. They barely knew one another and Felipe didn't know Jesus.

"Talk to me, Angel," Felipe whispered. "Tell me about your Jesus."

Moving over a couple of inches, putting more distance between them, Angelina turned to face him.

Jesus, please give me your words.

~~♥~~

Tiptoeing around the dining hall toward the back wall, Dean put a finger over his lips when he heard Felipe's voice. After listening long enough to know what the teenagers were discussing, he gave Sheila a thumbs-up. Taking her by the elbow, Dean gently guided her back to the front of the dining hall.

"Wh-why are w-we h-here?" Sheila whispered. "W-w-we n-need"—after closing her eyes tight for a few seconds, she opened them again—"t-t-to st-st-op th-them."

"No, we don't." Dean kept his voice low, not wanting to risk Felipe or Angelina hearing him. "Angelina is witnessing to Felipe. I'd stake my reputation on it. Sheila, your daughter is telling that boy about Jesus."

"R-r-really?" Sheila moved one hand over her mouth and her

eyes glistened in the moonlight.

"You've raised a wonderful daughter. There's no doubt in my mind that Felipe wanted to get her alone and kiss her, but she might be accomplishing what I haven't been able to do. Maybe she'll reach that boy on some level I can't."

Dean moved one arm around Sheila's shoulders, drawing her close in a hug of comfort. It felt so natural. He hadn't thought about it, hadn't planned it, and he was pleasantly surprised but gratified when Sheila laid her head on his shoulder. Her dark hair was soft and smelled better than nice. Felipe wasn't the only one thinking of stealing a kiss tonight. The idea had merit but it was much too soon and Sheila was skittish. Besides, he'd never been the kind of guy to take advantage of the situation.

Dainty and petite, Sheila appeared almost fragile, but he'd glimpsed how strong she could be beneath her demure demeanor. He'd known of her through TeamWork functions, but Dean had never met her until Lexa connected them and suggested they travel together to Albuquerque. They'd talked a few times to make plans for the trip, enough to know she didn't like speaking on the phone, perhaps because of her stutter. After only one day with Sheila, he was already growing accustomed to it. It didn't bother him, didn't annoy him, and he didn't feel sorry for her although he felt empathy for how others might react. The way she spoke was part of her and made her special.

He knew the basics about her husband—the kidnapping incident and that he'd been killed in a botched bank robbery—but he found it difficult to comprehend that this quiet, shy woman had been married to a hardened man with a criminal past. She seemed too sweet and untouched by what must have been a bad situation.

"M-maybe we sh-sh-shouldn't b-be st-standing h-here wh-when th-they c-come b-back out." Sheila moved away from him as if suddenly remembering she didn't know him well and shouldn't be caught in his arms if Angelina and Felipe came around the corner. She was right. They'd never live that one down.

"Sheila, do you want to work together at the church tomorrow?"

"I-It d-depends on wh-what I'm ex-ex-pect-ed t-t-to d-do."

"If it's okay with you, I'll see if I can get us assigned to the same area. What do you like to do?"

"I-I c-c-can p-paint or l-l-lay c-c-arpet."

"I know some of the Sunday school rooms need to be painted. How about that?" He tried not to get his hopes up too high, but this was suddenly something he wanted.

"I-I'd re-re-ally l-l-ike th-that, Dean." Sheila's smile made her even prettier. While she wasn't classically beautiful, her features had character. She'd earned the few worry lines between her brows and on the sides of her eyes, but her smile erased those lines. Her big, dark brown eyes—gorgeous and expressive—were one of her best features. She didn't look much older than thirty, so she must have been a teenager when she gave birth to Angelina.

He'd been told by a few ladies other than his mother that he was handsome. In this moment, Dean only cared whether or not *Sheila* found him attractive. At 37, he was a few years older than Sheila, but what did age really matter? They'd determined they lived within twenty minutes of one another—on a good day, traffic permitting. All the more reason to see if a relationship might be something worth pursuing.

"How about I walk you to the dorm and we can wait there together for the kids to return? I think they'll be okay. I suppose we should give them a little freedom while we're here," he said. "Show them we trust them unless they give us reason to believe otherwise. And pray that doesn't happen."

At first Sheila appeared hesitant but then she nodded and fell into step beside him. As they walked, a truth hit him: she hadn't stuttered at all when she'd said his name. Interesting. Made him wonder if there were psychological or physiological reasons.

The one thing Dean *did* know was that he liked the way his name sounded coming from Sheila. Very much. He hoped to hear it again soon.

Chapter 10

~~♥~~

Marta walked beside Eliot as they canvassed the perimeter of the campsite for the third time. They'd talked about nothing in particular. She appreciated how he invested himself in her life even though there were limits to what she could ask *him*.

"If a man asks questions about you and listens, *really* listens, it shows he cares for you." Those words had come from her mother after Marta admitted her ex-fiancé had betrayed her trust and then called off their engagement. Funny how much she'd understood in hindsight. Liam hadn't asked questions or listened for a number of months before his indiscretion with a shapely blonde fellow law student came to light. She'd been a fool for believing his lies far too long.

They kept their voices low and waved at Sam as he rocked on the front porch of his family's quarters. "You realize Sam will stay outside, rocking on that porch, until he knows we're tucked safely inside our dorms," Marta said.

Eliot grinned. "I wouldn't expect anything less from Papa Bear."

The night chill was settling in, bathing the camp in a fine mist. Marta was glad she'd changed out of her shorts and grabbed her hoodie before dinner. Not knowing what to do with her hands, she tucked them in the pockets of her jeans.

They stopped walking halfway between their two dorms. "I suppose we should call it a night," she said. "We have to be up early and it's going to be a long day. It should be an exciting day."

"Most definitely." The vertical line between Eliot's brows surfaced. "Marta, before you go inside, I need to ask you a question. An important one."

"Okay. What's that?" Marta hugged her arms over her chest. She shivered but not because of the temperature.

"Are you dating anyone? Seriously?"

She stubbed one toe in the ground and winced when she found

resistance. "No, I'm not dating anyone, seriously or otherwise." She hadn't been out on a legitimate date in over a year but didn't want to sound pitiful by admitting that sad truth. "I couldn't sit around pining away for you, now, could I?" She could have slapped her forehead. What possessed her to say such a dumb thing? Lowering her gaze, she hoped Eliot couldn't tell her emotions—giddiness combined with nerves—were waging war inside her.

"I can't imagine a man not wanting a second opportunity to spend time in your company. Or a third. And so on." He laughed quietly under his breath. "I think you get my point."

Marta hid her smile, thankful for the cover of darkness except for the moonlight. "Eliot, why don't you tell me what's really on your mind?"

Surprising her, Eliot reached for her hands. "I care about you, Marta. More than I think you know." His Adam's apple slid up and down in his throat. "What I can't seem to justify in my mind is how it could possibly be fair to you to start something I might not be able to finish."

A frown creased her brow. "Sounds ominous. Let's get something out of the way first. You're not sick, are you?"

"No, I'm not sick. I've never been healthier."

"Then you're talking about your job, aren't you?"

"Yes." After releasing her hands, Eliot raked the fingers of one hand through his short hair. "What I do can be extremely dangerous. I know that the Lord's protected me in situations I never would have survived otherwise, Marta. He's blessed me with insight and discernment, and there have been times when I've *felt* His presence and known He's right there beside me. That gives me an unbelievable comfort and hope that I can't even adequately express."

"I can't begin to imagine," Marta murmured, trying to absorb his words. "I guess my biggest question is why you go on assignments that you know can be so dangerous? I know you didn't like it when I asked that question after you first arrived, and I'm sorry I made you angry."

"You didn't make me angry, and I don't want you to feel like you have to apologize for wanting to know about my life." Lifting his face to the sky, Eliot's sigh was audible. "As simple as this sounds, the Lord gives me the desire to do it and then He *equips* me to do it."

"Meaning there aren't many others who are either capable or

willing to handle such dangerous…assignments? Is that even the right term?"

He nodded slowly and his gaze narrowed. "Yes, to both questions."

"Eliot, have you ever had to kill a man?" That question popped out unaware. Maiming went without question. She'd heard he'd broken a guy's leg and laid him flat on the floor with some impressive fighting when he'd rescued Mitch.

Eliot didn't flinch. "No, but I've come close."

She gulped. "You'd kill if you had to?"

"Yes, if duty called and for self-preservation. Same goes for self-sacrifice. It would depend on the circumstances. I still think I'll make it past the pearly gates one of these days."

She knew he was teasing or she'd address that last comment. "Are you military, Eliot?"

His expression was indecipherable. "I'm not at liberty to answer that question."

Would she never learn? "I shouldn't have asked. I can't seem to help myself."

Eliot cradled her face in both of his large palms and skimmed the sides of her face with his thumbs. "I've prayed for you every day, Marta." That comment came out raspy and edged with raw emotion.

"You have?" Her heart was poised to take flight.

When he chuckled, the sound warmed her. "Tell me I shouldn't be offended that you haven't prayed for me."

She placed one hand on his chest. "Of course, I've prayed for you, silly. It's just easier to pray if I know where you are and what you're doing. But that's not possible." Not that Eliot had been far from her mind since she'd met him.

"I guess it's like faith," he said. "We can't see God, but we know He's always there, loving and protecting us. You might find this difficult to believe, but you're the woman I've compared every other woman to since we first met."

"How, um, many women are we talking about?" Backing away, Marta held up one hand. "Strike that question. Doesn't matter. Wow, when you ask a girl to take a walk, you sure know how to steal her breath. Not that I'm complaining."

"There have been women, but not a romantic love interest." Eliot stared at the ground. "I'm not sure I know how to be in a relationship, Marta." His gaze moved back up to her. "Will you show me how?"

Something about his humility in asking that question, and the way in which he looked at her now, seared straight through to her heart. Stepping closer, Marta ran her fingers lightly over his beard. Such a handsome face, such expressive eyes. "In the past, you've tried not to show your true feelings. Why here? Why now?"

"During the drive from Texas to New Mexico, you were constantly on my mind. By the time I arrived here today, I'd decided I couldn't allow myself to get too close." His eyes softened. "And there you were, standing in that field. Beautiful Marta. So ready to spar with me. At the sight of you, I felt things I haven't experienced in a very long time, if ever. And then I heard your irresistible accent and your feisty, independent spirit came out to play."

"Eliot, are you saying..." Putting a hand to her forehead, she was consumed by a sudden lightheadedness.

"I'm saying that I know the value of every second, every minute. The way I see it, we have the opportunity for a lifetime in the next two weeks. This really is *our* moment, Marta. If you're willing, let's explore this attraction between us and see where it goes." He rested his cheek against her hair. "This isn't some spur-of-the-moment decision. I'm not looking for a fling, an affair, or a mission romance. No other woman has your fire, your intelligence, your ability to keep me in line and challenge me. You're funny. I love your beautiful eyes, your blonde curls, and your adorable nose." His gaze moved lower. "Your lips."

When he opened his arms, Marta willingly fell into Eliot's embrace. He wrapped those strong arms around her with surprising tenderness. She was surprised he didn't kiss her, but another part of her whispered that it was too soon.

Leaning her head on his broad, solid chest, Marta memorized the smell of him—a combination of the outdoors, a faint hint of lingering freshness from soap or laundry detergent, as well as something undeniably male and uniquely Eliot. A tear escaped. How long would she need to carry this memory of him? Sadness threatened to overtake her. Blinking hard, she tried to keep more tears at bay.

Pulling back, Eliot's strong arms still encircled her. "Why the tears?"

Sniffling, Marta shook her head. "I'm not crying. Not really."

"I've got a wet spot on my shirt to disprove that statement."

Marta glimpsed his dimple when it appeared beneath the stubble. "I have a question I hope you can answer."

"Go for it."

"Where do you live, Eliot? Physically live? Trust me, you can't imagine how silly I feel asking that question."

"I live all over the world, but my current home address is in Texas. Not far from Houston."

Marta stifled her gasp. "You mean all this time you've been so close—"

"Yes, but I'm away from home about eighty percent of the year on average." The regret in his voice was apparent. "It takes a strong woman to even want to be in my life."

She searched his eyes. "And you believe that I'm strong enough?"

"Yes. I wouldn't be saying these things to you otherwise. I'll tell you something else." With his arms still around her, he inched her closer. "You're the most unforgettable woman I've ever met."

Heat rose in Marta's cheeks. What could she say to that? She was still trying to wrap her mind around this entire conversation. "Thank you," she whispered. Of all the things she thought they might discuss on their first night together, she'd never have imagined such open honesty, such revelations, from Eliot.

"Well, you have to know you've pretty much spoiled other men for me."

He tilted his head. "That's a heady—not to mention intriguing—statement."

She laughed a little. "Trust me, it's all good. You're the singular most intriguing man I've ever met. And yes, unforgettable." For a second, she enjoyed the masculine pride that flittered in Eliot's expression at that statement, but she needed to keep going. "I've enjoyed every minute of getting to know you the past few years, but the truth is, we don't really know each other all that well, do we? We pass each other at various TeamWork events, spend a little time flirting and teasing, but some of those times are at weddings and funerals where emotions are running high and the adrenaline is freely flowing."

"True," he said, and nodded for her to continue. Eliot *did* know her well since he'd obviously sensed she wasn't done yet.

"Neither one of us is denying the mutual attraction between us. Now you're telling me you'd like us to pursue a relationship although you're not sure it's fair to me. You can't tell me what you do for a living except that your job can be extremely dangerous and your faith has carried you through situations you might not have survived otherwise. And although you live not far from Houston, you're not home most of the year?"

He leaned his forehead on hers for a few seconds. "Yes. That's pretty much it." His hold on her waist eased and he started to pull away.

"Stay right where you are, please." Eliot remained silent, waiting.

"All I know is that I've never felt safer in my life than I do right now, Eliot. I say bring on the creepy crawlies and the wild beasts! You put up with my sarcasm, you laugh at my dumb jokes, and you still somehow seem to like me. You're a brave man in more ways than one, it would seem." Tracing her fingertips over his forehead, Marta pushed aside a stray lock of hair. Then she moved them over his high cheekbones and down to his square, well-defined jaw. "I have a suggestion. Like you said, I agree that we should see how the next two weeks go. Then we can take it from there. We don't have to make any major life decisions tonight, do we?"

Those dark eyes bore into her with such tenderness it stole her breath. "Fair warning. I don't do anything halfway. I approach everything with a win-at-all-costs attitude. I'm sure that would intimidate a lot of women."

"Even so, you're not exactly an unlovable kind of guy."

"So," he said, the dimple resurfacing, "your answer is yes?"

Her heart in her throat, Marta nodded. "For the mission. Then if all goes well…"

He raised a brow. "Yes?"

Eliot had been so honest with her, and she needed to do the same for him. "If all goes well, then we'll go back home to Texas and I'll take the twenty percent you're offering."

His slow moving smile made her warm everywhere. "Not that we're making any major life decisions."

"Of course not." She lifted her chin, giving him the freedom and power to do what he wished.

Pressing his lips to her cheek, he whispered in her ear. "When I love a woman, I'm going to love hard. Passionately."

Oh my. Marta stepped back a few paces, wondering if she could stand upright and not fall in a heap at this man's feet. "That's not exactly a fair statement to say to a girl you haven't seen in a while." She brought one hand up to her burning cheek.

"That's why I need you to show me how to be in a relationship. Too much?"

"Just a little. It was, um…good. The problem, Eliot, is that it was *too* good."

"You'll probably consider this statement equally unfair, but as much as I want to kiss you right now, we need to wait. I can't take advantage of this situation no matter how much I might want to do that very thing."

Inside Marta, a little voice screamed for him to go right ahead. She stared at him, uncertain whether to smile or frown. "Who said anything about kissing?"

"You did. You see, Marta, your eyes don't lie."

"That's kind of arrogant, isn't it?" She hated that she was so transparent. Then again, Eliot was one of the most intelligent, perceptive men she'd ever known.

"Well, if there's not going to be any kissing going on tonight, I guess it's best if we say good night now and return to the dorms. Energized and ready to start this brand new relationship between us in the morning. I couldn't be happier. How about you?" As she walked past him, Marta brushed his shoulder with hers. Bumped, really. Flippancy had to work right now. Otherwise, she might very well topple over from all the emotions swirling in her mind.

Eliot's lips upturned and he grabbed hold of her hand and walked her to the door of the women's dorm. "Get some sleep. Tomorrow morning's going to come awfully fast."

"Right," she mumbled, unsure whether to feel rejected or appreciative that one of them was exercising caution and setting boundaries. "I'll look forward to finding out whether you're a morning person." Lowering her gaze, Marta attempted to extricate her hand from his, but Eliot increased his hold.

"If I'd kissed you tonight, I would have been hard-pressed to stop." He'd lowered his voice, and she was thankful in case any of the ladies inside were awake and could hear their conversation. They'd love it, but she wasn't in the mood to analyze anything. For what remained of the night, she simply wanted to savor this conversation.

"The tension was too high between us, and I also know my limits. For over two years, I've thought about kissing you. It will happen, Marta, but not tonight." He released her hand. "Now, off with you."

"You're actually *shooing* me? I suppose you're not going to leave until I'm inside the dorm?"

"That would be correct," he said. "In everything we've shared tonight, I didn't tell you the most important thing."

She stared at him. "I'm pretty much on emotional overload right now, so I can't even begin to imagine what you *didn't* say."

"Every moment I've spent with you has brought joy to my life. Falling in love has been the one thing in my life that's scared me the most. Until now."

Her heart swelled. A man who faced danger on an almost daily basis could be scared of falling in love? "I'm scared, too, Eliot. What do you say, let's be scared together?"

"Let me show you how I greet and sometimes say good-bye to the TeamWork guys and my Christian friends. It can work for us, too. At least for tonight."

"Instead of a kiss?"

Pursing his lips, she could tell he tried not to laugh, but his chuckle escaped. "Raise your hand and make a fist."

She raised her right hand and curled her fingers into a fist. "Now what? Please don't tell me you were greeting another woman like this and that's how you got the black eye."

"Repeat after me, please." Eliot brought his fist closer to hers and they lightly bumped knuckles. "Everything according to His purpose."

"Everything according to His purpose," she said. No doubt about his meaning there.

"Good night, Marta. Sleep well."

"Good night, Eliot. Same to you."

Slipping inside the dorm, she locked the door and then moved over to the side window. She watched as Eliot headed in the direction of the men's dorm a few hundred yards away. Pausing in the doorway, he turned and waved.

She returned his wave before moving over to her bunk, the first one closest to the door. She should go brush her teeth before going to bed, but for once, she decided against it. Getting used to the sharing arrangement for the facilities might take some doing and she didn't want to run into one of the men in the bathroom by accident. Not going to happen.

After undressing quickly, Marta tugged her nightshirt over her head and then slipped under the sheets. What a night.

As if I have a prayer of sleeping now, Mr. Marchand.

Tossing and turning in her bed, Angelina frowned. In her unrest, she'd managed to dislodge the fitted sheet. She climbed out of the bed and quickly tugged it back over the top right corner of the mattress. As she worked, her fingers touched something stuck between the mattress and the steel bed frame. Felt like a book. Dislodging it, she pulled out a small, well-worn paperback.

The pages were yellowed, some dog-eared. The woman on the cover was falling out of the top of her dress. A bare-chested, well-muscled man stood behind her, and the woman's chin was raised as if anticipating his kiss. The expressions on their faces, and the positioning of the man's hands, left little to the imagination. She might be naïve in some respects, but she'd seen this kind of book before. It definitely wasn't a Christian-themed romance. If they sold this kind of book in the grocery store where anyone—even kids could pick them up—could it really be all that bad?

Dare she open the book? No, she couldn't. Mama would kill her. Angelina darted a glance at her mom, fast asleep in the bed next to her. The light from the moon filtering through the window beside her bed illuminated the pages. With shaking fingers, Angelina opened it. What she read on the first page of the novel made her gasp. Covering her mouth, she looked around the room, satisfied everyone else was asleep—even Marta, the last one to come in tonight. She'd be humiliated if one of the ladies found her reading this…smut. Of course, she'd heard about books like this. Half the girls in her school talked about them. The guys had their magazines with pictures, and the girls had books that painted pictures with words.

Drawn by an irresistible urge, Angelina flipped through the book, pausing at a few of the folded pages. Her eyes widened and her pulse raced. She wanted to keep reading. Scary thought. Closing the book, she tucked it back where she'd found it. Maybe she should go take a shower but that wouldn't wash away what she'd read. What a mistake. Now the images and words might be stuck in her brain. It'd been written to grab attention, and it accomplished that purpose. Was this what pornography was all about? Wow. This stuff could definitely play with your mind.

Snuggling under the blanket, she closed her eyes tight and tried to concentrate. *Lord, I know I shouldn't look at that book. I'm sorry. I've never read anything like that before, and I know it's wrong. Why do people write things like that and why would anyone pay to read it? I don't understand it. Maybe they don't know any better. They don't know you the way I do, and that's why I need to stay away from it. Help me to be good. I don't want to think bad thoughts. Be with Felipe, too, Father. He's asking questions about you. He needs you. Help me to be patient and not too sarcastic with him. Help Felipe to keep his mind and his heart open to you. And help me to be his friend.*

"An-Angie? Ev-ev-ever-ry-th-th-ing o-ok-kay?"

She froze at her mother's words. "I'm fine, Mama. Sorry if I woke you up. Go back to sleep. I love you."

"I-I l-l-ove y-y-you, t-too, sw-sw-sweetie. S-s-see y-you in th-the m-mor-morning."

That was close. She had to find a way to get rid of that dumb book.

~~♥~~

Standing on the front porch, his elbows crossed on the railing, Sam heard a sound from inside. He turned, half-expecting one of the kids needed a drink of water or a hug of reassurance since they were away from their familiar environment.

Lexa stood on the threshold. She held the screen door open, waiting for him. "Everyone accounted for and tucked in for the night?"

He nodded. "Finally. I thought you'd fallen asleep."

"All your loud thinking out here kept me up." Giving him a small smile, she beckoned to him. She wore her favorite white cotton nightgown, also one of *his* favorites. Her beautiful blonde hair flowed around her shoulders and trailed down her back. Taking her hand, Sam ducked beneath the doorway and closed the door behind him.

With a deep sigh, he moved his hands around Lexa's waist and pulled her into his arms. He loved her softness, her curves, her warmth. He'd been waiting all day for some quiet time with his wife. When she raised her chin, inviting him, he lowered his mouth to hers. "In case I haven't told you lately, I love you," he said when they parted. "You've worked hard to get this mission off to a great start. I couldn't do what I do without you."

"Same to you." Easing out of his arms, Lexa climbed into the bed. "We wouldn't be here without you. I'm so proud of you for getting this mission together. It's going to be great."

Sam removed his Stetson and placed it on the small dresser. "By the way, Mom and Dad called this afternoon. They wanted to make sure the rest of the TeamWork crew arrived safely."

"That's nice." Lexa yawned and slid under the covers. "One of these days, I hope we can convince them to join us on another mission. They're the most active people I know for their ages."

Pulling his wallet and keys out of his pocket, Sam set them on the dresser. "That would be great, wouldn't it? They raised us kids on mission trips, after all." Along with his five brothers and sisters, he'd worked on TeamWork Missions projects in ten countries by the time he'd reached high school. "However," he said, unbuttoning the shirt he'd put on for dinner, "at the moment, they have a personal mission to pray some sense into my younger brother."

A slight frown furrowed Lexa's brow. "Let me guess. The astronaut brother?"

"You got it." Dropping into a chair, he began to unlace his work boots. "The *Earth to Will Project* is what Mom's calling it. I told her he'll come around. Right now he's caught up in the prestige and hoopla of being named as a shuttle commander for an upcoming mission. When we get back to Houston—speaking of hospitality— I'm going to invite Will and Carson on an overnight camping trip. Get the three of us together to go fishing like we used to growing up." After tugging the boots from his feet, Sam tucked them under the chair.

Lexa watched as he finished undressing and draped his clothes over the chair. "I think that's a great plan. Which reminds me, I should call your sisters and see how they're doing. Time to catch up. Now, switching gears for a minute"—she gave him a smile he found enticing although he knew that wasn't her intent—"based on what

I've witnessed today, we have three new romances—or at least the potential for them—going on in our camp."

"Hold that thought." After checking on the kids sleeping in the adjacent room, Sam pulled on his sleep shorts and a T-shirt before climbing into bed beside his wife. Stretching out to his full length, he chuckled when his feet dangled over the edge of the mattress.

Lexa laughed softly. "Another bed made by the Lilliputians."

"Not a problem. That just means I'll have to spoon my beautiful wife." He crossed his arms behind his head. "Eliot came to see me here in the office before dinner. He's ready to take the step with Marta, but he has some apprehensions. Valid apprehensions, as it turns out."

"Well, apprehensions aside, it's about time. I understand why he might be hesitant, but everyone can see how much he cares for Marta." Her brow furrowed. "Eliot needs to give himself permission to fall in love."

"Is that right? Like I was hesitant about starting something with you?"

Lexa playfully poked him in the ribs. "You needed permission, huh? Even if you did, look where that landed us."

Rolling toward her, he kissed the tip of her nose. "No place I'd rather be."

When she snuggled against him, Sam wrapped his arms around her. "Not to change the subject, but your meatloaf was a big hit tonight. I heard Cassie say there's only enough left for a handful of sandwiches if anyone wanders into the dining hall looking for a midnight snack."

"Thanks," she murmured before yawning again. "Did you thank Leah and Hannah for helping make your peach cobbler?"

"I did." Sam ran his thumb lightly up and down her arm. "I'm sure they had fun, and it tasted great." He chuckled, taking care to keep it quiet since Leah was a light sleeper. "I told them love was their special secret ingredient, but I didn't breathe a word about the carrots in the meatloaf."

"Smart man." Lexa stroked gentle fingers through his hair. "What you said tonight about extending hospitality was so heartfelt. I'm afraid it's a dying art with today's younger generation."

Closing his eyes, Sam sighed with appreciation. "Ah, that feels good." He heard Lexa's soft laughter. "What's funny?"

"I was thinking how old I sound talking about the younger generation."

His eyes fluttered open. "You're not old, baby. You're beautiful. Always." He kissed her again, being careful not to get anything started. Not tonight. They both needed sleep.

Lexa rested her head on his chest and snuggled closer. "I hate to say it, but if I try to pray tonight, I'll probably fall asleep in the middle of it." Lexa covered her mouth as she yawned.

"I've got it covered, baby." He felt Lexa's smile in the lift of her cheek where it rested on his chest. "Now," he said, patting her, "we have a long day ahead of us tomorrow. Let's get some sleep. We can continue this pillow talk tomorrow night."

"I'll look forward to it. Love you, Sam." Her lids were heavy with sleep. With a final kiss, she turned in the opposite direction.

"Love you more, Lexa." Within the minute, Sam heard the sound of her light, steady breathing. Curling himself around her, he spooned his wife. Then he continued his prayer, ending with the same one he'd prayed earlier in the afternoon.

Lord, remind us why we're here and what you want us to do.

Chapter 11
Day 2, Tuesday
~~♥~~

Felipe nudged Angelina's shoulder as he sat beside her at the breakfast table. "What's on your mind?"

She gave him a half-smile around a spoonful of milk-drenched cereal. "You think you know me so well, don't you?"

That increasingly familiar grin creased his face. "Yeah, I think I do."

"I found something hidden in my bed last night." Against her better judgment, she wanted to tell him to gauge his reaction. Telling the adults wasn't an option and no way would she ever let any of the kids see that book. That alone was reason to get rid of it.

"And?"

Felipe slathered a ton of butter on a blueberry muffin, making her frown. "You might want to take it easy with the butter. It'll clog your arteries and give you a heart attack."

"Yeah, right. When I'm like fifty. That's sweet of you to care about my heart health, Button Nose. So tell me what you found. I'm guessing it's not something dangerous like a knife or a gun or anything. Now a diamond ring? That'd be pretty sweet."

He could go on all day with that line of speculation. Inhaling a quick breath, Angelina plunged ahead. "It was one of those romance books that's really a…well, it's a sex book." Her last two words came out more of a whispered hiss.

"A *what?*" Felipe's shocked expression almost made her laugh. He wolfed down half the muffin in a couple of bites. Thank goodness he didn't choke on his food or repeat the "s" word out loud. That would definitely send one of the well-meaning TeamWork volunteers over to their table. Not that they were exactly watchdogs, like Felipe had called them, and they were giving them time to themselves. So, that must mean they sort of trusted *her* even if they didn't trust Felipe. Even Mama had backed off a little and that was a minor miracle.

"You heard me." She stared at the fresh fruit floating in her bowl of mostly milk since she'd finished the cereal. Using her spoon, Angelina pushed the lone strawberry around the bowl. Then she fished out the last banana slice and plopped it in her mouth.

"Did you read any of it?" Felipe watched her as he chased down his muffin with a second large cup of milk. No wonder he had such great teeth. The boy definitely got his calcium. Just like Mama.

"Not really, but I saw enough to know what it was." Angelina told him about the dog-eared, yellowed pages. "It was written like twenty years ago. I can't believe people wrote nasty books like that so long ago."

Felipe shrugged. "Why not? Sex has been around since the beginning of time. Adam and Eve had kids, right?"

"Yes," she said, spooning the strawberry into her mouth. "And one of their sons hated the other and killed him."

Felipe chewed a bite of sausage and eyed her. "What's that got to do with anything? You trying to change the subject on me?" When he caught her smirk, he laughed. "Okay, I'll play along. Why'd he kill his brother?"

"Mostly because he was jealous."

"So you're saying that murder has been around since the beginning of time? Like the world's oldest profession?" He leaned closer and lowered his voice. "That's prostitution, you know."

"You're disgusting. Is that all you can think about?" Angelina dropped her spoon into her bowl, splashing milk over the edge. Taking her napkin, she absorbed the spill.

"Hey, you're the one talking about that dirty book. Why'd you tell me, anyway?"

"It's not like there's anyone else here to tell," she mumbled. "I was just surprised to find it in a Bible camp. You know, when Adam and Eve disobeyed God, that started the whole sin thing. It's gone downhill from there." With one finger, she rotated it to represent a downward spiral.

After draining the last of his milk, Felipe set the cup on the table and smacked his lips. "These TeamWork ladies sure know how to cook."

"They should since Lexa and Winnie own a catering business."

"Sounds about right. Okay, Angel." Turning to face her, he propped one knee on the bench. "You want to give me a Bible lesson? Go ahead. Start with telling me what you mean by *the whole sin thing?*"

Sometimes she forgot Felipe really knew nothing about the Bible. In a way, he was like a child. Well, except for this group. The TeamWork kids probably knew Bible verses from the time they could talk. Not that they were little know-it-alls. They were all sweet and sometimes they said things that made the adults think. Mama told her that Christians were always learning and being refined and sharpened by each other in order to better understand how God works. That made sense.

Angelina wiped her mouth with her napkin. "Have you heard the story about Eve eating the forbidden fruit?"

"Back to Eve again, huh? Yeah, I've heard that story." Leaning one elbow on the table, he gave her his full attention.

"God told Adam and Eve they could enjoy anything in the Garden of Eden they wanted. There were two trees: the Tree of Life and the Tree of the Knowledge of Good and Evil. The only thing he told them *not* to do was eat from the good and evil tree. But they disobeyed God and did it, anyway. And then they were banished from the Garden of Eden forever."

"Why?"

"First the serpent deceived…them"—probably best not to play the blame game with Felipe as to whether it was Eve or Adam's fault—"and told them if they ate from that tree, they'd be like God and know the difference between good and evil." Angelina shrugged. "They were curious, like most people. It was exciting and unknown, so it was tempting to do something they'd been warned against."

Felipe frowned. "So sin is disobeying what God says to do or not do?"

Angelina eyed him over the top rim of her cup as she took a long drink of juice. "Pretty much."

"Okay, then, I have another question. Did *you* sin by reading that book? Couldn't you tell what kind of book it was by the cover? Couldn't you see that it wasn't what you should be reading as a"—he made air quote marks with his fingers—"'good, Bible-believing Christian'?"

She blanched. He'd caught her on that one. "Um, I guess I did. But that's not my point. And I didn't really read it. Only a little. You've heard of the Ten Commandments, haven't you?"

"A little or a lot, you still read that book. What's the difference? Sin is sin, right? I thought that's what you told me with your whole black and white speech."

"As I remember it, you're the one who brought up that up," she said. "Not me. *You* believe in the gray areas."

"Wait a second." Felipe stared her down. "You don't think I know what you're trying to do here?" Something in his dark eyes dimmed. He didn't sound angry, but he looked plenty perturbed.

"What?" Angelina lowered her cup to the table. "Felipe?" Her jaw gaped after he jumped up from the bench and stalked out of the dining hall. He didn't stop or look back, not once, even when Joe called out to him. What had she said?

Noting that Marta watched her, Angelina sighed. "What is it with guys, anyway?"

Marta shrugged. "I'm sure they say the same thing about us. Want to help clear and wipe down the tables with me?"

"Sure." She rose from the table, hoping she could focus on her work at the church this morning and not dwell on the conversation with Felipe. Maybe, just maybe, it was possible she needed an attitude adjustment every bit as much as he did.

Lord, keep working on me.

Eliot stopped the drill and grabbed another nail. Positioning it on the bookshelf in the Sunday school room, he paused as he heard someone—or something—cry out. When he didn't hear anything for another few seconds, he raised the drill, ready to resume his work. Then he heard it again. A loud whimper came from somewhere nearby. Was it animal or human? Someone, or something, was in pain. Putting the drill on the ground, he ran the back of his hand over his forehead and listened for more sounds.

"Ohhh…"

That was all he needed to hear. The voice was female. After pulling the goggles over his head, he tugged off his work gloves and tossed them on the floor. Sounded like the sounds came from near the ladies room around the corner.

"Ow. Ow ow. Ow ow ow."

Marta. And she was hurt. Not bad, but she was injured. "Marta? What's going on?" Eliot stood outside the restroom, hands on his hips. "Are you hurt?" Dumb question.

"I'm fine. Go away."

"Will not. I'm coming in."

"Eliot, stop—"

Pushing the door, he stepped inside. Barged in was more like it. Marta leaned against one of the two sinks, hands anchored on either side of the basin. Gripping it pretty hard based on the whiteness of her knuckles. She winced. "You don't listen very well, do you?"

"Not when you're obviously in pain. I don't see any blood. What happened?" His gaze traveled to the hammer lying by her right foot. "Did you drop that on your foot?" Chalk that up to his second dumbest question in less than a minute. Whatever finesse he had must have been left behind in that Sunday school room.

"No," she said between clenched teeth.

"Okay, then. Did it accidentally drop on your foot?"

"Not the time for semantics, Marchand."

"Not the time to be stubborn, Holcomb." Without another thought, he scooped her up in his arms. Then he glanced around the small room, wondering where he could take her. The hired workers were everywhere and he didn't want an audience. Not knowing what else to do, Eliot marched into one of the bathroom stalls and used his knee to close the toilet lid. Lowering himself onto the seat, he kept Marta on his lap. He wasn't about to allow her to wriggle away from him.

She'd moved her hands around his neck as he'd carried her inside the stall but now she loosened her grip and appeared embarrassed. "I'm feeling pretty stupid, and I'm not sure this is appropriate behavior."

"Nonsense. This is a medical assessment. And don't call yourself names." Lifting her leg—a long, shapely leg—Eliot awkwardly tugged off the tennis shoe on her right foot. This wasn't the time to admire her attributes, and he needed to focus. After pressing and gently kneading his fingers over the top of her foot, he then moved them to the bottom of her foot.

Leaning her head against his chest, Marta moaned quietly. "Eliot?"

"Shh," he said, continuing his task which had become more like a light foot massage than determining the extent of her injury. That moan had gotten to him. *Concentrate.*

"Before you kiss it and make it all better, it's not my foot. It's my knee. And it's the left, not the right."

He stopped his manipulation of her foot. "Oh. Why didn't you say so?"

"I don't know. It's painful, but I'm enjoying this more than I should." A hint of a grin curled the corners of her lovely mouth as Marta burrowed into his chest a bit more.

"I know what you mean." Man, did he ever. He never wanted to relinquish his hold on her. She fit perfectly in the curve of his arms. More than a physical attraction—although there certainly was that—she breathed new life into him every time their paths crossed.

The idea of coming home every day to a woman like Marta prompted crazy ideas in his mind—things like how it might be time to ponder changing jobs for something closer to home. *Whoa.* Where had that come from? They'd been on the mission twenty-four hours and now he was contemplating leaving his job?

"Everything okay in here? I thought I heard someone cry out."

Josh. The door opened and Eliot glimpsed the other man's boot-covered feet as he walked inside. If his voice hadn't tipped him off, the sight of Josh's fluorescent green shoelaces did. Green was his son Luke's request. Sam wore red shoelaces. Marc had vetoed Gracie's choice of hot pink, but then he'd relented with bright orange. Burying his face in Marta's great-smelling hair, Eliot fought off a laugh. Those guys would do anything for their kids. Rightly so.

Marta cleared her throat. "Not a problem, Josh. Everything's just peachy." With her close against him, Eliot could feel her smile. Never was he more aware of a woman.

Josh grunted. "Marta, what size shoe do you wear?"

Eliot shook his head and Marta bit her lip.

"Eight. Why?"

"I don't think I've seen you in work boots before. Or realized you have such big feet for a woman."

He should have known Josh couldn't leave it alone. "Go away, Grant."

"Sure, Eliot. Sorry to interrupt. Just wanted to make sure everything's under control."

"No worries. We're fine," Marta said. "I dropped a hammer and Eliot's administering first aid."

"I'm sure he is. Carry on." They both waited until they heard the door close behind Josh. Then they heard his laughter on the other side.

"Well, that was fun." Marta pulled away and stood up, running her hands over her rumpled T-shirt and shorts. "I hope you enjoyed it."

"I did. You did, too."

She snapped her gaze to his even as she pushed the stall door open and backed away from him. "I didn't drop a hammer on my knee on purpose to have you charge in here like a bull and try to play the hero, you know."

"I like being your hero. How'd you manage to drop the hammer on your knee, anyway?"

"There you go again. It slipped, okay?" As she raised her hands, a pretty pink flooded her cheeks. "It just happened and the head of the hammer bonked me on the knee on its way to the floor. At least I had the presence of mind or dexterity—whatever—to move out of the way or I really *would* be hobbling around." With a frown, Marta glanced down at her knee. "I hope it doesn't swell. That's all I need."

Eliot resisted a grin as he rose to his feet. "Want me to check it for you?"

"No, thanks."

"Then I suggest you go back to the dining hall and get some ice. It'll take down the swelling if there is any. Twenty minutes on and then twenty off. We could do it here but you should probably head back to the camp and keep off your feet and rest. If it still hurts or is swollen tomorrow, you can put moist heat on it. We can also wrap it, if you want, and you should keep it elevated."

"You're a walking encyclopedia, aren't you?" Running a hand over her hair, Marta frowned. "I didn't mean to sound critical. I know about the R.I.C.E. treatment for swelling. I was a competitive swimmer for years, but I also ran track and suffered a few falls that necessitated ice." She waved her hand. "I think I'll survive dropping a hammer on my knee."

Eliot's chest tightened when he glimpsed tears in her eyes. He hadn't expected tears. Coming from this woman, they could be his undoing. And he'd suspected she was an athlete. Even now, whatever she did to keep in shape was working. A woman who looked like Marta didn't have toned arms, thighs…everything else…without a serious commitment to fitness.

Focus.

"You must think I'm a real klutz." Was her lower lip trembling? He wasn't sure how to react, but it made her appear softer, more feminine than ever. Those soft, tousled curls were already doing a number on him. Combined with her gorgeous eyes—the intense natural color unlike any he'd ever seen—he was sinking fast into the irresistible allure of this woman. How she wasn't engaged or married was incomprehensible.

"Not true," he said. "You've always been coordinated from what I know."

"I appreciate your coming to check on me. In the ladies room, of all places."

Splaying his fingers on the door, Eliot glanced at her over one shoulder as he held the door open. "I would have come to make sure you're okay no matter where you were. For some reason, I seem in tune with you."

"Care to explain?" Her features revealed more curiosity than defiance, and she winced again.

"I wasn't the only one paying attention during our walk last night." He paused for effect. "Was I?"

"No." She glanced up at him with such a sweet vulnerability that it socked him straight in the gut.

"Marta, I never want to see you hurt. In *any* way."

He heard her sharp intake of breath. "I see."

Did she understand? He meant it, but he wasn't sure Marta was ready for him to mean it. He stirred out of his momentary musing. "The ladies room isn't the best place for this conversation. Would you like me to escort you back to the campsite?"

Shaking her head, Marta limped past him and out the door. "I should be fine, and I don't want to take you away from your work here. It's not that far." Although she ducked her head, Eliot caught her biting her lower lip. He'd witnessed a lot of injured people, many in a precarious state of losing either life or limb, but the sight of Marta biting her lip brought out every protective instinct.

"This could take all day. Allow me." Scooping her into his arms, Eliot headed toward the nearest side door, being mindful as he navigated the doorway and exited the building.

"You didn't give me a choice."

"You gave me no choice. I can't have you limping back to the camp and risking further injury."

"You seem to like carrying me around."

He chuckled. "You keep giving me valid reasons." He did like carrying her, enjoyed the feeling of her next to him.

"Again, not on purpose."

"I know that, but if you keep protesting, fair warning: I *will* call you a klutz."

Leaning her head on his chest, Marta breathed out a sigh. "By the way, I like that red bandana you're wearing. It's…jaunty. Strap on an eye patch and I'll call you matey. And I'm glad you shaved off the scruff although it would work with the whole pirate image."

Eliot smiled all the way back to the camp. But maybe he'd ditch the bandana.

Chapter 12

~~♥~~

Dean wondered if he'd ever have time alone with Sheila. Maybe that was selfish thinking since it wasn't his primary reason for being on this mission. Earlier in the day, Pastor Chevy and his wife, Lila, had warmly welcomed them and introduced the TeamWork volunteers to the members of his congregation.

After Dean asked Sam if he could be assigned to work with Sheila, he was half afraid she'd change her mind, turn him down, and choose to work with Gayle in the nursery instead. How could he compete with Noah's Ark? When she'd shown up in the elementary school room wearing that shy smile, he'd considered her presence a victory.

A couple from the One Nation Church, Tahoma and Kai, helped them in the morning and told them some history about the Navajos. "The Navajo use the name *Dine*, a term meaning people," Tahoma said. "The first Navajo Indians lived in the western part of Canada, part of an American Indian group called the Athapaskans. The traveled south and most of them settled along the Pacific Ocean. The Indians who settled in southern Arizona and New Mexico became different Apache tribes."

"They learned from the Pueblo Indians how to make their own clothes, blankets, and grow corn, beans, and squash," Kai said in her sweet, gentle voice. "The men were the hunters and warriors, and the women were the farmers who tended the livestock, cooked, and took care of the children. Their homes were called *hogans*, made of wooden poles, tree bark, and mud."

The couple told them about the 300-mile walk, called "The Long Walk," where more than 5,000 Navajo Indians were forced to walk to Fort Sumner in eastern New Mexico and the famous treaty of 1868 that gave them their own territory and freedom. "The Navajo reservation is the largest in the United States," Tahoma told them, "and most of the tribes live in their traditional territory. Athabaskan is the most spoken Native American language, but most Navajo Indians speak English because the Navajo language is very difficult to learn."

They'd all worked together to put down drop cloths and used painter's tape to protect the floors. The walls were textured, so they hadn't needed to dust or vacuum the walls, and that saved a step. As a result, their work went quickly and they'd finished priming the walls before lunch.

After eating the sack lunches provided by the TeamWork ladies, the couple apologized and told Dean they needed to leave. Secretly, he hoped no one else offered to help. Not that he hadn't enjoyed hearing about the Navajo Indians. He liked history as much as the next guy. Maybe he needed an attitude adjustment, but he couldn't help it. He wanted Sheila to himself.

Painting the wall in the elementary Sunday school room after lunch, Dean tried to concentrate. Someone had left a portable radio in the room. To fill the void of conversation, he turned it on. The only station that came in clearly played country. Not his favorite, but Sheila seemed familiar with many of the songs, so he enjoyed the soft sounds of her humming as the two of them worked together. To his untrained ear, she was in perfect pitch. He wondered if she stuttered when she sang lyrics. Perhaps that's why she hummed instead.

After a while, he'd had enough of the radio. He needed to generate some conversation in order to get to know her better. It could be that Sheila didn't say much because of the stuttering. He wanted to let her know that he accepted and valued her. He only hoped she wouldn't think he was coming on too strong or being too invasive into her private life.

"The outside of the church building looks great so far, don't you think?" He glanced over at her. "They did a good job, and I hear they're almost done."

"Y-y-yes." Without stopping, Sheila ran the paint roller over the adjacent wall.

"I know Sam wishes we could have come on this mission when he'd originally planned, but I guess it was hard to coordinate all of our schedules. And then Katrina hit and TeamWork had a big hand in the relief efforts there." He was stumbling over his words.

"S-st-ill a l-l-lot to d-do in-ins-side th-this ch-church. G-God al-al-w-ways kn-knows."

"Sure enough," he said. "The hired contractors and landscapers know what they're doing, and we're better suited to the inside jobs we've been assigned. Even though I've built houses with TeamWork before, working on a church building is a whole different beast." Poor choice of words. "Wait a second. That didn't come out right."

"I kn-know wh-what y-you m-m-mean." She darted a glance at him and giggled.

"What?" Dean paused in his work.

She gestured to his hair. "Y-you h-have y-y-yellow paint."

"Oh. Is it bad?"

"N-n-no. G-gives y-you a l-look of so-soph-phis-ti-ti-ca-cation." That last word was obviously more difficult for her, but her smile remained in place. He hoped he could make her smile a lot on this mission. For one irrational second, he wondered what it'd feel like if she'd put her hands on his hair, run her fingers through it. That was crazy.

"Better than white, gray, or silver, huh? Then I guess I'll leave it in for now."

Dean stole another glimpse of Sheila as she worked. Her medium-length dark hair was swept back in a high ponytail, making her look years younger. Sheila wasn't tall but she was well-proportioned. Her deep brown eyes held a hint of sadness he wanted to help erase if it was within his power. Not to mention her lovely but elusive smile completely captivated him. From what he could tell, the shy widow had no clue he found her so intriguing.

"D-did y-you go t-to N-New Or-Or-l-leans w-with T-TeamW-W-Work, Dean?"

Again, she didn't stutter when she said his name. Unfortunately, she'd asked him about something that had triggered deep feelings of guilt for the past month. More than anything, he'd wanted to join the guys to help in the Katrina aftermath. "No, unfortunately. Duty called and I couldn't get away."

"Wh-what d-do y-you d-do?"

"Have you heard of the stores called Leather?"

She lowered her paint roller into the drip pan. "V-v-very ex-ex-pens-sive s-s-stores? B-boots, pur-purses, s-s-add-les, and th-things l-l-like th-that? Re-real orig-orig-i-n-nal n-na-name."

He chuckled. "I can vouch the owner's logical and practical, but you're right. He's not very creative."

Her cheeks flushed. "I-I'm s-s-sorry. Y-you m-m-must kn-know th-the o-ow-ner w-w-well?"

"You could say that, yes." Maybe it wasn't fair to prolong telling her, and he enjoyed seeing the color bloom in her cheeks. "Quite well, as a matter of fact."

Sheila's eyes widened and she clamped a hand over her mouth. She pointed to him. "Y-you? Lea-lea-th-ther is y-y-our st-store, Dean?"

After lowering his paint roller into the drip pan at his feet, Dean bowed before her. "At your service." He straightened to his full height. At five-foot-nine, he was the runt of the TeamWork guys. Growing up, his mother had drilled the measure of a man speech—how height doesn't matter to God—into him. Along with that, as a single mother for most of his growing up years, Mama Rose had taught him the value of a dollar and that he could achieve anything in life. For those reasons, he'd made her a silent partner in his business, and made sure she was financially comfortable.

When he started to smooth down his hair, Sheila reached to stop him, putting her soft hand on his forearm. She pointed to the yellow paint and then motioned to his hair.

He laughed and she laughed quietly with him. "Thanks. Guess I don't need yellow sophistication streaked all over my hair."

"Ar-r-e y-y-your st-stores fr-franch-chis-ed?"

"No current plans to franchise although I've had plenty of offers." They both resumed their painting. He was pleased when she asked him a few more questions. He'd always enjoyed telling others about his store if they asked. "Grandpa Costas taught me to work with leather from the time I was a kid. I like working with my hands and find it relaxing. The business started out as a sideline hobby to make pocket money when I was in college. During my senior year, I employed a handful of people to work on my designs. They worked from their homes and then I'd sell them at flea markets, conventions, places like that. The Lord blessed my efforts and the business took off. So, when I graduated, I figured why not run my own business instead of working for someone else? Now I run the daily operations full-time."

Dean hoped Sheila wouldn't perceive any of that spiel as boastful. "I've found that if something's your passion, you can be successful if you work hard and follow that dream." Well, maybe *that* sounded pompous. Like something out of *How To Be A Success 101*.

"Th-th-at's won-won-d-der-ful. Wh-where are y-your s-s-stores?"

"The flagship store is the one in San Antonio. We have five more stores in Texas and two in Louisiana. The stores in Houston, Dallas, Austin, and Baton Rouge opened just this year. We have both downtown locations and suburban stores since our demographic is wider than you might suspect."

"S-s-sounds l-l-like y-y-your c-c-comp-pan-ny is r-r-real-l-y gr-gr-grow-wing."

He nodded. "It's amazing what city folks will buy, Sheila. The city slickers sometimes like to present the appearance that they've just come into town from the ranch. That's what I call my Urban Cowboy Collection. We also have a lot of clients who are true blue cowboys and ranchers."

Sheila smiled. "Th-the b-b-belts S-S-Sam w-wears? Th-th-those are y-y-your d-designs?"

"Most likely. Sam's been one of my best customers. He's bought belts as Christmas gifts for the TeamWork men, too." He chuckled. "Kevin, Mitch, Eliot, and Landon wear them. You might see one or two here on the mission. Sam and Josh bought purses for Lexa and Winnie for Christmas." He laughed. "I'm still working on Marc. I'm trying to convince him even Boston city slickers need a custom Leather belt."

Sheila smiled. "I-I l-l-like th-the w-w-way y-you s-s-say 'w-w-we' in-in-st-stead of m-ma-making it a-all a-a-b-bout y-y-you."

Dean appreciated her sentiment, but he wouldn't tell her about the store manager who'd embezzled more than ten thousand dollars from his San Antonio store in recent months. That revelation had made him seriously question his character judgment since he'd handpicked the man. On paper and in interviews, the guy had been impeccable, articulate, and presented himself as a person of integrity. His references had checked out fine. People could always get greedy or go bad somewhere along the way.

Determined not to allow the unsettling situation derail this trip, Dean had met with his attorney the day before coming to Albuquerque. Being advised to wait until they could obtain more sustainable evidence before firing the man had soured his stomach. Pursuing legal action wasn't something he relished, but he'd worked too long and hard to have someone steal from him and then walk away without punishment or repercussions. As the business owner, the onus was on him to figure out a way to prove his case against the man. Somehow he'd find a way.

"Th-that's v-very im-impress-ive." Retrieving her roller, Sheila began working again. Her strong, sure strokes suggested she'd done some painting before.

"You're very good at this. Looks like you could teach me a few things."

She gave him another shy smile but didn't respond. He couldn't shake the memory of their unexpected intimacy the night before. When Sheila had rested her head on his chest, he'd felt the strong need to take care of her. Protect her. It'd been a long time since he'd held a woman in his arms for any reason. Perhaps he'd gone too long without female companionship. Or it could be, as Sam suggested, that he'd been operating on autopilot the last few years.

When Cynthia broke off their five-year relationship, he'd stopped dating altogether and immersed himself in building his business. Erected barriers around his heart and told himself he didn't need a woman. Didn't need love. Didn't need a family. His tireless efforts for the stores had paid off, but—other than attending church—he'd been negligent of his personal life.

Make more conversation. Get her to talk. "Do you like being a social worker? That's very admirable although I'm sure it can't be easy. Did I hear you also help with runaway teenage girls?" When Sheila appeared startled, he hastened to explain. "Angelina mentioned it to Felipe and I happened to overhear."

She nodded and seemed to relax. "Y-yes. I d-do wh-what I c-can t-to h-help g-girls wh-who h-have l-left th-their ho-homes f-for wh-what-ever r-reason. A-b-buse, al-al-coholism, si-sickness. Th-there a-are a-all k-kinds of r-r-reasons, a-all k-k-kinds of h-hurt a-and h-heart-heartache. I ju-just w-want th-them t-to kn-know th-there a-are g-good p-pe-people in th-the w-w-world w-w-who c-care and w-w-want to h-h-help th-them and n-not ex-expect any-anyth-thing in r-ret-t-urn."

"Do you have family members nearby?"

Sheila's eyes widened and grew bright. She blinked hard as if to prevent tears from falling. What had he said wrong? If he'd offended her, his only defense was ignorance.

"N-not f-family w-w-who c-care t-to h-help or th-that I c-care t-to b-b-be ar-around."

"I'm sorry. I didn't mean to pry into your life, Sheila. It's none of my business. I have to say…"

She stopped her work, staring straight ahead, as though waiting for his next words.

"I think you're a very lovely woman." He hoped she understood those weren't empty words or words intended only to soothe or gain him any special favors.

Sheila bowed her head for a moment before meeting his gaze. "Th-thank y-you, Dean," she whispered.

"Would you like to sit together tonight at the prayer circle?"

After dipping her roller in the paint, she resumed working on her section of the wall. "I d-don't th-think th-that's a g-g-good i-id-dea."

"May I ask why not?" He might have come off as cross, but he hadn't expected that response.

She didn't answer. Uncertain what to say or do, Dean kept working on his section of the wall. Although he tried not to look at her, he couldn't help stealing glances.

"I-I-I'm d-d-da-m-maged g-g-goods, Dean."

He opened his mouth to protest, but stopped when she quickly brushed away a tear. "I-I'm s-s-sorry." Lowering her paint roller into the drip pan, Sheila quickly wiped her hands on a nearby cloth and departed without another word.

Staring at the empty doorway through which she'd disappeared, Dean wondered if he should follow her. Like a fool—or a coward—he stayed and finished the job instead. The entire time, he stewed. Was it wrong to want to know more about her? To want to spend time with her?

Maybe there's a reason you're still single. At the rate he was going, he might remain that way the rest of his life.

A short time later, Dean carried the paint supplies to the small sink in the corner of the classroom. "Lord," he said under his breath as he cleaned the brushes and rollers, "Sheila's hurting. You know that better than anyone. Please show me how to be her friend and help her."

Why would she consider herself damaged goods? Because of the stuttering? He didn't think so. No doubt it had to do with her no-good late husband. Call it a wrong heart attitude, but Dean pretty much hated that guy. Howard Morris had been blessed with a beautiful wife and daughter and he'd squandered it all away like a fool. What a waste of a life.

Dean begrudgingly added another request to that prayer. "Help me get over this anger I feel for a man I never met."

Sheila and Angelina deserved better. If he wasn't the right man to give them a better life, so be it, but he was willing to try.

Chapter 13

~~♥~~

Sam talked with Marc outside the church, comparing notes and discussing the various assignments for the week. The finishing touches were being put on the exterior of the building, and the current needs were to complete the sanctuary, fellowship hall, and the Sunday school rooms. The list was ongoing, and they needed to place their TeamWork volunteers where their unique talents could best be utilized.

Both men looked up as a black sedan with tinted windows made its way up the driveway to the church. As it came closer, Sam spied a gold seal on the driver's side door.

"Any idea who that is?" Marc moved beside him. "Looks official."

"I think we're about to find out. Pastor Chevy didn't tell me to expect company." Based on the fact the pastor left the property a half-hour ago, Sam figured he wasn't aware of a visit. "Can you read the seal on the door?" he said to Marc as the car stopped. He'd left his glasses in the small office in the construction trailer, not that they'd help him much now.

Marc's blue-eyed gaze narrowed. "It's hard to read, but looks to me like City of Albuquerque. Founded 1706."

A long-legged woman emerged from the vehicle dressed in a pale gray business suit and heels. The woman's brunette hair was short and she carried a briefcase.

"She's overdressed for a construction site, wouldn't you say?" Marc said under his breath.

Based on the firm set of her mouth, the woman meant business. Smoothing down her skirt with one hand, she ignored the catcalls from the hired construction and landscaping crew.

Turning in their direction, Sam gave the men a pointed stare. "Time to get back to work, guys." With a few grumbles, they did as he asked. Thankfully, they understood he was in charge whenever the other supervisors were away.

The woman closed the car door and gave them a curt nod as she approached. "Good afternoon, gentlemen. I'm looking for Pastor Cheveyo."

Sam removed his Stetson and walked toward her. "I'm Sam Lewis. My missions group, TeamWork, is here on-site helping to finish construction of the church. Pastor Cheveyo left a short time ago."

"Nice to meet you, Mr. Lewis." She extended her hand in a perfunctory gesture but then left her hand in his longer than he considered appropriate. Her gaze skimmed over him from the black Stetson he now held in his hand down to his dirt-covered work boots.

"How can we help you?" Sam narrowed his gaze. "I don't believe I caught your name."

"Stephanie Colton. How about the foreman for this project? Donald Morrison?" Brushing hair from her forehead in the slight breeze, she released a sigh. "Does he happen to be here?"

"He's been here all day, but he left a few minutes ago on an errand. I'm sure he'll return soon. Were they expecting you?"

"No, I'm afraid not. I happened to be in the area and thought I'd stop by to check the progress." Sam found that difficult to believe since the church was on the outer reaches of the city.

She moved her focus to Marc. "And you are?"

"Marc Thompson. Nice to meet you, Miss Colton."

"That's *Ms.* Colton." She frowned and glanced around at their surroundings, ignoring Marc's proffered hand. "I'm a member of the board for the City Commission on Indian Affairs. The Commission acts as a liaison between the City of Albuquerque and the Indian community. Our purpose is to bring Native American concerns to the City's attention."

Sam quirked a brow. "I'm assuming your visit means there are concerns about this worksite?"

In her heels, the top of Stephanie's head reached higher than his shoulder, but she raised her chin a notch. "It's been brought to our notice that there may be violations. Questions have been raised and complaints were recently lodged regarding proper adherence to standards and regulations." Her brown eyes bore into him. "Perhaps we could go to the office to discuss this matter in private?"

Beside him, Marc grunted.

"Of course," Sam said, "but first let me call my wife to come and join us. She can be here in ten minutes." He angled his head to the right. "The office is in the trailer if you'd like to have a seat."

"Help yourself to a cold drink while you wait," Marc said. "You look a little heated."

Sephanie arched a brow. "I highly doubt your wife will be interested in these matters, Mr. Lewis."

Sam cracked a grin. "You haven't met my wife." He'd never agree to meet one-on-one with a woman other than his TeamWork ladies, and even then, he preferred Lexa to be nearby if not in the same room. He'd seen too many accusations of impropriety and inappropriate behavior leveled against men in ministry. Ill-founded accusations or not, the resultant heartache and damage to a marriage could be profound. He'd vowed long ago, to the Lord and to Lexa, that he'd never subject her, their marriage, or their family, to that kind of nightmare.

Marc stepped forward. "If you'd called ahead, Ms. Colton, I'm sure Pastor Cheveyo or the foreman would have been here to meet you." Sam resisted a smile, appreciating his friend's directness. No wonder his advertising agency thrived. Marc didn't mince words.

"Fine," Stephanie said. "We'll talk here then."

Sam planted his hands on his hips. "Pastor Cheveyo filed every application and received all the appropriate permits for the construction of this church building. I'm sure if you check the records, you'll see that everything's proper and in good order. If you'd like, I'll go pull copies from the files in the office and bring them to you in order to back up that statement."

"I assume you're authorized to speak on behalf of Pastor Cheveyo?"

"He is. Would you like to see his credentials?"

Sam shot a look at Marc. Not the time.

"That won't be necessary." The corners of Ms. Colton's lips upturned. "This doesn't concern the permits since they are a matter of public record." Resting her briefcase on one knee, Stephanie clicked it open and retrieved a red letter-size file folder and handed it to Sam. "This is a copy of the City ordinance requirements for every worksite—"

"Excuse me"—Sam took the folder—"but speaking as a

member on behalf of the board, can you tell me whether these concerns stem from the Indian community itself, the community-at-large, or from the bureaucrats?"

"Mr. Lewis, the primary purpose of the Commission is to protect the rights of the Native American Indians in and around Albuquerque."

"So you've said."

"Those rights encompass this land, including its value and intended use."

Planting his feet apart, Sam crossed his arms over his chest. "The One Nation Church is constructing a church building for a congregation of Native American Christians. This will be a place where they can gather and freely worship, as is their right under law. Pastor Cheveyo informed me there are individuals—Native Americans as well as others in the Albuquerque area—who have been opposed to this project from the start, but they've raised the necessary funds, and I'm satisfied they've followed all the applicable laws, including obtaining proper credentials, licenses, and permits."

"I have a question if I'm allowed to speak."

Sam nodded. "Of course." Maybe he'd been a bit overzealous and she deserved to be heard.

"How is your organization—TeamWonder, is it?—involved in this project? We weren't informed of your presence here. Which in itself may be a violation."

"That's Team*Work*," Marc said.

"My mistake. TeamWork."

Trying to damp down his rising irritation, Sam briefly explained the mission and TeamWork's role, bolstered by supportive comments from Marc. "If there's nothing further, I'll take your business card and ask Pastor Cheveyo to contact you." He held up the red folder. "I'll make sure he gets this information. Good day, Miss Colton." Replacing his Stetson and running his fingers around the brim, he turned to go.

"Not so fast, Mr. Lewis."

Inhaling a deep breath, Sam turned back around. The woman was only doing her job.

"I've tried three times to contact Pastor Cheveyo—twice by phone and once by mail—but he hasn't responded. Out of obliviousness or by choice, I can't be sure. I stopped here today, admittedly on purpose, to see if I could find and speak with him directly. I wanted to make sure he's aware of the special meeting—an informal hearing, if you will—called for this Friday afternoon in the Office of the City Council to discuss this matter."

That surprised him, likewise the fact Pastor Chevy wouldn't have acknowledged her calls. "No, I'm not aware. May I ask what agenda matters have any bearing on this building project?"

"To discuss this worksite, the complaints, and the possible violations."

"It's a little late for that, wouldn't you say?" Marc stepped forward. "As Sam mentioned, all the proper papers were properly and timely filed. They were approved. Once ground was broken and the building supplies brought in"—Marc waved his hand around the busy worksite for emphasis—"what else is there to discuss? As you can see, the exterior of the building is nearly finished. It would seem the Commission is a little late to this party."

Marc couldn't know a thing about City ordinances in Albuquerque, and neither did he, but his friend was always there for moral support and could bluff better than anyone. He'd also given Sam a few seconds to regroup.

"As far as TeamWork Missions, Ms. Colton, if we've violated or breached any City ordinances, regulations, or codes, it's the result of blissful ignorance," Sam said. "I assure you, if that's the case, we'll make the necessary adjustments or corrections as soon as possible." Surely that answer would satisfy the woman, the board, the Commission, and any other interested entity that might present itself. "I also promise you this: we will not bow to pressure if these complaints are prompted by nothing more than petty judgments or prejudice." Maybe that statement was pushing the limits, but she'd disgruntled him.

The woman's brown eyes shot fire. "Blissful ignorance or not, I hope you can appreciate that we consider every complaint and take the appropriate steps to thoroughly investigate and resolve it."

"I do, and I know you're only doing your job. This is the first I've heard of any complaints, and I hope you understand that your visit took me by surprise."

Stephanie's eyes met his for a long moment. "It would seem you're a very passionate man, and that's always a good thing in my estimation, Mr. Lewis. I'd suggest you show up at the hearing and bring Pastor Cheveyo and the project foreman with you. Government Center downtown at two o'clock on Friday. Good day, Mr. Lewis. Mr. Thompson."

A moment later, Sam had another thought. "Ms. Colton? Wait up a second." At Sam's call, Stephanie waited by the car, resting one hand on the top of the door as he approached.

"To be clear, you're not telling us to stop any of the work here in the interim, are you?"

Stephanie shifted and lowered her gaze. "No. You're free to continue." The corners of her mouth twitched. "Read the report and I'd appreciate it if you'd advise Pastor Cheveyo to do the same. After Friday's session, we may need to reevaluate our next steps."

"TeamWork's general counsel, Joshua Grant, will be in attendance at the hearing. Pastor Cheveyo might also bring legal counsel."

"As you wish. Legal counsel's not necessary since it's an informal hearing, not an official judicial proceeding. But please feel free to invite whomever you'd like."

"Joshua Grant happens to be one of our mission volunteers as well as our attorney." Why that was important to add, Sam had no idea. For some reason, he wanted her to know.

Her gaze narrowed. "How nice for him. The more the merrier. Carry on, Mr. Lewis." With that, Stephanie gave him a tight smile before climbing back into the car and closing the door.

"That was interesting," Sam said as he walked back to where Marc waited. "Glad it's over."

Marc shook his head. "You can't see it, can you?"

"What's that?" Sam suspected what Marc meant, but he wasn't feeding into it.

"You're a beautiful man, Sam Lewis. Stephanie Colton couldn't stop staring at you."

"That was glaring, not staring. I probably came across as a little harsh, but she put me on the defensive."

"Understood. She wasn't exactly sunshine and roses." Marc put a hand on his shoulder. "I'd suggest having Lexa by your side at that hearing on Friday afternoon, my friend."

Sam grinned. "I'm sure Lexa will be there, but mainly because she'll want to be there on behalf of TeamWork. We'd better get back to work now." Removing the Stetson again, he headed into the church with Marc beside him.

"I've got to admire your stoicism," Marc said. "Her TeamWonder concept has merit, don't you think? Let's be superheroes. Grab some capes, masks, and fly around the world saving souls."

Sam laughed, appreciating his friend's humor. "Have you been sniffing the carpet glue?"

"Hey, you're the one who wore tights and a cape."

"You're never going to let me forget it either."

"What do you think that was really all about?" Marc said as they resumed their work inside the sanctuary a few minutes later. "Do you think this project's in any real danger of being delayed or shut down?"

"Not at this point. Sounds like a formality to me, but I'd still like to be there to support the One Nation Church. I'll give the report a cursory read and then hand it over to Josh. He'll let me know if there's anything to worry about." Sam frowned. "I'll talk to Pastor Chevy and see if there's any substantiation to Ms. Colton's claims that he's ignored the board's attempts to contact him. In the meantime, our mission is to help finish the church building."

Sam pounded the hammer into the wall with more force than necessary and he needed to be more careful. "If unseen forces are trying to thwart our efforts, they haven't faced my TeamWork crew or the One Nation Church members."

Marc grinned. "Amen."

Felipe plopped down beside Angelina later that afternoon. Startled, she closed the book and tucked it beneath her, praying he hadn't noticed the cover. *This is what you get for looking at that stupid book.* Nothing like getting caught red-handed. Ashamed of herself, she leaned against the tree behind her and tried to calm her breathing.

Pulling a rubber band from the pocket of his shorts, Felipe wrapped it around his hair, fashioning it into a ponytail that reached halfway down his back. He had really nice hair for a guy—shiny and healthy-looking.

"Aren't you supposed to be at the worksite now?" The tables and chairs arrived for the Sunday school rooms, and she knew he'd worked to unload and set them up at the church earlier in the day. She'd helped Amy and Natalie take the kids to the church nursery to help Gayle with the Noah's Ark mural. Later, they'd shared lunch and played with the One Nation kids. The kids were all either napping or having quiet time at the moment.

"I'm on my break." He grinned and nudged her shoulder. "I choose to spend my free time with you. That is, if you want. We can sin or whatever." Laughing, Felipe leaned away from her when she slapped his arm. "Hey, stop doing that, will you? I'm only teasing. So, what's up with you?" His voice sounded almost too casual and she wondered if he'd glimpsed the book.

Angelina pushed her braid behind one shoulder. "I'm on my break, too. I thought you were mad at me." Was he hot and cold or what?

Felipe leaned against the tree beside her. "I was, but I got over it. I figure this work camp will go faster and a whole lot better if we're not mad at each other, Angel."

"Can you tell me why you stomped out of the dining hall this morning?"

"I felt like you were preaching at me. You made me feel kinda stupid because I don't know stuff about the Bible. You're the one who pointed out I haven't had anybody tell me about it. Then I called you on the whole sin thing, and you turned it back on me." He crossed his arms. "I'm not the one reading that nasty book. Just sayin'."

What a hypocrite I am. A stab of guilt speared her. "I didn't mean to make you feel stupid, Felipe. I can tell you're smart, and I hope you can forgive me." She inhaled a quick breath and knew she needed to come clean. "You're right. I need to get rid of that book, but I'm not sure how to do it."

"You're forgiven." With those words, a whole new kind of guilt sliced through her by how easily and quickly Felipe was to forgive her. A lot of people who claimed to be Christians were quick to judge and held grudges against others. And never seemed to get over them.

"Just throw the book away."

Angelina shook her head. "Not safe. I feel like somebody would see it."

"Burn it?"

"We can't have a fire out here."

"Why don't you give it to one of the other ladies to get rid of it? To keep you from temptation and all that." Something in Felipe's eyes told her he knew she was sitting on that book.

Angelina shook her head. "Not on your life. No way I'll admit that I have it, no matter where I found it. I'm sure they'd believe me, but as forgiving as the TeamWork group is, I'd be embarrassed for the rest of my life."

"We could bury it somewhere."

"Where? I don't think that would work either. Someone would probably see us. I'll figure out something."

Turning toward her, Felipe raised one hand and gestured for her to do the same. "Repeat after me. I, Angelina Morris." He lifted his brows, waiting.

With a sigh, she raised her right hand. "I, Angelina Morris."

"Promise I won't read any more of that book until the talented, smart, and handsome Felipe Hernandez can find a way to get rid of the temptation."

She repeated his words, rolling her eyes and pretending to stumble over the flattering words about him. "You had a lot of fun with that, didn't you?"

"Sure did." When Felipe laughed, she realized how much she really *liked* the sound of his laughter.

"You need to relax, Angel. If everyone's as forgiving as you say, then they won't fault you."

"Maybe I should just stick the book back where I found it."

"Nah. Then in another twenty years, someone else might go through this."

"I know." It annoyed her that he was starting to sound like the voice of reason. Who was the better influence here?

"Hey, I found out that Mitch and Amy are brother and sister. And I could tell that Josh and Rebekah were related, but I didn't know they were twins. I think that'd be awesome to have a twin, especially one who's a girl. She could clue me in to how girls think." He winked at her. "But that's why I have you here. So you can tell me important stuff like that."

"You are so random." Angelina marveled at how his mind worked, switching from one topic to another in seconds. She watched as he scratched a spot on his left arm and then reached to scratch his leg just above the right knee. "Do you have fleas?"

"Very funny." Smirking, Felipe scratched his neck and then his left arm again. A few welts were visible on his exposed arms and legs.

"A little tip? You might want to lay off the cologne. In a place like this, it'll attract bugs, not girls. I think there's probably Calamine lotion in the first aid kit in the kitchen. Or check with Lexa or Winnie. I hear Lysol works, too."

He balked. "You trying to kill me? No way I'll spray that stuff on my skin to seep into my bloodstream. Besides, I think that's for sunburn, not bug bites. I might wear my cologne tomorrow night for the big dinner, though, in case I meet a cute Indian chick."

Angelina stiffened. "That's condescending in more ways than I can count. Besides, I think it's more politically correct to say Native American."

"You mean I can't ask one of them to take me back to her teepee? Or is wigwam more politically correct for you?"

"You're awful!" Angelina bit her lower lip so she didn't burst out laughing.

"You're jealous." He nudged her shoulder and winked.

"In your dreams." Although she'd never admit it, Felipe had hit uncomfortably close to the truth. "You'd better be on your best behavior when they come or you'll embarrass all of us." Angelina started to swat him but lowered her hand back to her lap. He was already bothered enough by the bug bites, so she'd give him a break.

"Oh, right. Heaven forbid I should embarrass any of the TeamWork people."

Angelina counted to three under her breath. "What's that supposed to mean? They've been nothing but kind and loving toward you. Please show some respect. A little gratitude wouldn't hurt, either."

"Hey, I respect them plenty, but come on, pretty girl. Nobody's perfect. You know there's got to be some skeletons hidden in their closets." Propping his knees, Felipe reached between them and tugged out a tuft of grass. He watched as the blades sifted through his fingers and floated to the ground. "No matter how many degrees they have, or how fancy their houses are, everybody's got skeletons."

"If people have skeletons, then that's between them and God, and it's none of our business."

Felipe slanted his gaze to hers and narrowed his eyes. "Answer this for me, Angel. Do you honestly believe God hears your prayers?"

That one was easy. "Sure. I know He does."

"But how? I mean, it's not like some big hand comes down from the sky and gives you stuff."

"That's because praying to God isn't about getting stuff." At least Felipe was listening as he repeatedly plucked out more tufts of grass. He always seemed to be doing something with his hands and rarely sat still. Was it a guy thing? A lot of boys her age did the same thing. In Felipe's case, maybe it was some kind of restlessness inside him that prompted his nervous energy.

He nudged her shoulder again. "I'm waiting."

"Remember how you asked me if I'd be your friend?" When he nodded, Angelina continued. "I've asked God to give me more opportunities to be your friend, and to be more understanding and patient."

Felipe stopped tugging out grass and stared at the ground. "You prayed about something like that? And you're not just talking about preaching to me? Not trying to convert me or whatever?"

That question was a little trickier to answer. "That's the kind of prayer I know He can answer." Maybe she should lighten up, like he'd suggested. "I'll only preach if you ask. How's that?" He'd asked her to tell him about Jesus, after all. She'd given him some things to chew on, and now was the time to lay off and give him some personal space. Sam always said to plant the seeds and then let God water them.

After brushing his hands down the front of him, Felipe jumped to his feet. "I'd better get going or one of the watchdogs will come looking for me. I promised Dean I'd do some work in the dining hall."

"Like what?" Angelina started to rise to her feet. Remembering the book beneath her, she plopped back down.

"I'm supposed to sand down the corners of some of the tables. Joe Lewis got a splinter in his finger and the mothers asked for someone to check it out. You ever had a splinter, Angel? Those things hurt like crazy."

He had a funny look on his face and darted a gaze to one side of her. *He knows.*

"A few. They're like paper cuts and annoying as anything. At least your finger doesn't hurt as much once you find it and pull the little bugger out."

Tilting his head, Felipe surveyed her. "You're cute."

So are you.

"Especially when you ramble on about stuff."

Angelina half-laughed, half-gasped. "You're the one who rambles! And stop saying the word *stuff* all the time. You really should vary your word choices."

Felipe's smiled grew wider. "You're even cuter when you tell me not to do *stuff*. How about that? I've got my own personal nag."

Shaking her head, Angelina reached for a nearby tree branch and threw it at him. Felipe caught it with one hand and twirled it between his fingers. "I kind of like it when you get after me, Cherub. But I'll deny I ever said that if you tell anyone."

She glanced up at him, her cheeks growing warm. "Thanks. I think."

"Want to come and help me? It'll go quicker and be more fun if we do it together."

"I should ask the ladies if it's okay. You go on, and I might show up in a little bit."

"Sounds good." Felipe started to walk away but then looked at her over one shoulder. "Oh, and Angel? I hope you're not getting any ideas by reading that book."

"Ohhhh…" Leaning her head in her hands, Angelina groaned. Whatever possessed her to tell Felipe about that book? Caught in her shame by the one person she really didn't want to know. Even more than Mama. The one solace was that Felipe wouldn't tell on her and rat her out. Revealing her secret wouldn't benefit him in any way. Would it?

On the other hand, she hoped he wouldn't hold it over her head.

Chapter 14

~~♥~~

Clasping her hands around her knees, Marta grimaced when she touched her sore left knee. As she waited for the prayer circle to begin, she thought about how wonderful Eliot had been in tending to her earlier in the day. After carrying her all the way back to the camp from the church, he'd taken her into the dining hall, lowered her carefully onto a bench, and ordered her to stay put. For once, none of the ladies were in the kitchen, and the dining hall had been quiet.

Soon after, he'd come out of the kitchen with an ice pack. Straddling the bench, Eliot had gently pressed the ice pack to her knee. They'd talked a little and he'd been sweetly attentive. She liked seeing the gentle, sensitive side of this man. He'd stayed with her until she assured him she'd be fine and ordered him to return to the worksite. Twenty minutes later, he'd departed with a promise to check on her later.

The ice had soothed her knee and she'd reapplied it again before dinner. Feeling guilty, she'd rested and read a bit on her bunk in order to keep her knee elevated. Thankfully it hadn't swollen much. If it had, she'd feel even worse about being so clumsy. Maybe she should stay away from tools and stick to projects that didn't involve heavy metal objects.

Marta startled when she realized Marc was speaking. She leaned forward on the bench, eager to hear what he and Natalie had to share with the group.

"We have some news," he said. "I think you all know patience isn't exactly my strong suit." Quiet ripples of laughter traveled around the prayer circle. "Some of you also know Natalie and I had trouble conceiving our second child. During that time of uncertainty, we contacted an adoption agency in Boston. Natalie and I went through the extensive process—interviews, paperwork, home visits."

"When I found out I was expecting, we never called the adoption agency to tell them to withdraw our application." Natalie reached for Marc's hand. "In case something happened with this pregnancy, we decided to keep it open as an option. We'd also indicated our willingness to adopt internationally."

Natalie spoke again. "Before we left Boston, we got a call from the counselor at the adoption agency. The counselor told us there's a child expected late next month who will need a home. A little girl whose mother is an unwed 15-year-old teenager. In...China."

A few collective gasps fluttered around the prayer circle. Sitting beside her, Marta saw Eliot smile and nod. For some reason, his response pleased her. Her gaze traveled across the circle to Angelina. She was almost 15. Old enough to be pregnant yet young and inexperienced in so many other ways.

Marc spoke again. "China's been widely considered as one of the best international adoption programs in the world. You might have heard there've been some scandals in the Hunan and Guangdong provinces of China with trafficking abducted babies. Since the beginning of this year alone, the counselor told me that more than twenty civil officials have been fired and baby traffickers have been sentenced to prison terms."

"We agreed to pray independently about it and then discuss it again early this morning," Natalie continued. "Neither one of us got much sleep last night. Not so much because the decision was a difficult one to make, but because we're excited by how perfectly everything has fallen into place." When her voice caught, she leaned against Marc's shoulder.

"Not that we've ever doubted God's perfect plan, and it's obvious His hand has been in this whole process," Marc said. "He's blessed us with a lot of love to give, a nice house, we're comfortable financially, and—"

"Gracie's been asking for a baby sister. More like begging and coercing." Gracie sat on her mother's lap, and Natalie kissed her cheek. "She takes after her daddy in that way."

Marc laughed. "Not only does Gracie want a baby sister, but she's insisting we name her Macy, Tracy, or Lacy. We're negotiating." His smile sobered. "The agency has given us the necessary assurances, and we have faith that an adoption would be aboveboard and sound. Friends, there's a baby girl in China who needs a family. So...*we're* going to be her family."

Marta jumped up with the other ladies as they all rushed over to Marc and Natalie. Winnie and Rebekah were first in line to throw their arms around their friends and hug them, and it seemed as though everyone was talking at once. Glancing at Sam and Lexa, Marta suspected they'd been tipped off to this news, especially when she caught the look shared between Sam and Marc across the circle. Those guys were tight. Josh slapped Marc on the back and they chatted like they'd been close friends for years, making it hard to comprehend that those two men had once weathered some deep personal rivalry and dissension.

"I can't tell you how happy I am for you and Marc," Marta whispered to Natalie when it was her turn. Giving her a hug, she planted a quick kiss on her friend's cheek. On the other side of Natalie, Gayle echoed her congratulations.

"Thanks," Natalie said. "Keep praying for us. We'll be raising two children close in age. Almost like twins, and we're not planning on finding out ahead of time if I'm expecting a boy or girl. Are we completely crazy or what?"

Wrapping her arm around Natalie's waist, Lexa joined them. "You'll be fine, and Winnie and I are always happy to give you long distance advice. Plus you know Sam's always willing to tell Marc a thing or two. I take it you'll be flying to China with Marc next month?"

"Try and stop me. As long as my doctor okays it, but I don't foresee any problems even though it's a long trip." Her daughter was standing next to her, and Natalie reached for her hand, giving it a squeeze. "Gracie's coming, too. We're hoping to have our new daughter home and settled in with us before the next little one arrives."

The group began to disband and their animated chatter faded into the quiet of the night. Cassie and Mitch were among the last to leave and Marta walked over to her.

"I think someone's waiting to speak with you," Cassie said. "How are things going?"

"Things are…wonderful. One thing about this TeamWork crew is that they know how fast a relationship can develop. This mission has already proven to be eventful."

"All it took was a weekend for Mitch and me. Think what can happen in two weeks." Cassie waved as she and Mitch started the walk back to the camp. "We'll catch up soon."

"You know it."

As she waved good-bye to her friends, Marta spied Eliot still sitting on the bench. He gave her an inviting smile. "Sit with me again if you're not too tired. How's the knee?"

She appreciated his concern as she sat beside him. "Sore but not swollen, thanks to your ministrations. Thanks again."

"Glad to hear it, and you're welcome."

Marta inhaled the scents of the trees, the night, the air. "We have such a terrific group, don't we? Really committed to each other. That's rare and special. Definitely something to treasure."

Eliot's gaze fell on her. "You're sounding contemplative tonight."

"I guess I am." She played with the string on her hoodie, wrapping it around one finger. "There are times when I wish I'd been in Montana on that personal mission to help Marc and Natalie."

"You hadn't joined TeamWork yet or I'm sure you would've been there." Eliot removed his jacket and draped it around her shoulders.

"Thanks, but what's this for?" Pulling the leather jacket closer about her, Marta enjoyed the masculine scent emanating from it. After this mission, she'd never smell a leather jacket again without associating it with Eliot.

"You shivered."

"I did? You're the most observant man I've ever known." She nudged his leg. "Maybe I should come to you each morning and ask you what I should be doing or how I should be feeling."

Although he chuckled, Eliot stared straight ahead. "I'm paid to notice details."

"No one's paying you now. Not that I'm not appreciative, but it's a little scary sometimes how you seem to know what I'm feeling before I do."

"That's not possible," he said. "You know how you're feeling. You don't think about it. Or you don't pay attention to it."

"Okay then." She drew in a quick breath. An undercurrent ran between them but far be it from her to understand what it was or what it meant. "Is something going on with you tonight? You're giving off a *something's bugging me and I'm not sure I want to talk about it* vibe. I vote we either talk about it or close up shop and call it a night. Start fresh in the morning."

Clasping his hands together between his legs, Eliot ducked his head. "It's not always about you, Marta."

She swallowed, stung by his words. "Trust me, I know that. Please help me to understand."

He turned toward her and their knees bumped. "No, I don't think you do. I'm not talking about you being egocentric or selfish. It's not a reaction to you or anything you've said or done. I'm talking about the fact that sometimes there are circumstances in my life that don't concern you."

"So," she said slowly, "you're saying this is really about you, not me?" Whatever *it* was.

"Maybe it's about both of us."

"You're not making much sense, Eliot. You told me you're on your own time for this mission. This is supposed to be the time for us to see if this"—she motioned between them—"has the potential to work."

"It is." Closing his eyes, he lifted his head to the night sky. "In a perfect world, I wouldn't have to keep leaving."

Marta's breathing slowed. "You're not leaving the mission so soon, are you?"

"I hope not." He met her gaze. "As of now, I have no plans to leave. I'm talking more in terms of my life outside of this mission. Sorry. I have a lot on my mind tonight."

"Let me take a wild guess," she said. "Things could change in a heartbeat, though, if you get a call. There's always the possibility that you might have to pull out of the mission and take off again. For who knows who long. Am I right?" Her heart sank when he nodded.

In that moment, a vision popped into her mind. She'd been eight, standing in the front hallway of her childhood home in Kentucky, begging her daddy not to leave on another trip. It was almost as though she somehow knew, in the deepest part of her, that it was the last time she'd ever say good-bye to him. The last time she'd ever see him.

Her father had once promised her that he'd always return. But that night, he'd kissed her mother, picked up his suitcase, and then walked out the front door of their two-story, three-car garage in suburban Louisville. Never to be seen or heard from again. He'd disappeared like the mist in the night air. And taken a large part of her heart with him.

Why did men always leave?

Liam left after they'd been together for years. He'd been the one who'd emotionally abandoned the relationship. And in every other way.

Eliot couldn't even stay for an entire TeamWork banquet.

Eliot's likely to do it again.

Maybe it wasn't fair to think that way, but that truth would always be there as long as he continued in his line of work. Whether or not it was his choice, he'd need to leave.

"But you promised," she breathed. Whether she was talking about her father or Eliot, or both, she couldn't be sure.

Raising both fists into the air, Eliot groaned, the kind of guttural, anguished cry that sounded as if it came from the deepest part of his soul. "Marta, you can't know how hard it is, how much it pains me, not to be able to share things with you."

"I can tell, Eliot, even if I don't completely understand. I was just remembering something about the night my dad left. He promised to always come home to us. Until that one night he didn't. And he never came back." Marta lifted her gaze to his. "That's all it takes. One time."

"I'm surprised I didn't know that about your dad."

"I don't tell many people." She shifted and avoided his gaze. "And I only tell my closest friends, those whom I trust implicitly."

He squeezed her hand and then released it. "I'm honored. You have no idea what happened to him?"

"No. My mom told us he died, but she's never shown us any conclusive evidence. No death certificate, no newspaper article telling of an accident, no death notice. Nothing. We used to beg Mom to tell us if he'd died, but then she'd run crying from the room. She's always refused to talk about him. My brothers and I finally stopped asking and we accepted that he was gone."

She shrugged and ran a hand through her curls. "We figured if he hadn't really died, he obviously didn't want us around. In a way, that was another kind of death. The death of our hope that he might return one day. In a way, it's like cancer. Before the diagnosis, you don't know what's wrong, but you have hope that everything will be all right or you wallow in self-pity and expect the worst. In my mind, the not knowing is the worst."

"I'm very sorry about your father, but not all men leave, Marta." Eliot leaned his forehead on hers. His skin was warm, and she felt the rise and fall of his uneven breathing. "All those things I said last night? All true, and I've never said them to another woman. Know this now: if anything ever happens to me, it's not because I don't want to be with you. I'll *always* want to be with you."

"I know." She *did* know. "Tell me something. Does your family know what you do for a living?"

"They know enough. They know it's dangerous and I have to be the one to contact them." His voice was barely above a whisper. "It's as much for their protection as it is for mine."

She gulped. "Would I be in danger if…?" She couldn't even finish the sentence.

Eliot wrapped her in his arms. "I'd do everything in my power to make sure nothing would happen."

Marta slowly withdrew from his embrace. "But that's not something you can promise, is it?" When he didn't answer, she lifted from the bench with a heaviness weighing down her heart. "I can't ask you to change your life for me, and I can tell that you love what you do."

"I do, but there comes a time to reassess priorities and weigh the options. It's not something I'll be doing in 15 years, but I don't want to lose you in the process."

"Then I suppose it's time for me to ask the 'Where do you see yourself in 15 years?' question?" She watched him carefully, waiting.

"I'd love to have a wife and family, a home in the suburbs. The American dream."

"What kind of job?"

"I have some ideas for creating an agency that helps others after they've suffered through a traumatic event."

She sat beside him again. "That sounds intriguing. Are you talking about a manmade event, or a natural disaster type of thing?"

"More manmade, but I've just started thinking about it recently."

"You'd be using your expertise and experience to help others cope with the aftermath?" She smiled. "Again, that sounds pretty psychological to me. Maybe you should go to school to be a shrink."

"I'll be too old by then, but this agency idea is a growing field and one where I could help make a difference in the lives of victims. My experience can play into it and be an advantage."

"In a way, it's a sad commentary that things happen that make such an agency a reality." She looked over at him. "So many people ask why God allows certain things to happen, but I think the question should be why do people do such horrible things to each other? In some cases, it's the ones who are supposed to love us the most who inflict the most damage."

Eliot didn't say anything for a long moment. "Unfortunately, you're right. Why do people bomb churches or gun down pastors in the pulpit in cold blood? There's always going to be opposition to what's right, and good, and just. In my mind, it boils down to ignorance."

"And the only answer is the saving power of Christ." When Eliot met her gaze, he nodded.

"You won't plan on eventually returning to your homeland, wherever that is?"

Eliot's eyes softened. "I love it here in the States, and my family has the means to travel at a moment's notice." That statement was telling, but Marta didn't feel as though she could ask further questions. Not tonight. Maybe as they shared more, he'd open up about his family. The only thing he'd revealed to her in the past was that he was an only child. At least she had that much.

"For the record, I don't want to wait 15 years to have a baby." With that said, she wasn't sure whether to laugh or cry.

"How many kids would you like to have?"

"A whole boatload when the time is right."

"Any idea how many your boatload would hold?"

She smiled a little at his question. "At least two or three, if not more. So, where does that leave us? What do we do now? I have to tell you, I'm pretty confused."

"We take it one step at a time. Look," he said, "we'll drive ourselves and each other crazy if we try to answer all of the questions. That's God's job, not ours."

She nodded. "You're right. You might need to keep reminding me, though."

"Same here. For now, I'd love the honor of walking you back to the dorm before I have to report back to the worksite." His use of the words *report back* might be telling. Or maybe she was analyzing everything way too much and trying to read meaning into what simply wasn't there.

When Eliot glanced up at her, sadness radiated in his eyes and in the slump of his broad shoulders. Rising to his feet, he offered his hand.

Marta put her hand in his. She hated how dejected he looked, but she didn't know what else to say. Could she give him assurances that she'd wait indefinitely for him? *Would* she wait?

She needed to pray. *Trust. Believe.*

"With God's help, we'll figure this out, Marta."

She squeezed his hand. "I know."

Chapter 15

~~♥~~

In his bunk, Dean leaned against the wall shortly after ten o'clock. He'd helped paint another Sunday school room after the prayer circle and now his neck was sore. After rotating his shoulders a few times, he flipped open his laptop, positioning it on his briefcase. It served as a decent makeshift desk. He should check e-mails, but he had something else uppermost in his mind tonight.

"Doing a little work, too?" From a few bunks down, Landon stretched out to his full length and crossed his arms behind his head. Landon had just closed his own laptop.

"Not this time. I wanted to do a little research before I go to bed."

Turning on his side, Landon eyed him. "I'm surprised we get such great Internet reception out here. Sam told me the former owner of the camp insisted on it so he could carry on his business when he was on-site. If it's not too personal, does this research you're doing have something to do with a lovely lady named Sheila?"

Dean gave into a grin as he fired up his laptop. "No comment. Journalists are used to hearing that, right?"

"Reporters, yes. I wasn't nicknamed 'Coop the Scoop' on the A&M newspaper staff for nothing. Sorry if I invaded your privacy."

"Not a problem, Landon. I'll invade yours. Everything okay with you and Amy?"

The other man grinned. "Couldn't be better, thanks. It's great to see her working with the kids, and then sitting with her at the prayer circle and stealing time together when we can. In some ways, it's like falling in love with my wife all over again. That can only be a good thing."

"You're an inspiration." Dean chuckled. "Eliot's right, though. You're all a bunch of saps."

That made Landon laugh. "I'm sure you'll find out one of these days."

"I dated a woman for a few years, but we were both more focused on our careers than a relationship. Well, that and the fact that Cynthia set her sights on the CEO of a pharmaceutical firm without bothering to tell me." Why he'd voiced that comment, Dean didn't know, but Landon was easy to talk to and he enjoyed his company.

"I'm sure you realize that if it was the right situation, it would have worked out." With another yawn, Landon slid under the covers. "All this physical labor shows me I'm getting older by the minute, but it's good for the soul. I'm pretty beat. Where'd you work today?"

"Painted the elementary school classroom this morning. I worked in another classroom tonight. I have the feeling I'll be dreaming in sunny yellow tonight."

Landon laughed and scrubbed a hand over his face. "Don't stay up too late. I hope it works out for you this time, Dean. Good night."

"Thanks. I'll see you in the morning."

Rolling over onto his back, Landon closed his eyes. The guy had seen straight through him. Was he that obvious around Sheila? Even if he was, did he care? Dean could answer his own questions with a resounding *no*.

Repositioning the laptop, Dean searched for *stuttering* and skimmed over the list of websites that popped up on the computer screen. Quickly scanning the lengthy list, he chose one and began to read how stuttering has been a subject of scientific interest, curiosity, discrimination, and ridicule. Moses stuttered, and a burning coal in his mouth had caused him to be "slow and hesitant of speech."

Seeing a biblical reference, Dean reached for his Bible and flipped to Exodus 4:10-13. *Then Moses said to the* LORD, *"Please, Lord, I have never been eloquent, neither recently nor in time past, nor since you have spoken to your servant; for I am slow of speech and slow of tongue." The Lord said to him, "Who has made man's mouth? Or who makes him mute or deaf, or seeing or blind? Is it not I, the Lord? Now then go, and I, even I, will be with your mouth, and teach you what you are to say. But he said, "Please, Lord, now send the message by whomever you will."*

Dean went on to read that stuttering—also known as stammering—is a speech disorder where the flow of speech is disrupted by involuntary repetitions and prolongations of sounds, syllables, and words or phrases. It didn't surprise him to learn there's a wide spectrum of severity and it has no effect on intelligence. He shook his head at the preposterous theories for the cause of stuttering: tickling an infant excessively, eating improperly during breastfeeding, allowing an infant to look in the mirror, cutting a child's hair before the child spoke his or her first words, having too small a tongue, or being the "work of the devil." The so-called cures were even more outlandish and included drinking lots of water from a snail shell and hitting a stutterer in the face when the weather is cloudy.

"Must be interesting reading."

Dean jumped. His laptop slid off the briefcase and onto the bed. He smirked as Eliot fell onto the bed next to him, laughing quietly. "Sorry, buddy. I couldn't resist. What's got you so engrossed? Don't tell me you're working."

"Not at the current time, no."

"I'm here if you need someone to listen."

Eliot was a close friend, so why not? "Since you asked for it, how about I read you some bedtime statistics?"

"Sure, but hold that thought. You keep reading and I'll be back in five minutes." Eliot grabbed his toiletry bag and darted out the door, being careful the screen door didn't slam behind him.

Dean continued reading. Aristotle theorized that stuttering was caused by a malfunctioning tongue. In 18th and 19th century Europe, surgical interventions—including cutting of the tongue with scissors, and other cutting of nerves, neck area and lip muscles—were used. Dean cringed at the thought. Anxiety, low self-esteem, nervousness and stress don't *cause* stuttering, although those things are often the result of living with a 'highly stigmatized disability'—whatever that meant—which can exacerbate the problem. While there are many treatments, including speech therapy techniques to increase fluency, there was essentially no cure for the disorder. That made him frown although he'd suspected as much.

Closing his eyes, Dean rubbed the back of his neck since it was sore from straining to read from the computer screen. Even though he was getting tired, he pushed on, anxious to learn as much as he could about the disorder.

"Okay, I'm all ears. Care to give me a heads-up?" Eliot tucked away his toiletry bag. After changing into his sleep shorts and a tank, he sat cross-legged on his bed, facing him. They greeted Josh and Marc as they walked in together, keeping their voices low so as not to disturb Landon, who'd fallen fast asleep. Mitch and Kevin weren't back yet. Dean assumed they must be spending a little private time with their wives. That's what he'd be doing, given the opportunity.

"You'll figure it out with this first sentence." Dean began to read. "In rare cases, stuttering may start in adulthood as the result of a neurological event—head injury, tumor, stroke, or drug abuse. Congenital and hereditary factors may also play a role, and children with a first-degree relative who stutters are three times as likely to develop a stutter. However, in certain studies, 40% to 70% of stutterers have no family history of the disorder."

"Do you know anything about Sheila's history?" Eliot said.

"No. All I know is that she stuttered during her first TeamWork mission in San Antonio. The same one where Sam and Lexa met. Listen to this," he said as he began reading. "Galen, known as the greatest physician of the Roman Empire, theorized that fear aggravated stuttering. Roman Emperor Claudius was initially shunned from the public eye and public office due to a perceived lack of intelligence because of his stutter. Aesop, the Greek author of fables, stuttered from infancy. Lewis Carroll, the author of *Alice in Wonderland* was afflicted with a stammer." Dean's eyes widened as he scanned the list of famous stutterers. "I had no idea some of these people stuttered."

Eliot reclined on the bed. "Give me some names."

"King George VI and Winston Churchill. Churchill suffered from a severe stutter as well as a lisp caused by a defect in his palate."

"And he was widely considered as one of the greatest orators of all time," Eliot mused. "You know about Moses, right?"

"Yeah. I just read the verses from Exodus. Did you know Tiger Woods is a stutterer?"

"Nope. Did not know that. Who else?"

"James Earl Jones, Mel Tillis, Jimmy Stewart, Julia and Eric Roberts, Bruce Willis, Sam Neill, Raymond Massey, Carly Simon, Anthony Quinn, Harvey Keitel, B.B. King, and even Marilyn Monroe. Also John Updike, Somerset Maugham, and Andrew Lloyd Webber."

"Interesting. Darth Vader? Marilyn Monroe? Those are surprising," Eliot said.

Dean read further down the list. "And what do you know? Charles Darwin made the list."

"Huh." Eliot's lids seemed to be growing heavier by the second.

"Get some sleep. I'm going to read a bit more."

"Sorry. We can talk more in the morning," Eliot mumbled.

"Sure. Thanks for listening."

"Anytime, buddy." Eliot rolled over.

As he read about the proposed modification therapies for stuttering, Dean started to doze. It all sounded clinical, complicated, and started to run together in his mind. Closing and storing his laptop beneath his bed, Dean extinguished the light and crawled under the covers. At least he felt more informed about stuttering, not that what he'd read helped him understand Sheila's specific case any better. If the opportunity presented itself, he might ask her about it sometime. Whether or not she'd stuttered from infancy, and even if she would always stutter, she was a perfect creation in Christ. If only he could help her understand that truth.

"You're not damaged goods, Sheila," Dean whispered into the darkness. "You are fearfully and wonderfully made."

Sam rocked on the front porch of his quarters with Hannah curled in his lap, and he hummed a new praise chorus Kevin taught them earlier at the prayer circle. He stopped when he detected sounds he couldn't define somewhere nearby. He waited. Yes, there it was again...a saw? Lifting from the rocker, Sam carried his sleeping daughter back to her bed. He tucked her in and bent to kiss her forehead and then did the same with Leah and Joe.

Satisfied all three kids were fast asleep, he shoved his shirt into his jeans as he strolled to the middle of the campsite and waited until he heard more sounds. This time, he heard muted voices. Sounded like they came from somewhere behind the dining hall.

Heading in the direction of the sounds, he stopped when he spied Kevin and Rebekah. They stood side by side, talking quietly. His shirt was off and his tanned skin glistened with sweat in spite of the cooler temperatures. Rebekah had a lightweight blanket wrapped around her and laughed at something he'd said. When Kevin pointed to something behind her, she retrieved a short, flat piece of wood. Sam smiled when he saw Kevin plant a kiss on his wife's cheek as he took the board from her.

"Should I ask or turn around and walk back to the campsite?"

Kevin and Rebekah glanced up at him, surprise written in their expressions.

"Hey, Sam." Kevin wiped one arm across his brow.

Sam glanced at his watch. Nearly midnight. "Kind of late to be out, isn't it?" Walking closer, he surveyed the supplies scattered on the ground.

"Give you one guess what we're doing." Rebekah shared a smile with her husband.

Sam moved his hands to his hips. "Considering all the lumber, I'd guess you're building a gazebo?"

Rebekah nodded. "You found us out."

"We didn't think you'd mind," Kevin said. "We want it to be a surprise for the One Nation Church."

"It will be." Sam's gaze narrowed. "It's a great idea, and I'm sure they'll love it. Not to put a damper on your little midnight rendezvous, but don't stay up so late that you'll both be exhausted. Kevin, maybe you'd better not handle any power tools in the morning. And it's getting chilly. Maybe you should put your shirt back on. Or get your wife to share a corner of her blanket."

"Thanks, Dad, but I'll be fine." Kevin lined up the board next to others, positioning it carefully. "We'll stop in another half-hour or so. Promise."

Rebekah smiled. "Kevin dreams about power tools, so I'm sure he'll be safe with one in the morning. Plus, this is a great way for us to spend some private time together. We figured if we're too tired in the evening, then we can get up early to work on the gazebo."

"Fair enough. As long as you feel you can get it done while we're here. Will it be your Rebekah's Heart design?" Sam had been proud of Kevin for patenting the design for the gazebo. That design had also earned him a ton of money. Humble and generous, Kevin had poured a lot of his profits back into TeamWork Missions.

"None other." Kevin nodded. "I premeasured and cut all the lumber at the store and brought it with me. I'm sure I can finish it, but if I see I'm running short on time, I'll ask for help."

Sam shook his head. How had he missed that load of lumber coming into the camp? "Lexa must know about this."

"You were at the One Nation Church in a meeting when we first arrived," Kevin said. "We pledged Lexa to secrecy. We'll tell the others in a few days when we need their help to get it over to the church. I figured we'd get it started here and then transfer it by flatbed truck later in the week. We can present it on Sunday morning after the church service and then finish it over there."

"Sounds like you've worked it all out. Carry on then." Giving them a wave, Sam turned to leave. Thinking better of it, he turned. "You know what? Private time or not, do you want some help tonight?" With a grin, he raised his hands. "I'm offering, so I'd advise you to take advantage. Unless you two kids would rather be left alone."

Rebekah smiled and beckoned him closer. "Sure. Come on over. You just missed Mitch and Cassie. They were here until a few minutes ago and are helping, too."

"Is Kevin okay?" Sam nodded to where Kevin sawed a board like his life depended on it. He'd been so close to his mother, and he was taking her loss hard. Rebekah would be a great comfort to Kevin since she and Josh had lost their father in the last few years.

"He will be," Rebekah said. "The physical release of building the gazebo is good for him."

"I'm sure it is. His dad doing all right?"

"Richard's lonely, as you might expect. It'll take time like everything else. My mom's reached out to him. When we talked a few days ago, Mom told me she invited Richard to join her at a Christian widows and widowers group. I'm hoping he will at some point."

Sam nodded. "It's only been a few weeks. He'll go when he's ready." Sam couldn't help but think of his own parents who were a little older than Kevin and Rebekah's folks. His father, Sam Sr., had suffered from hearing loss, dizziness, and occasional migraine headaches from Ménière's Disease diagnosed during his Air Force years. He'd kept himself in good physical shape and watched his diet. His mother Sarah's cancer scare a few years ago thankfully turned out to be a benign tumor.

"Thanks for putting together this mission for us," Rebekah said. "I'm looking forward to the fellowship time with the One Nation Church members tomorrow night. In case I haven't told you lately, I love you, Sam."

Emotion clogged Sam's throat. "I love you, too, Beck. Now, we'd better get to work or your husband's going to accuse us of slacking."

"May it never be." She turned back to the lumber pile.

"Beck, wait." Knowing her as well as he did, and working with her in the TeamWork office, Sam *knew*. Both Winnie and Lexa had mentioned that Rebekah hadn't been feeling particularly well since her arrival in New Mexico. The signs were there.

At his words, she turned. "Yes?"

"When's your baby due?" Sam's voice came out gruff with emotion.

"Six months. Early April." That response came from Kevin. Pulling his T-shirt over his head, Kevin joined his wife. He wiped his arm over his forehead and then kissed Rebekah's cheek. Leaning into the kiss, Rebekah reached for his hand.

"I know you've wanted this for a while now. I've been praying." Joy for his friends swelled his heart and Sam gathered both of them in a hug and said a prayer for their child. "Now, let me help you," he said, ending the prayer.

Entering his family's quarters an hour later, Sam caught sight of Lexa in their bed. He always found his wife at her loveliest during these times, with her long, blonde hair loose and flowing and the flush of sleep in her cheeks. Tired to his bones but also oddly energized after working on the gazebo, he quietly closed and locked the front door before dropping into the chair next to Lexa's side of the bed. He loved watching her sleep, so peaceful and content.

After unlacing and tugging off his work boots, he peeled off his socks as his thoughts traveled back to Lexa's first TeamWork mission in San Antonio. Feisty and stubborn, she'd challenged him like no other woman. Like a kid, he'd wanted to tug on that long braid of hers. Kiss her after that ornery goat spit on her through the open window of his old Volvo station wagon. All before they'd reached the campsite.

A believer from a young age, she'd been left on the doorstep of her faith without a clue how to *live* for Christ. During that summer, Lexa had blossomed as she'd learned to trust in the Lord's promises as well as Sam's love for her.

Rising out of the chair, he sighed. Yes, the Lord was merciful and poured out His grace so freely. Josh was covered in that grace. As was Marc. And Winnie. Eliot. Marta. Dean. Sheila. Each one of his faithful TeamWork volunteers was covered by the blood of Jesus. Fallible people who tried their best to live godly lives. *He* failed often, but he did his best to lead his group, armed with the word of God and His sweet promises. And prayer. Lots of prayer.

As parents, his crew now faced the daunting task of raising children in a world rampant with sin and temptation. But it was also a world of goodness, love, and overwhelming possibilities.

"Sam, are you ever coming to bed?" Lexa's voice was edged with sleep. Sexy. Turning over, she pushed aside the sheet, waiting as he stepped out of his shorts and shrugged out of his T-shirt. He grabbed his sleep shorts but stopped when she gave him a look he recognized.

Deciding to forego the shorts, Sam tossed them on the chair and climbed into bed beside his wife. Pulling Lexa into his arms, he nuzzled her neck, inhaling the sweet scent of her hair, appreciating her warmth. "You smell good, baby. Feel good." Turning on his side, he cradled her face between his palms and gently kissed her. "Taste even better." They'd been on the road and then in New Mexico for the past few days as they'd prepared the campsite. Caressing Lexa's arm, Sam smiled as Lexa wrapped herself around him, warming him in the chill of the night.

"Everything okay? Did one of the girls have a bad dream?"

"Everyone's fine." When he teased her lips with his in a way he knew she liked, her response was immediate and gratifying. A quick glance at the clock on the table almost made him groan. In three hours, Lexa would meet Winnie and some of the other ladies in the dining hall to start their breakfast. He'd get up with her and another day would begin. Somehow they'd make it through with very little sleep. He'd grown accustomed to getting short spurts of sleep and the occasional catnap when he was on a mission.

Lexa smiled against his lips. "Hmm. Someone's still awake." She lovingly stroked his face. "Something on your mind, handsome cowboy?"

He kissed her again. He needed to be quiet with the kids sleeping in the next room, but he'd missed his wife. Needed her. "I know it's late, Mrs. Lewis—make that early—but if you're not too tired, care to join me in a little after hours adult camp fun?"

Sam stifled his wife's laughter with a much more passionate kiss. It was the only way to keep the woman quiet. Based on her response, Lexa was more than willing. How he loved her.

Chapter 16

Day 3, Wednesday

~~♥~~

Sam awoke the next morning to quiet but insistent knocking on the outer door of their quarters. "Hang on a minute!" He shook his head, dazed with sleep, and glanced at the clock. Three-thirty. Sliding out of the bed, he pulled on his clothes. After first making sure Lexa was covered with the bedsheets, he opened the door. Eliot and Marta waited in the dark, both dressed in their sleep clothes and jackets with tennis shoes.

Sam flipped the switch on the wall, illuminating the porch. "Morning." Yawning, he stepped onto the porch and smoothed a hand over his unruly hair. "What's up? Do you two need an ordained man to marry you?"

"Not this time." Eliot's tone was serious, the set of his jaw firm. "Sorry to get you up, Sam, but we need you to come with us. There's something you need to see over at the women's dorm."

"Sure. Let me get my shoes. Just a second." Slipping back inside, Sam grabbed his tennis shoes from under the bed and shoved his feet into them. After pulling the door closed behind him, he fell into step beside Eliot. "Tell me what's happening."

Marta hurried to keep up with them. "I went to use the facilities about a half hour ago. When I came back, I saw something painted on the outside wall of our dorm."

"I thought we should discuss it before everyone else gets up," Eliot told him. A couple of minutes later, they reached the dorm. Rubbing his eyes, Sam stepped forward to get a better look. A large, crudely drawn eye was painted in bold red to the right of the door. The eye was inside a circle with an arrow pointing to the bottom line of the circle. An indecipherable drawing was in the lower right quadrant of the circle, possibly a large animal—a bear or a bull perhaps.

Studying it, he puzzled over its possible meaning. Why would

125

anyone have done this? Even more disturbing was the fact that someone had come into his camp during the early morning hours and gotten so close to the women.

Sam turned to Eliot. "An evil eye? I can't begin to identify the other things in the circle or guess their meaning."

"It's a warning," Eliot said. "I guarantee it's nothing good."

"The outer door was locked securely last night?"

"As far as I know," Marta said. "I think Beck came in after me. We can check with her when she wakes up, but I'm sure she would have locked the door."

"Right, and Kevin would have made sure of it." Sam moved his hands to his hips. "Have you checked the men's dorm and"—his pulse quickened—"Natalie and Winnie's quarters?" The women would naturally harbor concerns for their children.

"They're all clear. This is the only building affected," Eliot said.

Sam shook his head. "Any theories on who would have painted this symbol and why?"

"I did some quick research." Eliot crossed his arms over his chest and stepped to Sam's right, in front of the symbol. "The evil eye is a type of curse generally believed to bring sickness, death, bad luck, loss—"

"The evil eye symbol is prevalent in many cultures of the world, prompted by envy and jealousy," Marta said from Sam's left side. "Women and children are the most frequent targets."

Eliot frowned. "Pregnant women, to be specific, the ones generally considered the most innocent and vulnerable."

A blast of shock mixed with anger shot through Sam. "Sounds like mysticism and occultism to me. This kind of thing has no place in my work camp." When he stepped closer and raised his hand to touch the symbol, Eliot put a hand on his arm.

"Leave it for now, Sam. We need to alert the local authorities and they might want to dust for prints. Once they give the go-ahead, we'll paint over it."

Marta gasped. "Do you really think calling the authorities is necessary?"

Sam met Eliot's gaze and the other man gave him a slight nod. "Even though it's only paint on a wall, Eliot's right. It's vandalism and a scare tactic. I'd like nothing more than to march over to the supply room, grab a can of paint, and cover up this obscenity before the others see it." He ran a hand through his hair and blew out a breath. "I'll put in a call to the local sheriff and then I'll call Pastor Chevy to make sure nothing similar has happened on the church grounds."

They'd faced opposition in TeamWork camps before but nothing as blatant as this act. It could be nothing, but as long as it was under his control, Sam couldn't take any chances when it came to the well-being and security of the volunteers in his camp.

"You might want to mention this to Marc." Marta's sensitivity for Natalie resonated loud and clear.

"I will." Likewise, he'd mention it to Kevin and Rebekah. "The other women are bound to see the symbol when they leave the dorm in a couple of hours, if it's still here. Looks like we'll need to organize a rotation of the men to stand guard over the camp every night. Either that or we'll hire an outside security service." Sam quickly scanned the campsite. "We should station the guard in the middle of the camp where there's a good view of the women's dorm as well as the dorm for Winnie, Natalie, and the kids. Not only that, but we should probably have a male presence here in the camp at all times. Do you agree, Eliot?"

Eliot nodded. "I concur."

A deep frown creased Marta's forehead. "You guys are already putting in such long hours at the church. Sure, that ugly symbol spooks me a little, but that's probably the intent of the person who painted it. We can't give into fear or intimidation. I think the other ladies will be satisfied to know the authorities are being notified."

"Until we know differently, Marta, we need to view this as a potential threat," Sam said. "If one or more persons were brazen enough to come into our camp and do something like this, then we need to take it seriously. But if they're foolish enough to show up again, we'll be ready for them."

"You're right," Marta said. "To be honest, I think we'd feel safer if it's our own guys guarding us, not hired strangers."

"I'm sure our guys will *want* to be the ones standing guard in the camp," Eliot said. "I'll make up the rotation schedule. We'll make it work. However, I think we should hire an outside security service to watch over our vehicles and the plane, in case the vandals get any bigger ideas. I'll take charge of setting that up."

Sam appreciated Eliot's take-charge personality. "Good idea, and thanks. Let me know the cost and I'll reimburse you. If TeamWork can't cover the cost—"

"Don't worry about it. Consider it my contribution," Eliot said.

"You're a good man, Eliot. I'm glad you're here. Okay, let's tell everyone, men *and* women, to keep their cell phones with them at all times. We also need to check and make sure we have plenty of functional flashlights and extra batteries."

Eliot nodded. "Done."

Taking another sip of his coffee in the dining hall, Eliot noted the ladies seemed somewhat subdued. They smiled and interacted with the kids as usual but there was an undercurrent of unrest. He couldn't blame them. During his morning prayer, Sam briefly touched on God's watch care over them, but he understandably hadn't mentioned the symbol. Unduly alarming the others—especially with the children present—wasn't advisable until they knew more, if even then.

A gathering thunderstorm mirrored the mood of the group. Low hanging, dark clouds floated by outside the windows and he heard the distant rumble of thunder. Continuing to eat his sausage links and scrambled eggs, Eliot watched as Josh climbed onto the bench beside Sam. Josh was a deeper thinker but was usually jovial and easygoing. Not now. The two men kept their heads together, deep in discussion, for several minutes.

Across the table, Marta kept the conversation lively with Angelina and Felipe. The teenagers were amusing and their personalities played off each other in a fun way. Except for making an occasional offhand comment to let Marta know he was listening, Eliot didn't make much of an effort. After the worrisome events of the morning, he wasn't exactly in a conversational mood. Stifling a yawn, he swirled the last bite of his scrambled eggs in ketchup. He hadn't been back to sleep since the discovery of that evil eye symbol, and he'd pay the price later. Wouldn't be the first time.

"My dad used to do that," Marta said, nodding to his plate. "He loved scrambled eggs, and he always drenched them in ketchup."

He wanted to ask her more about her dad. If she was willing, he should be able to find out what happened to the man. Giving closure to families was what he could do, for better or worse. Most often the outcome was sad but expected. With Marta watching him now, Eliot wondered how best to respond. Wiping his mouth with his napkin, he wadded and left it in the middle of his empty plate. He was relieved when Angelina jumped off the bench with Felipe right behind her, leaving him alone with Marta.

"I'm not sure what to say considering your memories of your dad aren't so pleasant."

"It's not that, exactly." She took a quick drink of her cranberry juice. "I have a lot of good memories of my dad, Eliot. It was more that they just…stopped. When someone seemingly falls off the face of the earth, it's difficult to know what to think. Do you hope or do you mourn, and for how long? Do you declare them dead, hold a memorial service?" She ran one finger around the rim of the juice cup. "Do you move on with your life or remain in limbo indefinitely?"

"The only thing that's certain is that there are no easy answers. It's either a personal—or a family—decision." Lifting from the bench, Eliot scooted around the table and sat down beside her. He hoped she'd be receptive to his suggestion. "Marta, if you want, I can find out what happened to your dad."

She blanched. Her eyes were wide, but with hope or fear, he couldn't discern. "That's a very generous offer. I know I can't ask how you'd go about it or ask for any particulars, but would I need to hire you to do that?"

"Consider it a personal favor," he said. "I'd encourage you to ask your mother, and it'd be a good idea to mention it to your brothers."

"You're right. With men, it can be a pride thing. My brothers would want to know and agree to the plan, be a part of the process. Leaving them out isn't an option. You're fearless, aren't you?"

Eliot gazed straight into the one pair of eyes where he could so easily lose himself. Eyes which now held a rare vulnerability. A softness, a sweetness. Her guard was down. As much as he loved her feistiness, Eliot was deeply drawn to this side of Marta's personality.

"I have to be strong or I couldn't do what I do." He made sure to keep his voice low. "I have plenty of doubts about all kinds of things, but not about this. I can find out where he is or what happened to him." If human remains needed to be found, as long as the man's bones didn't reside at the bottom of the ocean or in a concrete slab, he could find them.

Marta nodded slowly and appeared deep in thought. "I don't know the first thing about how finding someone works."

"It starts with making a few phone calls. Based on what I find, I'd take it from there."

"I wouldn't expect you to travel anywhere." If Marta gave him the go-ahead, he'd travel anywhere on the planet to give this woman and her family the closure they needed.

"Expectations aside, I'll do whatever's necessary."

"I'm not sure if I should call Mom while I'm here or wait until I go back home to Houston. On the other hand, this is important enough that it might be best to schedule a family conference and fly home to Kentucky."

"Whatever you want," he said. "The offer stands now or later. Five or ten years from now."

She still looked overwhelmed and confused. "Thank you for the offer. That sounds somehow inadequate, considering the circumstances."

"I want to help you, if you'll allow me, Marta, but I don't want to overstep my bounds." He only wished he could give her good news, but he had a suspicion that was the one thing he wouldn't be able to give her.

"Well, we both need to get to it, I suppose. I'll see you over at the worksite." Marta glanced up at the window. "Looks like we might get wet today."

"Do you like walking in the rain?" He wasn't sure where that'd come from but maybe his instincts with Marta were better than he'd thought.

"Splashing in the rain has been one of my favorite things to do since I was a kid." Her smile stole his breath as she rose from the bench. "See you soon."

~~♥~~

Marta carried an empty serving tray back into the kitchen and deposited it by the sink.

"Thanks for helping, Marta," Lexa said as she transferred leftover sausage and bacon into plastic storage containers.

"You're not even on the cleanup schedule this morning." Winnie smiled from where she scrubbed a pan at the sink. "You definitely win the *Above and Beyond Award* for kitchen workers today."

"Glad to do it," Marta said. "No awards necessary."

Gayle helped her store the leftovers in the refrigerator a couple of minutes later. "Are you okay? You look worried."

"Let's go outside." Marta slipped out the back door with Gayle right behind her.

"Whew. It's humid this morning," Gayle said. "It's one of those days where I wonder why I bothered taking a shower. Maybe the rain will cool things down." Her gaze bore into Marta's. "Tell me. Did something happen that's upset you?"

"Oh no, nothing like that. Eliot just offered to help me find my dad." Other than Sam and Lexa, Gayle was the only other person she'd told about her dad's disappearance. She'd surprised herself by telling Eliot so soon.

"That could be a good thing, right? When did you tell Eliot?"

"At the prayer circle last night. He said something that made me think he might be leaving the mission and then a vision of my dad popped into my head. I guess it was a God thing because it's not like I go around freely telling people." Marta inhaled a deep breath. "Okay, I have to tell you something else or I'm going to burst."

"Go on. I'm listening."

"Eliot wants a relationship. With me."

Gayle's green eyes widened and she put her hand over her mouth to muffle her squeal.

"Shh. Be careful with the squeals, happy or not." Marta laughed as Gayle swept her into a warm hug. "With that weird symbol setting everyone on edge, the guys might come running out here to make sure we're okay."

"At least they're protective, and I can't help it. I'm so happy for you!" Slightly taller than Marta, with her classic features and every hair in place, Gayle always looked effortlessly glamorous. If she wasn't so wonderful and down-to-earth, and solely based on appearance, Marta might assume she was snooty and pampered. Gayle had never been forthcoming about her background, and she'd learned not to ask questions. But it was more than obvious that her close friend had been born to privilege.

Marta pulled out of the hug. "Remember, I was there for the whole *Gee, Eliot and Marta should really get together* discussion in the kitchen the other day. I had no idea Eliot would make any kind of proclamation of his feelings this soon. I mean, we've never even been on an official date, Gayle!"

"Eliot has always struck me as a very in-command, take charge kind of man. Strong and authoritative. A born leader."

"He's all those things from what I can tell. On the one hand, he's not sure how to be in a relationship. He was sweet when he admitted that, and I found it endearing. Then he went on to explain that a relationship with him comes with…complications."

Gayle's smile sobered. "Complications? Like what?" She frowned and slid one hand down to her hip. "Please don't tell me there's strings attached. *Long* strings. If so, I need to have a little chat with that boy. I won't allow anyone to string you along, my friend."

"Oh, calm down already. Not strings, exactly, but he did confirm—as we suspected—that what he does for a living is dangerous. And that he's gone a lot, which we knew based on past experience." Marta held her tongue before telling Gayle that Eliot lived not far from Houston. Maybe she shouldn't be spilling any of his secrets and should limit her comments about Eliot to Lexa and Sam. Surely they knew.

This is so confusing, Lord.

"Well, that's a huge step in the right direction, right? And what else?" Gayle quirked a brow and gave her a knowing look. She was very good at those.

"No, we haven't kissed. He had a very good reason why not"— Marta shot her a *don't ask* glance—"but if he doesn't initiate one soon, I might have to grab the man and plant a big one on him."

"I imagine he's had some experience in that department."

"Okay, that's not helping." When Marta had teased Eliot about his girlfriends around the globe, she'd only been half-joking.

"Sorry for the momentary detour. Are you going to take Eliot up on his offer to help find your dad?"

"I'd like to have him find out so my family can finally have closure. Eliot told me I should talk with my mom and brothers about it first, and he's right."

"Is he offering to help while he's here on the mission or after he goes back to work? We both know Eliot's job is no nine-to-five desk job."

"Whenever I say the word. He said he could make some calls

and take it from there. Eliot made it clear he'd do whatever it takes to find Dad." Tears welled in her eyes. "Or find out what happened to him."

"Honey, it's okay." Gayle put a hand on her arm and squeezed. "I didn't mean to make you cry."

"You didn't. I guess it just hit me all at once." When her tears spilled onto her cheeks, Marta quickly wiped them away. "I haven't thought about trying to find out what happened to my dad in so long."

Gayle nodded. "I think you're right that it's a God thing. From what you've told me, you loved your father, and I can't imagine what it felt like to have him disappear like that."

Marta took the tissue Gayle dug out of her jacket and thrust in her hand. "Thanks for always being here for me, Gayle."

"That's what friends are for. You're one of my biggest encouragers and I love you like a sister. Good thing we like each other since we work together. And now, would you look at us? We're on our vacation together, and where do we go? On a mission trip with our employers!"

"Yeah." Marta wiped her eyes. "We're either overly dedicated or crazy. Maybe a little of both."

As if in answer, a loud clap of thunder sent them hurrying back into the kitchen.

Chapter 17

~~♥~~

Sam caught Eliot's eye and angled his head toward the door of the dining hall. Excusing himself from his conversation with Dean, Eliot headed their way.

"One of the men from the One Nation Church is here," Josh told him as the three men walked out of the dining hall together. "Harry's familiar with mysticism, ancient Indian culture, that kind of thing. He's going to give us his interpretation of the symbol."

Sam glanced at the sky as more thunder rumbled. "Hopefully before this storm breaks."

An older gentleman dressed in work clothes and a denim jacket met them in the middle of the camp. After Josh made the introductions, they walked to the women's dorm.

Harry studied the symbol for a minute before speaking. "It looks to be a type of curse, a warning." Harry pointed to the irregular circle. "The circle symbolizes a number of things, including life, unity, completion, cycles, infinity, and spiritual energy. This symbol," he said, pointing to the arrow inside the circle, "symbolizes woman. And this"—he pointed to the creature-like symbol—"represents childbearing and motherhood. In most cases, it would indicate a woman with child. The evil eye and the 'x' in the corner of the circle are warnings that caution should be taken and that someone is watching."

"Why would anyone wish them harm?" Josh sounded incredulous. "Do you think we're a target because of our connection to the One Nation Church or the fact that we're a Christian-based missions group?"

Harry shrugged. "Hard to say, and I don't mean to alarm you. There are some in the area who are superstitious and still believe in these old symbols. The main thing to remember is that they're generally harmless."

Sam cleared his throat. "Harry, I'm asking for your gut feeling.

Do you believe the women here in our camp are in any real danger?"

"Hopefully it's nothing. Pastor Chevy told me you've alerted the authorities. That was the best thing to do. Still, I'd advise you—as a safety precaution—to be vigilant and keep a good eye on the women while they're here. You don't want to take any chances."

"We'll do that." Josh shared a glance with Eliot.

Sam nodded. "Thanks, Harry. I appreciate you coming out to the camp and lending your insight."

Eliot stepped forward and shook the man's hand, thanking him, and Josh followed suit.

"I'll be praying." Harry darted a quick glance at the sky. "I'm gonna make a run for the church and try to beat the rain. Let me know if you need anything else."

As Harry departed, Eliot turned to Sam and Josh. "Supposing this symbol *is* a warning against pregnant women, I have to wonder why it was painted here on the women's dorm instead of outside the building where Winnie and Natalie are staying."

Sam said nothing for a long moment, confirming his personal theory. "I'm guessing it's because we might have more than one woman expecting in the camp? Sam, if more of the ladies are expecting, we should know sooner than later."

"I think we need to talk with a few of our couples," Sam said. "Let's go."

When they walked back inside the dining hall, everyone had gathered around two of the tables. Eliot did a quick survey of those assembled. All in the TeamWork camp were present except for Angelina, Sheila, Felipe, Dean, Gayle, and the children. Meaning that he and Marta were the only two single persons in the building. He knew Sheila and Dean had already headed over to the worksite, so he assumed Gayle was minding the kids with the help of the teenagers.

Seeing them come into the dining hall, Lexa rose to her feet. "We're discussing the symbol and its ramifications. As you can imagine, there have been rumors and speculation. I thought it best if we address the concerns and questions before this goes any further."

Eliot had always admired Lexa. She was every bit the perfect helpmate for Sam and a great mentor for the ladies.

"Good idea. I'm glad you're all here," Sam said. "Josh, Eliot, and I just met with one of the members of the One Nation Church familiar with symbols, and he gave us some insight."

Standing to one side of the room, Eliot listened as Sam explained what Harry told them. Even though Sam was tactful and took care with his wording, a number of the ladies gasped and appeared pale when he mentioned the symbol's possible warning. Then Sam nodded in Eliot's direction, telling them that he'd be posting a security schedule for the men to guard the camp for the duration of their mission. Upon hearing that news, several of the women visibly relaxed. So did their husbands.

Eliot kept a careful eye on the body language of the various couples. The blinks, the hand gestures, the quirks, the squirms—all could be indicative of inner calm, turmoil, or a state of agitation. Based on his observations, Rebekah was also expecting and Amy was a strong possibility. Besides Marc, Kevin and Landon seemed more attuned to and attentive to their wives than usual. That was saying a lot. These guys paid attention to Sam's marriage book. He'd gifted all the TeamWork men, married or not, with a personal copy. His own autographed copy had been collecting cobwebs. Might be time to dig it out. Couldn't hurt.

Eliot cleared his throat. "If any of you have a preference for nights to stand guard, let me know. Otherwise, I'll post the rotation on the bulletin board." He pointed to the wall behind him. "Please check the board every day for changes or notes and come to me with any questions. One final note: if you have an updated cell phone number, be sure and give it to me."

Lexa moved to stand beside Sam and slipped her hand in his.

"We'll pray together as a group in just a minute, but if any of you feel that you'd rather leave the camp, we'll understand," Sam told them. "It's your call. Your top priority is to your wives and your unborn children. It's my firm belief that the enemy can't bring anything that the power of God can't overcome. His army will triumph over evil. If you need to talk, come talk with Lexa or me. We're here for you."

"Amen." Marc stood and addressed the group. "'For God has not given us a spirit of timidity, but of power and love and discipline.' That's a verse of scripture I've always followed, especially when I quit playing Triple-A baseball and started my sports advertising agency. Facing the unknown is always difficult, especially when you feel unseen forces might be plotting and working against you. This symbol is probably nothing more than a scare tactic. That's not to say that we shouldn't take it seriously. Most of you know that my dad played in the NBA. Because of his high profile, our family received a few kidnapping threats targeting my sister and me, especially when we were little. Nothing ever materialized, but my dad took the threats seriously and ramped up security. After he left us, my mom continued to exercise caution. I think the security rotation here at the camp is a great idea, and I'd like to volunteer to take the first shift."

Kevin and Rebekah stood up next. "I volunteer for the second shift," he said. After Rebekah handed over his Bible, Kevin pulled out a bookmark and began to read. "This is Psalm 91:5-10: 'You will not be afraid of the terror by night, or of the arrow that flies by day; of the pestilence that stalks in darkness, or of the destruction that lays waste at noon. A thousand may fall at your side and ten thousand at your right hand, but it shall not approach you. You will only look on with your eyes and see the recompense of the wicked. For you have made the Lord, my refuge, even the Most High, your dwelling place. No evil will befall you, nor will any plague come near your tent.'"

Kevin closed his Bible. "TeamWork has always stood on the promises of God. Let's continue to do so, united and strong." He moved his arm around his wife. "Rebekah and I were going to wait before making an announcement, but we decided to go ahead and tell you that we're expecting our first child in six months."

Eliot shared a smile with Marta as everyone jumped to their feet and ran over to hug and congratulate them. Landon and Amy followed suit a couple of minutes later while everyone was still on their feet. Landon cleared his throat and Amy winked when a few of the women clapped and the buzz of excitement started all over again.

"One of my favorite verses has always been, 'I will say to the Lord, my refuge and my fortress, my God, in whom I trust!' Landon nodded to his fellow Texas A&M alum. "Not to steal your thunder, Kev, and we haven't confirmed this with a doctor yet, but—"

"*Now* he gets long-winded." Mitch laughed, shaking his head. "Just say it already, bro."

"We're pregnant!" Amy said, beaming. Pulling her into his arms, Landon kissed his wife.

"For the record, Cassie and I aren't pregnant—*yet*. Give us a little more time," Mitch said. Cassie blushed as Mitch kissed her.

All over again, everyone erupted with exclamations of joy and hugs all around. TeamWork. Good or bad, they were there for each other. Fighting the battles and weathering the storms together. What a great group of people.

While Eliot shared a kinship with his comrades, they drifted in and out of his life. Without hesitation, they'd lay down their life for one another in a heartbeat. They understood the fragility of life. The same with his dear friends gathered in this room with him now with one major distinction: *these* people held hope for eternity. Most of his comrades refused to embrace the truth of a Savior who died for their sins, and it was that knowledge that most grieved his heart.

Beside him, Marta smiled. "The next generation of TeamWork is growing by the minute, wouldn't you say?" The weariness in Marta's expression, combined with smudged shadows beneath her eyes, evidenced her lack of sleep.

"They're following the Lord's command," Eliot observed as he saluted Landon and Kevin. "Part of the plan. First comes love, then comes marriage, and then everything else falls into place."

Sam called for their attention. "Anyone else have an announcement of impending or repeat parenthood?" He glanced around the room. "Anyone? Please speak now."

Winnie raised both hands. "Don't anyone look at me! I ain't birthin' no more babies, Miss Scarlett. At least not anytime soon."

"Ditto," echoed Lexa in an emphatic tone, prompting more laughter.

"The mission's not over yet," Marc teased. Josh balled up a napkin and tossed it at him.

"Okay, troops. It's time to pray," Sam told them when the group finally quieted down. Forming a circle, they all joined hands. "I appreciate your good humor. While we can always trust in God's promises and His watch care over us, it'd be good for all of us to be a little more vigilant and protective of one another during this particular mission."

As Sam began his prayer, a loud clap of thunder sounded.

Marta inched closer and reached for Eliot's hand. Eliot grasped it firmly in his own. He'd hold on as long as she allowed.

Lord, keep us all safe.

Chapter 18

~~♥~~

Glancing at the number that flashed across his cell phone, Eliot figured he should take the call. He stepped into the men's room and walked into a stall, closing the door as he listened to the man on the other end of the line.

"*Oui,*" he said, keeping his voice low. The acoustics in bathrooms weren't optimal for keeping a conversation quiet. "*Je serai à Paris la première semaine du mois de mars. Nous pourrons discuter de nos plans plus en détail à ce moment-là.*" Eliot listened a bit more. "*Merci. Oui. J'apprécie votre appel et je contacterai à mon arrivée. Au revoir.*"

Disconnecting the call, he tucked away his cell phone. As he came out of the men's room, he nearly barreled over Marta. "Whoa. Sorry." He planted both hands on her shoulders. "You okay?"

"Fine. I'm not a stalker or anything, but I saw you come in here. I suppose it wasn't the brightest idea to follow you to the men's room, but I wanted to see if you'd like to have lunch together." Marta's flushed cheeks indicated either embarrassment or guilt. Even if she understood French, Marta couldn't have any idea what he'd discussed.

"Sounds good." He loved that *she'd* initiated the invitation. This day was getting brighter by the minute. "Is it still raining? I've been inside all morning." By some divine intervention, the thunderstorm had held off until they'd reached the church before unleashing on the area with a good, soaking rain. The lights inside the church had flickered a few times in the past few hours, but thankfully they'd never lost electrical power.

"The rain's stopped and it's kind of muddy, but I'm game if you are," she said. "There's a picnic table to the back of the church, but the benches might be a little damp."

"If you don't mind grabbing a couple of sack lunches and bottled waters for us, I'll find some plastic to cover the benches so our clothes don't get soaked."

"See you then!" With a wave, she departed.

As Eliot approached the table a few minutes later, Marta waited. Scooting out of the way, she thanked him as he spread the plastic covering over the bench.

He waved his hand. "After you, fair lady. Do you mind if I sit beside you?"

"Suit yourself." Marta's grin was playful and inviting, making his lack of sleep a moot point. "Even though I don't want to think about that creepy symbol, tell me what's happening back at the camp." She handed him a sack lunch followed by a chilled bottle of water.

"Thanks." Reaching for her hand, he prayed for their food. "The sheriff's deputy came out but there weren't any viable fingerprints. Whoever spray painted it wore protective gloves. We got some photos of it. The security rotation is already in effect and Marc's there now. Sam called a little while ago and told me he'll personally make sure that symbol is gone by dinnertime."

Marta chewed a bite of her sandwich. "I don't like the idea of an outside security service, but I also detest that a silly symbol is taking our guys away from their work here at the church. Whoever did this painted it on purpose, and I think they wanted to scare us."

"I'm afraid your assessment is correct." Trying to lighten the mood, Eliot winked. "You sure you're not a detective?"

She scrunched her nose in a very cute way. "Hardly. I sure don't envy Winnie, Natalie, and Lexa having to explain the symbol to their kids. Being a parent can be hard enough."

"The TeamWork children are special," Eliot said. "Even if they haven't been on mission trips before, and as young as they are, they've been raised to understand there are varied cultures and many different beliefs, spiritual and otherwise. From what Marc said, the kids are okay. They're asking questions, but I didn't get the impression that any of them are frightened."

"Well, that's good, considering it's big, red, and pretty scary looking. I'm sure how a kid reacts is a reflection of how their parents react to a potential threat. So, in that regard, kudos to our friends. Your honest answer here, Eliot: do you think we'll ever find out who painted that symbol?"

Eliot pondered his answer as downed half his water bottle with one long swig. He hadn't realized how thirsty he was. Several water bottles sat on the table, and it was a good thing she'd had the foresight to bring along extras. "It's my experience that if someone wants to cause trouble, they'll keep trying until they eventually achieve the results they want."

Marta frowned with obvious displeasure. "Then how can we combat it?"

"We can't."

Her frown deepened. Giving her false hope would be worse.

"Marta, all we can do is manage the moment, so to speak, and then deal with situations as they come."

"Is that what you do in your regular line of work?"

Eliot narrowed his gaze. She wasn't being cagey or coy, and this was a question he could answer. "Yes, for the most part." Learning to strategize and anticipate what was coming next also figured into the equation. Best to keep Marta on track with current events. "For one thing, that's why we're scheduling three-hour shifts," he said. "Sam's worksite schedule allows for time off for everyone from time to time, anyway, so we have enough guys to cover. And he also told me something that was pretty awesome."

"What's that?" Marta's eyes sparkled. Like the crispness of the air after the rain. Fresh. Clear.

He snapped to attention. "Pastor Cheveyo is going to send over some of his men from the church to help guard the camp, too." He removed the plastic wrap from his sandwich and opened the bag of potato chips.

"That's great." She bit into a carrot stick. "So nice of them."

Eliot nodded. "Since we've all gotten to know a number of the One Nation Church leaders, Sam thought it'd be okay with the ladies. He checked with Lexa and Winnie before giving the okay. So," he said, chomping into a chip, "where have you been working today?"

"Here, there, and everywhere. I helped Gayle for a while but that woman knows exactly what she's doing and doesn't need anything more than my scintillating conversation. The kids are going to help her paint something on the mural later on, though, and I think that's terrific." She took a handful of chips from his bag. "Amy and Beck were here earlier to take measurements for curtains, so I helped them with my mathematical skills. Currently, I'm working in the kitchen with some of the One Nation ladies, and we're lining the kitchen drawers and cabinets. It's more difficult than you'd think. The adhesive on that liner paper is fierce."

"You're a multitasker. I like that." Eliot bit into an apple. When it was juicier than he expected, he grabbed a napkin and swiped it over his chin. "I got an interesting call this morning."

"The one in the bathroom?" Marta said. A flash of guilt surfaced in her expression before she chomped into her own apple. Convenient.

"No," he said, shaking his head. "It's been a busy morning. The Albuquerque International Balloon Fiesta is going on now. I have a buddy from university, Tyler, who's a pilot of one of the balloons, and he asked if I wanted to come out to Balloon Fiesta Park and be a chaser. He said I could bring a friend, so I immediately thought of you. I thought it'd be a good opportunity for us to spend some time together away from the camp. What do you say? Are you game?"

"Seriously?" Marta brightened. "Sounds like fun. Tell me more."

"It's the largest ballooning event in the world. Not to mention the most photographed. The launch field is 78 acres, which is the equivalent of 54 football fields. They're expecting over 700 balloons this year, people from all over the world, and there's always food and activities. We'd have to start out before the crack of dawn, dress in layers, and you'll need to take sunscreen since the field is at a high altitude, increasing the risk of sunburn. If we decide to do it, all we have to do is fill out registration forms online and e-mail them. If you'd like, I'll bring my laptop to the dining hall tonight and we can take care of it before the prayer circle."

"What exactly does a balloon chaser do? I have this vision of when I was five. I jumped and tried to reach the sky after a cluster of my birthday balloons escaped my hand and floated away. I cried, and my oldest brother, Thom, walked to the store and got me some more. He was my hero for a while after that." She gave him an impish grin. "I go off on rabbit trails sometimes. Sorry."

"Stop apologizing. Like I said, I admire your spontaneity." Eliot stopped. "Wait. Are you done? Because if you're not…" He ducked and laughed when she tossed her apple core at him.

"In answer to your question, a balloon chaser helps to inflate the balloon and works with the pilot on the launch. Then the chaser follows the balloon's progress from the ground, meets up with the pilot when he lands, and then helps deflate the balloon. I figured I could take the tank and drive us there. Tyler said his balloon should be easy to spot among all the rest, a good thing when you've got a lot of balloons in the air at the same time."

"What's the design on his balloon?"

"It has the Texas state flag on it. Some of the balloons have shapes."

Marta grinned. "That just begs for a corny joke about the size of Texas, but nope. Not going there." Her smile quickly faded. "If it's on Sunday, we'll miss the church service."

"I know, and that's regrettable. It's the only day Tyler will be there this year. I'll speak to Sam. Of course, if you'd rather not—"

"Are you kidding? It sounds like a once-in-a-lifetime opportunity, Eliot. Sam will understand. If he gets cranky about it, I'll speak with Lexa and she'll give us a hall pass."

Eliot laughed. "Sounds like a plan." He stuffed his empty chip bag, apple core, and napkin inside the sack and tossed it in the trash can.

Marta held out her palm. "Feel that?"

A raindrop plopped on his head. Then another. "I do now."

"Come on." Tugging him by the hand, Marta dragged him off the bench. She ran a few feet away, lifted her head to the sky, and spun in a slow circle.

Watching her, Eliot marveled at her zest for living. Marveled at *her*. "I love your joy, Marta."

She stopped spinning. "Then come and share it with me!"

As the rain started to fall, light but steady, they splashed, danced and laughed. Eliot couldn't remember the last time he'd had such pure fun.

Dean rounded the corner of the Sunday school room where Sheila helped to lay carpet. Her hair was pulled back in a high ponytail, the same as always when she worked at the church, and she wore denim shorts and a pink T-shirt. Concentrated on her task, she didn't see him standing in the doorway until one of the women said something to her. Glancing up at him, Sheila gave him a small smile. Angling his head toward the hallway, he arched a brow.

"Hi," he said when she came out to meet him seconds later.

"H-h-hi, Dean." They walked further down the quiet hallway.

"Do you have time to take a break now? I was hoping we could talk. I'll bring fresh fruit and bottled water." He gave her his best smile, hoping either the enticement of spending time with him or a healthy snack would convince her to accept his invitation.

When she checked her watch, he noted something about her watchband. What do you know? The band was one of his designs and a Leather original. "C-c-can y-you g-g-g-ive m-m-me a-a-b-bout t-t-ten m-m-minutes?"

"Sure. Sounds good. They've put a few picnic tables under the trees to the side of the church. I'll meet you there."

Not wanting to stare as Sheila walked toward him at the appointed time, Dean fiddled with his watch to give him something to do. "Thanks for meeting me," he told her as she climbed onto the picnic bench across from him.

"I-it's a n-n-nice b-b-break."

"Help yourself to anything you'd like." He waved his hand at the assorted fruits, water, and juices decorating the top of the picnic table.

She smiled. "A-are y-y-you ex-ex-p-pecting a c-c-crowd?"

"I guess I went a little overboard, huh? I wanted to make sure to give you a well-rounded selection." He'd noticed at their meals in the dining hall that she ate healthy—whole grains, few starches, nothing fried or greasy. Not that he was overweight, but he could stand to lose a few pounds. Since he'd turned 37, the calories liked to congregate around his middle. The long hours spent in his office had him eating out and getting takeout more often than not. The physical labor this week had been quite beneficial even though it rendered him sore most nights. Totally worth the discomfort, though.

Sheila eyed the fruit as if weighing her options.

"I got the fruit from Lila in the kitchen," he assured her. "It's all been washed."

"I-I'm n-n-not w-w-worried." Choosing a green apple, she bit into it and winked. "S-s-sour," she said, laughing. She wiped her chin with the back of her hand when a tiny bit of juice dribbled. "T-t-tell m-me w-w-what y-you w-w-were g-going t-t-o s-say."

He tilted his head and eyed her curiously. "You're perceptive. I was thinking how I haven't been getting as much exercise as I should back home. I've been too busy with the stores and working long hours." If he was admitting to being out of shape, he might as well stress his strong work ethic to balance it out. "It might be a good idea to join a gym with Felipe. He seems to like working out." Twisting the cap off a water bottle, Dean took a long drink.

"I-I've b-b-been pl-pleased t-t-o s-s-see h-him d-d-doing s-s-some of th-the h-h-heavy l-lif-t-ting h-here a-at th-the w-w-worksite." Sheila took another bite of the apple. "H-h-he's l-l-lean b-b-but s-s-strong." She smiled around another mouthful of that apple. With her lips moistened from the juice, it was all Dean could do not to stare. He'd never realized eating a piece of fruit could be so…appealing.

"Keeps him out of trouble, at least," he said, breaking out of his musing. "I noticed your watchband. From what I could tell, it's from Leather. One of my designs, if I'm not mistaken."

Sheila turned her wrist and studied it for a few seconds. "Y-y-you're r-r-right! I-I re-re-p-placed i-it a f-f-ew m-m-months a-a-go. I-It's a L-l-leather d-d-design." She seemed genuinely pleased.

"May I see it?"

When she offered her wrist, Dean admired how small and dainty it was. He pointed to the design on the underside of the band. "See the tiny heart by the signature 'L' logo? I add a heart to all of my designs in honor of my mother, Rose. We tried to make a rose, but being so small, it didn't translate well."

Leaning closer, Sheila nodded and looked up at him. "I-It's b-b-beauti-ti-f-f-ul. W-w-when d-d-did s-s-she p-p-pass a-a-w-w-w-ay?"

He couldn't help his grin. "She didn't," he said quickly when Sheila gave him an odd look. "I'm happy to report Mama Rose is alive and well. If she's not, then there's some crazed woman who calls and gets on my case if I don't show up for dinner once a week. She's really taken to Felipe and is great with him. He likes her a lot, too. Better than me, I'm afraid."

"Y-y-your m-m-mother l-l-likes F-F-Fel-l-lipe b-b-better th-than y-you?"

"No. I meant Felipe likes Mama Rose better than me." His eyes widened. "I hope you don't think I'm a pathetic, almost middle-aged loser who lives with his mother."

She laughed. "Y-y-you're n-n-not p-p-pathetic a-a-nd I-I'm s-sure F-F-Fel-lipe l-l-likes y-y-you. H-h-he j-j-just d-does-s-n't kn-kn-o-w h-h-how t-t-o sh-show it."

"I'm not middle-aged yet, either. Just so you know. At least I hope I'm not, but I suppose it's dependent on my life expectancy."

He ran a hand over his hair, thankful he still had a lot of it with no bald spots. "I seem to have a tendency to say dumb things in your presence." What was *wrong* with him?

Dean hoped his smile conveyed how grateful he was for her faith in him. The same way he could tell Sheila was thoughtful and kind. Gentle. A great mother. At first he'd thought she was a bit overprotective, but he'd been a teenage boy once with hormones in overdrive when he was around a pretty girl. Felipe talked a good game, but he seemed to genuinely like Angelina. From what he'd seen at the camp, they were becoming friends, and that pleased him.

"Sheila, I'm going to lay it on the line here and state my case."

Tilting her head as she chewed, she nodded for him to continue. She didn't appear scared and she wasn't running away. That in itself was encouraging.

"I like you. Very much," he said. "Above all, I'd like for us to be friends and spend more time together once we get back to San Antonio." He met her lovely brown eyes and held her gaze. "But, I'd be lying if I said I didn't want more. We're both consenting adults and—"

"Dean!" Coughing, Sheila cupped one hand over her mouth. "W-w-what a-are y-y-you s-s-sug-g-gesting?"

"What do you...?" He held up one hand. "Oh, no, no, no. Sorry. Bad choice of words. Please don't misunderstand." Dean shook his head, praying under his breath she didn't think he was some kind of leering pervert. "I hope that what I lack in articulation skills, I make up for in other ways. Sheila, the other day, you told me that you're damaged goods. If you're willing to share, I'd like to know why you feel that way. Because the way I see it, that's not true at all."

He could see her swallow the last bite of her apple. Lowering her gaze from his, she grabbed a napkin from the table and wrapped the apple core inside it. Finally she spoke although she still didn't look him in the eye. "Th-there a-are pl-plenty of w-w-omen w-who've n-n-never b-b-been m-mar-r-ried, n-never h-h-had a ch-child. Y-y-you sh-should f-f-find one of th-them."

"I might not *want* one of them."

Sheila's eyes grew wide, but she remained quiet.

"First of all, your heart might be damaged, but that's not your soul. It shouldn't define who you are or prevent you from finding happiness. You've triumphed over the past and you're strong and independent. You've survived, you have a terrific relationship with Angelina, and a satisfying career. Don't you see? The most important thing is that you're whole in God's eyes, and I want you to know that you're also whole in *my* eyes."

Sheila's eyes were moist, and he hoped his words had reached her in the way he'd intended.

"Dean, m-m-my f-f-family f-f-forced m-m-me t-to m-marry H-Howard."

"Did you love him? I'm sorry," he said. "I have no right to ask that question. Or expect an answer."

"I-I th-th-thought I l-l-loved h-him, a-a-and th-then I-I g-g-got p-p-pregn-n-nant wh-when I-I w-was b-b-barely 16." She lowered her voice. "H-H-Howard w-wanted m-m-me t-t-to a-a-b-b-ort th-the b-b-bab-by. H-He g-g-grew t-t-to l-l-love An-Angel-lina, b-b-but I-I w-w-was v-v-very pr-pr-o-t-tect-t-tive of h-her."

"I can understand why. You're a terrific mother." Compassion filled him for this woman, and he stretched his hand across the table. After only a few seconds, Sheila put her small hand in his. Wrapping his fingers around hers felt natural, as though he'd been doing it all his life. Even when he was dating Cynthia, he'd never felt an emotional connection with his ex-girlfriend the way he did with the woman sitting across from him now.

"I'm sorry you had to endure all that, Sheila. Sounds to me like you were never allowed to enjoy your youth or the freedom to make choices for yourself. And I figured you must have been a child bride."

"Y-y-you've n-n-never m-m-married, Dean?" She carefully eased her hand away from his. He wanted to grasp hold of her again, but pushing the issue didn't seem advisable.

"No. I had a serious relationship for a few years. Turns out we wanted different things."

"I-I f-f-ind th-that s-surp-p-r-rising. Y-y-you're w-w-wond-d-derful a-a-and v-ver-ry h-h-handsome."

He smiled, thrilled by the unexpected compliments. "Thank you. I'm glad you think so."

"M-m-maybe y-you l-l-looked in th-the w-w-wrong p-p-places."

Feeling bold, Dean squeezed her hand. "Or maybe the Lord knew I'd find the right person through TeamWork and He kept blinders on me for all these years."

Sheila withdrew her hand. "I-I sh-sh-should g-get b-b-back t-to w-w-work n-n-now."

"Sheila—"

Jumping up from the bench, she took off at a fast walk, headed in the direction of the church. Dean beat his fist against his forehead a few times. "Way to go, Costas." He'd been making headway and then he had to spout something that made her run away. Again.

Lord, it's not supposed to be this difficult, is it?

Slowly getting up from the bench with a heavy sigh, Dean retrieved the cardboard box he'd left on the ground and began to put the fruit and bottles in it to return to the kitchen. He moved slowly, his motivation sapped. But he'd hang onto her comment about him being handsome. That was headway. He'd found out more about her relationship with Howard. Although he wasn't surprised, he was thankful she'd opened up to him. That, too, was headway.

He'd keep on trying, an inch at a time, if needed. Whatever it took. He hadn't built his business by walking away from adversity. Not that Sheila was a business deal, but she was definitely worth the wait.

"Dad, I've got a problem."

Joe only called him Dad when he wanted a heart-to-heart chat. His boy was almost four going on forty. He took things so seriously. His TeamWork reports could wait. "Sure, son. Want to go sit on the porch and talk?"

"Uh huh." Joe walked beside Sam from the office and out onto the porch. The early evening had cooled a bit and a slight breeze rustled the leaves of the towering trees.

In a few minutes, he'd walk his children over to the dining hall for dinner. He'd put in an appearance earlier but Lexa had shooed him out, telling him everything was under control. The tantalizing aromas of food filled the air. The ladies of the One Nation Church had been cooking for hours, and they were all in for quite a feast tonight.

After Joe dropped into one of the rockers, Sam took the other. "Tell me what's bothering you."

"Gracie."

"Ah." Resting one elbow on the arm of the chair, Sam began to rock as he stared out over the expanse of the camp. Maybe it was no surprise that—as the son of two former financial planners—Joe already exhibited signs of an analytical, logical mind. Sam's brother, Will, was Joe's personal hero these days. When he'd first heard Will had been named a shuttle commander for an upcoming NASA mission, Joe had whooped and hollered and declared he wanted to be an astronaut. No doubt they'd be paying a lot of visits to Johnson Space Center.

Sam glanced over at Joe. "How's that arm?" Since they'd arrived at the camp, Joe had complained that Gracie punched him at every available opportunity. He knew Natalie and Marc were working with their daughter to try and control her inclination to sock Joe, apparently Gracie's sole target.

Joe rubbed his fingers over his upper right arm. At least no bruises were visible. "Sore. Like always when Gracie's around. It's good she lives in Massa…."

"Massachusetts. Why do you think she hits you?"

Scrunching his features into a frown, Joe appeared to consider the question. "'Cause she's mean."

"Is she mean all the time?"

"No. She's nice to Hannah and Leah. And Luke. She wants to carry Emily around like she's *her* baby. Chloe thinks Gracie's okay when she's not bossy."

The corners of Sam's mouth quirked. "And what do *you* think?"

"I think Gracie hates boys."

"That could be it, although I doubt it's as strong as hate. Do you like Gracie? Even though she's a girl?"

"Sort of. If she'd stop hitting me all the time, I might like her better. I don't hate her." Joe's feet didn't reach the porch floor, so he scooted to the edge of the chair. Pushing off with both feet, he began to rock.

"You know, Joe, sometimes girls hit boys for the opposite reason. Maybe Gracie punches you in the arm because—deep down inside—she secretly likes you."

"She sure has a funny way of showing it."

Sam laughed. "You know, your mother wasn't sure she liked me all that much when she first met me, either. It was at our first TeamWork mission together outside San Antonio."

"Did Mommy hit you?"

"She did, but it was an accident. We had a flat tire on the old Volvo station wagon—the one in the garage out back at home in Houston—and I was trying to fix it. When Mommy tried to hand me a wrench, it slipped out of her hand and hit my leg."

"So she didn't *mean* to do it." The implication from Joe being the situation was different since Gracie intended to hit him. Smart boy.

"No, no. It was heavy and slippery. But she sure made a big impression on me. And I think Gracie's made an impression on you."

Joe tilted his head. "What's that mean?"

Sam chuckled and ran one hand over his chin. "It means I started liking your mother."

"Because she hit you?"

He wasn't doing the best job of explaining. "Mommy got my attention, but then she kept my attention because she was different from all the other girls. In a good way."

"Yeah. Gracie's different, too, but does that mean I have to like her?"

Joe asked insightful questions that helped to keep Sam sharp. He learned from his children on a daily basis, and that was one of his favorite parts of being a father. "As a Christian, we're told in the Bible to love one another. I always try to do that even when people do things I don't like."

"Like what?" Joe rocked away in his chair and looked at him with wide-eyed innocence.

"They lie or they cheat. Or they do something they know could hurt someone else and they do it, anyway."

"Yep." Joe shook his head with a sad expression. The compassion in his boy—even for Gracie—warmed his heart. They wouldn't be having this discussion now if he didn't care.

"Sometimes it's hard to like people, Joe. All God asks is that we try. Be patient with Gracie. God's working in her heart just like He's working on you and me."

Joe nodded. "Makes sense. My tummy growled. Is it time to eat?"

"So did mine." Sam lifted from the chair. "Let's go get your sisters and head on over to the dining hall. Thanks for the talk, son."

"Anytime, Dad."

Chapter 19

~~♥~~

Walking into the dining hall, Angelina's stomach growled. Embarrassing. She darted a glance at Felipe, hoping he hadn't heard. "It smells great in here, doesn't it? I'm starving. The ladies of the church have been cooking all afternoon."

"Me, too," Felipe said, rubbing his hand in circles over his stomach. "This dinner is a great idea. I'm ready to eat."

Sam and Lexa talked with Pastor Chevy and his wife, Lila, over by the long tables of food. The TeamWork kids and the children from the One Nation Church—about twenty or so from what Angelina could tell—circled each other. They were cute together and she had no doubt they'd all make friends very soon.

"I hope Hannah doesn't ask if any of the little girls are named Tiger Lily," she said to Felipe. "And Luke probably thinks they all wear moccasins and hide in pine trees."

Felipe cocked his head. "*Peter Pan*, right?"

"Yep." Angelina suppressed a grin when she caught a whiff of his cologne. She watched as Gracie approached one of the little girls. "Would you look at that?"

"What am I looking at?" Felipe whispered back.

She nodded to Gracie. "Gracie's playing nice. That's sweet."

"Don't act so surprised. Gracie's a cool kid. Now Chloe? I swear that one's gonna grow up to be a lawyer like her dad. Did you hear her argue for more mashed potatoes with Mrs. Grant the other night? How old is she, anyway?"

"She's seven and the oldest of the TeamWork kids."

"Well, that little girl is scary smart. Chloe sure convinced me," Felipe said. "I'd have given her the whole bowl of potatoes. And all the gravy."

"The little boy over there"—Angelina pointed to where Joe talked with a group of boys who looked to be about his same age— "just gave Joe a miniature bow and arrow set. Looks like he's giving it to him as a gift."

"Look out. The ladies will probably be all over that. I had a fake gun as a kid and look how I turned out. I'm sure the TeamWork mothers don't want to raise any juvenile delinquents."

"Mama's very good with a bow and arrow. She was on an archery team and won trophies."

Felipe stared at her. "Your itty bitty mom?"

"Yes." Angelina laughed.

"Your dad must have been tall, huh?"

"Yeah, pretty tall." She didn't want to talk about Papa; it might spoil her good mood before dinner. "This mission is good for all the kids," Angelina said. "Sam and Lexa will probably take their kids on mission trips around the world before they're much older."

"Yeah, unless Mrs. Lewis keeps popping out babies." Felipe frowned when she swatted his arm. "Easy on the arm, will you? I'd like to keep it for a while longer. I see some kids about our age." He bowed before her. "Shall we go and make their acquaintance, Lovey?"

Angelina played along. "Yes, let's do." She hooked her arm through his and they headed across the room. In spite of getting after him, she liked the way Felipe had referred to Winnie and Lexa by their married titles. That showed respect, and she was proud of him. From the corner of her eye, she caught Mama watching them. Again. She loved her mother more than anyone, but she was beginning to believe Felipe was right with the watchdog description. Mama was the worst of all. Dean wasn't as tough with Felipe. Maybe Dean would keep Mama distracted.

Angelina introduced herself to one of the girls and then motioned to Felipe. "This is my friend, Felipe Hernandez."

"I'm Amitola. Are you engaged or married?" Amitola was taller than most of the other teenage girls, and her dark, thick braided hair hung nearly to her waist.

Angelina gaped. "Um, no. Definitely not. No. Not even a couple." She tossed a glance at Felipe. "*No.*"

"Don't let Angel fool you," Felipe said. "She's hoping to get a kiss from me before this mission is over, but I'm holding out on her. Right, Sweetums?"

Angelina ignored Felipe's wink and Amitola appeared amused. "We're both from San Antonio and met right before this mission, so we've only known each other a few days. Are you"—a quick glance at Amitola's hand revealed a ring with a pretty blue stone—"engaged?"

"Yes." She held out her hand for Angelina to see. "My ring is a sapphire. I chose it instead of a diamond."

"When are you getting married?"

Amitola smiled. "In June this coming summer."

"How old are you?" Felipe said.

Angelina shot a *be good* glance in his direction. "I apologize for Felipe's rude behavior. He can't seem to help himself. He has a little"—she circled her finger on the side of her head—"mental incapacity."

Felipe snorted and Amitola giggled. "My fiancé, Avonaco, is right over there." She pointed to a good looking guy who appeared to be a few years older, maybe in his early twenties. When Amitola turned, Angelina glimpsed pretty flowers interwoven in her hair that she hadn't noticed before.

"He's talking with his father and some of the men from TeamWork. In answer to your question, Avonaco is 20, and I'm 18."

Mama had married Papa at a young age, but Angelina couldn't imagine getting married until she was in her late twenties, if even then.

"Avonaco's an awesome name," Felipe said. "What's it mean?"

"It's Cheyenne, and means lean bear."

Angelina smiled at the other girl. "Your name's very pretty. What does Amitola mean?"

"In Navajo, it means rainbow, but it's usually a boy's name. According to tradition, rainbows are miracles. Because they appear as if from nowhere and then slip away into the sky, there are some who believe rainbows have magical properties and that it's a spirit. The scientific explanation is that a rainbow is sunlight that's bent and reflected by raindrops."

"Didn't know that." Felipe grinned. "I think Amitola translated means smart one." At least he redeemed himself a little with that comment.

"Thank you." Amitola smiled. "My personal belief is that rainbows are the jewels of God's creation and they're created by God to remind us of His majesty. Rainbows give us hope and optimism."

"That's beautiful." Angelina warmed to Amitola even more. She had a lot more poise and maturity than most girls her age.

"Well, boy's name or not, Amitola sounds pretty girly to me," Felipe said. "I like it for you. Now Avonaco? That's a strong name. Masculine." He darted a glance at Avonaco. "Seems fitting."

"Do the members of the One Nation Church come from different tribal nations?" Angelina said.

"With a few exceptions, most are Navajo," Amitola told them. "The Navajo are the largest recognized Native American tribe in the country, and their reservations are spread through the four corners of Arizona, New Mexico, Utah, and Colorado."

Thrusting his hands in the pockets of his shorts, Felipe surveyed the tables laden with food dishes of all kinds. "Looks like there's some good grub. Rainbow, do you and Lean Bear want to sit with me and Baby Cakes? Is that allowed?"

"Of course." Amitola smiled. "If you want to find a table for us, I'll be there with Avonaco shortly."

Angelina watched as the other girl walked in her fiancé's direction. Her movements were controlled and graceful. By comparison, she felt like such an immature, gawky little kid.

Sam welcomed Pastor Chevy, Lila, and the members of the One Nation Church. Pastor Chevy greeted them and prayed for their meal. Lila and Lexa then directed everyone to be served table-by-table. Angelina smiled to see how the kids were all interacting well together, about twenty in all, including the TeamWork kids.

"Whoa. This is like Thanksgiving. No reason to go home hungry tonight." A couple of minutes later, Felipe handed Angelina a plate and they began to make their way around the various dishes on the tables. She found his comment intriguing but now wasn't the time to ask him about it.

The ladies of the One Nation Church had prepared American as well as Native American foods: turkey, cornbread, cranberries, blueberries, mush, corn, many types of beans, tomatoes, and peppers, posole—a hominy stew with chile—as well as a variety of meats and seasonal fruits. Another smaller table held an assortment of desserts.

After filling her plate with food, Angelina waved to Amitola, gesturing for her and Avonaco to join her at a nearby table. Next, Angelina poured a cup of half-lemonade, half-iced tea at the drink station. Then, on second thought and deciding to be nice, she poured a cup of milk for Felipe. She figured that's what he'd choose since he guzzled it at every meal except breakfast.

"What do you think, Sweet Cheeks?" Felipe sat down next to Angelina and surveyed the heaping mounds of food on his plate. Picking up his fork, he attacked his food with gusto.

Protesting his newest nickname for her would only spur him on. Pretending to ignore it might work. "About what?" Angelina stared at her plate and silently debated where to start. This might be a case where her eyes were definitely bigger than her stomach. No way could she eat all this food without ending up with a major stomach ache later on that night. Better to just sample a little bit of everything and be safe about it.

"This marriage business," Felipe replied. He tilted his head to where Amitola and Avonaco stood in the food line. "I could go for some of that myself." He gave her a lazy grin. Did they teach boys that grin in school?

"You're nuts. Absolutely crazy." Boys could be so obsessed with the dumbest things. "If you ask me, they're way too young. There's too much to see of the world, too much to do, too many other people to meet."

Felipe slowed his chewing. "So, what are you saying? You're not going to get married until you're too old to enjoy it? That's right, though. Women hit their peak later than guys."

"You're on dangerous ground," Angelina warned, avoiding his gaze and stabbing a bite of food. "Very shaky. Don't spoil it. You've been doing better."

He grunted. "Yeah, sorry. How old are we talking here?"

She pushed his milk closer. "Here. I got you a drink."

"Thanks. You're too kind." He took a quick sip. "Dare me to spike it?"

Angelina put down her fork. "Please don't tell me you're serious." Not to mention in milk? That sounded all kinds of gross.

"I brought a bottle of vodka. It's over in the dorm, and I could run and get it. Come on. Live dangerously for once in your life. Or are you going to run and tell Sam Lewis on me?" That sounded a little like he was mocking her.

She lowered her voice. "You seriously smuggled booze onboard an airplane?"

"Yeah, why? Is that illegal or something? They sell it in on airplanes, don't they? Relax. I put it in Dean's suitcase. When we got here, I pulled it out before he could find it. No sweat. I've got it under my bunk. It's not like I brought a whole suitcase full of liquor."

Angelina leveled her gaze on him. "We'll talk about this later." Frustrated beyond belief, she shook her head. "You'd better be good or so help me. . ."

Felipe shrugged. "You've got your dirty book. I've got my own temptation. To each his own, right?" His eyes bore into her.

"I thought we were over that."

"Apparently not. Do you still have that book?"

She heaved a sigh. "I'll make you a deal. I'll destroy the book if you get rid of the vodka."

"Kiss on it?"

"You're a pig."

He scoffed. "I'm a growing boy. I need my sustenance."

"Not that kind of pig."

Felipe threw back his head and laughed.

I'm a failure, Lord. What now? She'd tried to be a good influence on him, but Felipe hadn't been receptive. Beating him over the head hadn't worked. Backing off apparently wasn't working well either.

"By the way, I like your hair that way, Dumpling."

Self-conscious, Angelina touched the loose ends of her hair. Instead of braiding it or putting it back in a ponytail, she'd left it down for dinner. "Thanks. What's with all the nicknames tonight?"

He shrugged and took a long drink. "Something to liven up our relationship."

What relationship? "Just don't say dumpling. That makes me sound…fat and, well, doughy."

"Would you rather I call you Centerfold Girl? Pudding Pop?"

Good grief. "Dumpling's fine." She turned her attention to her food since Amitola and Avonaco were headed their way.

Please behave, Felipe.

Angelina was pleased when Felipe interacted well with their guests. He asked polite questions and talked about his classes in school enough to indicate he paid attention and might be a halfway decent student. She still wasn't sure whether to trust him for the entire meal and prayed under her breath that he wouldn't say or do anything to offend Amitola and Avonaco.

"Angel tells me she doesn't want to get married for a long time. How come you two are getting hitched so young?" Felipe held up a hand. "I'm not judging. That just means you get to do stuff and it's all good and legal." Chewing his food, he shot Angelina a grin. She wished she could sink through the bench onto the floor and disappear.

Amitola lowered her gaze and Avonaco answered. "Our parents had an informal agreement when we were younger. For business and financial reasons, they've always wanted us to marry."

Angelina couldn't believe it. "What? You mean like an arranged marriage? That's not fair. You can't let them do this! You should be allowed to make your own decisions about who you marry." Crossing her arms, she stared from one to the other. "How can you be so calm?"

Felipe patted her on the arm, as if to calm her down, which irritated her even more. "Are your parents members of the One Nation Church?" he said.

"No, and they're not happy with us for joining the church." A shadow crossed Amitola's face. "We didn't mean to upset you, Angelina."

"Please understand that arranged marriages are a thing of the past," Avonaco said. "We appreciate your concern, but we're not allowing our families to push us into anything. We're free to marry whomever we want. And we have freely chosen one another." When Amitola gave him a loving smile, he covered her hand with his on the tabletop.

"Well, I think it's great!" Felipe raised his cup in a toast. "Here's to the two of you. To our new friends, Rainbow and Lean Bear. Wishing you many happy years together, happiness, good health, prosperity, children. All that good stuff." All four of them raised their cups and joined in the toast.

Next, Felipe held up a piece of bread. "Does this bread have a special name?"

"Fry bread," Amitola said. "In our family, it's tradition to eat it with every meal."

"Well, it sure is tasty."

Angelina shook her head. "You must really like your bread."

"Yep." Felipe grinned at her around a mouthful of the fry bread. "Why do you think I work out so much? Have to keep my figure."

Feeling her cheeks grow warmer, Angelina lowered her gaze to the food on her plate. Why did he say things like that? To embarrass her or to get attention? "There's so much, it's hard to know what to choose next."

"One thing at a time, Sugarplum. Here. Try this." Before she could stop him, Felipe tore off a large piece of the fry bread and stuffed it in her mouth.

Laughing, Angelina pushed it into her mouth as she chewed. "You're right. That's really good." She bit into it again, pulling it out of Felipe's hand with her teeth. His eyes lit with surprise.

"Did you see all the fresh produce?" she said to him a minute later. "Sam's going to love the peaches. His idea of Heaven probably has roads lined with rows and rows of peach trees."

Felipe eyed her closely. "You really believe in Heaven?"

Her eyes widened and she paused in her chewing. "Sure. Don't you?"

"No, and I don't believe in the alternative, either."

She wondered if there was any wiggle room in there somewhere. Here we go again. "Why not?"

"Believing in that stuff is for sissies. When you die, your flesh rots, and your bones turn to dust." He snapped his fingers. "Then poof! You're gone."

"What a lovely image." Angelina frowned.

"The idea of Heaven gives us hope," Avonaco said, and Amitola nodded in agreement.

"Exactly. Even if our body is gone, we believe that our soul still lives on. If it doesn't, why bother? What about your soul, Felipe?" For whatever reason, Angelina couldn't let it go. "Your eternal destiny?"

"Why do you care?" Felipe shook his head as though in disbelief. "We're all out for number one, Lamb Chop."

Avonaco rose from the bench and helped Amitola to her feet. "If you'll excuse us, we're going to get more to drink. Would you like anything?"

"Milk, please. Much obliged." Felipe handed his cup to them, but Angelina declined. She hoped Felipe hadn't made them feel uncomfortable to the point where they'd avoid them the rest of the mission. She'd already started to look forward to sitting with them at the church service on Sunday.

As soon as the sweet young couple walked out of range, Felipe started in again. "Come on, Angel. All that destiny talk sounds like Romeo and Juliet. Fate and all that." He nudged her shoulder. "Those two kissed. Plus they did lots of other stuff, and she was younger than you are."

Angelina gritted her teeth. "Felipe?"

"Yes, Angel?"

"Do yourself a favor and shut up. Enjoy this wonderful feast and please don't feel obligated to say anything else."

Stabbing another forkful of his food, Felipe smiled. "As you wish."

She was thankful he didn't call her another nickname. If he had, she might have followed Gracie's lead and punched Felipe in the arm. Unlike Joe Lewis, he'd definitely deserve it.

Chapter 20

~~♥~~

Pastor Chevy's wife, Lila, sat across from Lexa. They'd finished their dinner and talked quietly while their husbands were engaged in conversation. A quick glance at the kids confirmed they were occupied and having fun with their new friends from the One Nation Church. Gayle had offered to sit with them and everything was under control. Life was good.

The ladies of the One Nation Church had presented handmade jewelry to each of the TeamWork ladies, and brightly painted wooden *katsina* dolls, as well as hand-carved wooden flutes, for the kids.

"Traditionally, the katsina dolls are teaching tools," Lila explained. "They're carved representations of the *Katsinam*, the spirit messengers of the universe. For that reason, if you'd rather your girls not play with these dolls, we will understand."

"Our girls think they're very pretty and colorful, and they're a good reminder of our time here in New Mexico. We encourage our children to embrace different cultures. They're strong in their faith and aren't threatened by beliefs different from their own."

Lila nodded to table filled with all the TeamWork children. "Your children are very well-behaved."

"Thank you," Lexa said. "Your children are grown?"

"Yes. We have two sons, both in their twenties. They live in Arizona within five miles of one another." Although she couldn't be sure, Lexa thought she detected a trace of sadness.

"That's nice," Lexa said. "May I ask how you came to be a Christian?" From what little Lila and Pastor Chevy had shared during dinner, they'd only come to know the Lord in the past decade. To think they'd assembled a group of Native American believers and raised enough money for the church building in a relatively short time was a testament of their commitment to telling others about their faith in Christ.

The dark-haired woman smiled and pushed a strand of hair away from her eyes. She'd been cooking most of the afternoon, and her round, pretty face was still flushed from the heat in the kitchen. She appeared to be in her mid-forties.

"There was a five-day revival in Albuquerque eight years ago, and Cheveyo and I decided to go one night. I think we were more curious than anything else. My husband is a policeman, and he'd been hurt in a shooting. I'm thankful his life was spared, but it shook his self-confidence."

Lila glanced at her husband. "He was difficult to live with and didn't want to be relegated to a desk job. A friend of his from the police precinct invited us to go to the revival or we wouldn't have gone. As we listened to the preacher, he presented a very clear explanation of how and why Jesus died for us on the cross, the power of forgiveness, grace, and redemption. That night, Cheveyo and I went to the altar together. With all the stress after his injury, I almost walked away from the marriage. But on that night, I renewed my commitment and then God renewed our marriage."

"What a wonderful testimony of God's grace," Lexa said. "Is Cheveyo still a police officer?" If Sam had mentioned the pastor was a police officer, she must have forgotten. More likely, he told her when she'd been busy or had her mind focused on other things.

"Yes, he's now a part-time night duty officer at the station. The church is more his full-time job. A few members of our church are also police officers. That's a brotherhood that's also quite special in a very different way."

Lexa smiled, reminded of her late father, Michael Clarke. "My father was a police officer in Houston, so I understand the life of a public servant. Are either of your sons police officers?"

"No, they chose accounting. They both wanted the type of desk job their father never did."

"I take it your sons weren't at the revival with you and Cheveyo?" Lexa worried she'd overstepped her bounds by asking the question, but the other woman didn't seem to mind.

"No." Lila said with obvious regret. "We didn't raise our boys with any type of faith system other than the traditions of our parents and ancestors. And, because they don't understand our faith, we don't see them often. They won't come to visit, even though they grew up in Albuquerque, and I'm afraid they don't want much to do with us. Our oldest son, Kohana, has two young children now, and it breaks our hearts not to know them." The other woman's eyes welled with tears. "I should be reading them stories and Cheveyo should be bouncing them on his knee."

Lexa moved her arm around Lila and drew her close. "Sam and I will certainly pray for your sons' hearts to be softened, especially Kohana's. We'll pray that you'll be able to see your grandchildren. God can accomplish so much if we ask. Trust me, it's a lesson I had to learn. But if we trust in His promises, He can accomplish miracles that we can't even begin to imagine."

"I know," Lila told her, smiling through watery eyes. "I've seen some of those miracles. I never would have believed we'd be building this church today. I believe God brings those to us who will impact our lives, for good and bad. But, in the case of TeamWork and your husband, in particular"—Lila reached for Lexa's hand, squeezing it for a long moment—"God brought us a true warrior of the faith. Thank you for the gift of your time, your efforts, and your love."

A few minutes later, Kevin pulled out his guitar and led them in a few songs. Then Pastor Cheveyo and Sam presented a short devotion together. As the two men took turns reading scripture and speaking, Lexa sat back in her chair with Hannah on her lap.

"I'm reading from 1 Corinthians, verses 5 through 9," Sam said. "'What then is Appollos? And what is Paul? Servants through whom you believed, even as the Lord gave opportunity to each one. I planted, Appollos watered, but God was causing the growth. So then neither the one who plants nor the one who waters is anything, but God who causes the growth. Now he who plants and he who waters are one; but each will receive his own reward according to his own labor. For we are God's fellow workers; you are God's field, God's building.'"

Pastor Chevy smiled. "The members of our One Nation Church have done the planting. The TeamWork volunteers have watered those plants, but it's the Lord who's now going to bring growth to our efforts here."

"Daddy and the other man are talking about the Bible," Hannah whispered before planting a wet, sloppy kiss on Lexa's cheek.

"They're also talking about you, me, Leah, and Joe." Lexa tapped the end of her daughter's nose with one finger, smiling at the way she scrunched her cute little face. Leaning close, she whispered in

Hannah's ear. "They're saying how all of us are working together to build a special place to worship God here in New Mexico."

Hannah glanced up at her with wide blue eyes. "I help?"

"Yes, honey. You're here to love and support your daddy, me, and our TeamWork friends, and help make things for the kids' Sunday school rooms."

All by itself, the smile that spread across her daughter's face was worth the trip.

Chapter 21
Day 4, Thursday
~~♥~~

During her mid-morning break from helping the kids, Angelina leaned against the tree. After eyeing her tote bag for a few seconds, she grabbed it and pulled out the book. She'd managed to make a cloth cover for it with some of the fabric leftover from making curtains for the church. No guilt there. She'd come up with every excuse in her own mind to justify her reading material. It was wrong, but she couldn't seem to stop reading the book.

"Hi, Angel."

Startled, Angelina moved one hand over her chest as she glanced up at Lexa. Sliding from her lap, the book landed on the ground, open, face up. Her cheeks burned with shame.

"May I?"

"Sure. Have a seat." Snatching the book and stuffing it in her bag, Angelina shifted to make room.

"I feel bad that I haven't had much time to spend with you." Even the kindness in her mentor's tone pierced Angelina with guilt. "Chloe and Gracie showed me the crayon holders you all made out of the old coffee tins. The girls told me they were your idea. It was a good one."

"Thanks." Angelina relaxed a bit. "We had fun. Of course, the boys protested the ribbons and lace. I think their tin with the fire engine turned out really cute."

"Yes, it did." Lexa settled beside her, leaning back against the tree. She exhaled a long sigh. "It's good to take a break for a few minutes, isn't it? Some of us are going into town soon, if you'd like to come."

"Sure. Sounds like fun."

"We're going to buy fabric for curtains in the nursery, preschool, and elementary Sunday school rooms. I talked over ideas and color schemes with Lila last night at the dinner, and we have a clear direction. If we can find a Noah's Ark print, we're going to use that for the nursery to coordinate with Gayle's mural. I hear you've helped Gayle a bit with the mural. Are you keeping up with your artwork these days?"

Angelina nodded. "Art's my favorite subject in school." She wondered if she should tell Lexa about Felipe's books but decided against it. He might not want anyone else to know. He still hadn't shown her any of his work, but if she kept asking, hopefully he'd give her a peek.

"I'm glad your mother was able to arrange it so you could join us, especially during the school year."

"One of the weeks is a break, anyway, but they were pretty cool with it."

"That's good. I noticed you were reading. I'm glad to see you still enjoy that."

"I do. I still remember you reading to me in the TeamWork camp." Feeling her cheeks grow warm, Angelina lowered her gaze.

Lexa paused a long moment.

Oh oh. Yep. She's on to me.

"Angelina, I hope you know those books aren't representative of real life." Lexa leaned her head down, trying to gain her eye contact. Embarrassed, Angelina refused to look her in the eye.

"How did you know?"

"I made an educated guess. I also caught a glimpse of the title. Dead giveaway." With a gentle touch, Lexa placed one hand under her chin. "Look at me."

Lexa waited until she lifted her gaze and then dropped her hand. "I'm going to tell you something that might surprise you. When I arrived at that first TeamWork camp in San Antonio, I had a trashy romance novel in my purse and a few more few stashed away in my suitcase. If I was going to be there for eight weeks, I felt like I needed something to help me relax after building houses or working in the schoolroom all day."

Angelina drew in a quick breath, finding that difficult to believe. "Really? You?"

Lexa smiled. "Really. A couple of the books were sweet, innocent romances, but most of the books were full of sexual situations, fantasies, and poor representations of what a real life romantic relationship is like."

"Lexa, can I ask you a question?"

"Anything." Lexa meant it, too. In some ways, talking with Lexa about the book, and telling her about Felipe, would be easier than with Mama.

"If I'm only reading it and not doing anything with a boy, is it so wrong? I found it tucked beneath the bed here at the camp. It's not like I brought it with me. See, Felipe says things to me sometimes, and it makes me curious. Not bad things, exactly, and I'm sure he'd tell me more if I asked. He hasn't done anything with me that he shouldn't, either, but I can tell he's experienced with girls. I don't know any details—and I don't want to *know* details—but he gets...I don't know, all these feelings stirred up inside me." She was rambling, but she felt the need to try and explain herself. Not that there was any valid excuse.

"Good feelings that make you all tingly and excited inside? And I'm guessing this book makes you feel the same way?"

"Yes." Although it was a difficult admission, she had to be honest. She owed it to Lexa since she'd been so open with her. A thought flitted through her mind of how Lexa had defended her against her harsh aunt in the San Antonio marketplace all those years ago. She'd stood up for her when most people would have backed away and not taken a stand.

"Let me tell you what I've learned about that type of book, sweetie. The so-called hero has enjoyed a number of sexual encounters with women. He can be brooding and closed or outgoing and flirtatious, but he's the kind of man every woman supposedly wants—tall, handsome, and virile. When he meets the heroine, for whatever reason, he decides she's the one he's been waiting for his entire life. He only wants her and suddenly he gives up his bad-boy ways. He takes her into his bed and makes love to her. And again. And then one more for the road."

Angelina couldn't help her giggles. The corners of Lexa's mouth lifted and then she continued. "Something eventually happens to break the lovers apart, but then they find their way back to one another and ride off into the sunset to their happy ending."

"That sounds like you and Sam without the sex stuff." Angelina giggled when Lexa quirked a brow. "I mean, Sam's very handsome and you're so pretty. From what Mama says, when you two met, it's like you both knew you were meant to be together."

Lexa smiled. "It wasn't exactly like that, but what I want you to understand is that the romances in those books are fueled by hormones and a desire for a physical relationship. That's lust, and it's the opposite of how the Lord wants us to love someone, especially before marriage."

"How do you know you're…compatible or whatever…if you don't…?" When Lexa's brow lifted, Angelina hastened to explain. "I'm not saying it's right or anything. I'm just curious since you're being so honest."

"It doesn't mean we can't be physically attracted to someone. That's a part of us that will always be there. But we need to learn to exercise self-control and develop a healthy respect for everything about the other person apart from how good they can make us feel when we're touched in an intimate way. More importantly, we need to be touched here." Lexa put her hand over her heart and her expression softened. "God works out the details and honors those desires if we honor Him and make wise decisions."

"Some people think you shouldn't even kiss before you get married."

Lexa nodded. "True. That's a decision everyone has to make for themselves."

"Okay, then, how about Josh and Winnie?"

Lexa had started to say something else but that comment stopped her. She was silent for a long moment as if gathering her thoughts. "Josh had a problem," she said finally. "But he recognized it, confessed his sin, and got straight with the Lord. He's always been a good man, and he was a Christian, but he made mistakes."

"They had a daughter together, but he didn't marry Winnie until Chloe was four years old."

"Josh didn't know about Chloe for a few years," Lexa said. "Winnie had a rough upbringing and her grandmother basically raised her. Winnie considered Chloe a gift that God had given to her. She'd always loved Josh, but for a long time, she had no expectations for them one day becoming a family. Amy and I were with Winnie when Chloe was born, and Sam and I always prayed that Josh would come back one day. When Josh did return, a few years later, he made his apologies in private to those he'd wronged, the way God tells us to do. But he made sure to get his life in order before he married Winnie." Lexa sighed. "Real life is sometimes as complicated as a book."

Angelina nodded. "I know. Josh is great, and so is Winnie. All the TeamWork couples are like the best people I've ever known."

"Josh is a flesh-and-blood example of a true hero, Angelina. He faced his weakness and repented of his sin, and he's been forgiven unconditionally by God. That's what Jesus does for us."

"What makes Sam your hero, Lexa? I mean, I know he's great and everything, but what makes him stand out in your mind?"

"Sam's deep faith is at the root of who he is—his integrity, honesty, dedication to me and the kids, and to TeamWork." Lexa hadn't even needed to think about her answer. "And even though my daddy made it hard to get to know him, I always knew he loved me. He was a hero, too, because—like all public servants—if called upon, he wouldn't hesitate to sacrifice his life for someone else."

"That's pretty awesome," Angelina said. She hung her head, suddenly overwhelmed with memories of her dad. "Sometimes it's hard for us to forgive like God does. I guess that's why He's God, huh?"

Lexa smiled. "You're right. And that's why we're human. God knows your struggles. Just be sure and talk with Him about them. I'd suggest that you talk with your mother, too. She loves you, and she'd want to know what you're feeling. Don't be afraid to share them with her."

"I know. I guess it's hard, too, because the rest of the world doesn't look at having sex as bad. They look at it as normal. Fun. Accepted. You're weird if you *don't* do it."

"That's true, but look at how messed up a lot of people are in the world," Lexa said. "They might be beautiful, or rich, or intelligent, but that doesn't mean they're immune from things and don't have hidden issues. I'll tell you a secret. A lot of those people are insecure and hurting. The world sees what most people *want* us to see. They're seeking acceptance, or confirmation of their self-worth, or beauty, or love. As Christians, we know they won't find those things unless they first find the kind of love and security that can only come from the Lord."

Lexa reached for her hand, grasping it tightly. "I'm going to ask you a question, and I hope you'll answer me honestly."

"Okay." She had nothing more to hide, so why not?

"Have you ever given into the pressure before? To have sex or to do anything else you didn't want to do?"

"No."

"I didn't hear you."

Angelina knew full well that Lexa heard her the first time, but she raised her chin and repeated it in a stronger tone. "No."

Lexa released her hand. "That's my girl. Stay strong. You've always been independent, even when you were that tiny little seven-year-old in the work camp. I'm proud of you and the young woman you've become. In part, spending time with you during that camp—in all your sweet innocence—helped convince me to get rid of those books. I'd encourage you to check into the Christian romance novels out there that are full of good, solid men who don't use women for the wrong reasons. Books with God-honoring characters and stories that will uplift you."

"You know, Lexa, I can see hero qualities in Felipe. I mean, I know he's only 15, but he's not all bad. He's just had some bad breaks in his life. But he's handsome, and he's smart. I don't want to see him go back home and steal more cars, or do anything else he shouldn't. I don't want to think about him being with other girls, either." Angelina couldn't believe she'd admitted that last one out loud, but it was the truth.

"Keep talking with Felipe, and praying for him."

"I told him about Jesus, and he's changing. I know he is, Lexa. Felipe asks me questions, and I can tell he's thinking. But," she stammered, "sometimes he says things I don't understand."

Taking her hand, Lexa squeezed. "I agree with you. I can see the potential for great things in Felipe. He's coming from a broken family home. Even though both of his parents are still alive, they've made some bad decisions. It doesn't mean they can't straighten out their lives, get clean, and stay out of trouble. They can still make a family with Felipe, but it means they have to *want* to do it. That's the biggest stumbling block. A lot of people don't have the strength of character to do it, even if they say otherwise. I'd encourage you to pray for his family, too."

"I will. Thanks for not judging me, Lexa." At least Lexa hadn't looked at her like she'd been doing something wrong by reading that book. Even though she had.

"That's not my place. You're young, and we all have to make our own mistakes, but if I can help you by giving you real-life examples to help, that's what I want to do. And you know what?" Lexa slowly rose to her feet and dusted off the back of her jeans.

"What's that?" Angelina rose to her feet beside Lexa. She found it so weird that she was taller than her mentor now.

"Felipe has a sparkle in his eyes when he looks at you. The same sparkle I see in your eyes. I think you'll be just fine, and I'll be praying." With a small wave, Lexa started to walk away.

"Lexa, wait." Reaching into her tote bag, Angelina pulled out the book. "Can you get rid of this for me, please?"

A small smile creased Lexa's face. "We can walk to the dumpster together now, if you'd like. I have some food scraps we can dump on top of that book. We can bury it real good."

Relief flooded through Angelina. "Perfect. Let's go."

Chapter 22

~~♥~~

Hallo mein Freund. Ja, richtig. Ich bin ende November in Berlin und in der ersten Januar wache in München. Alles ist in Ordnung. Ich rufe dich an wenn ich wieder zurück nach Park komme. Richtig. Vielen dank und auf Wiedersehen.

"Eliot? You in there?"

Sitting on his bunk as he disconnected the call, Eliot smiled at the sound of Marta's voice outside the screen door. Her accent was a combination of her Kentucky roots mixed with a Texas drawl. Definitely appealing, and uniquely Marta.

She knocked again. "Eliot? I know you're in there. Was that German?"

He chuckled. And proceeded to tell her in four languages that she should stop eavesdropping.

"Show off. Want to come and help me set the tables for dinner? Cassie called and said the ladies are running late."

"Sure. Need me to strap on an apron and whip up some mac and cheese?"

"Funny man." He heard her soft laughter. "I'm tempted to say yes to see if you'd follow through on that threat. Winnie left casseroles, veggies, and bread with strict instructions for when to put them in the ovens. I think I managed to do that successfully since no one's called the fire department."

"Yet. Are you sure the ovens are turned on?"

"Listen, I feel silly standing out here talking through a screen. Please come outside or I'm going to barge in there right now and drag you back out here with me."

"Is that a threat? In that case, come right on in."

He didn't hear anything for a few seconds then laughed when she appeared at the window closest to his bunk. Cupping her hands near her eyes, she pressed her face up against the screen. "On the count of three…"

"I don't startle easily, if that was your intent, but you drive a hard bargain. Hang on. I'm coming." Stuffing his phone into the pocket of his jeans, Eliot rose from the bed and walked over to the screen door. He stepped outside and gave her his best smile. "My, my, aren't you looking fetching this afternoon?"

"Thanks." She looked a little off-balance. He'd tuck away the word *fetching* for future use since that compliment brought a pretty flush to her cheeks. "You just saw me a couple of hours ago at the church."

"Yes, but you didn't have…this…on your cheek a couple of hours ago." Marta's eyes widened when he skimmed the pad of his thumb over her cheek, dislodging dirt. "Were you playing in the dirt again?"

"I was helping to build a fort over at the church for the kids, if you must know. Then I made a fool of myself by leaning on a window screen to get some oblivious guy's attention."

He pulled back as if offended. "Oh, I'm not oblivious to your charms. Trust me."

"And you seem to like touching me," she said, her cheeks coloring an even darker pink. "Oh, never mind." With a sassy glance at him over one shoulder, Marta stomped off in the direction of the dining hall. She cried out in surprise when he caught up to her and put his hands around her small waist, stopping her. Lurching slightly forward, she leaned back against his chest with her hands resting on his arms. Nice. He wouldn't mind staying in this position until his pulse slowed. Or forever sounded pretty good, too.

"Shall we dance?" Turning around, Marta moved her hands around his neck and looked up into his eyes.

"I think we already are, in a manner of speaking." His eyes roamed over her face, drinking in her features. Ah, she was lovely. Until she pushed against his chest and stepped back a few steps.

"Eliot, why haven't you kissed me? Is there something repugnant about me? Do I have bad breath? Body odor? Talk too much? Laugh too much?"

He raised his hands and balked. "How about I'm waiting for the right moment? Is that acceptable to you?" He liked that she'd brought up the subject of kissing. Seemed it was all he could think about lately when in her presence.

"Not sure. Sounds rather lame."

"You seem pretty independent," he said. "Kissing is a two-way street. You can initiate a kiss, if you want. I won't stop you." Crossing his arms, he waited.

"I happen to think the man should be the one to make the first move when it comes to kissing. Or pretty much most things in that…part of life."

"Oh, is that right?" Eliot laughed. "I just called your bluff. You're a whole lot more old-fashioned than you want me to believe."

"What if I am? Is that a problem for you?" Turning, she took off at a fast walk toward the dining hall.

"Here we go again." Within seconds, he caught up to her again and tugged her into his arms. "You are completely enticing, Marta. You have sweet breath from what I know, and you smell pretty, just like a woman should. And yes, sometimes you talk a little too much, but you can never laugh too much."

"Well, okay then. Are you done?"

"Oh, not by far, sweetheart. As they say, we've only just begun. One little kiss. But that's all." The corners of his mouth curled. "Try not to get too carried away." Leaning forward, he enjoyed the way Marta moistened her lower lip with her tongue as her long, dark lashes fluttered. Oh yeah, this would be fun. Lowering his head, Eliot ever-so-slightly touched his lips to hers and then brushed his mouth over hers. He'd meant to tease her, but he was the one suffering. Such sweet torture he'd never known. Against his every instinct, Eliot released her.

Marta staggered a bit, appearing slightly dazed. "You're teasing me."

"And what do you call what you're doing? Want another one?"

"Yes, please."

Oh, he liked it when a woman told him what she wanted. Years ago, that meant so much more than a kiss. *Lord, forgive me. Keep my thoughts pure.* He couldn't allow his thoughts to go there. He couldn't disrespect Marta. Still, he'd give her the kind of kiss that would wipe the memories of any other men she'd kissed from her mind. Forever. Yeah, that might be arrogant, but—since Marta had asked—he wasn't going to ignore her request without giving her what she wanted. Those soft blonde curls, those luscious lips, that gorgeous smile. How had they waited this long?

"Come with me." Eliot took her by the hand. "I'm not going to do this standing in the middle of the camp for anyone, including wild animals, to see us."

"I think the wild ones are the two of us. By the way, your eye is healing up nicely from the looks of it."

"Nice of you to notice." Pulling open the door to the dining hall, Eliot ushered her inside. He leaned against the inside front wall and threaded his fingers through her hair, luxuriating in the silkiness of her blonde curls. Marta raised her chin in expectation. She tempted him without conscious effort just by virtue of everything about her.

"Are you sure this is what you want?" It took every ounce of self-control he had not to crush her mouth under his without waiting for her answer.

"Very much." The heat radiating from her eyes was undeniable.

"You're dangerous for me, Marta. Maybe we should wait...?" What was he saying? Maybe he was delirious with her nearness.

"We're not other people."

"True enough. I, for one, am very glad about that." The way she moved her fingertips along the side of his face and traced his dimple...that was good. Combined with the look in her eyes, Eliot was helpless. If she were the enemy, he'd be dead by now and wouldn't even care. Being with Marta was worth it.

Lowering his lips to hers, Eliot teased her a little before settling into the kiss. He cradled her face between his hands, murmuring her name as he kissed her, enjoying the feel of her smile against his mouth, the softness of her lips on his. Every fiber in his being screamed to deepen the kiss, but he forced himself to pull away. "We need to stop." Leaning his forehead against hers, he tried to steady his breathing.

"I know." She planted both palms on his chest, her breaths ragged. Even that urged him to kiss her again and keep on kissing her. But he couldn't, no matter how much he wanted it. No matter how much Marta wanted it. One thing he knew: they were good together. Not that he'd ever doubted it. That kiss only confirmed it, but it made him want more. Want *her*. He should have known better. Greed and hunger for this woman could consume him if he didn't stand steadfast. He'd be doing a lot of praying later on tonight.

Eliot heard voices approaching the building. It was too late to think, too late to react.

"I don't know why you think—" Cassie stopped just inside the door, her blue eyes growing wide as she spied them. Right. Nothing going on here, with his fingers tangled in Marta's hair, and with her hands on his chest.

"Oh. Sorry. Let me, um, go back outside and come back in again in a few seconds. Give you a little time to…regroup."

He'd been so engrossed in kissing Marta, Eliot hadn't heard the group coming back to the dining hall. Not good. He needed to refocus his energies. *Now* would be good.

"No, it's fine." Marta moved out of Eliot's arms and smoothed a hand over her curls. He'd enjoyed playing with those curls and they were more tousled than ever. He didn't care that they'd been caught but hoped Marta wouldn't be mad or upset. They were adults and that kiss had been coming on for years, not just a few days. Even if Cassie hadn't caught them together, with Marta's messy hair, flushed cheeks, and breathy voice, it was a dead giveaway to what they'd been doing. Not to mention her lips were full and rosy and she had the dazed look of a woman who'd just been thoroughly kissed. He probably looked pretty goofy himself, but he didn't care. That kiss had been better than anything he'd imagined, and he'd done a whole lot of imagining since he'd met Marta.

Stop or you'll drive yourself crazy, man. Averting his gaze from Marta, Eliot looked at Cassie. "What happened to your hair?" When she blanched under his scrutiny, he felt like a heel. "Sorry. I didn't mean that the way it sounded. You look good." Based on Cassie's frown, he was only making it worse.

"Smooth," Marta said under her breath as she walked all the way around Cassie. Her auburn hair now reached her shoulders instead of falling almost to her waist. "I have to say, you look adorable, but what made you decide to cut your hair?"

Cassie grasped hold of her shorter locks. "We went to a couple of fabric stores to get some supplies. There was a hair salon nearby that was offering free haircuts in exchange for donations for Locks of Love. You're making me nervous. I hope Mitch doesn't hate it."

Marta gave her friend a quick hug. "It's only shorter and you cut it for a great cause. Mitch will love you even more for that."

True enough, but Eliot also hoped Mitch wouldn't freak. Since they'd been in New Mexico, his new friend had mentioned how much he loved his wife's long hair and how he'd asked her to promise she'd never cut it. He wasn't sure whether or not Cassie had ever made that promise. The way he saw it, hair was hair, and Cassie could always grow it long again. What was the big deal? Plus Mitch didn't strike him as a shallow guy by any stretch of the imagination.

Angelina bounced in next, clearly happy with her new, chin-length cut. Eliot chuckled when Felipe strutted in right behind her. That kid put in a lot of time trying to hide his insecurities. Felipe's long ponytail was now gone and his hair was cut higher than his ears. He looked good, much more put-together.

"Hey, dude." Felipe bumped fists with Eliot. "What do you think? Do I look less like a punk?"

Eliot cracked a grin. "You look sharp, man."

Cassie clapped her hands, startling him. "Okay, everyone. Let's get ready for dinner. Casseroles are in the oven, right?"

Marta saluted. "Yes, boss."

"Great. I gave Lexa and Winnie the night off. Amy and Gayle are coming over in a few minutes to help in the kitchen. If you two"—she nodded to Eliot and then at Marta—"can behave yourselves, why don't you set the tables?" She motioned to the teenagers. "Angie and Felipe, you come with me and we'll get started on the lemonade and iced tea."

"Cassie, you could fell a battalion of troops with that sweet Alabama accent," Eliot said. "They'd fall all over themselves to do your bidding."

Cassie laughed. "Yeah, right. Your flattery comes a little too late, Mr. Marchand. The napkins and supplies are in the cabinet right behind you."

"You take the table on the left and I'll take the one on the right," Marta said. After opening the cabinet, she handed over a stack of paper plates.

"Race you?" This should be fun.

"I'm not that juvenile." She avoided his gaze and started to work.

"Sure you are. That's one reason we're so good together. Come on. It'll be fun." Standing a few feet away from his assigned table, Eliot tossed four plates like flying discs onto the table with precise aim. Not bad considering he was out of practice.

"You're good." If he wasn't mistaken, admiration shone in Marta's eyes as she started to set her table. "I'm glad they're not breakable."

"Quiet. You're slowing me down." Soon enough, he was

finished with that task and headed back to the cabinet counter to retrieve cups and napkins. "Here," he said, tossing a package of paper cups and a handful of napkins toward her. "Make yourself useful."

"Eliot!" She caught the cups but the napkins floated through the air and landed on the floor. "Now look what you've done. We can't use those napkins now that they've been on the floor."

"Sure we can." He quickly scooped them up from the floor. "The three-second rule applies." He put one finger over his lips. "No one else ever has to know. It'll be our little secret." He started to put the napkins on the table with methodical precision just to spite her.

"That rule's only for food. Better napkins than food, I guess," she said. "Still, how do you think the mothers here in the camp would feel knowing the napkins their precious children are pressing against their mouths spent time on the floor?"

"I was on clean-up duty last night, and I'll have you know that I swept up so well that baby Emily could eat off the floor." Opening the package of cups, he placed one at each place setting. "Winnie and Lexa don't seem preoccupied with such things. Natalie, maybe, but what do I know? Besides, don't kids at camp eat bugs and worms? At least one a day for added protein?"

She laughed. "I suppose you think it builds up their natural immunity." Marta motioned to the package of napkins. "Give them to me. I'll replace the ones that fell on the floor and finish. You can do the silverware."

"Why? They're just fine, Marta."

"No, they're not. Give them here, Eliot. Hand them over. Gimme. Now," she insisted, one hand out, the other on her hip. Cute. This woman was getting to him, inching herself into his heart one little jab, one little quirk, one little smile at a time. Not to forget that one unforgettable, over-the-top kiss. Best kiss of his life. Hopefully, he'd passed Marta's lip-lock criteria. Based on her eager response, she'd been pleased.

"This is a pretty inane conversation all the way around. Although," he said with a shrug, "it could be amusing to tell our children someday." He couldn't resist teasing her.

"You're a child sometimes. Insufferable and arrogant." Her smile belied her words and she'd handily won this round.

After snatching the offending napkins from the table, Eliot handed the stack to her.

"Thank you." He watched as she deposited them in the trash can. "Please be more careful with this stack. No more throwing things." She handed him a new stack of napkins.

Fine. He'd show her. As she continued working on her table, Eliot could tell she watched from the corner of her eye. He made a big show of pulling out one of the napkins, folding it first one way and then another. Turning it over, he continued to fashion a shape from the plain white paper napkin.

"What are you making?" Ah, he'd made her curious. Good.

"Ta-da!" He walked toward her. "Hold out your hand."

"But..."

"Just do it, Marta. For once in your life. And close your eyes. It'll add to the effect."

With a sigh, she obeyed. Squeezing her eyes tight, she held out one hand.

He deposited the paper napkin swan in her open palm. "Okay. You may open your eyes now."

She looked at it silently for a long moment before looking up at him. "That's really impressive. Where'd you learn how to do that? Jail? I hear the inmates have a lot of time on their hands."

He couldn't help it. Eliot roared. "You're precious, you know that? Matter of fact, that'll be your new nickname. I think I'll suggest it to Sam. Seems like he has nicknames for most of the women, so it's about time you have one, don't you think?"

Marta stared at him and shook her head. "Any more tricks up your sleeve? Any other animals or shapes you can make out of plain paper napkins? Wow me with your folding prowess. It's quite fascinating."

"We don't have time for my whole repertoire, but I'll show you something else." He pulled another napkin out of the package. Marta stepped closer, watching closely as he quickly fashioned a flower. Arranging the petals, satisfied with his efforts, he bowed low and offered it to her.

"Don't think this is a compliment or anything," she said, "but that's a unique talent. No doubt the Lord is pleased with your napkin folding abilities."

Eliot swallowed his satisfaction at that little bit of a compliment. "Think the kids will appreciate my napkin creations? Let me make a few more and then I promise I'll be good and help you put out the silverware."

"I can handle it," she said. "You just keep on making those napkin animals and flowers."

"I'll do that."

As Sam prepared to leave the worksite, his cell phone rang. Pulling it out, he glanced at the display. "Hey, Kevin. What's up?"

"Sam, I'm at the hospital with Rebekah." Something in Kevin's tone alarmed him.

Sam's pulse accelerated at a rapid-fire pace. "Tell me what's happening." He noted Marc's look of concern as he sat on one of the pews installed in the sanctuary earlier in the day.

"She started feeling faint and then she had some spotting. She didn't black out and the bleeding wasn't heavy, but I thought it best to have her checked over by a doctor. Mitch and Cassie are here with us."

"Has the doctor seen Beck?"

"Not yet. We're waiting in an exam room now." Kevin's voice, usually so strong, wavered. "I overheard one of the nurses mention the possibility of an ectopic pregnancy. Don't mind saying that was one of the worst things I've ever heard in my life."

Ectopic? From what little Sam knew, an ectopic pregnancy was one that couldn't develop full-term and posed a potentially serious health risk to the mother, both now and for future pregnancies.

"Let's pray," Sam said. Leaning forward, elbows on his knees, he bowed his head. "Father, we pray for Rebekah and her child, and for your will to be done. Be with the doctors as they assess her condition. Give Rebekah comfort and help her to know that you are in total control. You hold this little one in your hands, Father, and he or she belongs to you, no matter what happens. Be with Kevin. Give him peace and help him to be a source of strength for Rebekah. Thank you for Mitch and Cassie and their friendship, especially in this time of need. We ask these things in the name of your precious Savior. Amen."

Ending the prayer, Sam cleared his throat. "Thanks for letting me know, Kevin. Do you want me to come to the hospital? I can bring Josh and Winnie with me."

"There's not much you can do here. Prayer is what we need most. I've talked with Josh, so he's aware of what's happening, too."

"Be sure and call as soon as you know anything." Sam scrubbed one hand over his jaw and chin, exhaustion threatening to overcome him. Marc tapped him on the shoulder and gestured to the phone. "Hang on a second if you can, Kevin. Marc's here and wants to say a few words." Before handing him the phone, Sam covered it with his palm and gave him the basics.

"Kev? Hey, it's Marc. Listen, you might remember the same thing happened to Natalie out in Montana. Beck's going to be fine, buddy. You've got to believe that." As Sam listened, Marc said a quick prayer, too. "Call us if you need anything, okay? We can be there. Just say the word."

"Thanks. I'm glad you were here." Sam pocketed the phone.

Marc dropped down beside him. "I'm sorry, Sam. This must bring back some bad memories for you."

"Bittersweet, really. We have to look at whatever happens as God's will. He's blessed us over and above what we ever expected." Sam still felt a pinch near his heart whenever he thought of the baby they'd lost early in Lexa's first pregnancy. Always would, most likely. He slapped his knee. "Let's wrap it up here and then you can tell me more about your trip to China."

Fifteen minutes later, the two men walked side-by-side for the short walk back to the camp. Marc told him about the plans for their adopted daughter as well as for when their baby was born. "Natalie's leaving her teaching position next month and taking an indefinite leave while the kids are little. Gracie's in school a few hours every day, so that'll give Natalie more time to bond with the new babies."

Sam took a long draw from his water bottle. "Are you going to find out if you're having a boy or girl?" He thought Lexa told him they weren't, but he couldn't remember.

"No, because it doesn't matter. I've learned to be thankful for what I'm given."

"Amen, brother."

Marc checked his watch. "I know it's only been a little while, but think we should put in another call to Kevin?"

"You read my mind." Sam pulled out his phone and punched the speed dial.

Chapter 23

Eliot dropped onto his bunk and pulled out his cell phone. No one else was around, so he retrieved the latest message and listened. With the time difference, he'd need to return the call later. His schedule was filling up quickly, and along with other assignments bound to come his way, he wouldn't be home much. Wouldn't be around to romance the lovely Marta. Wouldn't be any closer to establishing a solid relationship with her. That reality made him frown.

He looked up as Dean blew into the dorm looking none too happy. "What's up?"

"Name it." The other man dropped onto his bunk and stretched out. Putting both hands over his face, he growled with obvious frustration. "Why is it so hard to try and talk with people?"

"Are we talking female or male?"

"Both." Dean sat up on the bed and then swung around to face him. "Let's start with Sheila. I'll admit I'm not a Romeo like most of the TeamWork guys, but it seems like I put my foot in my mouth every time I try to talk with her."

"Well, at least it's a foot covered in fine leather." Eliot chuckled and held up one hand. "Sorry, that was bad. I'm sure Sheila can tell you're sincere. That goes a long way with a woman."

Dean ran his hand over his jaw. "I started to point out the obvious facts that we're about the same age, both single, and consenting adults. You should have seen the look on her face. You'd think I'd asked her to jump into bed with me."

"Hate to tell you, but a lot of women would probably have the same reaction." Dean looked a bit steamed. Positive reinforcement was needed to diffuse his friend's agitation.

"Give me a break, Eliot. I don't say things like that, but now she's avoiding me."

"Relax. Sheila probably thought it was amusing." When Dean's frown deepened, Eliot figured he was only digging the hole deeper.

Again. Not his best afternoon. "Look, you're a great guy with a lot to offer a woman. Do you think you might be coming on a little too strong? Sheila had it rough with her first husband from what I hear, and she's probably skittish around men. More skittish than most women."

"So you're saying I should treat her with the proverbial kid gloves? That's what I've been trying to do. I guess I've been out of practice too long. I even mentioned the heart symbol on my designs is in honor of Mama Rose, and Sheila got the impression she'd died. My communication skills obviously leave a lot to be desired, and that's putting it mildly."

Eliot couldn't help but laugh at that one. "Concentrate on being her friend and pick up on her cues. Once she knows you better, I'm sure she'll open up more."

Dean shot him a grateful glance. "I hope you're right, but I'm bad when it comes to talking with women. Next topic: Felipe. That kid doesn't like me, and I don't know what to do about it."

This topic was tougher. "You might try not treating him like a juvenile delinquent."

Dean's brows lifted. "Need I remind you that's exactly what he is?"

Eliot was used to being more blunt and factual. Perhaps he'd been too strong in his assessment. "I think we can all see that Felipe's not a bad kid. He's a classic case of being a product of his environment. Haven't you noticed how much he's grown in the short time he's been here in the camp? He's relaxing and getting to know everyone. The last couple of days, he's volunteered for jobs over at the worksite and seems eager to work each morning."

"Yeah, I guess so." Dean's brow furrowed. "So, again, what's your suggestion to get him to open up more and not treat me like I'm the scum of the earth?"

"That's a little extreme, isn't it?"

"I don't think it is. Felipe answers me with monosyllables and short grunts. I'd like to have a decent conversation with him one of these days about something more meaningful than the weather. Look, Eliot. I'm not trying to be his friend, but I'm also not his parent. I feel kind of stuck as to my boundaries. A temporary guardian's not a parent and yet I'm supposed to exercise some kind of parental-like authority."

"I'm sure it's tough. There are no real rules when it comes to a situation like this, but he *is* part of your family. You don't necessarily have to be buddies with him, and you're right that you need to maintain his respect as an authority figure. Felipe needs a structured family unit, although I'm sure he doesn't understand that. What's he interested in? Sports? Music? Usually the best way to get someone to open up and talk is to generate discussion about something they like. Ask questions. Show interest."

"Other than a certain pretty teenage girl here in the camp, I don't really know what he likes." Dean scratched his head. "Sad commentary on my quasi-parenting skills, huh? He's been with me a while now, and I should know the answer to the simple questions."

"Why not ask him what he likes?"

"I could try. Knowing Felipe, he'll accuse me of prying in his life."

"Let him. Persist." Eliot smiled. "Doesn't hurt to ask, does it?"

Dean met his gaze. "No, I guess it doesn't. It's worth the risk of being shot down. Again."

"Want to pray about it?"

Dean's expression visibly relaxed. "You know, that'd be great. Best suggestion yet."

Chapter 24

~~♥~~

Dean's eyes widened in surprise when he entered the dining hall and noted Angelina's shorter haircut. Then he spied Felipe beside her and his mouth gaped. For the past few months, he'd been trying to get him to cut his hair. More power to Angelina. He glanced about the room but didn't see Sheila. For now, he needed to concentrate on Felipe. Bolstered by his shared prayer with Eliot, he felt ready to tackle the challenge.

Sliding onto a bench across from the teenagers, Dean pasted on a smile. "Nice haircuts. What prompted this change?"

Angelina explained how they'd come upon a Locks for Love promotion at a hair salon when they'd gone into town with the ladies. As she talked, Dean darted several glances at Felipe. The teenager remained silent with the same scowl he always wore in his presence. It wasn't like he was an ogre or mistreated Felipe. Could be the kid didn't like him because he represented authority and a father figure. Since his dad was a sore subject for Felipe, it could be a transference issue. Seemed like an uphill battle, but it was one he was willing to keep climbing.

His relationship with his own dad had been rocky until his dad died five years ago, so maybe he could tap into those feelings to try and reach Felipe. There had to be a way, and he was determined to find it.

"I'm proud of you, Felipe," he said. "You're helping out a cancer patient. That was a very unselfish, generous thing to do."

Felipe drummed his fingers on the tabletop and seemed surprised by the compliment. "Yeah. Thanks."

Josh welcomed everyone a few minutes later. "In case you haven't heard, my twin spent a little time in the hospital earlier, but I want to assure you that everything's fine. Beck's back in the camp and she'll be staying with Winnie and Natalie so they can keep an eye on her for a few days. Kevin's here now and wants to say a few words. Then we're going to ask that you wait and let him go through the food line first." Stepping aside, Josh nodded to Kevin.

Kevin's eyes were bright as he glanced around the room. "You know, it seems there's always a blessing to be found, even in situations that sometimes seem overwhelming. Like Josh said, we had a scare earlier today. I don't mind saying that I've never been so frightened in my life. Not that I ever doubt God's promises or His will, but this hit close to my heart. It's no secret that I've wanted to be a father for a while now. The same for Rebekah becoming a mother. I wanted to share with you that the tests they ran on Beck revealed something we didn't anticipate."

Like everyone else, Dean leaned forward, waiting.

"The doctors told us what to watch for and monitor once we get back home, but there's no reason Rebekah shouldn't carry to term and have a healthy, safe delivery." Kevin broke out into a huge grin. "It's all good, and we couldn't be more thrilled to announce that Rebekah and I are expecting twins!"

Dean cheered and clapped along with everyone else. Some of the guys stomped and whistled and the ladies ran over to Kevin. He chuckled under his breath as they hugged him and then bombarded him with advice and questions. This crew had to be the best support group anyone could ever want.

An unexpected stab of envy hit Dean. Who was he kidding? He could barely bond with Felipe. Then again, Felipe had come to him with a whole set of teenage problems built up through the years. Forcing himself off the bench, Dean joined Angelina and Felipe as they congratulated the first time father-to-be.

"Okay, next on the agenda," Josh said after the buzz of excitement died down, "you might have noticed some new members have joined us for dinner tonight. Mitch, could you introduce your friend?"

"Very funny." Mitch wrapped his arm around Cassie. "My wife, as well as Angelina and Felipe, all donated a foot or more of their hair to Locks of Love today."

"Kudos to all of you!" No one clapped louder than Josh. "Now, before I pray and we eat this wonderful meal, I have a very important announcement." He held up one hand when Marc suggested he talk while they ate. "Hang in there, Thompson. Natalie, if you want to go fill a plate for yourself, Gracie, and your biggest kid over there while I talk, you go right ahead."

Natalie shook her head. "That won't be necessary." She placed one hand over Marc's mouth and nodded for Josh to continue.

"Next Tuesday night, beginning at seven o'clock sharp, right here in this dining hall, I will be your host for the first annual"—Josh nodded to Felipe and asked for a drumroll, to which the teenager gladly obliged—"TeamWork Talent Show! Winnie put a sign-up sheet on the bulletin board so don't fall over yourselves to get over there, people. If you belch like a hippo or play a symphony with your armpits, sign up. Every one of you has talent, and I know because I've seen it or heard it. For instance, if you'll notice the napkin creations on the tables tonight, those are courtesy of Mr. Eliot Marchand, ladies and gentlemen. Now *that*, my friends, is some awesome talent."

"You're not the master of ceremonies yet." Landon's comment generated laughter. "Great job on the napkins, though, Eliot." Eliot acknowledged the compliments with a wave from where he sat next to Marta and Gayle. Ah, the singles table. Dean had considered moving over to join them but then Sheila stole his total attention when she quietly slipped onto the bench beside him. Never had he been so happy to see her, and he hoped she was feeling kindly towards him. He highly doubted she'd come to sit by him only to ignore or chastise him. Then she'd disappeared again.

"It'll be your time to shine," Josh continued. "Discover your creative gene and find a way to entertain us."

Sam rose to his feet. "Just one more announcement."

Several of the volunteers turned their heads toward Marc. "Why are you looking at me?" Then he groaned in an exaggerated way, making everyone laugh again.

"I think you'll like this announcement," Sam said. "After the church services on Sunday, everyone has the rest of the day free. The world-famous Balloon Fiesta is going on, and the longest tram ride in North America is right here in the Sandia Mountains. We'll need to keep the security rotation in place, but do what you want until Monday morning when we resume our work schedules both here and at the church. Just be safe and have fun."

Josh asked the blessing for their meal and then invited Kevin to start and form the food line at the front. When Dean got into the line behind Angelina and Felipe, he caught sight of Sheila coming out of the kitchen. She chatted with Amy as they put baskets of fresh-sliced bread on both tables. She passed by him on the way back to the kitchen again, and he reached out to her, touching her on the arm. "I hope you'll sit with us tonight."

"I-I'd l-l-like that." Those three words, combined with Sheila's sweet smile, gave him renewed hope.

"Dean," Sheila said once they were settled at the table with their meals and drinks. "I-I'm s-s-sorry. I-I'm s-s-sorry t-t-to k-keep r-r-run-ning a-a-w-w-ay f-f-from y-y-ou. Y-y-ou're o-o-only b-b-being n-nice."

Dean's pulse skipped a couple of beats. "I didn't mean to make you uncomfortable."

"I-I-I kn-know. I-I-I've p-p-put u-up b-b-bar-riers f-f-for t-t-too l-long."

"Does that mean I can ask you to spend some time with me and you won't run away?" Dean held his breath, wondering if he should have phrased that thought in a different way. He'd drive himself crazy if he second guessed everything that came out of his mouth.

"Y-y-yes."

He slowly released a breath. So far, so good. Might as well keep going. *Here goes nothing.*

"Did you hear what Sam said about being on our own on Sunday?" Dean kept his voice purposely low, not sure he wanted the teenagers to overhear. If he got shot down again, he didn't particularly want witnesses to his humiliation.

Sheila nodded but glanced across the table at Angelina and Felipe. The kids were behaving themselves and she visibly relaxed. That was a good sign. She always seemed tied up in knots when those two teenagers spent time together, which seemed to be most of the time. Other than physically separating them, or sticking close by them—or sitting on them—what more could he do? Trying to keep Felipe away from Angelina would do a lot of damage to his already precarious relationship with his charge. From all accounts, and from what he'd personally witnessed, they were getting along well and Felipe treated Angelina with respect. Sam told him he thought they were good for each other.

A sudden case of nerves overtook him, but Dean pushed forward. "If you really want to go to the hot air balloon race or on the tram, I'll understand. Both of those things sound like a lot of fun." He was sabotaging this before he'd even stated his case.

Focus on the positive.

"W-w-what d-do y-you h-h-have in m-m-mind?" Sheila smiled and her dark eyes sparkled. Selecting a slice of bread, she offered the basket to him. Dean shook his head and handed it across the table to Felipe. That kid loved his bread.

Sheila's enthusiastic response spurred him on. "I want to cook you dinner and invite you to be my guest here in the dining hall on Sunday evening. Hopefully everyone else will want to scatter to the winds so it'll only be the two of us." He couldn't believe he'd confessed such a thing to her. "Only if you want. We could tell Sam…" Seeing her coy grin, he hesitated. "Did I say something wrong? What are you thinking?"

"G-go o-on."

Looking into her eyes, Dean's breath caught. Sitting this close to her, Sheila's eyes were the loveliest shade of brown he'd ever seen. Rich, expressive, passionate. Okay, maybe that last one was more his wishful thinking.

"I'll put candles on the table if it doesn't violate the fire code, I'll find a tablecloth, and I insist on doing all the cooking. We can even dress up in our Sunday best, if you'd like." He stopped, hoping he hadn't already pushed her too far. When he heard her soft laughter, he paused. "I'm doing a lousy job of convincing you, aren't I?"

"W-w-who s-s-said I-I n-n-need c-c-con-vincing?" Sheila's eyes held a smile when she lifted her chin, meeting his gaze. "I-I th-think w-w-we sh-sh-should vol-volunt-teer t-to s-s-stay h-here on S-Sun-d-day."

~~♥~~

"Sam?"

"Come in, Winnie. I'm back in the office." Although it was nice to be needed, his time to catch up on paperwork was often interrupted. His crew always seemed to know his schedule and when he was in the office. At the moment, it was between dinner and the devotional time at the prayer circle. If one of his volunteers needed him, for any reason, they were his top priority.

Appearing in the doorway, Winnie gave him a coy smile. He recognized that smile. He was in for trouble. Lexa's best friend, the

Mother Hen of the TeamWork crew, had hatched a new plan of some kind, most likely.

"What's on your mind? Have a seat if you'd like."

"I won't be long. I need to get back over to the dining hall before your wife thinks I've deserted her. Have you thought about what you'll be doing for the talent show?"

"Nope. Not a thing, especially considering Josh's announcement at dinner was the first I've heard of it."

"You don't mind, do you? I guess we should have cleared it with you first. I'm sorry."

"Not a problem," he said. "It'll be fun. I figured I'd just sing with one of the kids or dance a jig."

"I have an idea I think is pretty great. Bear with me and hear me out before you say no."

Sam laughed and sat back in his chair. "Do I have a choice?"

"Not really. Hold on." Winnie darted around the corner and, when she reappeared, she held something white in her hands. Looked like a one-piece jumpsuit. Satin. With sparkly things all over it.

He almost choked as she unfolded it and held it up for him to see. "Tell me you aren't serious."

"I said to hear me out." One hand slid to her waist. "As long as I've known you, Sam, you've always been a fair man. If you sing one of Elvis's love songs to Lexa, she'll swoon and everyone else will love it! A man who humbles himself—"

"Sometimes proves himself the fool. You want me to be an Elvis impersonator." It wasn't a question. "What's Josh doing?"

Winnie batted her baby blues at him. "He's the emcee, master of ceremonies—whatever he's calling it—why?" Something lit in her eyes that gave him hope.

"Make you a deal. I'll wear the getup and croon like The King if Josh wears something equally ridiculous. It's only fair, right? And make sure Marc's outfitted in something interesting, too. Tights would be especially good."

Tilting her head, Winnie appeared to be considering the option. "In order to get you to agree, I was thinking more along the lines of talking Lexa into wearing a cheerleading outfit. Don't men always like that?"

Sam grunted. "Give me some ideas for Josh."

Winnie broke out into a wide grin. "Trust me, I've got something for him, too. He just doesn't know it yet. You know my husband. Josh will play it up to the hilt. And so will you. And Marc? Goes without saying. Don't you worry. I'll take special care of him, too."

"Did you bring that costume with you from Houston? Have you been planning this all along?"

"Of course not, but I think it's inspired. We found a thrift shop near the fabric store in town. The timing couldn't have been more perfect. Being early October, they'd just put out a rack of costumes, and we had our pick of the best. Cheap prices, too."

"Glad to know you were frugal in your misguidedness." Sam chuckled. "I'm fine with it, Winnie. Lexa wasn't a party to"—Sam waved his hand at the costume—"this? It'll be a surprise?"

She laughed. "Lexa went to the hair salon with Cassie, Angie, and Felipe. Trust me, she has no idea. I smuggled everything back to the car without her seeing anything, and I swore everyone else to secrecy. Part of the fun will be seeing the look on Lexa's face once she gets a glimpse of you in this jumpsuit. Like I said, she'll be swooning once you start singing. Not to mention how surprised everyone else will be."

"Don't remind me. I'm sure they'll never look at me in quite the same way again."

"No, they won't." When Sam gave her his most piercing look, Winnie smiled. "They'll have even *more* respect for you than they already do."

"If you say so. I wonder why Lexa didn't get her hair cut for charity." He was glad she hadn't, but he would have supported her if she had. Not that he would have had a choice. He'd never seen his wife with hair shorter than the middle of her back.

"Um, maybe you should ask Lexa that question. Far be it from me to answer." Winnie brightened again. "Hold on a second. I can't believe I almost forgot to show you the best parts of the costume. I left them on the bed."

"Parts, plural? There's more?" Sam almost groaned. If nothing else, Winnie was always creative.

After darting around the corner, she came back into the office and stepped close to his desk with a yellow plastic bag in her hands.

Reaching inside it, she pulled out…fake hair. Sideburns. Followed by dark sunglasses.

"There'd better not be fake chest hair in there," he warned.

"Don't be silly." She stuffed something back down inside the bag. "Guess we don't need that."

"I'm not shaking my hips or anything else, either. Only Lexa's privy to that. Just so we're clear."

One of Winnie's trademark giggles slipped out. "Whatever you say. You don't even have to try and imitate Elvis. You can sing in your own wonderful voice. But you might want to say one of his signature lines in a deep voice. Think about it."

This time Sam did groan, but he knew it wouldn't do any good to protest. He'd already agreed to play along with Winnie's plan. Scheme was more like it. "I suppose if I'm really doing this, I need to complete the whole persona that was Elvis, huh?"

"And that's why I love you. Thank you, Sam. Much obliged. Really. Truly."

Before he could respond, Winnie departed. She knew him well, all right. In spite of the teasing he knew he'd endure, he'd make it a memorable performance. Lexa would enjoy it, and so would the kids, even though they'd probably never heard of Elvis Presley.

The thought of the smiles on their faces was all the reason he needed to make a fool of himself. After all, it wouldn't be the first time.

Chapter 25

~~♥~~

Sam was glad to turn over the reins to one of his volunteers at the prayer circle every other night. Especially tonight. After the time of singing, Mitch started the devotional. Stifling a yawn, Sam curved his arm around Lexa and she leaned against him. She had to be as tired, if not more, than he was.

The City Council hearing downtown was tomorrow afternoon, and he wanted to be well-rested for whatever that might bring. He had no idea what to expect. It could either turn out to be a bureaucratic nightmare for the church or prove to be a classic case of much ado about nothing. In any case, his prayer was that—whatever happened—it wouldn't impede the great progress they'd already made at the church. He'd hate to have come this far only to be stalled in their efforts. That seemed a far-fetched scenario. Most importantly, he didn't want anything to prevent the One Nation Church from worshipping in their beautiful new sanctuary.

Mitch rose to his feet with his Bible. "Galatians 6, verses 7 through 10 are familiar to us. 'Do not be deceived, God is not mocked; for whatever a man sows, this he will also reap. For the one who sows to his own flesh will from the flesh reap corruption, but the one who sows to the Spirit will from the Spirit reap eternal life. So then, while we have opportunity, let us do good to all people, and especially to those who are of the household of faith.'"

When Mitch motioned to his wife, Cassie joined him as he addressed the group. "Sam and Lexa have encouraged us to share our news with the group. And no, like I said before, it's not *that*." He paused as laughter moved around the circle.

"The Lord expects our best in all we do," Cassie said. "As most of you know, Lexa and Winnie graciously gifted me with a week-long course at The Institute of Culinary Arts in New York when Mitch and I were navigating our cross-country relationship. I'm sure it had nothing to do with the fact that they wanted us to get together." She paused while several laughed. "I'd originally planned on studying elementary education, but now my plans have changed."

Mitch set his Bible on the bench and took Cassie's hand. "We're pleased to announce that Cassie will be continuing her education at The Institute of Culinary Arts."

"And the best news? After my graduation, I'll be heading up the New York branch of Doyle-Clarke Catering!" Cassie beamed and Sam's heart swelled with pride for Lexa. She and Winnie had worked hard to establish and grow their business, and now the fruits of their labor were being reaped.

As the volunteers offered their congratulations, Dean walked around the circle and crouched behind Sam. "I'm sorry to bother you, especially during the prayer circle, but we might have a problem."

Sam nodded. "We're done. I'll be right there."

Lexa gestured for him to transfer Leah, currently asleep on his lap, to her and mouthed *I'll be praying.*

"Eliot and Felipe are back at the men's dorm," Dean told him as they started in the direction of the camp. "Felipe opened his backpack after dinner and something fell out of it and onto the floor. Sam, it was a can of red spray paint."

A chill ran through Sam, but he chased it away.

"Felipe swears he's innocent and knows nothing about it." The worry in Dean's voice was painfully apparent. The poor guy felt responsible. While Sam understood, he couldn't blame Dean for feeling that way.

"Eliot supports Felipe," Dean said, "but I didn't handle it so well and said some things I wish I hadn't. Of course, that doesn't help my relationship with Felipe. Since I'm the one who brought him here to the camp, I feel responsible. If you want us to leave, I can't blame you, Sam. I sure don't want any of the women thinking that Felipe will cause trouble for them."

Sam shook his head. "Don't jump to conclusions. I'm siding with Eliot on this one."

Dean's brows lifted. "You don't think he did it?"

"No. Call it my gut instinct. I have no idea who did, but there's got to be an explanation."

"But he stole a car—"

"He's starting to bond with some of our guys. He and Angelina are friends. In case you haven't noticed, the kids all love him." Sam's voice was gruff but he couldn't help it. That's what exhaustion always did to him. "The thing that worries me is that someone got into our camp a second time, and now maybe even into the men's dorm. How did that happen? When?"

"I have no idea." Dean sounded equally frustrated.

"Let's go talk with Felipe, but I need you to go easy on him."

Dean grunted. "I thought that's what I'd be saying to *you*, Sam."

"Gayle, I think Eliot's from Great Britain or Europe. Or at least somewhere overseas."

"This I have to hear." Gayle's knees bumped hers as she turned to face Marta on the bench. Everyone else was chatting as the prayer circle ended, and the kids were running around the circle, extinguishing the lit candles inside the luminarias. "Give me details."

"It was only something little, but to me it might have been telltale," Marta said. "He's been asked to be a crew chaser at the Balloon Fiesta and invited me to go with him on Sunday. Which means we'll miss the church service since we have to be out at the field before the crack of dawn."

"Get there faster," Gayle urged with a gentle smile. "I'm not talking about Sunday morning, although I'm sorry you'll miss it. The part about Eliot." She laughed under her breath.

"The friend who invited Eliot to be a chaser is a friend 'from university,' as he put it." When Gayle's passive expression clued her in that she found nothing odd in that statement, Marta pushed on. "You know how people from Great Britain and Europe use the word university without the word 'the' before it?"

"Yes, but are you sure he didn't stick the word in there somewhere? Or maybe it was implied?"

"Let me think." Marta rubbed her fingers in circles against her temples, rocking back and forth on the bench. She wondered why Eliot hadn't made it to the prayer circle. Hopefully his absence meant nothing significant in terms of camp security. Dean had come only long enough to get Sam, and then the two men left together.

"I'm pretty sure he said, 'My friend from university.'" She looked at Gayle in triumph. When no response was forthcoming, she raised her hands. "If I said to you, 'Oh, by the way, I got a call from Lydia, my friend from university,' wouldn't that sound a little odd?"

"Well," Gayle said slowly, "I sort of see what you're saying, but I'm not sure that I'd automatically assume he's from Europe just because he forgot the word 'the.' The man has no clear accent. If he's from outside the U.S., he does a great job disguising it. I've known plenty of people from foreign countries who've been in the States for years, but there's always a trace of their original accent."

Marta stared at her. "Who *are* you, Gayle Ferrari?" She shook her head. "What does it say about me that I know very little about my boyfriend—if that's even what I should call him—and I don't know much about one of my very best friends? That's you, girlfriend, in case you're wondering." With a sigh, Marta rose from the bench. "I guess I'm grasping for something that's not there."

Gayle stood up beside her. "Honey, you know I'm as curious as you are, but don't drive yourself crazy trying to figure out the man. Just try to enjoy his company."

"He said a French word when he first arrived at the camp. That might be something."

"What was the word?"

"*Oui.*"

Gayle covered her mouth. Now she was laughing at her?

"Okay, so that's not exactly evidence," Marta grumbled. "But the biggest clue? I overheard him on the phone at the church, and I could have sworn he was speaking in French. *Fluent* French this time."

Gayle laughed. "You sound like you're trying to piece together clues."

"Because that *is* what I'm doing!" Marta could tell the others were waiting for them, so she started walking.

"I think you need to resolve yourself to the fact that if you're in a relationship with Eliot, you need to be patient and accept whatever he's willing to give. I guess the big question here is whether or not you can do that."

"It'd be easier if Eliot would give me something to hang onto, Gayle. A tidbit about himself that he shouldn't share with me. But he will, anyway, because he cares for me and he trusts me." Marta frowned. "Don't look at me that way, please."

"I'm not looking at you in any particular way. That's you being paranoid."

"Speak then. I can feel your disapproval a foot away."

"Part of loving someone is accepting them as they are." Gayle's words were slow, purposeful. "Eliot shouldn't have to prove anything. I can't imagine what it's like to love someone and yet feel like you don't really know much about him. It's a very odd situation. But I feel like I know Eliot well enough to know that he's conflicted. You know he'd tell you if he could, Marta. It's probably killing him that he can't say anything."

"You know, Eliot said that very thing."

"See? There you go. The way I see it, Eliot's taking a big risk," Gayle said. "His job is dangerous and he's not around much. He's putting a lot on the line by investing himself in a relationship with you. He's not purposely hiding anything from you, and it's not that he doesn't trust you. You're also taking a huge risk, and I admire you. It can't be easy for either one of you. That's probably what's kept you apart this long or it might have happened before this trip."

"He kissed me today, Gayle. I kissed him. We kissed each other."

"Well, it's about time!" Marta felt Gayle's hands on her shoulders and then she was being drawn into a warm hug. "I'll be good and won't ask." Gayle released her.

"It was...great. Best. Kiss. In. The. History. Of. The. Planet."

"Oh, be still my heart. That good, huh?" At first Marta thought Gayle was being flippant, but her voice was full of emotion.

"If I didn't know I was falling in love with Eliot before, I know it now. Not just because of the kiss, either. There's a lot to admire and love about Eliot." Oh, it felt good, *really* good, to openly admit it to someone else. Liberating.

"I knew it all along," Gayle said with a wry grin. "*You* just needed to know it. Here's a little tidbit about me that very people know: Gayle is short for Gaylen."

"Really?" Marta smiled. "That's beautiful. Why don't you use it?"

She shrugged. "I've been called Gayle for so long that it stuck."

"Well, thank you for telling me. I feel like I know you better already," Marta said. "Feel free to tell me anything about yourself. Anything at all. Lay it on me."

Gayle laughed. "I'm sure I can come up with a few more."

Turning over on her side, Lexa watched Sam as he slept. She must have dozed off at some point because she didn't remember him coming back to their quarters. His dark lashes feathered on his cheeks, and his breathing was quiet and even.

Lexa thought over her conversation with Angelina earlier in the day. "God works out the details."

"Something on your mind?" Without opening his eyes, Sam rolled toward her.

Only a whisper in the dark, and yet he'd heard. "No. I'm sorry I disturbed you."

"You didn't. I have some kind of internal radar set to your personal setting." Sam's lids fluttered open. "Do you need to talk?"

"You first. Tell me what happened tonight."

"Lexa, it's late. Even my bones are tired."

"The quick version?"

He groaned lightly and rolled onto his back, crossing his arms over his chest. "Someone managed to get hold of Felipe's backpack and guess what they put in it?"

"I have no idea."

"A can of red spray paint."

Lexa gasped and stared at him, open-mouthed. "I hope you don't think Felipe painted that ugly symbol. He might be somewhat rebellious, but he's got a good heart."

"I never thought he did, and Eliot agrees. Felipe's a jokester but he wouldn't do something like that for spite or to play a prank. One reason I know he didn't do it? He expressed concern about what happened to Beck and questioned whether that evil eye symbol could have brought bad luck."

"In its own way, that's sweet, don't you think? I'm sure you set him straight."

"I tried. He's asking questions, and that's a good thing. This episode is another reason I'm glad we've got the security detail in place."

"Do you have any idea how the spray paint got into Felipe's backpack?" she said. "Other than someone going into the men's dorm?"

"When Eliot asked him that, Felipe said he'd taken his backpack to the dining hall. He left it in the kitchen while he helped carry out the breakfast serving trays."

Lexa thought back over the day. "That seems like a decade ago."

Sam chuckled. "Tell me about it."

"You know, that's right." Lexa lightly snapped her fingers. "Felipe left his backpack under the preparation table. He probably left it there while we were all eating, too, and the screen door was unlocked."

"It's always unlocked. Anyone could have come inside." Tugging his pillow from beneath his head, Sam put it over his face and groaned.

Lexa watched, fascinated, and somewhat amused. She'd never seen him react like that before. "Are you done?" With a light touch, she skimmed her finger down the length of his arm.

He pulled the pillow away from his face. "Lexa, you know one of my biggest aggravations in life is feeling helpless. It seems like Satan works overtime in these camps. Shelby was killed outside a TeamWork camp, then there was the kidnapping situation with Howard and Sheila, and..." Sam scrubbed a hand over his face. "Now someone out there—or a group of people—are trying to drive us out of this camp."

"Or drive us crazy trying. But we won't let them."

Lexa's heart lurched at the weariness in his face when Sam turned his head and met her eyes. "I've heard that a few people have said behind the scenes, but never to my face, that I'm a curse at the TeamWork camps. Supposedly, there are volunteers who don't want to work with me."

She hated to hear such a thing and hoped it wasn't true. "If that's the case, then they have more fear of man than faith in the strength of God's promises. Lila was right when she called you a strong warrior. Satan would love nothing more than to see you fall, but you've got the spirit of the Lord and some pretty awesome men standing with you. The Lord will prevail."

"I know. Thanks, baby." The deep emotion in his voice tugged at her heart.

Lexa ran her hand over his unruly dark waves, smoothing them.

"Your turn," he said. "As long as we're awake and sharing. What's on your mind?"

"I had an interesting discussion with Angelina. If you can believe this, she found a romance novel beneath her bed here at the camp. From what little I could see of it, it looked pretty spicy."

Sam readjusted his pillow and surprised her by grinning. "You've never been to this camp before, have you?"

She laughed. "You're never going to let me live that down, are you?"

"Not as long as I can help it. And I'm going to keep reminding you what I said in that first work camp after I discovered your dirty little secret." She'd never forget the moment Sam found one of her romance novels partially hidden beneath her pillow.

"Dirty little secret." Lexa sighed. "As I recall, you told me that real life is a whole lot more fun."

He chuckled. "And don't you agree?"

"You know it. It's definitely never dull. Angelina had some good questions, and I did my best to counsel her about the difference between lust as it's portrayed in those types of books and love in the real world."

"Three kids later, I'd say we have a good combination of the two." Sam rubbed his hand over his jaw, rough with new growth, and turned heavy-lidded, sleepy eyes on her. Those sexy smile lines surfaced on either side of his mouth, and his gorgeous blue eyes locked on hers.

"You know what I mean. I counseled her about finding a man who's a true hero, and we talked a little about Felipe. She likes him, but she doesn't understand some of the things he says." Lexa laid her head on Sam's shoulder and traced light circles on his chest. "She wondered how a person could know they're compatible with someone else if they've never…"

"Given it a trial run?"

Lexa pulled back, wide-eyed. "Yes. I told her God works out the details."

"Yes, He does. Do you think she took your words to heart?" Sam threaded his fingers through hers.

"I think so, yes. She also gave the book to me and we buried it deep beneath a heavy pile of smelly garbage."

"You're a good woman, Lexa Lewis. I have a question for you. Why didn't you get your hair cut for charity?"

She hadn't expected that question. Neither was she sure she

wanted to answer. "For one thing, I know how much you like my hair long."

"True, but I'm just surprised since it was for a good cause."

"I have a confession, Sam. I recently had my hair colored for the first time. You can't donate dyed or chemically processed hair."

"You did? When?" He took hold of one of the long strands of her hair. "It looks the same."

She blew out a sigh of relief. "Good. That's the point. I had a mini freak-out over it a couple of weeks ago when I found a white hair. Winnie and Marta had to talk me down from the ledge."

"One little hair, Lexa? I've had silver hair at my temples for years, and I had them the first time we met."

"That's not even a fair analogy. It's different for a man." Lexa crossed her arms and tried not to pout. "Silver hairs make you look handsome and distinguished, but that ugly white hair just made me feel old. It starts with one little hair here and there, and then before you know it, you wake up one morning to find they've multiplied. Don't even get me started on eyebrow hairs, or"—she mock shuddered—"chin hairs."

He laughed. "If it makes you feel any better, I'll love you any way you come."

"Thanks, but as much as it's under my control, I'm going to keep pace with you so when we go out, people don't make comments about that distinguished looking man and his little old mother."

"It'll never happen. Older sister maybe." He ducked and laughed when she swatted him with her hair.

"I'm so happy for Kevin and Beck," she said as they prepared to go to sleep. If they wanted to function in the morning, they needed rest. "When you told me she was in the hospital, I prayed like a maniac. I'd hate for that sweet couple to…" Unable to finish the sentence, tears filled Lexa's eyes.

"I know, baby."

"Sam, will you hold me?"

"Always." He wrapped her in his arms.

Chapter 26

Day 5, Friday
~~♥~~

After lunch, Sam guided his Volvo station wagon onto the highway. Headed toward Government Center in downtown Albuquerque, Sam noted that Eliot followed right behind him in the Hummer with Marta in the passenger seat. When Eliot had offered to come, he'd readily accepted in the event any security issues would be raised. Pastor Chevy had provided him with a copy of the complaint after Stephanie Colton's visit and filled him in on more details. After a quick read-through, Sam handed off the complaint to Josh.

When Sam had first mentioned Stephanie Colton's claims to Pastor Chevy, the pastor claimed no knowledge of receiving any mail or a phone call. "The church mail is being routed to our home. It could be that Lila didn't realize what it was and assumed it was junk mail. As far as the phone call, I'd need to know what number Ms. Colton tried. Please be assured that I would have responded to her communication had I known." That was all Sam needed to hear. He'd seen enough odd occurrences with TeamWork mail and phone calls, so nothing was outside the realm of possibility.

"So, what's your take? Anything we need to worry about?" Sam said to Josh, who was seated behind him in the Volvo.

"The one sticking point that might have some validity is the short line of trees that was torn down to pour the foundation for the church. Based on that, be prepared for a discussion of possible land encroachment or violation of property lines. It's all vacant property, and it's a done deal, so that point will be negotiated and a resolution reached, if necessary." Josh pulled at the collar of his shirt.

Sam adjusted the level of air conditioning and negotiated changing lanes. "That seems like a completely unrelated issue in terms of Native American rights. Do we know the source of these so-called complaints?"

"A group calling themselves 'Extant' filed all the complaints and concerns."

"Extant?" Twisting in her seat, Lexa directed her question to Josh. "Doesn't that mean *still in existence?*"

"Right. I had Eliot dig into their background. He says the group is legitimate but there's also a rogue fringe element that's caused some trouble in and around the Albuquerque area in the past."

"Meaning?" Sam raised a brow. That didn't sound good.

"Vandalism, petty theft, that kind of thing. I can't say for sure, but according to Pastor Chevy, it's possible there might be a group of locals who don't want a Native American church in their region." Josh met Sam's gaze in the mirror. "They could also be opposed to TeamWork's presence in helping to build the church." He shrugged. "Anything's possible."

Enough to come into their work camp and spray paint a symbol outside the women's dorm? Enough to sneak the can of spray paint into Felipe's backpack? Sam kept those thoughts to himself and shelved them for a later discussion with Eliot.

"What else?" Sam said. "Stephanie Colton indicated there was more than one complaint."

"The second issue is that there are some who believe the Native Americans weren't offered equal opportunity for the jobs at the worksite. Pastor Chevy has all the documentation substantiating the bid process and the hiring of the construction and landscape crews."

Sam frowned. "In that case, it seems the hired crews would be the focus of the complaints and not the One Nation Church."

"Agreed," Josh said. "Because the Commission's focus is protecting the rights of Native Americans, this could have been a potential issue since Pastor Chevy and the church leaders hired the crews. They originally tried to hire an all Native American crew but there weren't enough applicants qualified or trained to do the work. It's to our advantage that Pastor Chevy was extremely thorough in documenting his interviews and kept detailed records. I think it'll be easy enough to shoot down these claims."

"I don't get it," Lexa said. "If this group doesn't want a Native American church in the first place, then why would they bother making a claim that not enough Native Americans were hired for the construction?"

"That's the part that doesn't make much sense." Josh pushed up farther on the seat. "If that's the case—and we don't know that it is—it's probably a stall tactic to try and delay completion of the project. It would have been better if TeamWork had been informed of the prior complaints against the One Nation Church. Not that it matters much now."

"They apparently didn't feel the claims were valid or had any basis," Sam said.

Lexa sat back in her seat with a slight frown. "The construction foreman plans on being at the meeting?"

"He'll be there with Pastor Chevy and their attorney." Sam smiled at Lexa's interest. His wife was a silent—sometimes *not* so silent—partner in their TeamWork administrative matters. She'd always been a vocal advocate for the organization, and he loved her for it. On the rare occasions when he'd been called into court, Lexa had insisted on attending the sessions. Same with this meeting. As if reading his mind, his wife reached for his hand and squeezed.

"In some ways, this hearing seems like a waste of time since the church building is nearly completed," Josh observed.

"As Stephanie Colton told us out at the worksite, it's the responsibility of the board to investigate all legitimate claims or complaints." Sam noted the highway sign for their exit coming up in two miles.

Lexa reached for her purse on the floorboard. "Who's Stephanie Colton?"

"A member of the board for the City Commission on Indian Affairs." Sam checked the clock, pleased to see the early afternoon traffic was light and they were making good time. "The Commission acts as a liaison between the City of Albuquerque and the Native American community. She'll be there this afternoon."

Lexa glanced at the display on her cell phone. "I have a message from Winnie."

"Everything okay?" Josh said.

"I think so. Hang on." She listened for a moment. "She wanted to let us know they're taking all the kids to a natural spring to cool off since it's really hot this afternoon. Beck's feeling fine and is going, too, as long as she promises not to lift any of the kids. Lila told us about the spring at the dinner the other night and suggested it'd be a fun place to go. It's apparently a well-kept secret among the locals and it's only ten minutes away. Angelina and Felipe are going along to supervise the kids since the ladies aren't planning to get in the water."

"That'll be good for them," Josh said. "Luke hasn't been sleeping well and he's been keeping Winnie up at night. He's a fireball of energy that won't quit. Maybe playing in the spring will wear him out."

"Plus Angelina and Felipe will have a chaperone." Sam chuckled at Lexa's skeptical expression. "I'm teasing, but it never hurts to keep an eye on them. It's obvious they're getting along better now than when they first arrived."

"Yes," Lexa said slowly, "but just because they're the only two teenagers in the camp doesn't necessarily mean they're doing anything they shouldn't."

"True, but Felipe's a normal teenage guy, Lexa," Josh chimed in. "Best to keep an eye on them."

Sam glanced back at Josh again. "Anything else we should know before the meeting?"

Josh chuckled. "Yes, but take this one for what it is. Seems they're short a few Port-O-Lets at the worksite."

"Excuse me? Someone complained about *that?*" Lexa shook her head and stared out the passenger window, but not before Sam heard the amusement in her tone.

"I wouldn't even tell Marc about that one," Josh said. "I can hear the bad jokes now."

Laughing, Sam almost missed the exit until Lexa pointed it out.

Angelina loved hearing the ladies talk about babies. Rebekah and Amy asked lots of questions, and Winnie and Natalie told them funny first-time mom stories. She couldn't help wondering about her own birth since Mama never said much. Maybe it was a painful time since she'd been so young, and talking about it would bring back bad memories of Papa.

She tuned out the childbirth tips and focused on eight-month-old Emily cooing on Winnie's lap. Then she checked on Hannah and Leah napping on a blanket beneath a large tree. When the subject of breastfeeding was raised, she'd heard enough. Jumping up, Angelina excused herself and carefully made her way down the short embankment leading to the water.

Chloe waved and called to her. "Come in with us, Angelina! We're playing Duck, Duck, Goose."

"Is it cold?" Stepping to the edge of the spring, Angelina removed her tennis shoes and gingerly dipped her toes in the clear water. Tall trees blocked some of the light and warmth from the sun, but the temperature was cool without being too cold. The kids hadn't protested, so she needed to be as brave as they'd been.

"Aw, get in here already or it'll be Duck, Duck, Chicken, and you'll be it!" Felipe flapped his arms and made squawking noises, making the kids giggle. His hair was slicked back from his forehead, emphasizing his strong cheekbones and making him look older. He'd stripped off his shirt and wore shorts in the water, but the kids all had on their swimsuits. Chloe told her they'd stayed in a hotel with an indoor pool when the Lewis and Grant families caravanned to New Mexico. At least these kids had been taught to swim at an early age.

When Luke and Joe imitated Felipe with the squawking, Angelina laughed. "Look out, people, I'm coming in!" She waded into the stream in her shorts and T-shirt. Maybe it was a good thing she hadn't brought a swimsuit. She would have felt self-conscious with Felipe's gaze on her. He was definitely looking, and his smile made her stomach do a little flip-flop.

For the better part of the next forty minutes, she and Felipe kept the kids occupied with water games. The kids all seemed to love him, and she liked how he took a personal interest in each one of them. He asked Gracie if she ever went into the Prudential Tower in Boston to her daddy's office. Asked Joe if he ever swiped a cupcake when Lexa wasn't looking. Made Chloe and Luke laugh with his impressions of their favorite cartoon characters.

"You're really good with them," Angelina said as they sat on a large rock by the stream and dried off in the afternoon sun. The kids were wrapped in towels and either dozing or listening as Rebekah read them a story. "Have you been around many kids?"

"Not really. They're cool. Sometimes I think kids are a lot more honest than adults."

Angelina considered his words for a moment. "I think it depends on the type of people you know. Felipe, you made a comment the other night that made me wonder about something. I know this is a personal question, but I feel like I know you well enough to ask."

"Sounds intense. Ask away. I have no secrets from you, Sweet Potato."

She smiled at the nickname. Call her crazy, but she was becoming accustomed to them. "You mentioned not going home hungry. Did you ever do that?"

"No," he said, "but I was hungry *at* home. We didn't go out much, if you know what I mean. I was home by myself a lot. With some of the assorted step-siblings sometimes."

Angelina's stomach turned and she felt a little sick. "Felipe, you didn't have enough to eat?"

"Sometimes. It's not a big deal, Angel. Really. You kinda get used to it and make do, you know? Mom finally got us on some government program but us kids had to go out and get the food ourselves."

Something inside prompted her to ask the next question. "Do you know how to cook?"

Felipe looked over at her so fast she almost laughed. "What makes you ask that?"

"Because I'm getting to know you, and my guess is that—if you had other mouths to feed in the family, especially younger ones— you'd be the kind of guy who'd provide for them. Am I right?"

Felipe started to say something but then hesitated as if debating whether he should answer.

"You can't fool me. Underneath all your bravado or whatever, you're an okay guy." Was that a touch of pink in his cheeks?

"Did you hear about what happened last night?"

"About what? I guess I didn't. Is everything okay?" A chill ran through her. What now?

"I found a can of red spray paint in my backpack. I swear to you, I had nothing to do with it."

Angelina gulped. "Is it the same kind that was used to paint the evil eye symbol?"

"How should I know? I didn't do it. That's my point." He sounded defensive again.

"I believe you, Felipe. What did Sam say?"

Something in Felipe's expression softened. His guard lowered long enough for her to glimpse the naked emotion beneath his usual smirk. "He, um, said he believed me. Eliot backed him up. Dean?

Not so much." The bitterness in his tone surfaced.

"I'm glad you didn't get in any trouble, Felipe. I think Dean will come around. You just need to give him a little more time. He needs to see the real you. For all I know, he has trust issues."

He laughed a little. "Listen to you. You sound like a shrink, Buttercup."

"You can't use that nickname. That one belongs to Chloe." She was glad to hear him laugh again. "Felipe, has anyone said anything to you about my dad?"

"No." His gaze met hers and she could tell he was intrigued. "Tell me."

"He was kind of like your dad, I guess. I mean, Papa was in and out of jail, too. So don't go thinking everyone in my life is a fine, upstanding citizen."

"Yeah? Sorry to hear it, but maybe you can sort of understand my life better."

"Of course I can. Let me tell you a little story. On my first TeamWork mission, Papa tried to kidnap Mama and me. I was seven, and the work camp was just outside San Antonio."

"No fooling? Why'd he do that?"

"Because Mama was trying to get away from him. During the bad times, he…uh, hit her sometimes. Mama used to say he was all talk and big dreams. When things didn't work out the way he wanted, he took it out on her. I remember she had a broken arm once and a few bruises here and there. She'd make up excuses, but I could tell. Mama's not careless or clumsy."

Felipe shifted into a sitting position and wrapped his arms around his knees. "That's pretty awful. I'm sorry, Angel. My parents aren't much to speak of, but they never pounded on me. Or on each other. So, your mom was hiding out with you at the TeamWork camp?"

She nodded. "I think her biggest fear was that Papa would start in on me. He never did, though."

"I thank God he didn't," Felipe muttered. That was the first time she'd ever heard Felipe thank God for anything.

"I remember Mama crying one night. She was rocking me back and forth, and I think she did it more to comfort herself than me. I didn't really understand what was happening. I just knew Mama's heart hurt."

When Felipe reached her for hand, Angelina gave it to him after first glancing over her shoulder. The ladies and kids were all occupied and partially hidden from view.

"I don't care if they see us." Felipe's voice was quiet. "Can you tell me what happened when he kidnapped you?"

"He kidnapped Mama from the work camp, and then Sam and Lexa came after us. Papa tied up Mama and Sam, and then he stole Sam's car to drive to my aunt's house in the city to get me."

"Whoa," Felipe said. "No wonder you hate people who steal cars."

Removing her hand from his, Angelina wiped away a tear. "Hate's a strong word, Felipe. Lexa insisted on going with Papa, and she got Papa's gun away from him."

"Mrs. Lewis? That's impressive. I don't see her as the type to pack heat."

Angelina smiled a little. "She didn't, but her dad was a cop and she knew how to handle a gun. Papa didn't know Lexa had taken his gun and he started to pull it out at a convenience store later on when he had Mama and me in the car. I don't think he really would have tried to kill anybody, but he liked to threaten people. The clerk pushed one of those silent alarm buttons, and that's when the police caught up with us and threw Papa in jail."

"That's quite a story, Angel. I never would have guessed you'd been through something like that."

"I don't talk about it much. Lexa and Sam risked their lives for Mama and me." She met his gaze. "And you know what? They'd do the same thing for you or anyone else in trouble."

"Yeah, maybe," Felipe said, frowning. "What happened with your dad after that?"

She blew out a sigh. "After he got out of jail, things got better for a while. That was the pattern. And then he hooked up with some bad guys again. They turned on him and shot him in a bank robbery. Whether or not they did it on purpose is anybody's guess."

If only Felipe knew how hard it was to tell him the story without breaking down in tears.

Felipe's shoulders slumped. "Man, that's rough. If you don't mind my saying, I'm kinda surprised your mom would be with a guy like that."

Angelina shrugged. "She got pregnant with me when she was

really young and her family forced her to get married. She always told me that, deep down, Papa wasn't a bad person. He just had mixed up ideas of right and wrong and what he should do to earn respect and love. So he kept making dumb decisions and mistakes."

"She never divorced him?"

She shook her head. "Mama made a commitment, and she didn't want to break it."

"Hitting a woman is never right, Angel. Of all people, God would understand that."

"I know." A tear slipped down her cheek and sadness overwhelmed her. "I told her God wouldn't expect her to stay in a marriage like that. Papa didn't honor the vows he'd made to Mama. Mama was right about one thing, though. Papa was a good dad to me. He never mistreated me, and he said I was the one bright shining light in his life, and the one thing he did *right* in his miserable, sorry life. *His* words."

Felipe pulled her into his arms and Angelina didn't resist. "I can understand why he felt that way, and I've only known you a few days."

She leaned her head on his shoulder for a few seconds before moving away from him.

"Did your Papa know God? From what you've said, I'd have to guess he didn't."

"No," she whispered, steeling herself not to cry again. "Not that people didn't try." She wiped away another tear and met his gaze. "Sometimes, no matter what you do or say, some people don't want to hear the message. I want *you* to hear the message, Felipe."

"Why do you care so much about me?" The way he looked at her, Angelina could tell he really needed to hear her answer.

"Because," she said, her voice rough, "Papa didn't have hope when he died. I want you to have the kind of hope that he never did. Hope for what's beyond this life."

She could tell he didn't get it. Right then and there, Angelina resolved that if it was the last thing she ever did, she'd make Felipe understand.

"Thanks for caring about me," he said.

"Felipe, I hope you don't believe that being my friend will somehow make you a better person. 'Cause it doesn't work that way."

"I think it sort of does. I don't have all the answers, but I know one thing."

"What's that?" The compassion she glimpsed in his eyes touched something deep inside her, making her pulse jump.

"Just being around you makes me want to be a better person."

More tears stung Angelina's eyes. "That's the nicest thing you've ever said to me. There's hope for you yet."

He smiled. "You think so? Stick around."

Chapter 27

~~♥~~

Pastor Chevy waited for them as they found the meeting room. After a brief discussion, Sam put his hand on the small of Lexa's back as he ushered her into the meeting room. She loved it when Sam did that; it was a protective gesture, as if he was saying *this woman belongs to me*. Some women wouldn't appreciate that sentiment, but with Sam, he always treated her as his equal. She was a cherished partner, not his possession.

After they found seats near the front, a tall, pretty brunette dressed in a power suit with a short, pencil-thin skirt approached. Without a doubt, this must be Stephanie Colton.

"Mr. Lewis," Stephanie greeted him with a small smile, offering her hand, her gaze showing appreciation for how handsome Sam looked. "It's good to see you again. Thank you for coming."

Sam rose from his seat and shook her hand. "This is my wife, Lexa." Releasing the woman's hand, he turned to her. "Lexa, this is Stephanie Colton."

"It's nice to meet you." Lexa waited to see if Stephanie offered her hand. She did not.

Stephanie turned to Josh. "I assume you're the general counsel for TeamWork that Sam mentioned at the worksite?"

"Joshua Grant. Nice to meet you." After shaking her hand, Josh excused himself and strolled across the room to speak with Pastor Chevy and the foreman, Donald Morrison.

Stephanie's brown-eyed gaze settled on Sam once more. "Mr. Thompson decided not to join the party this afternoon? He might have added some welcome humor to our proceedings."

Sam chuckled. "No, he's keeping things under control at the worksite. There's a lot to be done, and we saw no reason to stop the work because of this meeting."

"I'm sure," Stephanie said, giving him a small nod. "We'll be ready to begin in a few minutes."

Lexa bristled a bit. She was used to women admiring Sam on a regular basis, but most females weren't so blatant. To their credit, the guys had acted professional and had done nothing to encourage her. Stephanie must have met Marc at the worksite, and she was now making it a point to introduce herself to Eliot.

Sam slipped his arm around her and whispered, "You're a hundred times the woman she is."

Lexa leaned into the curve of his arm. "I didn't say a word."

"You didn't have to," The warmth of his lips tickled her ear. When Sam squeezed her shoulder, it unsettled her even more.

When she felt Stephanie Colton's eyes on her, Lexa wished Winnie were sitting beside her for moral support. But no, it was probably best that her friend wasn't here. Winnie was feeling self-conscious enough these days about not losing the baby weight she'd gained with Emily. Although she'd stepped up her exercise regimen and limited her portions, Winnie couldn't seem to shake those pesky extra pounds.

Not that Lexa was jealous of the long-legged brunette board member sitting at the front of the room. In seven years of marriage, she'd rarely had a reason to be jealous. Sam was a very attentive husband, but in the presence of Stephanie Colton, it was difficult not to feel somewhat frumpy by comparison. Stephanie made it a point to cross her legs, and Lexa cringed when the other woman's skirt hiked even higher, visible beneath the table.

Lexa lifted out of her chair as Josh returned to sit beside Sam. "How about some water?" Engaged in conversation, both Sam and Josh nodded. She headed toward the pitcher of ice water and plastic cups on a nearby table.

Marta came to her side and reached for two empty cups. "So, this should be fun, huh?"

"I'd say so." Lexa poured the water for her.

"Thanks." Marta took a sip from one of the cups and met her gaze above the rim. "Lexa, why does a woman like that intimidate me?" When Marta moved her gaze to the front of the room, Lexa didn't need to turn around to know she was looking at the youngest, tallest female board member.

"Probably because we're giving her too much power in allowing her to intimidate us." Lexa poured water for Sam and Josh.

Marta's brows lifted. "We're? Meaning you feel the same way?"

"In some respects, yes. But we're the ones with the power in this situation, Marta. Acting insecure and jealous can turn a man in the opposite direction. We'll be better off if we focus our attention on supporting Pastor Chevy and the One Nation Church. That's the reason we're here." Lexa hoped her smile softened her words. She didn't want to come across as chastising or judgmental in any way because she totally understood Marta's concerns.

"I wish I could be as generous in spirit as you." Marta took another sip of water. "Forgive me, Lord, but what I see is a woman who's looked at all three of our TeamWork men like they're her personal eye candy."

"From my experience, women who look at men that way are lacking something in their personal life," Lexa said. "Not that I know Stephanie Colton or am making any judgments."

"What she seems to be lacking is a man or she wouldn't be looking at our guys like that." Marta frowned. "Sorry. I know that sounds judgmental."

"I think if you dig beneath that cool, somewhat tough exterior, you might discover a wounded, hurting heart. It's in her eyes, Marta. Mark my words, there's something there. An insecurity, perhaps."

"Could be," Marta mused, finishing her water and tossing the cup in the nearby trash can. "I just wish she didn't feel the need to wear that short of a skirt."

Picking up the cups of water, Lexa gave Marta a wink. "If I had an afghan, I'd give it to her to cover her legs. We wouldn't want her to get a chill, after all." As she walked away, she heard Marta's soft laughter.

She *was* only human after all.

"Let the circus begin," Eliot said under his breath, sitting back in his seat and resting his chin on one hand. He listened as Pastor Chevy introduced himself, Donald Morrison, One Nation attorney Martin Long, and then Sam and Josh.

"I wonder why they didn't introduce you," Marta whispered.

"I'm a peripheral player, so there's no reason. I also specifically asked Sam to make sure I wasn't introduced."

"Why not?" Marta shifted in her seat. "Oh. Would that blow

your cover?"

"No comment." Was she being sarcastic or teasing him again? Hard to tell from her tone of voice, but she'd been rather prickly on the way downtown. He'd never known Marta to be moody, but he could tell something was weighing on her mind. Maybe he could draw it out of her on the way back to the camp. He only hoped this proceeding didn't last for hours. Being a Friday afternoon, surely these people would want to wrap it up sooner than later and get their weekend started.

A haggard looking older man sat at the head table. "All right, ladies and gentleman." With a small wooden gavel, the man lightly tapped the table a couple of times. "Let's begin, shall we? Welcome and thanks to all of you for joining us today. For those visiting with us tonight, I'm Clarkson Traylor, President of the City Council. The Council is the legislative authority of the city. It is our responsibility to adopt all ordinances, resolutions, or other legislation conducive to the welfare of the people of the city. The Council is made up of nine members, elected on staggered terms, with four or five districted Councilors elected every two years."

Mr. Clarkson proceeded to introduce the other members of the City Council, as well as the three members from the Commission on Indian Affairs, including Stephanie Colton, the woman Eliot knew had talked with Sam and Marc out at the worksite.

"The purpose of this meeting is to discuss complaints that have been lodged against a building project at a site located on the east side of the Sandia Mountains. To give you a brief history, application was made by the members of a Native American group called...."

Pastor Chevy rose to his feet. "The One Nation under God Church, Mr. Traylor."

"Yes. Thank you." The man's dark eyes beneath his glasses encompassed the assembly, numbering about fifty according to Eliot's quick headcount. Mr. Traylor went on to report that all of the necessary licenses and permits had been duly, timely, and appropriately filed and approved on behalf of the One Nation Church.

"In answer to your question, it's imperative that I keep a low profile," Eliot said in low tones, leaning close to Marta. "Not bring attention to myself." Her hair smelled so good he wanted to bury his nose in it. That was a first. He was going soft, but for once, he didn't care. Being this close to Marta and not kissing her was growing increasingly difficult. Awareness of her shot through him. They were both dressed in the best clothes they'd brought to the mission camp, making him wish they sat across a dinner table with fresh flowers and candlelight.

"Imperative? You're not exactly the kind of guy who can blend into the background."

Eliot chuckled. "Glad you think so. And you're not exactly a 'blend in' type of woman either."

"Ms. Colton," Mr. Traylor said next. "If you'd be so kind, please read for the record the ordinances regarding the Commission on Indian Affairs for the benefit of those in attendance tonight."

"Neither is she, from all appearances," Marta said. "Her skirt's too short."

Coming from Marta, that comment surprised Eliot. "You think so?" He leaned slightly forward in an attempt to regain her eye contact. Acting stubborn, she resisted giving him the satisfaction.

Stephanie Colton rose to her feet—at least five foot eleven in her high-heeled shoes—and began to state her case. "In order to promote the health, safety and general welfare of its citizenry through the creation of a Commission on Indian Affairs to serve as an advocate of Indian affairs to investigate, study and consider..."

Eliot tuned out the woman's slightly nasal, irritating monotone. Sparring with the woman beside him would make this hearing a whole lot more bearable.

Marta shifted in her chair again. "It's not jealousy, if that's what you're thinking. Women like that always drive me crazy."

This should be fun. Sure sounded like jealousy. "Should I ask why?"

Stephanie Colton droned on. "...the subject of Indian conditions within the City of Albuquerque, including, but not limited to, matters of employment, education, economy, health, environment, government and access to services in the City."

"She's uncommonly tall," he observed. "It's probably difficult to find skirts that are long enough for her—"

"Spare me, Eliot. Her physical attributes are clearly on display for all to see."

"So are yours at times. You wear shorts at the worksite. And in the camp. And sleep in them, too, judging from our middle of the night adventure."

Marta's eyes widened and her lovely mouth gaped. "What do you expect me to do? Roll myself in bubble wrap to keep you from staring at me?"

"No," he said, trying not to laugh. "For one thing, no matter how much bubble wrap you'd use, it'd still be see-through. Don't be ashamed. You have great legs."

"I am *not* ashamed. I hope you don't think I purposely—"

"Ah, and now we're back to the slinky lavender gown."

Based on Marta's quiet laughter, he was relieved she apparently found this crazy exchange amusing. Flirtation. Whatever it was between them, it was pretty great. Energized him. Settling into his seat, Eliot tried to concentrate on the proceedings, but Marta was way too distracting.

He moved his gaze slowly around the perimeter of the room. A few townspeople sat to one side, but no one stood out as appearing unfriendly, hostile, or in any way threatening. If any of the members of the Extant group were in attendance, they were keeping a low profile. That didn't surprise him. They weren't exactly the type of group to wear matching T-shirts with the name of their group emblazoned across their chests. That was more TeamWork's style.

Apparently satisfied that all the formalities had been dispensed, Mr. Traylor asked Stephanie to present her next point. Then Stephanie began a discussion of labor and employment practices.

Marta leaned closer to Eliot. "Let me get this straight. Is she claiming the Native Americans weren't given equal opportunity for employment at the worksite?"

"Pretty much. But they shot it down."

Pastor Chevy rose at that point and addressed the room. "I can assure you that every attempt was made to hire Native American Indians for the available paid jobs at the building worksite. At the time, the particular requirements for the positions were specific in terms of operating the heavy equipment in order to bulldoze and level the land, and quite frankly, no Native Americans applying for the positions possessed the necessary training, skills, or proper licensing for the project. If needed, I can produce evidence of our efforts to advertise and interview for the positions. That's when we hired Donald Morrison"—Pastor Chevy nodded to the foreman—"and he brought in his crew to complete the job that we'd already started."

Mr. Traylor glanced at Stephanie and the other members of the Commission. They all shook their heads. Seemingly satisfied that providing evidence would not be necessary, he told Pastor Chevy as much, thanked him, and then asked him to take his seat.

Beside him, Marta stifled a yawn. Eliot blinked hard a few times himself. Pulling out a small pad of paper, she initiated a game of Hangman. He won twice and she won once.

Another discussion ensued regarding the proposed landscaping around the church structure and possible violations of land use by tearing down an existing line of trees on the southeastern corner of the property.

Marta passed a note to him. ARE YOU ARE BORED AS I AM?

Chuckling, Eliot crossed out her words and wrote MORE.

She nodded and mouthed *We are such big kids.*

He mouthed back *You love it.*

Once again, Pastor Chevy rose and introduced a man sitting next to him as the landscape engineer hired to assess the situation prior to the groundbreaking for the church. The engineer quoted from a City ordinance before pointing to his schematic of the property, highlighting the line of trees and telling them the line was outside the lines of protected property for demolition purposes.

Marta sat up straighter. "Oh goody. Exhibits."

Eliot loved Marta's sense of humor and use of sarcasm. His right arm brushed against hers as he sat forward, elbows on his thighs. Neither one of them moved. When he chanced a quick peek, Marta turned her head at that precise moment. Their gazes locked and held.

"What?" she whispered.

He swallowed, wishing he could speak his mind. For once in his life, he couldn't. The time and the place didn't lend itself. "Hold on and brace yourself, Marta." He forced a grin. "They haven't even broached the Port-O-Let shortage issue yet."

Brilliant, Marchand. Way to impress a woman, talking about portable bathrooms.

"Whaaat?" When Marta laughed and then clamped a hand over her mouth, her response earned them chastising glances from several of the Council members.

"Although they didn't come forward, I feel sure a few of the men in the back are members of the Extant group," Eliot told Sam and Josh when the meeting concluded a good forty minutes later with a slap on the wrist for a few minor violations having nothing to do with hiring practices or a line of trees torn down. Two more Port-O-Lets would be brought out to the worksite by Monday.

"Sam?"

"Ms. Colton." Sam nodded to her as the woman approached.

"I'm thankful everything worked out in a manner satisfactory to all the parties involved. TeamWonder is free to continue your work at the worksite."

"That's Team*Work*," Josh said.

Eliot quirked a brow when Stephanie smiled at Sam as if they shared a private joke of some kind. "Of course it is," she said. "I'll check in on Monday to make sure the Port-O-Lets have been delivered."

"The first worship service will be held at the church this Sunday," Sam told her. "You're welcome to come and join in the celebration. And now, if you'll excuse me." Walking toward Lexa as she emerged from the ladies room with Marta, Sam slipped his arm around his petite wife's waist.

And that's the way it's done. Sam's response to the attractive woman's flirtation by inviting her to the church service was classic. No wonder Sam wrote marriage books. Stephanie Colton had taken the hint and moved farther down the corridor to speak with some of the City Council members.

Marta walked over to him. "Was she conceding victory?"

"For everything but the Port-O-Lets." Eliot told her about Sam's invitation to join them at the church service.

Marta smiled. "Papa Bear strikes again."

"From the research I did before coming to the meeting, Extant's game is intimidation aimed at minorities," Eliot told them in the parking lot.

"What's their issue? Your best theory," Sam said.

Eliot knew Sam didn't expect him to have all the answers, but he depended on him to lend him the benefit of his experience. "Seems no minority is beyond their focus. The members come from all walks of life and professions, mostly Caucasian, primarily male, and with an average age range from 25 to 55."

Eliot stuffed his hands into the pockets of his khakis and glanced around the area. Most everyone seemed to have cleared the area. There had been a group of five men who'd sat at the back of the room. As soon as Clarkson Traylor's gavel sounded, they'd risen from their seats and quickly departed.

"White Supremacists?" Josh said. "Please Lord, no."

"Not quite as extreme," Eliot said, "but from what I've read, some of their known actions have been prompted by racism. I'd look at this group as the poor man's version of the KKK or other white supremacy groups. Extant isn't as highly organized. They have fewer members and less violent tendencies. What we need to keep in mind is that the bigger white supremacist groups normally form smaller factions in order to carry out their dirty deeds. The members seek out likeminded people. Meaning this Extant group could be large and a few of their members have targeted TeamWork and the One Nation Church to harass. Unfortunately, there's no way of knowing how dangerous they could be or how far they're willing to carry out any threats. Bottom line, we should take their presence seriously, press on with our work, and be aware they can do some damage."

"Do you think they might try to damage the church building? Where does it stop?" Sam ran a hand over his brow. "I guess my question would be how we can try and reach these people where they live, so to speak?"

"We need to always be on alert," Eliot said. "I've told our crew—both the guys and the ladies—to report anything suspicious while we're here in New Mexico. I'm glad we've hired the security service to watch over our vehicles and Landon's plane. Otherwise, I'd advise you to do what you always do."

"Right." Sam nodded. "Then I'd say we need to keep praying."

Eliot's gaze met Sam's. "Sounds good. That's what we'll do."

Chapter 28

~~♥~~

After returning to the camp, Sam changed back into his jeans and T-shirt. With a quick kiss, Lexa hurried off to the dining hall. Hearing animated voices from the softball field to one side of the camp, Sam headed in that direction. His eyes widened as he turned a corner of the camp.

"Mom? Dad?"

Sure enough, Sarah Lewis was up at bat and swung at the ball, proving once again why she'd been a four-year scholarship softball player at the University of Texas in Austin, the alma mater for Sam and both of his younger brothers, Will and Carson. Will had been offered a scholarship at MIT, among other prestigious engineering schools, but he'd preferred to remain in Texas before joining the Air Force.

The ball connected and soared high into the air, sending several players scrambling for it. Instead of having one of the kids run the bases for her, Sarah took off at a run.

Moving his hands to his hips, Sam chuckled as his mother rounded the bases like a woman half her age. He moved his gaze to his father. The look on Sam Sr.'s face as he watched his wife spoke volumes. Spying him, his father motioned for Sam to join him.

Sprinting over to him, Sam gave his dad a hug. "Hey there. What a nice surprise. You had to come all the way to Albuquerque to show off Mom's softball expertise?" He made sure to stand on the left side of his dad, his better ear with the hearing aid. His father had initially been stubborn and resistant to getting it, but Mom had finally convinced him a number of years ago.

"You know it, son. We figured this was as good a place as any."

"How are you feeling these days? Any migraines lately? Dizziness?"

"No. Same as always," Sam Sr. said. Still limiting the salt and caffeine. As long as I get plenty of water and sleep, eat well, and limit the stress, I manage to keep it under control."

"Good," Sam said. "I hope this altitude and climate won't cause you any trouble."

"It might actually be better here in New Mexico. I have medication if I need it." Sam Sr.'s gaze narrowed and he whistled as his wife after she rounded third base and headed toward home plate. "Would you look at her, son? I'll never tire of watching your mother. Beauty and poetry in motion, isn't she? Sarah's as energetic as she was all those years ago on the UT softball field."

"Yes, she is." Sam cheered along with the kids and his dad as his mother rounded home plate, stomping on it and raising her fisted hands in the air. When she reached them, Sam pulled her into his embrace and kissed her cheek. "Great to have you here, Mom. You're looking as beautiful as ever."

"Thanks. I didn't come to Albuquerque to show off, you know." Putting one hand over her abdomen, Sarah seemed slightly out of breath. "Good to know I can still run a little. To be honest, I wasn't sure I could do it. And don't you dare use the word spry, either. That word's reserved for old people."

Sam laughed. "I wouldn't think of it. You'll never be old. You're radiant."

Sam Sr. kissed Sarah's cheek. "Yes, she is. Awesome as ever, Tomboy."

"Thanks, Captain." Sarah slipped her hand into her husband's as Sam had seen his mother do many times through the years. Somehow, the poignant gesture resonated even more with him this time. Maybe it was seeing his dad's hearing aid although a hearing aid was nothing compared to so many other things they could be facing. With some of the TeamWork members losing parents in recent years, it put things in perspective. Made him thankful they lived nearby in Houston and they saw one another often.

"You looked great out there," Sam told her. "I'm sure the kids would be glad to do the running for you, if you want."

"Never. I'm getting older, but I'll keep running on my own speed as long as I can." Cupping her son's chin in one hand, Sarah gave him a kiss on the cheek. "You're looking as handsome as ever, Sam. A little tired, but I know that'll be the norm while you're here."

Sam eyed his Mom. "Did you mention to Lexa that you were coming? She didn't say a word."

"No, this was all our doing. Your dad and I thought a little road trip might be fun. Do a little sightseeing and maybe lend a helping hand where it's needed at the church or here in the camp."

"Well, it's great to see you. Welcome. Do you have a place to stay?"

"Starting tomorrow," his mother said. "We hoped you might have a place we could curl up for tonight. If not, we'll head farther down the highway."

"You're here, so don't think for a second that I'll send you looking for a hotel room. I can't promise anything fancy, but you can have our quarters. Lexa and I will camp out with the kids tonight," Sam said without hesitation. "They'll love it. It'll be another adventure."

"I don't mind putting you out," Sarah told him with a grin, "but I don't want to inconvenience Lexa." He laughed, appreciative of how his mother was always mindful of Lexa's feelings. His wife and mother shared a great relationship. Mom had taken Lexa under her wing when he'd been on the year-long overseas mission. Both women were of similar temperament—feisty, passionate, and not afraid to speak their minds. Great qualities that helped to keep him straight.

"Trust me, she won't mind," Sam said. "How long can you stay?"

His mother smiled. "We caught wind of the TeamWork Talent Show on Tuesday night. Your dad and I thought we might stay for that."

"I hope you'll want to participate."

Sam Sr. nodded. "I'm sure we can come up with something. We caught wind that you were downtown at a City Council meeting this afternoon. Everything okay?"

Sam chuckled. "Nothing a few more Port-O-Lets and minor adjustments at the worksite won't cover. A group brought claims against the worksite and needed them aired publicly by a board that oversees issues related to the Native American community."

"There's always a critic in every crowd," Sam Sr. said.

"Lexa told us about the evil eye symbol." His mother didn't sound overly concerned although she'd always been a fierce prayer warrior, especially where her children were concerned. Sarah brushed strands of honey blonde hair away from her forehead in the breeze.

She refused to allow her hair to go gray, silver, or white. After their discussion about her single white hair, Lexa would get a kick out of knowing that about his mother, if she didn't already. His father's hair—still full and only slightly thinning at the crown—was now peppered with distinguished silver, mostly at the temples, same as his own.

"No worries. We won't give into the bullies. So, how are Caty and Carson?"

"They're both doing great and send their love," his father said.

Sam glanced at his mother. "And Will?"

"I'm afraid your brother's lost in the clouds as usual these days." Sarah leaned against her husband's shoulder.

"Don't know if we told you that NASA confirmed that Will's shuttle will be *Pursuit*, and his mission to the International Space Station will be for six weeks. He'll be blasting off in two years." Sam Sr.'s voice was full of pride for his second son.

Sarah smiled. "I remember telling your father as we sat by Thornton's Creek all those years ago in Rockbridge that it'd be one of the scariest—but greatest—things in the world if one of my children would ever travel into space. That was before I knew I'd marry the handsome Air Force captain who made a habit of following me to that creek."

"We're all proud of Will," Sam said. And he was. His brother would make history for the United States and the space program. For the world. "He'll come around, Mom. Give him time. He's caught up in the whole NASA thing. It's no small feat to be named as a shuttle commander. We all know that's been Will's mindset and singular purpose since he was a kid."

"I know." Sarah's brown-eyed gaze uncharacteristically avoided his. "I'm thrilled and proud, of course, but a bigger part of me can't help but be sad that he seems to have…"

"He'll come back to the Lord, Sarah." His dad visibly tightened his hold on his wife. "He hasn't forgotten his faith."

"He's *neglected* his faith, and that's just as bad." Sarah shook her head. "It's more than that. Will has no personal life. He should be socializing. Do you know that boy says affirmative and negative instead of yes and no in everyday conversation?" Sarah shook her head. "That's not normal."

Sam couldn't help it. He laughed. "I imagine it is for an astronaut."

When he caught his mother's quick glance in his direction, Sam held up both hands. "Hey, I'm trying to do my part in the grandchildren department, but you'll get no announcements from me today, folks."

Sam Sr. smiled. "Thanks for doing your part, son."

"We'll keep praying for Will," Sarah said. "If he's going into space as the space shuttle commander, then he's going to show the world who's boss while he's up there. And I'm not talking about William Jordan Lewis."

"I share that prayer, Mom. What do you say we play some more softball and show these kids how it's done?"

Sarah brightened at his suggestion. "Splendid idea! I think I have my breath back now." Sam hated to see her upset, but he understood Will was uppermost in her mind. Today was one of the rare times she'd voiced those concerns.

"Sarah's been worried about you, too," his dad said in low tones as they walked to join the batting lineup. "The opposition to your TeamWork project here has troubled her a bit. It's not easy being a mother."

"I know," Sam said. "So far, the threats haven't amounted to anything. And Mom makes everything look easy."

Standing beside him, Sam Sr. nodded. "You've got that right, son. And so does Lexa."

~~♥~~

"I definitely need a hot shower. It seemed warmer at the worksite tonight."

Lexa glanced up from where she sat reading in the chair closest to her side of the bed. Sam was in the process of pulling his shirt over his head. She watched as he stepped out of his shorts. All the physical work he did both at home and here at the camp kept him sculpted and buff. She tugged on the collar of her blouse, fanning herself. While she enjoyed the sight of her husband, the timing wasn't good, especially tonight.

"What were you working on?"

"Dad came over with me and we were nailing down the pews." Sam picked up his dirty clothes and deposited them in the laundry basket outside the bathroom.

She grinned. "There's a pun in there somewhere but far be it from me to think of it tonight. All I know is, I'm going to need to make a trip to the laundromat early next week before we're overrun with stinky laundry."

Sam laughed. "Is that a personal observation about the way I smell tonight?"

"No," she said. Expecting him to go into the bathroom, she was surprised to find him lounging against the doorframe of the bathroom. "Do you need something?"

"Do we need to talk?"

"About?"

"Stephanie Colton."

Lexa glanced at her watch and tried not to frown. What could she say that wouldn't make her sound insecure or jealous? "I don't know why you'd think that. Your parents are due to show up in an hour. I've changed the sheets and everything should be ready for them."

"The One Nation guys got the teepee all set up and ready to go." Sam ran his hand over his hair. "The kids think it's the greatest adventure yet."

"I'm sure they do." Lexa put her book on the nightstand. "I have a feeling that teepee is going to be a permanent fixture for the rest of the camp." She'd wanted the kids to stay in their quarters with Sam's parents, but once the One Nation men offered to construct the teepee, the kids could barely contain their excitement. It would be fun, but she hoped they'd get some sleep.

"I think you're right," Sam said. "The kid in me has embraced the idea. Eliot's on guard tonight, by the way. The guys are doing an awesome job with the security rotation. Now," he said, "speak to me. Stop staring at my chest and tell me what's on your mind."

"Okay, so you caught me. It's not fair staring at how gorgeous you are and trying to have a coherent conversation."

"You realize I'm in my skivvies here." Sam raised a brow and gave her a grin Lexa recognized when he was feeling playful and fun. "You could strip down, too, and then we'd be on an even playing field. But at least you'd smell better."

Sliding out of the chair, Lexa walked across the room. Sniffing the air around him, she wrinkled her nose to tease him. "You're right."

Cupping her face in his hands, Sam leaned close. "I will never stop pursuing you, Lexa. No one else is like you. The Lord created me for you—and you for me—and I love you. Never forget that."

After a prolonged kiss, Lexa released a sigh of contentment. "Kind of hard to forget after that kiss." This man never ceased to amaze her. The way he could read her was a little scary, but always, Sam considered her needs and those of his family first.

She patted one hand on his chest. "I love you, too, Sam, but you'd best go take that shower."

When he laughed, his smile lines surfaced. "Is that your polite way of telling your husband he stinks?"

"Your words, not mine."

Watching her, Sam tilted his head. "I think I like that look in your eye."

Ah, he really *could* read her. At the moment, she appreciated that quality very much. "The kids are playing games in the dining hall, and your parents are talking with Winnie and Josh. The others are all settling in for the night, and"—Lexa trailed one finger over a smile line and then down to his chest—"I'm feeling very supportive of water conservation tonight. Plus, I'm a good back scrubber."

A telltale gleam surfaced in Sam's eyes. He gave her another quick kiss. "You're being naughty, Mrs. Lewis."

"Nah. Just spicy."

He glanced at the clock. "We've got a limited window of opportunity. Don't be long, baby. And lock the door."

Try as she might, Marta couldn't sleep. She startled when she heard something hit the window above her bunk. What was that? She shuddered to think it might be a large bug. When she heard it again, thinking it might be Eliot since he was on guard duty, she hopped out of bed. After putting on her hoodie, she shoved her feet into her house shoes and then unlocked and opened the door a crack.

"Eliot, is that you?"

"It is I." His deep voice came from her right. "You need to be careful. You never know what kind of hooligan might be lurking about."

Even in the dim light, Marta could feel Eliot's gaze on her. "Is this a shameless ploy?"

"Yes," he said, chuckling under his breath, stepping forward. "It worked to get you to come outside."

Marta shivered and crossed her arms over her middle. "All it took was a few pebbles thrown on my window." She shook her head. "I'm a discredit to womanhood."

"Not at all, but I hope you wouldn't come outside for just any guy."

"Are you fishing for a compliment, Mr. Marchand?"

"Depends." He shrugged. "Do you have any compliments for me tucked away in the pockets of those…really cute sleep shorts?"

"I was right. You *are* shameless."

"I plead guilty." He waved his hand to the side wall. "I brought folding chairs and bottled water. Will you join me for a chat? If you're not too tired, that is."

"Let me go and change into my sweatpants," she said. "I'll be back out in just a minute."

Eliot smiled as she returned. "Good to know you're a punctual woman."

"I do what I can." Marta settled into the chair he'd set up for her. "Tell me what's on your mind, Handsome Hooligan." She liked the way the night breeze ruffled the short waves in his hair, and the scruff on his face was appealing in an unkempt, rolled-out-of-bed way.

He handed her a water bottle. "Tell me all there is to know about Marta Holcomb."

"Okay, let's see. Where to begin? My birthday is March fourth, and I'm older than 21. According to my mom, I could swim before I could walk. I won 34 trophies for swimming and 15 for diving before college, not that anyone's counting. My favorite color has always been yellow. I love sunflowers, daisies, and orchids. I love Italian food—my mom owns a small Italian bistro back home in Kentucky—and I can eat more meatballs than my brothers in one sitting. I'm not really proud of that fact, but for whatever reason, I thought it was worth mentioning."

"Older brothers, right?" Eliot said. "Thomas, spelled T-h-o-m, is the oldest and…" When he raised his head and closed his eyes, Marta could tell he was trying to remember. "Give me a clue?"

"You take medication for the…"

Opening his eyes, he snapped his fingers. "Of course! How can I forget. Paine!"

"Right. As you might imagine, I'm immensely grateful for *my* name considering my brothers' first names combined are the same as the controversial revolutionary who published *Common Sense*."

"Which challenged the authority of the British and the royal monarchy," Eliot said. "Thomas Paine's discourse was the first published work to openly ask for independence from Great Britain, so it was significant. My question is whether or not your parents did that on purpose?"

"Believe it or not, it was a fluke since neither of my parents were history enthusiasts. Thom owns an insurance agency and does very well for himself and Paine is a professional student. Both live in Kentucky, and neither one is married. I'm the defector who left the Bluegrass State to move to the wide open spaces of Texas for college. And then decided to stay."

"That's a very good thing for TeamWork. And for me, if you don't mind my saying."

"I don't mind your saying." They shared a grin. "Are you tired of this bedtime story yet or do you want a few more parting tidbits?"

"Please proceed, but I shouldn't keep you up too much longer."

"You're not keeping me up," she said. "In my opinion, the whole idea of beauty sleep is highly overrated, both in theory and principle. Let's see, what else can I tell you? I absolutely adore corny love songs from the 60s, 70s, and 80s. The cornier the better. I rent a small house in Houston, not far from Sam and Lexa's house. Gayle and I had moved into Cassie's condo when she and Mitch got married, but then Gayle decided to buy it. Although I love Gayle like a sister, I do much better living on my own."

"Why's that?"

"For one thing, my regular bed buddy is a huge St. Bernard who goes by the name of Barney. I know the name's highly unoriginal, but it fits my overgrown puppy."

"I'm sure it does. I'd love to have a pet someday, preferably a dog. A big one named Brute. Brute and Barney could be buds." Eliot chuckled. "How old and how many pounds is Barney?"

"He's five years old, weighs almost 180 pounds, and is extremely protective of me."

"Glad to hear it. I like Barney already."

"I just have to watch it sometimes because he has this crazy idea that he's a lapdog."

They heard a noise and Eliot sat up straighter, at full alert. Mitch and Cassie walked into view, hand-in-hand. Talking quietly, they stopped to share a prolonged kiss beneath a tall tree.

Marta curled up in the chair and shifted to face Eliot. "It's kind of hard not to look at them, isn't it? They're too adorable."

"We could follow suit," Eliot suggested. "How about it?" He leaned toward her, puckering his lips in an exaggerated fashion.

"You big goof." Marta waved as Mitch and Cassie came closer.

"Good evening, comrades," Mitch said. "Hope all's quiet on the home front tonight."

"It was until your unbelievably loud smooching woke me up." Eliot angled his head to the Bible Mitch carried. "I see you've got the Good Word there. You two doing a little studying?"

"We like to spend some private time together every day," Cassie said. "Early morning or late at night seems to work best."

"Just be careful." Eliot sounded much more serious. "Don't wander too far from the camp."

"Duly noted," Mitch said. "You might want to look the other way now because I fully intend to give my beautiful wife one more good night kiss."

"I don't know if I can stand it!" With a mock groan, Marta covered her face with her hands like the kids did whenever they witnessed one of the couples sharing a kiss. With the TeamWork crew, amorous behavior was more commonplace than not. "Good night, sweet lovers," she said after Mitch released Cassie's hand.

"Same to you." Cassie scooted inside the door of the dorm before Marta or Eliot could respond.

"Big difference, *Mrs.* Jacobsen." Marta called out in a loud whisper before turning back to Eliot. "No comments, please. I realize I can be a little juvenile sometimes."

"So can I, remember." Eliot laughed quietly. "I think they're on to us." He held a long stick in his hand and absently made a cross-hatch in a patch of dirt, softened by the recent rains.

"I'm suddenly feeling brave." She took the stick from him. "I'm going to toss out a question and you can answer if you're so inclined. Or not. Your prerogative."

"This could be dangerous but go for it. Let's see what happens."

"Where were you born? United States or abroad will suffice since I'm sure you can't give specifics." She dropped the stick on the ground between their two chairs. Unless they were going to play Tic Tac Toe, it'd lost its appeal.

"Abroad."

"Ah," she said. "As I suspected. How many languages do you speak?"

"I suppose that answer would depend on your definition of speak. Fluently? Four. I'm also proficient enough in a few other languages to ask for a glass of water and the price of an apple at the corner market."

"Which four languages?"

"French, German, Italian, and Spanish."

She smiled. "You forgot English. If it's not your native tongue, that is."

He angled his head toward her. "Very astute. But I choose not to answer that one."

"Fair enough." She'd keep going with a few more questions. "What brought you to the States?"

He hesitated long enough that Marta figured he wasn't going to answer. She started to retract the question when he answered. "To attend university."

So her assumption that Eliot was from overseas was correct, but she hadn't guessed that he'd attended university in the States. "Which one?" She might be pushing it with that one.

"Suffice it to say Ivy League, but that's all I can say." Eliot had already revealed more than she'd expected and probably more than he should.

"Excuse me?" She whistled under her breath. "I knew Mitch went to Harvard, and Marc to Yale, but I had no idea. Seems we've got ourselves a few blue bloods in our TeamWork camp."

"Something wrong with that?"

She looked up at him quickly. "Not at all. What did you study?"

"Foreign relations."

"Oh," she said. "That makes perfect sense from what I know."

"Foreign relations applies every bit to relating to a woman such as yourself as it does to maintaining a friendly rapport with other nations."

"That's a very politically correct answer. Why did you need that kind of training? That's what I'm wondering."

Eliot sighed. "To prepare me for my career."

"Oh, so you're a spy," she teased, nudging him with her elbow.

"I can't say anything more, Marta. Really."

"Because if you told me, then you'd have to kill me, right?"

"Something like that."

"So, are you like James Bond? Do you have any fun little gizmos or gadgets? Cars with ejector seats? A beautiful, sexy woman in every port?"

Eliot chuckled. "No, but I've had some interesting adventures. That's the second time you've mentioned my so-called girlfriends around the globe. I thought we'd settled that misperception. Let's keep moving forward. Tell me more about your education."

"Not much to tell. I was a good student but my mom didn't think I applied myself or I could have been brilliant. Her words, not mine. You know I went to Baylor University, but you probably don't know I earned a full-ride swimming scholarship."

"That's very impressive, but it seems natural for someone who could swim before she could walk. What's your specialty?"

"The 800 Freestyle and the Butterfly were my best events."

"Which tells me you have endurance, strength, and stamina."

Pulling up her knees on the chair, Marta wrapped her arms around them. "You also know what I do for a living, but what you *don't* know is that I smuggle state secrets in muffins."

"That's a very commendable choice. The school, not the smuggling." The corners of Eliot's mouth upturned. "What's your degree?"

"Geophysics."

Eliot choked as he took a drink from his water bottle. "So, my next question would have to be why—"

"Why am I working for Lexa and Winnie's catering business? I do a lot of the accounting work for Lexa now, so I'm putting my mathematical skills to good use. Since Cassie moved away, I've taken over the front office duties. I coordinate events and interact with existing and potential clients, put in bids for big jobs, order supplies and enlist extra staff for big events. I enjoy it, and I still help serve at the occasional catering event. We have a regular staff of part-timers now, and they've just hired a new office manager."

Marta shrugged. "To be honest, there aren't many positions for geophysicists that appeal to me. The jobs are few and far between unless I want to man the controls at the local planetarium. I'm happy keeping the books for Doyle-Clarke Catering and baking the occasional muffin. I'll have you know my blueberry muffins are to die for."

"I'm sure they are. I'll have to try one sometime. State secrets included or not."

Although he didn't smile, Marta could hear the amusement in Eliot's tone. "It's okay to say you're surprised, Eliot. That's about the only thing they allow me to bake."

"Okay then, I'm surprised. You had me way back at trophies, but why geophysics?"

"Call me weird, but I've always loved math, science, and the study of the earth. I love the study of meteorology and astronomy, in particular. Can you keep a secret?"

Eliot grunted. "I'm an expert at it."

"I've been talking with one of the TV stations in Houston about a weekend meteorology job."

He shifted in his chair. "That's great. Which station?" When she told him, he nodded. "Adding a beautiful blonde on the weekends makes perfect sense to me. They could use some fresh blood, so to speak."

"I have a screen test next month. If I get the job, I'd start early in the New Year. I'm not sure whether to tell Lexa and Winnie yet. Gayle's the only other person other than you that I've told."

"Are you saying I'm special?" His wink made her heart soar.

"No." She laughed quietly. "I'm saying that nothing may come of it. They're my friends, too. I'd like to share this news with them so they can pray for me, but they're also my bosses and sign my paychecks. I'm sure you can see my conundrum here."

"I can. As much as I know they'd hate to lose you at Doyle-Clarke Catering if the job comes through, Lexa and Winnie would be pleased for you. You'd be at TeamWork events, so it's not like you'd lose touch. And you go to the same church, as I understand it."

"True. Jensen Callahan—the new girl we've hired as the office manager—seems more than capable of taking over in my place. Rumor is she can cook, too. A certified double whammy."

"Sounds to me like the Lord is paving the way for something to happen so you can move on."

"Could be. Don't get too excited for me yet. Since it's a weekend job, there's the possibility that I could still work for Doyle-Clarke during the week. Depends on what the TV station's looking for, I suppose." Marta tucked hair behind both ears. "I'm nervous about the screen test, but I'll give it my best shot."

"I'll be praying for you, Marta."

Her pulse sputtered. She'd always been the kind of girl who lived in the moment, the here and now. Once they went back to the "real world," the Lord only knew what would happen, including with Eliot. She quickly dismissed that thought. This evening was too special to dwell on anything sad.

With every muscle protesting, Marta reluctantly rose from the chair. "I'd better say good night. Thank you for the wonderful chat. Since we don't share a normal dating relationship in any sense of the word, I think you should know that I consider this a date."

"So do I." Eliot drained his water bottle, recapped the bottle, and set it on the ground.

"I already broke a big dating rule with you," she said, lifting her shoulders. "*Huge*, actually."

"Should I ask?" When Eliot rose from his chair, Marta's heart jumped. Lacing her fingers through his, he walked her to the door—all of two feet.

"Kissing before the first date. It's unheard of. I hope you can still respect me."

"Always. But if you think about it," he said, "we talked on the way to the camp when I first arrived. Then we had what I'd call a major, life-changing talk after that first prayer circle. That's two dates in one day, right? Got to count for something." When she nodded, he continued. "Then we shared the hammer and ice incident. And then the middle-of-the-night episode—"

She laughed. "I like your reasoning."

"Marta, I've been falling in love with you since the moment we first met. And each time we've spent together since has reinforced those feelings. My mind and body have been going at such warp speed at times that I needed this mission to slow down and focus on you. On *us*," he amended.

She inhaled a quick breath. Eliot's words thrilled her. Should she pinch herself to see if this conversation was really happening? He took her other hand in his and guided both her hands around his neck. *Smooth move, Mr. Marchand.*

"Thank you for sharing more about your life with me," she murmured. "I realize that's a big risk for you, and I want you to know how much I appreciate it."

He leaned close and touched his lips to hers. "Is that all?" His arms moved around her.

"Are you teasing me again?" Marta smoothed one hand over his hair. The light from the moon brought out the highlights in his hair, and the strands were soft under her fingertips, making her want to sink in with both hands.

"Yes. I kind of like teasing you." His voice was deep, low, teasing.

"Kiss me again, please?"

Eliot's lips met hers. His kisses made her deliciously, deliriously dizzy.

As they parted, Marta was thankful his arms still circled her waist. "At the risk of sounding like a girl in a fairy tale, I can't believe this is happening."

"Oh, this is definitely happening." To prove his point, Eliot kissed her again.

A long moment later, Marta released his hand. "The here and now is a beautiful place to be."

Chapter 29

Day 6, Saturday
~~♥~~

"Is this where you want the gazebo, Pastor Chevy?" Sam worked with his TeamWork men to position the partially constructed gazebo to the side of the church. One of the One Nation men had transported it from the campsite in his large, flatbed truck.

"Yes, thank you." The other man smiled and addressed Kevin. "Thank you for making this lovely gazebo and donating it to our church, Mr. Moore. The women, in particular, are very pleased with this addition."

"TeamWork's all about promoting love," Marc said. His sentiment was met with knowing smiles from several of the other men.

"Which brings me to our next project," Sam announced. "After lunch, I suggest we go on a shopping expedition."

"Are you talking about more building supplies?" Mitch said. "I can help you." Kevin and Landon echoed their agreement.

"I have something a little more personal in mind, guys. We're halfway into the mission, and I can tell you natives are getting a little restless." Sam's statement was rewarded by a series of grunts and chuckles. "We've been working hard, and it's time to take a few hours off. I'd like to suggest that you each pick out a special gift for your wife. Gear it toward her unique interests. Whatever helps her to relax, makes her feel pampered, makes her feel pretty. That kind of thing."

Marc nodded. "Sounds like Rule Number Three. Show her your love in a physical, tangible way."

"I've pretty much imprinted those rules in my brain," Landon said. "They've come in handy."

Josh smiled. "You like them so much you're publishing Sam's books." He turned to Marc. "I don't even want to see what you'd pick out for your wife."

Marc laughed. "Try to keep up, will you?"

"We'll tell the ladies we're going to the home supply store for pipe fittings and that should do it. Once they hear that, I can guarantee none of them will want to come along." Sam paused while the other men laughed. "We'll only be gone a couple of hours, and they won't suspect a thing. It'll be good for our marriages, and that's always a good thing."

"When do you suggest we give the gifts to our wives?" Ah, that from Kevin, practical as always.

"Don't you mean *where?*" Marc said.

"I've got a plane. I can take reservations." Several of the guys laughed at Landon's suggestion, but it might have been inspired.

"I guess the nature of your gift will dictate how much privacy you'll need." Sam chuckled. "You'll figure it out. I'll leave it up to you. I know you're a creative bunch."

"We learned from the master." Marc saluted him as he headed for the church.

Hands on his hips, Eliot tossed Sam a broad grin as the others departed. "I'm sure you'd like us to take over security at the camp while the rest of you lovebirds are at the mall? Great idea, by the way."

"You might want to catch some more sleep, Eliot. You were only supposed to handle a three-hour shift last night, but you were standing guard last night and again when we climbed out of that teepee." Sam rubbed the back of his neck and chuckled. "In my wildest imagination, I never would have believed I'd be saying a sentence like that."

"Not a problem," Dean said. "You can count on us, Sam. Eliot's coasting on love fumes as it is."

Eliot smirked. "Speak for yourself, Romeo."

"Do you want some iced tea?" Angelina asked Felipe. They'd played a couple of games outside, and now the kids were coloring at tables in the dining hall. Winnie had stopped by a few minutes ago to get Emily and Luke for their naps, and Lexa should be coming soon to get Leah and Hannah.

"Sure, but not milk this time. Thanks, Love Bunny."

Laughing, she shook her head. "Don't let the kids hear you say that."

"Yeah, right. Get real, Angel. These kids hear plenty of nicknames from their parents."

On her way to the kitchen, she saw Gracie hand a crayon to Joe. Good. She didn't feel like mediating between them today.

A couple of minutes later, Angelina handed Felipe a cup of iced tea and dropped down onto the bench beside him.

"What's that you're drinking?" he said.

After she explained it was called an Arnold Palmer—half-lemonade and half-iced tea—he asked to try it. "Not bad," he said, smacking his lips. "Tart and sweet, like someone I know sitting with me now."

"Very funny."

"Angel, did you know that one of the survivors at The Alamo was a little girl named Angelina?"

She blinked in surprise. "Seriously? I had no idea. I've only been to The Alamo once with a school group. I'm surprised I didn't know that. How'd you find out?"

"Our resident history expert mentioned it to me when we were working over at the church the other day."

She laughed. "Let me guess—Sam?"

"Right. Anyway, she was only a baby. Two years old. Her name was Angelina Dickinson, and her mama's name was Susanna. Have to tell you, if her name had been Sheila, that would have been pretty weird. After the battle at The Alamo, a Mexican general offered to adopt Angelina, but Susanna refused to give her up. I thought about that, and I know your mother wouldn't ever give you up, either. But my mom? If she had an offer like that, she'd probably jump on it."

When Felipe said things like that, it made her heart hurt. "Felipe, I've been wanting to ask you about something."

"What's that?" After taking a drink, he turned to face her.

"You mentioned step-siblings when we were out at the spring. Can you tell me a little about them?"

His grin faded fast. *Oh oh.* What had she said now? She didn't mean to make him sad, but she also wanted to understand more about his life so she could be a better friend.

"Yeah, I've, uh, got a few half-siblings and some step-siblings.

I've kind of lost count."

Angelina tried to keep the shock from her voice. "You honestly don't know how many brothers and sisters you have? How...tragic." She'd prayed for a baby sister or brother for years. Mama was still young enough to have another baby. She'd noticed the way Dean looked at Mama, and he didn't have any kids. She liked Dean, and Mama deserved to be happy. Maybe there was still hope.

"They're all bad news," Felipe said, breaking into her reverie. "Like my folks. Mom's been married three times that I know of, and Dad's been married at least twice. I try not to think about any of them."

"How are your step-siblings bad news?" Maybe she shouldn't push it, but she wanted to know.

"In and out of jail. Drug possession for the most part. Drugs are stupid." Wrapping his hands around his cup, he nodded to the kids. "Look at them. Do you think they have any idea how bad some people have it?"

She followed his gaze. The kids giggled together, their laughter filling the otherwise quiet dining hall. "Probably not, but why would you want to take away their innocence? They're happy. They'll find out soon enough how hard the world can be. How people aren't always nice even if they seem that way on the outside. Those kids are stronger than you might think, though."

"Yeah? What makes you say that?"

"From what I know, not one of them cried or got scared because of that symbol." Angelina looked back over at Felipe. He stared straight ahead, but she could tell he was lost in his own world.

"One of the guys I hung out with back home took an overdose a couple of weeks ago."

The sadness in Felipe's voice about broke her heart. "I'm so sorry." She had no idea he'd been struggling with something like that since he'd been here in the camp.

"Me, too," he said after taking a drink. "He was one of the guys who *borrowed* the car with me that night. I thought Marco would be the one who'd make something of himself. He was a lot smarter than me."

Shifting on the bench, Angelina turned to face him. "Sorry to say this, but he wasn't all that smart if he took drugs."

"I think it was an escape for him. He had it rough. Problem is, nobody knows if Marco meant to kill himself on purpose or not."

"You've had it rough, too. Drugs are a cop-out. What's *your* escape, Felipe?"

"I've done some things I'm not proud of, Angel. I tried drugs, but they made me do stupid stuff. I play soccer sometimes." He drummed his fingers on the cup. "And…"

"And?" Angelina prompted.

"Promise not to laugh?"

"I promise." She sipped from her drink.

"That promise thing didn't work out so well before, but I'll tell you anyway. I like to write stories. Short stories mostly."

"Really? That's great, Felipe!"

Her enthusiasm made him visibly brighten. "You don't think it's too weird?"

"Of course not. For one thing, it shows you have an active imagination. Not that I doubted it for a second. What kind of stories do you write?"

"Okay, this part might sound strange."

Angelina held up one hand. "Don't even tell me if it's— "

He snorted. "Not *that* kind of story. Get your mind out of the gutter. I like to write stories for kids."

That was the last thing she expected to hear. "Kids? You mean like chapter books?"

"Picture books about families. For younger kids. Books to let them know it's okay if their family's messed up. To encourage them to make something of themselves." He lowered his voice. "To tell them that the bad stuff doesn't mean they can't be successful or do whatever they want in life. That kind of thing."

"I imagine that must be difficult to write about since most books for kids are usually happy and light. Unless things have changed since I was a kid."

He grunted. "They're not singing barnyard animals or anything, but I like to think it might give them hope." He glanced at her as he took another drink. "Are you saying you don't think I should?"

"I'm not saying that at all." She tried to think of how to put her thoughts into words that wouldn't offend him. The way Felipe watched her, Angelina could tell how important her opinion was to him. "I admire you for attempting something like that. You've had a rough time of it and you're trying to help others. That's a wonderful thing. Can I see your work sometime?"

"Maybe. If you're nice to me." He grinned at her as he took another drink.

"I like drawing, you know. If it's for kids, you must have illustrations in your books, right?"

"You mean pictures? I will if I ever get to that point."

"Did you bring anything to the camp with you?"

He tossed her a wary glance as if debating whether to tell her. "I have a notebook where I jot down notes and stuff. I have a couple of stories with me."

"Can I see them sometime? Maybe I can help you with the illustrations."

He appeared to consider her suggestion and then a wide grin spread across his features. "You'd really do that for me, Blossom?"

She smiled at the endearment. "I wouldn't offer if I wasn't serious. How many books are we talking about?"

"Not sure. Six…seven, maybe. Maybe I'll show them to you sometime."

Angelina smiled. "I'll look forward to it."

~~♥~~

"Well, if it isn't Josh Grant." The woman's voice was husky, female, and came from behind them as Sam and Josh walked in the shopping mall's main corridor.

Josh's jaw tightened. "Stay with me, buddy."

"I'm right beside you." Both men turned around at the same time.

A tall, leggy blonde—dressed to kill in a black dress—click-clacked in unbelievably high-heeled sandals on the polished floor. As she approached them, she rested one hand on her hip. In her other hand, she carried a small pink-and-black striped bag. Her lips curved as she reached them.

"Hi, Josh. Do you remember me?"

Removing his Stetson, Josh nodded to the woman. "Hello, Victoria."

Her smile grew brighter as she eyed him. "Sugar, you look better than ever." The woman moved her dark-eyed gaze to Sam, making him feel on display as she sized him up, down, and all around.

"Who's this tall drink of water?"

"This is my friend, Sam."

She nodded. "Very nice to meet you, Sam."

"Victoria." He tipped his Stetson with his left hand so she couldn't miss his wedding ring. Josh hadn't given her his last name, and for that, he was thankful. Best to get this awkward run-in over so they could be on their way.

Victoria moved her gaze back to Josh. "What are you doing with yourself these days?"

"I'm the general counsel for a Christian missions organization called TeamWork. I live in Houston with my wife and our three kids. I trust you're doing well, Victoria, but we're on a limited time schedule and need to keep moving." Turning to leave, Josh hesitated when she put one hand on his forearm.

"Don't run off so fast. What brings you handsome gentlemen to Albuquerque?"

Sam sent up a silent prayer of thanks that their wives weren't with them on this fun little shopping trip. On the other hand, Winnie and Lexa could probably handle this run-in with one of Josh's former female friends better than their husbands.

"We're helping to build a church." The muscles in Josh's cheeks flexed.

The woman's eyes widened. "Is that a fact? That's surprising. You weren't much into…building anything a few years ago. Do you have a few minutes to buy a parched girl something to drink?" She'd directed that comment to Josh alone.

"Afraid not. We really need to go." Josh's voice was firm. "Good-bye, Victoria. Take care of yourself."

"I live here in town if you'd like to reconnect while you're in Albuquerque, Josh. For old time's sake. Let me give you my card." She opened her purse and pulled out a card, offering it to him. "No strings attached."

Josh sighed and ran a quick hand through his hair. "Victoria, I'm not going to take your card. I need to tell you something."

She tilted her chin upward to meet his gaze, sending her long, silver earrings swinging. "Tell me, Josh. Anything you want, sugar."

"I'm a different man today than I was a few years ago. You're as beautiful as ever but do yourself a big favor."

"I thought that's what I was trying to do," she said, pouting.

Josh motioned for Victoria to follow him over to a quieter side corridor with fewer shoppers. This conversation should be between the two of them. "Stay, Sam," Josh called to him when he started to walk away. "I won't be long."

With a nod, Sam did as he asked, planting himself a few feet away. If nothing else, he hoped his presence would be a good source of moral support for his friend.

"Victoria, when we met, we were both trying to find ourselves." Sam appreciated how Josh lowered his voice and offered no encouragement she could misinterpret. "We went about it the wrong way. Sexual gratification won't solve the ache of loneliness. It feeds your physical needs, but if you don't feed your heart and your soul first, then you'll be left feeling empty every time. I've been there, and it's not pretty. I don't want to see that happen to you. You deserve better."

She frowned. "I'm glad you've found what makes you happy, but that doesn't mean it's what I need. I'm…happy with my life."

"You might not want my advice, but I'm going to give it to you, anyway," Josh said. "Find a group and get involved—a service-oriented group is great. Helping others is the best place to discover your God-given talents and it allows others to get to know you. The *real* you, Victoria—who you are and what makes you unique and special. Along the way, I'll pray you'll find a man named Jesus. He's the only One who can give you what you're seeking."

"What's that, Josh?" Victoria's eyes were wide.

"Love. Acceptance. Hope. There's a big, beautiful world out there when you know where you're going for the rest of eternity."

She stared at him. "Are you for real?"

He smiled. "Last time I checked. And so are you. Take care, Victoria. I'll pray that you find the very best in life."

"Thanks," she murmured.

Josh replaced his Stetson and Sam followed suit. They walked in silence until they reached the preappointed meeting place near the center of the mall. Sam knew his friend well enough to know when he needed personal space.

As they dropped into chairs a few minutes later, Josh scrubbed a hand over his face. "I suppose that was bound to happen at some point." His smile was tired. "I can't believe I was telling an ex-lover to find Jesus, standing in the middle of a shopping mall. In

Albuquerque."

"You handled it well." Sam gestured to Josh's bag. "Before you give Winnie her gift, you might want to destroy the business card Victoria dropped in your bag."

"You've got to be kidding me." Digging around in the small bag, Josh pulled out the card. After staring at it for a few seconds, he crumpled it in his palm and tossed it in a nearby trash container. "Thanks for being here, Sam."

"Goes without saying, brother. We have about twenty minutes before we meet up with the other guys. Why don't we pay a visit to that lingerie store? Lexa would like something new."

Sam's suggestion was met with an unexpected frown from Josh. "I'm not sure that's the best idea for Winnie. She's feeling self-conscious enough these days since she hasn't lost all the baby weight."

"Then think pretty instead of slinky. They have other things."

Josh's steps slowed as they approached the store. "I hate shopping in these places."

"I can't say I'm too fond of them myself," Sam said. "We're doing this for our wives."

"Good for my marriage, good for my marriage, good for my marriage," Josh said under his breath as he squared his shoulders and they entered the store. "Let's do this."

Chapter 30

~~♥~~

"I thought I'd find you here." Felipe approached where Angelina sat beneath her favorite tree between dinner and the prayer circle. His hands were behind his back. "Here. This is for you." He handed her a small, flat package wrapped in shiny pink paper. A huge pink, green, and white polka dot bow sat on top.

"Really? Thank you!" After closing her Bible, she put it on the ground beside her. "What's the occasion?" She turned it around in her hands. "How pretty!"

"The other ladies got gifts. I wanted you to have something, too."

"That's very thoughtful of you." Angelina smiled as Felipe sat beside her and leaned against the tree. She wouldn't point out that it was the *husbands* of the ladies that bought them the gifts.

"Go ahead. Open it." Felipe smiled like he had a secret he couldn't wait to share.

"Okay. Thanks." He watched as she removed the bow and then began to remove the wrapping.

"Eliot and Dean took me to one of those Jesus stores after the other guys got back from the mall. The lady at the store wrapped it for me."

She'd wondered where he'd gone. When she pulled away the paper, she spied a book nestled inside. "What a beautiful cover." Smoothing one hand over the front of the book, she smiled. "This looks like historical fiction."

"What, like from the 80s?" He gave her a sheepish grin. "The lady picked it out."

"A little further back in time." She smiled and he winked. Looking at the back of the book, she skimmed the description. "This sounds great. I'll start reading it tonight."

"It's supposed to be about people traveling across the country on wagon trains, so yeah, I guess it's set in the olden days." He scratched his head. "Sounds strange to me, but the lady said it's real popular. She said ladies like reading about a simpler time, or something like that. It's got some romance in it, too. I figured that was the one to get since you like that kind of book." Rolling his eyes, Felipe's laugh sounded nervous. Seemed there was a first time for everything. "Look in the front."

"Okay." Turning it over again, she lifted the cover and spied a message printed in uniform capital letters. ANGELINA, I HOPE ONE DAY YOU'LL CONSIDER ME WORTHY TO BE YOUR PERSONAL HERO.

Angelina stared at the words, so touched she was momentarily unable to speak.

"Do you like it?"

"Yes, um, very much." A lump stuck in her throat and she nodded. "It's one of the best gifts anyone's ever given me. Thank you, Felipe. I really appreciate it."

He held her gaze. "Welcome, Angel. I got something else at that store, too."

"What's that?"

"Eliot bought me a Bible, and guess what?"

"What?" She enjoyed his enthusiasm. Earlier in the week, she never would have believed something like this would happen. She'd always heard how God could work miracles in people's hearts, and this seemed pretty close to it. Sometimes it took years.

"If you can believe it, the store had Bible covers made by Leather. Dean bought one of his own covers to put on my Bible. Isn't that a kick?"

She shook her head. "You lost me. What do you mean?"

"Have you heard of the chain of stores called Leather?"

"Sure. Who hasn't? Why? Does Dean work for Leather?"

Felipe's grin grew broader. "I guess you could say that. Angel, Dean *owns* those stores. All of them, as far as I know."

She gulped. "Dean Costas owns Leather? I had no idea. He must be...rich." She'd never know to look at him that he had money—he dressed like a regular guy and didn't throw his weight around. But neither did Marc Thompson or any of the TeamWork guys. There wasn't a deadbeat in the bunch.

"Dean does all right for himself." Felipe watched as she tucked the Christian romance book back inside the wrapping paper. "He's got a nice house, and his car's one of those classics. He'd never let me borrow it." He shot her a grin. "I brought something else, too. Hang on a second." Felipe reached behind the tree and brought out an empty bottle.

Angelina gasped. "Is that what I think it is?"

"Don't worry. I didn't drink the vodka. I dumped it. There's a patch of grass near the men's dorm that'll either grow like crazy or wither away and die fast."

She giggled. "I wish I could have watched you get rid of it."

"We could have had a little ceremony. You told me you buried that book beneath a pile of trash, and I believe you. Now I'm asking you to believe that I got rid of the booze." Propping his hands on his knees, Felipe leaned close. Close enough to envy those insanely long lashes that fringed his gorgeous dark eyes. She caught a whiff of his cologne.

"Lexa is my witness," she said. "Not that it negates from what you did."

A slow, lazy grin creased his lips. "Does that mean you believe me?"

"I think I do." She cleared her throat. "Just don't get any ideas."

"Oh, I have all kinds of ideas for us, Angel. Wanna know what I'd like to do now?" His lips parted slightly, and his gaze roamed over her face.

Her heart in her throat, Angelina swallowed. He smelled so nice. He looked handsome with his new haircut. Felipe leaned in. So did she.

"Angelina! Wh-what's going on h-here?" Mama approached them, fire in her eyes. Beside her, Dean appeared more annoyed than angry. Not a good situation.

"Whoa. Your mom hardly stuttered at all," Felipe said under his breath.

"She doesn't stutter as much when she's all fired up."

"Seriously? Why not?" Was that really all Felipe could think about right now?

"Hormones or something. Adrenaline. I don't know." Rising to her feet, her cheeks burning, Angelina avoided her mother's gaze and focused on Dean. She silently implored him to mediate on their behalf. He might be her best hope to mollify Mama's anger since he'd want to stay on both Sheila and Felipe's good side.

"F-F-F-el-l-lipe, I-I'm n-n-not s-s-ure wh-whether t-t-to g-g-ive y-y-you a t-t-tongue l-l-lashing or h-haul A-A-Angel-lina a-a-w-w-way r-r-right n-now." Mama's gaze traveled to the empty vodka bottle on the ground at Felipe's feet. "Wh-what is th-that b-b-bottle?"

"It was a vodka bottle, but I didn't drink it. Just 'cause you don't trust me, Mrs. Morris, don't go thinking the worst. I'm not like Angelina's father."

Oh no. Wrong thing to say, even if it was true. Angelina flinched as the color drained from Mama's face.

"Felipe, for once, can you please not say the first thing that comes into your head?" Hands on his hips, Dean turned aside and rubbed one hand over his forehead. Then he moved to Mama's side. "Sheila, I can vouch that he didn't drink any of it."

Felipe glared at Dean. "Yeah? How do you know? I thought you'd be the first one to jump down my throat."

Angelina's gaze shifted to Felipe. She didn't like his surliness, but his defensiveness had kicked in. He always felt like he needed to defend himself because of his background and past behavior. She wanted to help him if she could.

Before she could say a word, Dean spoke. "I found that bottle right after we arrived at the camp." His eyes bore into Felipe's, unwavering.

Felipe's jaw went slack. "Then why didn't you say anything, man?"

"Sounds like Dean's on your side. Take it easy." Angelina put her hand on Felipe's arm.

"I wanted to see if the vodka disappeared a little at a time," Dean said. "I know where you stashed it in the dorm, Felipe. I've checked that bottle every day, and I could tell you haven't touched it. Based on your current behavior, you seem to be in full possession of your faculties. Your hormones might be in overdrive, but you're definitely not intoxicated. If you say you didn't drink it, then I believe you."

Sheila watched and listened, wide-eyed, before addressing Felipe. "D-d-did y-you o-o-f-f-fer m-my d-d-daughter al-al-co-cohol?"

The muscles in Felipe's cheeks flexed. "No, Mrs. Morris. I did not."

Please, Mama. Believe him.

Angelina stepped forward. "Felipe didn't offer me any of the vodka. He made a deal with me."

The other three turned to her. Might as well throw herself under the bus. If Felipe was going down, she'd go right along with him. Willingly. "I found a book under my bunk here at the camp."

Sheila's eyes grew wider. "Wh-what k-k-kind of b-book?"

"A dirty one. Smutty."

"Some would call it soft porn." Felipe crossed his arms as if prepared to do battle. "Erotica." Angelina almost groaned at that last word and shot him a *so not appropriate* look.

Sheila sputtered and put her hand on her forehead, swaying slightly. Angelina noticed the corners of Dean's mouth curl slightly as he stepped behind her mother and put one hand on her shoulder. She knew Dean's presence comforted Mama or she'd never allow him so close. *Physically* close. As far back as she could remember, her mother had only had one date each with two different men since Papa died.

"I learned my lesson, Mama." Angelina raised her chin and met her mother's gaze. "I won't make that mistake again."

"I told her if she got rid of the book, then I'd get rid of the vodka," Felipe said. "Angel told me last night that she'd ditched the book. She kept her part of the deal, so I brought the bottle to show her that I'd emptied it. And not into my stomach," Felipe added. At least his tone didn't sound churlish. Angelina appreciated his efforts to explain himself. She was equally proud he hadn't used the words *I swear* anywhere in their conversation.

"Felipe gave me a gift." Retrieving the book, Angelina held it up for her mother to see. "Look, Mama. It's a Christian novel. Historical romance."

Sheila moved her gaze to Felipe and, if she wasn't mistaken, Angelina glimpsed a softening in her mother's expression. "Th-that's a l-l-lovely g-gift. B-b-but th-that st-still d-does-s-n-n't ex-exp-p-plain wh-what y-y-you w-were d-doing."

Angelina's anger surged after that comment. "I'm not a child! I'm 14 years old." She wanted to stomp her foot, but that would negate her point that she was growing up. "Most girls my age have kissed a boy. Or done a whole lot more than that. Kassidy Turnbull had a baby three months ago, so I don't think kissing is such a big crime."

"Way to go, Cupcake." Felipe scooted closer.

"Don't call me that," Angelina hissed.

"Okay, truce everyone!" Dean held up one hand. "I think we all need to take a deep breath and step back. Angelina found a dirty book and learned a valuable lesson. Felipe smuggled vodka into the camp but didn't drink it. You two kids need to be careful and respect Sheila's wishes as Angelina's mother."

"I respect your wishes, Mama, but I'm not a little girl, anymore. You can't protect me forever or keep me from making my own mistakes." When her mother met her gaze, Angelina glimpsed nothing but love. Her eyes filled with tears and she blinked hard so they wouldn't fall.

Dean cleared his throat. "I think the important thing to remember here is that none of us are perfect. The sooner we acknowledge that and move forward, the better. I hope we can all be friends when we get back to San Antonio, but we need to communicate with each other. Felipe, do you have anything else to say?"

Felipe stared at the ground for a long moment before nodding to Mama. "Look, I know my track record isn't the greatest, Mrs. Morris, and I meant no disrespect with that comment I made. I'm sorry, and…uh, I hope you can forgive me."

Angelina breathed a sigh of relief when the tension in her mother's features relaxed, especially since she'd seemed on the verge of exploding a few minutes ago. The expression on Dean's face was priceless, as if he couldn't believe he'd heard an apology from Felipe.

Felipe moved his gaze to hers, and Angelina's breath caught in her throat. "Angel's beautiful on the outside, but she's just as pretty on the inside. She's the best girl I've ever known. And yes, I'd like to kiss her. But you TeamWork people are doing something right when it comes to marriage and relationship stuff, so I figure I should pay attention." Felipe shuffled his feet on the ground and looked back up at Mama with a grin. "If you could give me a heads-up as to how long that might be, that might be kinda good." He shrugged. "Before I can kiss her. Once. I'd be real gentle."

If Mama and Dean hadn't been standing with them, she'd grab Felipe and give him a kiss. A nice long one right on the lips. She wouldn't know what she was doing, but she'd sure try.

Sheila stepped forward and offered her hand to Felipe. "I-I f-f-forg-g-ive y-you." After only a moment's hesitation, Felipe reached out to her.

"I know what we could do." Dean nodded to Sheila and then angled his head toward the dining hall.

Angelina stared at Dean and then back at Mama. Beside her, Felipe did the same. Some weird unspoken language must be going on between the two adults. She darted a glance at Felipe, and he gave her a wink. That was pretty daring with Mama standing right in front of them, but she appeared to be considering Dean's suggestion, whatever it was.

Crooking a finger in their direction, Sheila indicated for them to follow. "C-c-come w-w-ith me."

~~♥~~

"T-t-take th-that!"

Dean laughed as he launched a water balloon at Felipe. Once Sheila and the teenagers heard his plan, they'd grabbed the balloons and started filling them. Within minutes of starting their water fight, the other kids had come running.

All around him, the kids squealed with delight as Felipe took it like a man and then staggered around like he was dying before falling to the ground. Chloe and Gracie teamed up to pelt their dads, and Joe and the twins ran around in circles, chasing after Emily and Luke. When Emily teetered and fell over, Chloe ran over to her. After helping her baby sister to her feet, she held on to Emily's hands, making sure she was okay before she let go. Like mother, like daughter.

Gracie and Chloe seemed every bit as tenacious as their fathers as they teamed up on Luke and Joe. Dean smiled as the little boys retaliated. Luke showed signs of a good pitching arm and Joe's aim was spot-on.

Splat! A red balloon hit Dean in the face, soaking him. "You're going to get it for that one!" Laughing, he glanced down at his soaking wet shirt and started after Felipe.

"Hey, it wasn't me!" Felipe held up his hands with a big grin and then pointed to Sheila.

"Y-you r-r-ratted m-me out!" Sheila's eyes were bright as she grabbed a green balloon from the supply on the ground and launched another one at Felipe. The balloon hit him square in the chest, exploding and spraying water all over him.

"Ah, you got me! I'm a dead man. Again." Felipe staggered backward and slumped to the ground. Chloe ran over to make sure he was okay. Bless that kid's heart. Wiping water off his face, Felipe smiled and assured her he was fine. He'd never noticed how good Felipe was with kids. Maybe he should pay closer attention.

"This is war!" Gathering a balloon in each hand, Dean charged Angelina and Sheila. For a fleeting second, he wondered if he should have mercy on them. Nah, they could handle it. Angelina had already soaked him too many times to count. The same for Sheila.

"This is for felling my comrade!" Taking aim, Dean whipped a green balloon at Sheila's lower legs and, within a split second, sent a yellow balloon sailing toward Angelina. He might be out for revenge, but he'd never purposely pelt a woman anywhere above the knees.

He caught the glance shared between mother and daughter before they both reached for a fresh supply of balloons and came running after him. He was in trouble now, but oh, how he loved it.

Chapter 31

~~♥~~

Standing in front of the mirror, Lexa twisted her new necklace this way and that, admiring the lovely setting featuring the birthstones for the twins and Joe. She didn't wear much jewelry, but the few pieces she had were well-made, including this one. She'd commented on a similar necklace a friend at church had worn on Mother's Day, and Sam must have remembered. He'd probably spent too much money on it, but she loved it and would wear if often.

Earlier in the afternoon, he'd slipped into the kitchen while she washed pans in the sink, lost in thought and humming away. Sneaking up behind her, he'd moved his arms around her waist and kissed her neck. She'd elbowed him and squealed so loud that Eliot came bursting through the door at a run. Before she knew it, the kids were all crowded in the kitchen doorway, staring at her with wide eyes. She'd let Sam explain his way out of that one.

When things had calmed down, they'd shared a good laugh. "I hope I didn't hurt you, but that's why you sent the TeamWork ladies to that self-defense class," she'd told Sam.

"Right. To ward off amorous husbands. The other guys got things for their wives, too."

"That's one way to make sure everyone's in a good mood tonight," she'd told him. "You are such a romantic."

"I do my best. I write books about keeping wives happy, so I need to set the example." Giving her a wink, he'd swiped a few fresh vegetables from a serving tray and departed.

Lexa's gaze fell on the pale pink nightgown she'd found draped across her pillow when she returned to their quarters after dinner. That gift was more for his benefit, and the sight of it made her smile.

Glancing at her watch, she called to Sam in the bathroom. "Sam, we need to get moving or we'll be late for the prayer circle. Are you still planning on saying a few words before your dad gives his devotional?" Not hearing a response, she knocked on the bathroom door. "Sam? Are you ready?"

"Lexa…"

Opening the door, she gasped. Curled in a fetal position on the floor, Sam clutched his stomach and writhed in pain.

"Sam!" Kneeling beside him, Lexa wasn't sure whether or not she should touch or move him. He'd been fine 20 minutes ago. "What's wrong? Tell me." Food poisoning immediately came to mind. She prayed they hadn't served food that had spoiled or they could have a nightmare on their hands if sickness spread through the TeamWork crew.

"My neck," Sam rasped. "Something bit me."

"Let me take a look." Sure enough, he had a small but distinct red welt on the left side of his neck. He'd had mosquito bites before but nothing that prompted this kind of reaction. His forehead was damp with sweat and his face was flushed.

He began to tremble. Was he having a seizure? Fear shot through her since Sam was rarely sick and she'd never seen him suffer from anything worse than the flu. That'd been bad enough. "I'll be right back. I'm going to get help."

"Joe!" Lexa ran through the bedroom and into the kids' bedroom. Her son glanced up from where he played with a set of blocks. "Can you run over to the dining hall and get Mimi? Tell her Daddy needs her and that Mommy said to come quick. If Mr. Mitch is there, ask him to come, too. Then I need you to stay over in the dining hall with your sisters and Angelina, okay?"

"Yes, Mommy." Without another word, Joe took off at a run.

Lexa returned to the bathroom and soaked a washcloth with cool water. Sitting on the floor, she cradled Sam's damp head in her lap and pressed the cloth on his cheeks and forehead, hoping it would give him relief. "Lord, be with him. I pray it's nothing serious," she murmured under her breath.

"Ohh… I'm going to be sick."

Moving out of the way, she felt helpless as Sam crawled over to the toilet and lost the contents of his stomach. After he was done, she mopped his brow again with the damp washcloth and stroked his hair. Other than taking CPR certification classes for TeamWork, she didn't know how to deal with many medical emergencies. She was thankful Sarah was in the camp, and likewise Mitch, since he'd had medical training.

"Not now," he said, shaking his head.

"What?"

"The hair. Not now."

"Oh. Sorry. Force of habit." Lexa withdrew her hand. "I'll go get you a water bottle. You need to stay hydrated, and hopefully you can keep it down."

"That'd be good." Sam's voice was hoarse. No doubt his throat felt pretty raw.

"It looks like a nasty spider bite," Sarah said a few minutes later after she'd examined the spot on her son's neck. "Sam, do you know how long you've had it?"

"Not a clue. Sometime today, I guess, but it hasn't bothered me until now."

Sarah lightly touched the welt and the surrounding skin. "Does this hurt?"

"Yes." His features creased in pain. "Like a little sledgehammer. My head hurts and my entire chest aches. It's crazy that such a little bite can bring me to my knees." Sam's gaze fell on Lexa. "Like you, baby. You're little, but you brought me to my knees."

Lexa stared at him. "Maybe it's best if you close your eyes and rest now."

"We should take him to a medical clinic or an ER to have them check him over," Sarah said. "We can't know what bit him, and we need to make sure that it wasn't a brown recluse. My best guess is that it was a brown widow spider. The good news is that they're rarely poisonous to the point of being life-threatening."

"That's comforting," Sam mumbled. "You're discussing me like I'm not right here." He pointed to himself. "Tall guy on the floor."

Mitch had taken his pulse and finished a quick assessment. "It appears the bite on his neck is the only one."

"Thank you, Lord," Lexa said.

Sam began to sing. "The first bite is the deepest…"

Mitch laughed and shook his head. "Sam, I never would have believed you'd be singing a Rod Stewart song, wrong lyrics or not. All the more reason to get you checked out."

Sam waved one hand in the air. "Would you let the man have his music, people? That song's been around a long time."

"So has Rod Stewart," Lexa said. "I'm relieved you're apparently going to live, but I think you might be a tad bit delirious." When both Mom Lewis and Mitch smiled, that went a long way toward easing her trepidation.

Groaning again, Sam crossed his arms over his midsection. "Lexa, I have all the respect in the world for you having to go through childbirth. I'm sorry I did that to you, baby."

"No, you're not, but thanks for the empathy." Lexa exchanged an amused glance with Sarah.

Mitch rose to his feet. "I'll go get the guys to help with Sam and then I'll run out and get my car."

"No need," Sam protested. "I'll walk on my own speed. Better give me a bag, though."

Lexa pressed the cold cloth over his forehead again. "I'll go get a bag, but you rest until the men come to take you out to the car."

"Lexa, are you telling me to shut my trap?"

"No, but I think the Corny Spider bit you."

"I'll stay with Sam," Sarah said. "Mitch, you go get the car and Lexa, you go round up a few of the guys to help get him in the car. That way we'll get Punchy Sam to the hospital faster."

"Listen to Mom. She's the TeamWork Queen." Sam winked at Lexa. "Other than you, beautiful girl."

"I'll bring the car as close to the camp as I can." Mitch darted out the door.

"Mom, would you tell Lexa it's A-Okay that she colored her hair?"

"Sam! Don't go spilling my secrets!" Lexa shook her head. What kind of spider *was* that, anyway?

"Mom doesn't want anyone to know she's colored her hair for years, so there you go. Another thing for my two favorite women to bond over. You're both beautiful, and if coloring your hair makes you feel better, even to cover up one little white hair"—he aimed a pointed glance at Lexa—"then I say, go for it." Sam's eyes widened and the color drained from his face. "Look out. I think I'm going to be sick again."

"You go get the men and I'll take care of Sam," Sarah said.

"I'll be right back with reinforcements." Lexa hurried out of their quarters and headed to the dining hall.

~~♥~~

Within five minutes, Marc crouched by Sam's head and shoulders. Landon was at his feet, and Kevin and Josh were on either side of her husband. The men talked quietly together and then carefully assisted Sam to his feet.

"Sam, put your arms around Josh and Marc," Sarah instructed.

"I didn't know you cared." Sam leaned his head on Josh's shoulder. "The road is long…"

Lexa clamped a hand over her mouth. He was singing again? She'd never seen Sam drunk, but his behavior now came pretty close. Loopy Sam was actually kind of fun, but from a spider bite? Who knew? Even with Sarah's assurances, Lexa was antsy and nervous. Getting him to the hospital was uppermost in her mind.

"Is he singing 'He Ain't Heavy, He's My Brother?'" Marc looked about to burst with laughter.

"That's right. He's my brother!" Sam raised a fist in the air and then let it fall as he leaned heavily against Marc. "Feeling a little lightheaded."

Josh readjusted Sam's position from the other side. "Take it easy there, Sam."

"Let's get moving, slow pokes, or I'll start singing again," Sam mumbled. "I could be dying here."

"No, you're not. But you're punchy and need to see the doctor." Lexa held the door of their quarters while the men carried Sam onto the porch and then out to where Mitch waited beside the car. The motor was running and all the doors were wide open. After grabbing her purse, Lexa hurried beside Sarah and they climbed into the car. Sarah sat in the front with Mitch and Lexa sat in the back with Sam, cradling his head in her lap.

Mitch pulled up to the Emergency Room entrance a short time later. He'd told them it was the same hospital where they'd brought Beck. Asking them to wait in the car with Sam, Mitch darted inside and within minutes, a male staff member arrived with a wheelchair and assisted Sam from the car. Lexa took hold of Sam's hand as they transferred him to the wheelchair and pushed him toward the automatic doors. From there, the nursing staff took over.

"Don't worry. They'll take good care of him, and Sam will be fine." Sarah looped her arm through Lexa's as they entered the quiet Emergency Room waiting area.

"I'm so glad you and Mitch are here," Lexa said. "Thank you,

Mom." The area was quiet with only a few people scattered about the room, and instrumental music played quietly in the background. Most of the others were reading magazines or talking on the phone. A television was playing but no one seemed to be watching.

Lexa approached the desk and handed the insurance card to the nurse. "Am I allowed to go back with my husband?" she asked after taking care of admitting Sam. "They just wheeled him in."

"Of course. He's waiting to be seen by the doctor now."

Mitch had joined Sarah and they sat in nearby chairs. "You go on, Lexa," he said. "We'll wait here."

"Are you sure?"

"Go," Mitch and Sarah both insisted.

Following the nurse, Lexa walked through the large room with curtained-off patient areas and a large staff station in the middle. When she spied Sam, tears misted her eyes. He looked so tired. Sitting beside him on the edge of the bed, she smoothed a lock of dark hair away from his face. All the singing must have worn out Serenading Sam. He'd graced them with a medley of songs in the car, and Sarah had recognized them as camp songs from the old TeamWork missions.

Sitting beside her husband, Lexa held his hand, thankful for the quiet as she waited for the doctor.

Ten minutes later, Dr. Robinson completed his examination. Sam had answered the doctor's questions to the best of his ability, and Lexa told him about the campsite.

"It would appear your husband was bit by a widow spider, but we can't be certain if it's from the western black widow or the brown widow. The effects are very similar, and they both have neurotoxic venom that travels through the bloodstream and can attack the vesicles at neuromuscular junctions."

Lexa cringed at the mention of the word *venom*. What he said sounded serious, but what did she know of medical terminology? "Please just tell me if he's going to be all right."

Dr. Robinson's expression softened. "He should be fine, Mrs. Lewis. Sam's in excellent health, and he should recover quickly. While every widow spider is capable of biting and injecting venom, most are harmless. Their fangs are too small, and their venom is too limited, to cause more than swelling, irritation, and itching. Only five percent of these cases prove to be fatal, and that's generally due to an underlying heart disorder. A spider bite of this type is most dangerous to senior citizens and children."

"I'm not a senior citizen...yet," Sam said. "Give me time."

Thank you, Lord. She could breathe now. "Thank you, Dr. Robinson. Sam's mother is in the waiting room as well as a good friend who's a member of our TeamWork group. Do you mind speaking with them, as well?" In case she forgot something important, Lexa wanted Sarah and Mitch to hear the physician's report.

After Lexa made the brief introductions, Dr. Robinson confirmed Sarah's theory that Sam's bite had most likely come from a brown widow spider. "Sam's experiencing effects similar to a severe flu with muscle aches and a general rundown feeling," the doctor said. "Widows typically build their webs in areas that sit undisturbed for long periods of time. From what Mrs. Lewis told me about the campsite where you're staying, it sounds like Sam could have encountered a brown widow in any number of locations there. The good news is that widows are usually not aggressive. They will bite if handled or threatened, especially if an egg sac is present. I'd warn the others in your camp that this has happened, and if possible, keep the children in the newer and more open areas of the camp."

"Thank you, Dr. Robinson," Sarah said.

Mitch shook the doctor's hand. "We'll be extra vigilant."

"Be forewarned that Sam will probably be agitated and restless for the next few days, especially in the next 12 hours or so. The best course of treatment is to apply ice to the wound to control inflammation and you can also use aloe vera to soothe the area. The wound site should be kept clean, and you can give him over-the-counter pain relievers."

"So, no further medical treatment is necessary?" Lexa said.

Dr. Robinson shook his head. "From the information you provided, he's up-to-date on his tetanus booster. In cases with severe symptoms, there's a drug we can administer, but it's no longer used routinely. Antibiotics aren't recommended unless an infection develops, but the likelihood of that happening is rare. He might have some localized pain in the abdomen, and watch for cramping, nausea, fever, perspiration, tremors, and possibly elevated blood pressure. If any of those develop with any severity, or if you have any questions whatsoever, feel free to call."

"Please tell me you have written instructions," Lexa said.

The doctor smiled. "Of course. His symptoms should improve within 24 hours, and then Sam should be able to resume normal activities within a day or two." Dr. Robinson's gaze encompassed all three of them. "If you'd like to stay with Sam, that's fine, but we should limit it to two visitors at a time."

"You two stay with Sam. I'll wait out here," Mitch told them. "I need to call the others, anyway. They'll want a full report." His eyes widened. "Wait a sec. Didn't Sam take out the trash after dinner tonight?"

"Yes," Lexa said. "Dr. Robinson, could the lid or handle of a trash can be a breeding ground for a widow's egg sac? The garbage cans sit under the overhang at the back door of the dining hall."

Dr. Robinson nodded. "It's a good possibility, yes."

"If that's the culprit, I'm thankful none of the kids were bit," Lexa said. "They usually have the job of gathering and taking out the garbage every night."

"I'm on it, Lexa," Mitch assured her. "Hopefully no one will get ambitious tonight and dispose of any more garbage before we can check them out." Cell phone in hand, Mitch walked a few paces away.

"Our phone number is on the form the nurse will give you." The doctor led Lexa and Sarah back to the curtained area where Sam was resting. "I'll check on him again in a few hours. We'd like to keep him here in the ER for observation for another hour or two, but then we can release him then if he exhibits no further symptoms."

After thanking Dr. Robinson, Lexa turned to Sarah. "I guess now we wait. As I'm sure you know, Sam does many things well, but he's not a very good patient. To tell you the truth, I think I prefer Corny Sam."

Sarah nodded. "I know what you mean."

"I heard that," Sam said from the bed.

"You rest, young man." Sarah winked at Lexa. "Remind me

to tell you about the time I assisted in a childbirth back in Rockbridge, and the reaction of Sam's dad."

"For tonight's entertainment, I could sing again."

Lexa laughed. "Sam, please tell don't tell me you're going to wear a blonde wig that looks like a spiky pineapple and sing 'Do Ya Think I'm Sexy?' for the talent show."

Sam laughed and then coughed. "I might. I guess you'll just have to wait and see."

"I said rest," Sarah reiterated. "No singing for now. Or laughing. Or talking."

"Spoilsports. You two are no fun." Sam frowned, but at least he closed his eyes.

"Yep," Lexa said. "Cranky Sam has now arrived."

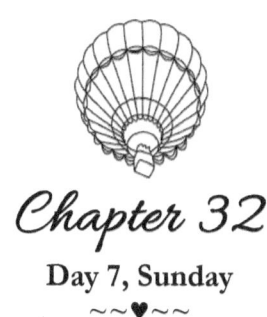

Chapter 32
Day 7, Sunday
~~♥~~

"I'll bet the smartest chickens in the coop aren't even up at this insane hour."

Eliot stole another glance at Marta as she trudged beside him on their way to the Hummer. In her jeans, T-shirt, athletic shoes, and medium weight jacket, she looked great. Sporty and athletic. A dark green Baylor Bears baseball cap covered her head, and her curly blonde ponytail cascaded out the back.

"Don't think I don't know what you're doing over there," she said. "Even in the dark, I can feel your eyes on me."

He chuckled. "I have no idea what you're talking about."

"Fine. Am I dressed appropriately? I followed your rules—sturdy, flat shoes with good traction, long sleeved wool jacket, no nylon outer clothing because it creates static electricity, and no drawstrings."

"You're fine, and I was thinking how great you look," he said. "And those aren't *my* rules. They're for everyone."

"Oh. Thanks for the compliment. Did you bring the leather gloves for both of us?"

"Check. They're in the backpack."

"I hope you got a smaller size for me."

He glanced over at her as they walked. "Trust me, I know the size of your hand and how well it fits in mine. If your hand *was* as large as mine, we'd have a real problem."

"On our hands? Ha! I'm so annoyingly 'punny' at this hour. No wonder I'm not a morning person. You sure know how to flatter a girl. Nice to get compliments this early." She skimmed her gaze over him. "You look great, too."

"What? This old thing?" As usual, he wore his jeans and a blue T-shirt, but he'd tossed on his leather jacket. He'd brought just enough clothing for the trip—no more, no less. Traveling around the world taught a guy how to streamline a wardrobe real fast.

"Too bad you're so tired," he told her. "I was going to offer to let you drive my tank." Teasing her, Eliot tossed his keys in the air and then caught them one-handed.

Marta perked up immediately. "Yes, please. I'd love that! The power! The speed! Oh, the places we could go!"

He laughed and, being purposely annoying, dangled the keys as enticement in front of her face. "On second thought, maybe not. I've witnessed all the yawning you've done in the short, ten-minute walk from the campsite. Didn't you get enough sleep last night? I warned you we'd be up before the crack of dawn."

"Hey, I tried," she protested. "Suffice it to say that Landon was on guard duty last night and Mr. and Mrs. Warnick were enjoying some time together. The night before, it was Kevin and Beck, but at least she's feeling up to a little canoodling with her husband." Marta punctuated her words with yet another yawn. "Who am I to stand in the way of true love? I think it's simply swell."

"Where I come from—if they're doing it right—kissing doesn't make enough noise to keep someone else from sleeping."

"It was all the quiet laughter and talking. My bed's closest to the door."

"Ah," he said. "Gotcha." In a quick move, she tried to wrest the keys from his hand, but he'd anticipated it and thwarted her efforts.

"You're good. Do we have time to stop for coffee on the way to the Balloon Fiesta? Please?"

"Yep." As they reached the Hummer, he checked his watch: 4:38 a.m. Right on schedule. "We don't have to report to Tyler until 6:00. If you can wait, let's get some food once we reach the festival area."

"I can wait for food, but I definitely need coffee. Trust me, you don't want to be around me until I've had my first cup."

He chuckled. Even silly and sarcastic, Morning Marta was adorable. "Thanks for the warning." Pulling out his key fob, Eliot clicked to unlock the doors. "You already know caffeine's my poison of choice. You do have a valid driver's license, right? I'm counting on you."

"Would you like to see it?" She started to unzip her small backpack.

"Not necessary." When he held up the keys, she smiled and held out her palm. Opening the driver's door and ushering Marta inside, he showed her a few of the controls and then helped her adjust her seat. Then he climbed into the passenger seat beside her as she started the engine.

"What a sweet ride. This tank is awesome, Eliot. I bet it cost a pretty penny, but would you listen to that engine purr!" Marta's grin was addictive. He'd thought he might have qualms about her driving his Hummer, but surprisingly, he didn't. His Hummer was his baby, and he spent more time in it than he did his condo. As a swimmer, Marta must have great reflexes. More importantly, he trusted her.

She adjusted the rearview and side mirrors. "Okay, you'd better give me some basic directions before we head out. Then we're off."

Listening intently, Marta nodded as he gave her the basic directions. "There might be some Fiesta traffic, even at this hour, but it shouldn't take too long," he said. "Should I say a prayer before we head out?"

"Good idea." Marta bowed her head and Eliot began his prayer. "Give us a good day at the Balloon Fiesta, Father. Keep everyone safe, both in the air and on the ground. We pray for Sam to heal quickly and that he can attend the worship service this morning. Thank you for your many blessings to us. We ask these things in Jesus's name. Amen."

"Amen. Thanks. That's something about Sam getting bit by that spider, huh?" She pulled out of the parking area and headed down the narrow gravel road. "I know I joke about creepy crawlies, but that hit a little too close to home. I hope no one else irritates that mama spider."

"At least it wasn't something worse."

"Have you ever been bit by a widow spider?"

"No, but I've been bit by a poisonous snake and a few other assorted disgusting creatures."

Marta gasped, and he could tell it was genuine this time, not feigned. "Well, thank the Lord you didn't lose anything vital. At least not that I know of."

He laughed and shook his head. "No worries."

"Any alligators?" she said. "With those huge jaws that snap down on their prey, and those big, sharp teeth." She shuddered. "They scare me almost as much as snakes."

"You can rest easy. No gators. Next topic? There are certain things I'd rather not discuss before I've had my morning java. If you don't mind, I'm going to lower my window and let the wind whip through my tresses as you drive."

Marta shot him a grin. "Sounds good. Think I'll do the same. And I'll pull into the first convenience store we see unless there's suspicious looking characters lurking around outside."

"Define suspicious."

"More tattoos than teeth for starters. Sloppy hygiene habits and visible weapons are another."

Eliot laughed. "You must hang around some interesting places in Houston."

A few minutes later, they departed a convenience store with their coffee cups in hand, medium-sized for her and extra large for him. They'd started a fun debate in the store with several customers—surprising how many there were for that hour of the morning—over the best flavoring to add. Eliot took his straight up and black, the stronger the better. Marta insisted she couldn't possibly drink coffee without Irish Crème or French Vanilla flavoring. Not surprisingly, her opinion won out. Bunch of sissies. When he was thirteen, his dad told him black coffee would put hair on his chest. Whether or not it was the caffeine, it worked, so he'd been drinking the stuff ever since.

"I'm surprised you don't have more of an inflection in your voice when you speak English," Marta mused as they began to see signs for Fiesta Park. "You could pass for an American, but now I know better."

Better to steer her away from that line of thinking. Early on, he'd worked like a dog with a linguistics coach to erase all evidence of his native French accent. Not that he was ashamed of his home country in any way, but it was a necessity in his line of work. Kind of like creating a blank slate upon which to write the story of his life. At times he wondered if he'd lost *himself* somewhere along the way. In his lowest moments, he always came back to the one thing in his life that was constant: his faith.

"Great job driving the tank," Eliot said as she parked and they exited the Hummer at Fiesta Park.

"Thanks, but the tank made it easy." Marta tossed him the keys, which he pocketed. "Oh, look! There's a sign for Vendor Row. I'm assuming that's the place to go get some grub." She inhaled deeply as they walked closer and rubbed her hands together. "It smells like…"

"Roasting chiles," he said. "Chile's the defining ingredient for New Mexican cuisine. It comes in two varieties: red or green. Are you okay with spicy foods?"

"It's generally not a problem."

"In restaurants here, they'll ask if you want red or green. If you want to sample both, you say, 'Christmas.'"

"How fun is that?" Marta said. "Lila told us a lot of their food is a blend of Native American foods like blue corn, squash, chile peppers, and pork. Everything I tried at the dinner the other night was very good." On the way to Vendor Row, they walked by tents, booths, trailers, TV station trucks, and radio booths. People were milling about, drinking coffee, and—in spite of the early hour—an excitement hovered in the air.

"Look, Eliot!" Smiling, she pointed to a few of the balloons in the early stages of being inflated. "This is so exciting."

"Why don't you sit at one of the tables, and I'll go get us some breakfast burritos. It's one of the specialties here." A few minutes later, he returned with a hot, wrapped burrito. "Here you go. I also brought you a water bottle. We can get more coffee, but I thought you might want this." Once she sampled her first bite of the burrito, Eliot figured she might need the water.

"Do you mind if I sit next to you?" he said. "Since it's cold, we can huddle while we eat."

She smiled. "Have a seat. Thanks for this huge burrito. You might have to help me finish it."

Moving his arm around her, Eliot prayed for their meal, pleased when she snuggled next to him. As he took the first few bites of his burrito, he kept a close eye on her as she bit into hers.

"This is really good," she said. A few seconds later, her eyes widened and she reached for the water bottle and downed a third of it in one long drink.

"The level of spice can be an acquired taste."

"No," she said, fanning her mouth. "It's fine. Just, um, a little unexpected."

"Should I get another water bottle for you?"

"That might be advisable. Thanks."

Ten minutes later, they headed to the prearranged area to meet Tyler. "I take it that noise is the sound of the balloons being inflated?" Marta said.

Eliot sighed in appreciation. The only thing more exciting was to see the glorious and colorful balloons rising and then floating across the sky—majestic and graceful.

"You're right. It's the butane torches firing the hot gases," he told her. "It uses hot air first to begin the inflation and then when it gets enough room inside the huge bag, the pilot fires up the fuel at full power and the heat does the rest. When the bag reaches its full size, the operator shuts down the flame and then intermittently fires it up to keep the balloon full of hot air."

"Hot air ballooning has been around for a long time, hasn't it?" she said.

"I know a little about it. I can share a few tidbits, if you'd like."

"I'm all ears. I'd love to hear it."

"A scientist named Pilatre DeRozier launched the first hot air balloon in 1783. His passengers were a sheep, a duck, and a rooster. The balloon stayed in the air for 15 minutes before it crashed. Two months later, a couple of French brothers launched a balloon from Paris and flew for 20 minutes. That was considered the birth of hot air ballooning. In 1785, another French balloonist and his American co-pilot were the first to fly across the English Channel, a benchmark in ballooning history. And for your last interesting tidbit: our scientist DeRozier, the world's first balloonist, unfortunately met his demise at his own attempt to cross the Channel."

"Oh no!" Marta said. "What happened?"

"He had an experimental design using a hydrogen balloon and a hot air balloon tied together, and"—he closed his fists, bumped them together, and then opened them—"sadly, it exploded half an hour after takeoff."

Marta's lovely smile faded and her eyes clouded. "That's absolutely tragic."

"Yes, but he died doing what he loved." He shrugged. "Oh, here's one more that's not so sad. One of the French brothers, Jean Pierre Blanchard, became the first person to fly a balloon in North America in January 1793. George Washington was present to see the balloon launch."

"Ah, so he was *President* George Washington at the time."

Eliot nodded. "That would be correct. It launched in Philadelphia and flew across the Delaware River to New Jersey." He grinned. "Of course, George had already been there, done that with the whole crossing the Delaware thing, so he declined to ride in the balloon."

She laughed. "Fascinating. You know, Eliot, from what you've told me, the French were heavily involved in the history of hot air ballooning. I wonder if they teach kids something about it in their history lessons…over there."

He shoved his hands in the pockets of his jacket and looked the other way. "You're not getting anything out of me, Marta. Give it up."

"Eliot, how *do* you know all this stuff? Seriously this time." When he didn't answer, she tilted her head and tried to catch his eye. "You've been here before, haven't you? To the Balloon Fiesta?"

Might as well admit it. He met her gaze. "A couple of times, yes. Tyler's participated in a few races."

"And is Tyler in a race today?"

"Nah," he said with a wide grin. "Today's just for fun."

"And you've obviously memorized a pamphlet with the history of ballooning."

Laughing, Eliot raised both hands. "Busted. You're on to me."

She angled her head to some of the staff as they walked farther into the huge Fiesta Park. "Who are those people running around in the black and white striped zebra shirts?"

He laughed. "That's exactly what they're called. Zebras. They're the launch directors who help launch the balloons every morning."

"What a fun job. How long does the Fiesta run?"

"Nine days, I believe." He smiled and waved as he spied Tyler up ahead, standing by his collapsed balloon on the ground beside him. After the introductions were made, they listened as Tyler gave them instructions and told Marta about inflating and then chasing the balloon.

"Sounds pretty easy to me," she said. "How long does it take to get all the balloons inflated and in the air?"

"It generally takes about two hours, start to finish. We have almost 700 balloons this year," Tyler said, "and about 300 of those are from New Mexico."

Eliot enjoyed Marta's enthusiasm as the balloons started being inflated all around them. "This is one of the most awesome things I've ever seen," she said. "You look in one direction and see a daisy, a tree, an orange, assorted cats and dogs, and…"

"Something wrong?" Eliot followed her gaze and couldn't help his laughter. "Marta, don't tell me you're afraid of clowns."

"Not usually, no. But when they're *that* big? Yeah, it's a little freaky." She brightened. "Oh, look over there, Eliot! It's a peach! Sam would absolutely love that! I can't wait for the sun to come up so I can take some photos."

They worked together to inflate the balloon as Tyler pointed out the various parts to Marta. "The tank's 20 gallons and it's inside the wicker basket, also called the gondola," he said. "It has a hardwood base and there's a leather scuff pad at the bottom and a padded suede trim on the upper rim of the basket." He showed her the instrument panel, including a champagne console, and explained in brief terms about the double burner system, the blast valve, envelope attachment block, and the fuel hose, among others.

"Do you need a pilot's license to fly a hot air balloon?" she asked.

"Yes, either a private of a commercial license. I'm a private pilot."

"I see. And one more question?"

Tyler grinned. "Ask away."

"Why do the balloons take off at sunrise?"

"The winds are most favorable the first few hours after sunrise or before sunset. They can only fly in stable air. The sun heats the earth, creating thermals, during the day. In certain climates, balloons can fly all day because the sun never gets hot."

A short while later, Marta's smile grew wider as the balloon inflated. "This is so awesome!" she called to him. "How tall is the balloon when it's fully inflated?"

"Almost 27 meters," Tyler said, shouting over the sound of the butane torch. "It's one of the tallest ones launching today."

"Of course it is—it's the State of Texas, after all." Marta laughed. "Sorry, I couldn't resist. Let's see, 27 meters would be...over 88 feet. Wow!"

"The flight will be a little over an hour and a half," Tyler told him, and Eliot nodded.

"My head is now officially spinning," Marta said as they finished fully inflating the balloon. "What time is sunrise?"

"Should be a couple of minutes after seven." Eliot checked his watch. "Tyler's launch time is 8:30, so we can walk around and get some photos, get some more food, whatever you'd like to do. Then we should head back to the tank to get ready for the launch."

"And then the chase begins?" Marta was so lovely, and all over again, Eliot appreciated her enthusiasm for people, for life, for TeamWork, and for the Lord.

He loved her pure joy. Loved *her*.

Unable to resist, Eliot kissed her. "And then the chase begins."

Chapter 33

~~♥~~

"Sam Lewis, where do you think you're going? You get back in that bed right now."

Crossing her arms, Lexa stared down her husband. "It's a good thing you're not laid up often. I don't know how I'd keep my sanity. The doctor said to have you rest and lay low for a day or two."

"Nothing doing." After opening the top drawer of the dresser, Sam pulled out a fresh shirt. "I didn't come to New Mexico to help finish the One Nation Church only to stay in bed and miss the first worship service."

"I know, but you were in the hospital emergency room last night. And then you were sick again in the night."

"I'm well aware of that." An odd expression crossed his face and he swayed a bit. Reaching for the dresser, he clutched the edge.

"Sam, you're still feeling the effects from that nasty spider bite and need to rest. I don't think Pastor Chevy wants you to christen his brand new sanctuary. It's not like you're supposed to lead the service. Kevin's helping with the music and TeamWork will be well represented."

With a frown, Sam tossed the shirt on the chair. In a few steps, he fell onto the bed, crosswise, flat on his back. "Is that not leading the service comment a crack? If so, it's defeating your purpose. That challenge only makes me want to go even more."

"No, that wasn't a crack. It's called reality, dear husband." Tapping her foot on the floor, Lexa moved her hands to her hips. "Don't make me go get your mother. I won't hesitate to do it, if needed."

"Don't do that. Please. It makes my head hurt." He opened his eyes. "I'm talking about the foot tapping. I'm a grown man and don't need my mommy. I only need you, fussy and demanding as you are. Always need you, Lexa." His attempt at a grin fell short. Clamping one hand on the back of his neck, Sam closed his eyes. A fine line surfaced between his brows as he pinched his fingers over his nose. "Getting up from this bed is the hardest thing to do right now." His eyes fluttered open. "Did you put lead weights on my feet during the night?"

"Come on. Let's get you settled." Walking over to the bed, Lexa took hold of his hand and tugged. "If I didn't know better, I'd think you were drunk last night and have a hangover this morning. The doctor didn't warn me the side effects of being bitten by a widow spider would be so interesting."

"I just get punchy when I'm not feeling well. Strange phenomenon. Ask Mom. She'll tell you."

"She already did. Last night when you were treating us to your rendition of 'Strangers in the Night.'"

"That was an odd choice, wouldn't you say?"

"Oh, I don't know. I'd rate it a little higher than 'I'm Gonna Wash That Man Right Out of My Hair.'"

He snapped his gaze to her. "Please tell me I didn't."

"Okay then, I won't. Don't let it threaten your masculinity." She suppressed her grin. "All the more reason for you to stretch out. Come on now. In we go." Lexa watched as Sam crawled under the sheet and then she pulled up the lightweight blanket and tucked it around him.

"That's what I get for Mom listening to all those musicals when I was growing up."

"I think you secretly loved them but don't want to admit it."

"You would say that since *The Sound of Music* is your favorite movie. Remind me to keep Joe occupied the next time you watch it." His smile sobered and he fixed his gaze on her. "Lexa, I want you to go to the church service. Just put a bucket or the trash can by the side of the bed and I'll be fine." He'd already swallowed a couple of pills to help with the head and muscle aches. So far, he hadn't wanted to eat anything, but he'd kept down the water.

"I'll pull the cooler over here so you can get more water if you need it, but are you sure?"

He nodded. "Positive. I'd suggest changing out of your nightgown before you go, though. Don't want any of the other men to see you in it. That's for my benefit alone."

Even with the stubble on his face, and not feeling well, Sam was the most handsome, appealing man in the world. "Only for you, Sam."

"And I thank God every day." Yawning, he turned on his side, giving her a sleepy-eyed half smile. "Please give Pastor Chevy my best and let him know I'm there with them in spirit. I hope someone's recording the service so I can listen to it later."

"I'll check into that. I'm sure they will."

After hurriedly changing into the one dress she'd brought on the trip, Lexa darted into the bathroom to braid her hair and finish getting ready. Picking up her Bible, she pressed a kiss to Sam's cheek. It was warm, but he looked less flushed and wasn't perspiring.

"God works out the details," she whispered. "Love you."

Angelina stole a glance at Amitola and Avonaco as the church service began. They were such a cute couple and seemed so...*adult*. They'd probably be having babies in the next couple of years. Her gaze moved to Felipe sitting beside her, and she admired his profile. Turning his head, he gave her a smile. Before she knew it, he slipped his hand over hers. At first, she thought about withdrawing her hand, but she liked it. His hand was warm and it made her feel appreciated and protected. She'd never held hands with a boy.

He's not a Christian. Quietly, Angelina slipped her hand away from his and avoided looking at him, knowing the question she'd see in his eyes. His new Bible was on his lap and she'd helped him find a few verses of scripture as they'd been read.

He's learning and growing, Lord. I know he is. Bring him to you in your way, Father, and in your time. She liked how Pastor Chevy had asked Kevin and Cassie to lead the music and worship portion at the beginning of the service. "Isn't it cool being here for the first service in their new church?" she whispered to Felipe.

"Yeah," he said. "It's the first time in a church for me. Ever."

That truth hit her like a gust of wind in the face. Angelina felt the color rise in her cheeks. She'd been going to church for so long with Mama that she couldn't imagine being their age and never having been in one before. Reaching for his hand again, she squeezed it. "I'm glad you're here now. With me." When he glanced over at her, she couldn't read what was in his eyes except to tell that the effects of the service weren't lost on him. Gone was the flippancy, the teasing, the disregard for the things of the Lord. Replaced by an understanding, and maybe an acceptance. Her breath caught.

Interestingly enough, Pastor Chevy's message was all about teamwork. Grabbing a pen from the pew in front of them, Angelina pulled the outline from the church bulletin and prepared to fill in the blanks. She noted that Amitola did the same.

"In order for teamwork to function effectively," Pastor Chevy told them, "each person needs to put aside their own needs." Reading from his Bible opened on the podium, the pastor quoted from Philippians 2:3-4. "Do nothing from selfishness or empty conceit, but with humility of mind regard one another as more important than yourselves; do not merely look out for your own personal interests, but also for the interests of others."

Angelina's mind wandered to what she'd heard about the infamous TeamWork brouhaha. Lexa had told Mama how the volunteers tore into each other during the weekend Mitch and Cassie met. Amy thought her brother and Cassie had impulsively gotten married, but it was all a huge misunderstanding that brought out repressed feelings between different members of the group. That's what tension and pent-up feelings could do. Christians weren't immune to grudges and bad feelings. In a way, she wished she could have been a fly on the wall at the brouhaha, but maybe it was better that she hadn't been there.

According to Lexa, the volunteers had hashed out everything and aired their grievances. In the end, they were stronger for it. As a social worker, Mama always stressed the importance of communication. That was the key, just like Dean had also stressed when he and Mama caught her and Felipe about to kiss. The TeamWork volunteers were fiercely committed to each other and to their faith. They loved each other. They encouraged one another. More importantly, they didn't walk away from tough situations like a lot of people would do. They stuck it out, talked with each other, and worked out their differences.

Felipe pressed his lips next to her ear. Having him so close was almost as intimate as a kiss. "What are you thinking about?"

"TeamWork," she answered. It was true, after all. He pointed to his outline, indicating she'd already missed the first two words to fill in the outline.

"He just talked about cooperation and how two is better than one." Felipe kept his voice low. "I like that idea."

So, he *was* flirting, and in a church service, no less. Pastor Chevy went on to talk about having a dedicated commitment to the objectives. Feeling as though she was copying from a test, Angelina glanced at Felipe's outline and wrote down the reference for Ecclesiastes 4: 9-12. The pastor ended the message by talking about Paul and Timothy's ministry, and then telling them how Solomon was an example of someone who knew the advantages of teamwork when the temple was built.

"A team must be coordinated by a strong leader," Pastor Cheveyo told them. He prayed for Sam, especially that the Lord would quickly restore him to full strength and health.

"Thank you for coming today," Amitola told Angelina as they walked out of the church together and into the bright sunshine. She glanced up at the blue sky and smiled. "The warmth of the sun seems as though the Lord is giving His blessing on our church."

"I'm sure He is." Feeling a sudden urge to hug Amitola, Angelina did just that. "I wish God's blessing on you and Avonaco as well as on your church."

"If you give me your home address, I'll send you an invitation to our wedding."

"That would be awesome." Avonaco handed Angelina a piece of paper he pulled from his shirt pocket and Angelina scribbled it down for her. Beneath it, she wrote her e-mail address. "In case we don't see each other again before we leave," she said, handing Amitola the piece of paper. In her heart, she knew Amitola would follow through on her promise. Leaning close, she whispered, "Pray for Felipe. This was the first time he's ever been in a church."

"We've been praying. We'll keep praying."

Pulling away, Angelina smiled at her new friend. "Are you sure you're only 18?"

Amitola laughed. "For another few months. I'll be 19 when we marry."

"I liked what Pastor Chevy said about the cord of three strands," Felipe said as they stood outside the church together.

"The verse from Ecclesiastes that Pastor Cheveyo read is one that we've picked to be read at our wedding," Amitola told them.

Angelina was relieved Felipe didn't bring up the verse in that section that said if two lie down together, they will keep warm. Her lips twisted. No doubt he'd have his own interpretation.

After thanking Pastor Chevy and speaking briefly with Lila after the worship service, Lexa left the sanctuary. The kids were practically jumping up and down in their excitement to go to the Balloon Fiesta. Sam and Sarah had attended the service and planned to take their three grandchildren to the Fiesta. Marc, Natalie, Josh and Winnie planned to take their families, as well. Amy, Landon, Mitch and Cassie all planned on riding the Sandia Peak Tramway, and Angelina and Felipe planned on going with them. Like the adults, the teenagers had worked hard in the past week and deserved a day away to relax, have fun, and do some sightseeing.

Sheila and Dean had volunteered to take security duty for the rest of the day. Besides that, Lexa was aware that Dean wanted to spend some private time with Sheila. According to Sam, that sweet man was cooking dinner for Sheila in the dining hall. She'd grab something quick for sandwiches and share a quiet dinner with Sam in their quarters. Or maybe take the Volvo and bring something back. As much as she'd like to go the Balloon Fiesta or ride the Tramway, reading and resting sounded like a great way to spend the rest of the day.

Lexa stopped short as she spied Stephanie Colton talking with Winnie and Amy over by the parked cars. This morning she wore black dress slacks, an ivory silk blouse, and a single strand of pearls. Had Stephanie attended the service?

Is this how you work, Lord?

"Mrs. Lewis!" An older teenage boy hurried toward Lexa, holding a CD in a paper sleeve. "This is the CD of the service to give to your husband."

Lexa smiled as she took it from him. "That was fast. Thank you for making it so quickly."

"Glad to do it. Tell Sam we hope he's back here at the church tomorrow but not to push it if he's not ready."

"I'm sure you won't be able to keep him away."

Inhaling a quick breath, Lexa turned back around, bolstering herself to speak with Stephanie. As Lexa approached, Stephanie's brown eyes narrowed. "Ms. Colton. I'm so happy you came to the service today."

"I enjoyed it. Call me Stephanie. I'll be honest, Mrs. Lewis. I was hoping to see your husband again."

Lexa bristled at the nerve of the woman as she drew upon every ounce of grace she could muster. If Ms. Colton was this bold in speaking with her, Lexa could only imagine what she might have already said or implied in her conversations with Sam. Sam could handle himself well, and she trusted her husband, but she hadn't come to New Mexico to verbally spar with another woman about Sam.

Amy and Winnie excused themselves. She could handle whatever Stephanie Colton might say or do, but a little reinforcement might have been nice. If the TeamWork ladies had been at the City Council meeting, they'd be standing with her now. That thought gave her small comfort.

"I was disappointed Sam wasn't here," Stephanie said. "I couldn't imagine why not since I know how important this church building is to him."

Lexa nodded. "Yes, it's important to all of the TeamWork volunteers."

"The ladies told me that Sam was bit by a brown widow. Please give him my sympathies and best wishes for a quick recovery. I've known people who've suffered from spider bites. Depending on the type of spider, they can be potentially harmful and very painful if left untreated."

"I'll tell my husband you asked about him. I'm sure he'll feel better in a day or two. I'm definitely not going to give him a bell."

Stephanie laughed, and it relaxed her features, softening them. "Sam strikes me as the type of man who won't allow anything to deter him from what he wants."

Lexa wondered if steam might come out of her ears at this woman's audacity. *You brought her here, Lord. Help me to be gracious.* Was she reading too much into everything Stephanie said? Even if she was, for once she was thankful Sam wasn't at the service. Never would she have believed she could ever *think* such a thing.

"If you could give Sam a message for me, I would appreciate it."

"What's that?" Lexa was beginning to lose patience. *Upper hand, Lexa.* However, if the woman offered to come out to the camp and bring Sam chicken soup and spoon feed it to him, she might very well scream. Knowingly or not, purposely or not, this woman pushed all of her wrong buttons.

"I wanted to let Sam know that I received what he sent to my office."

What? Was the woman purposely egging her on? Lexa met the other woman's gaze levelly. "What did he send?" She regretted how that question would clue Stephanie in to the fact that she hadn't been privy to the mailing. The overwhelming urge to know trumped any potential embarrassment or humiliation.

"To be more specific, the envelope was mailed from his TeamWork office in Houston," Stephanie said. "When I got back to my office after Friday's hearing, I found a package with all kinds of information about your organization. At first I thought Sam might be trying to recruit me." The corners of Stephanie's mouth upturned. "I'd mistakenly called it TeamWonder. After I opened the package, I realized he wanted me to understand better why your group is here in Albuquerque, as well as TeamWork's mission and its purpose."

Lexa laughed. "TeamWonder sounds about right."

Opening her handbag, Stephanie pulled out a small Bible, the same type the TeamWork main office bought by the hundreds and distributed for downtown Houston projects and on certain missions. "Sam also had this Bible sent to me. I've never had anyone try to give me a Bible before, Mrs. Lewis. Seems there's something about me that puts people off. I come across as too strong." Brushing dark bangs away from her forehead, Stephanie turned her gaze to the surrounding Sandia Mountains, majestic in their morning glory, before focusing on Lexa once more.

Lexa raised her chin. "What do you believe, Stephanie?"

The other woman hesitated before answering. "Honestly? I've always believed in my own abilities more than in a higher being. But now? Maybe it time to explore Christianity. It's something I need to learn more about so that I can make an informed decision."

Lexa nodded to the Bible Stephanie held in her hand. "The Bible has all the answers you'll need. If you have any questions, feel free to call me." *Not Sam. Me.*

Stephanie's features eased into a slow smile. "Understood. I might just do that. I also have the correct contact information now for Pastor Cheveyo and his wife. Seems our records were incorrect. Thank you, Mrs. Lewis."

"Call me Lexa, and you're welcome."

Stephanie nodded. "I'm glad we talked."

"Me, too." Surprisingly, considering the turn of the conversation, Lexa *was* glad.

"Mommy, we wanna go!"

Lexa hurried over to her children where they waited with Sarah and Sam Sr.

"Who was that woman?" Sarah asked, glancing over at Stephanie as she climbed into her car.

"I'll tell you on the walk back to the camp. Once we get the kids changed into their play clothes, they'll be ready to go."

Sarah nodded. "Why do I have the feeling my son is involved?"

That made Lexa laugh. "Because he usually is. Let's go see how our patient is doing."

Chapter 34

~~♥~~

"Dean, do you have a minute?"

Dean turned, surprised to see Josh as he walked back to the camp after the church service. "Great service this morning, wasn't it?"

"Terrific. I only wish Sam could have been there, but I hear they taped it for him."

"That's good. You wanted to talk to me?" In some ways, Josh intimidated him. This mission had gone a long way toward helping Dean feel more comfortable with the other TeamWork guys. Other than going out to Montana, he hadn't been able to join as many missions or projects with Sam and the crew as he would have liked. Instead, he'd worked a few inner-city missions closer to home in San Antonio.

Josh fell into step beside him. "I'm not sure if anyone ever mentioned to you that I'd helped Sheila back in that San Antonio work camp years ago. The one where her husband kidnapped her."

"I caught wind of it. I haven't asked any questions, and I don't know any specifics. Maybe it's better that way."

"I understand, but I feel the need to explain a few things," Josh said. "If I'm not mistaken, you like Sheila. As more than a friend."

Dean nodded. "Yes, I like Sheila. Very much." As irrational as it seemed, and although it was way too soon, he was falling in love with her.

"Look, I'm not trying to pry into your business, Dean. Are you aware that Sam threw me out of the camp?"

What does this have to do with Sheila? This exchange felt awkward, and he had to wonder where Josh was headed with it. He was a purposeful guy, a straight-up guy, so he should hear him out. No doubt he had a point to make. "Yes, I heard about that. Sorry, man. I'm glad everything got worked out."

Josh chuckled under his breath. "I was what got worked out. I had some issues that I needed to work through and get straight with the Lord. It took me a few years, and I can't tell you how happy I am to finally be back with the TeamWork crew on a mission."

Dean nodded. "You have a wonderful family, Josh."

"I've been blessed beyond what I deserve. I wanted you to know that—in spite of my past bad behavior—nothing happened between Sheila and me in that San Antonio work camp. I can't explain it except to say that her fear was almost palpable, and I wanted to help her. Sheila was like a little bird, scared of everything. She looked down at the ground when she walked. Lexa befriended her as much as Sheila would allow, but she didn't talk to anyone unless they tried to draw her into conversation. No one in that work camp suspected Angelina was her daughter. She was hiding her out in the camp, and we all knew her as Margarita."

Dean hadn't known that part of the equation. Something in Josh's words alerted him that there was more to it. "You knew, didn't you?"

Josh nodded slowly. "I sensed Sheila was in trouble, and I asked her if she needed help. She told me how Howard sometimes hit her...sorry," he added when Dean winced. "Sam had some money in the safe, and I knew the combination. I borrowed the money and gave it to her to get away—with the full intention of returning it in a couple of days—but then Howard found her and Sam threw me out of the work camp. There was a lot happening in that work camp."

"I guess so," Dean said.

Both men stopped walking. From Josh's conflicted expression, Dean could tell the other man was concerned that he understand *why* he'd tried to help Sheila. "I'm not sure what to say, Josh, except that I'm glad you tried to help her."

"Sheila's a lot different now than the woman she was in San Antonio."

"How so?" He had a pretty good idea but wanted to hear it directly from Josh.

"She's stronger in her faith, for one thing. With Howard gone now, she's free from the chains of the past. She's more independent and sure of herself. I know her family life growing up wasn't good, and I don't know that the situation is any better now, but she and Angelina are doing very well on their own."

Dean nodded. "Yes, they are. What is it that you really want to say, Josh?"

Josh met his gaze. "I'm saying I think the Lord's brought both of you to the mission camp for a purpose. I'm saying I'll be praying for the two of you and the Lord's will."

"Thanks. I'm cooking dinner for Sheila tonight in the dining hall. Winnie made a tablecloth for one of the smaller tables, and I'm making her my special chicken enchilada casserole."

Josh chuckled and they resumed their walk. "A man who cooks? She won't be able to resist you."

"I hope you're right."

Marta bent her knees and propped her feet on the dashboard as Eliot drove. She dipped her head and peeked out the front window to check on the progress of Tyler's balloon. Hard to miss that one with its huge Texas state flag. They were all beautiful, but with the multiple balloons with rainbow colors, she imagined it could get confusing. Her gaze moved to the walkie talkie radio on the console between them. Periodically, Tyler checked in with them, and it was his preferred method of communication.

"Oh, look! It's Tyler! There he is!" She pointed out the front window. "You know, I don't think someone who's color blind could be a chaser. Unless there's some way they can compensate for distinguishing the colors. I wonder if that's in the rules. I have them right here. Wanna hear some of them?"

"Sure. Lay them on me," Eliot said. Her rabbit trails seemed to amuse him and kept things lively.

"Always be courteous and friendly," she read from the brochure. She skimmed a few more. "Be aware of and respect any pets or livestock. That's definitely an important one. And we *cannot*—that's underlined, bolded, and in all capital letters—cut any fences or force locks. We always have to make sure gates and fences are left as we found them. And look, it says here that we should check the area for litter and take it with us." She looked over at him. "Does that mean I have to pick up the trash left behind by someone else? That hardly seems fair."

"I guess if you're a responsible citizen, you will."

"As long as I don't have to cut a fence, open a gate, or disrespect any livestock to get to it, I suppose I can." She laughed at the look Eliot shot her way. "You're not wishing you hadn't brought me, are you?"

"I can't imagine being here with anyone *but* you, Marta."

"And yes, I sort of led you into that one, didn't I?"

"You're very good at it," Eliot said. "The rules about livestock and the gate cutting and forcing locks are there for a reason. We can't know where the balloon will land, and we have to go and meet it no matter if it's in a cow pasture or a backyard swimming pool. Landowner relations are very important, and they like the pilots to get permission to land, if possible."

"Have you ever actually been up in a hot air balloon?" Following Eliot's lead, she looked out the window.

"Tyler took me up in one once."

"What's it like?"

"Surprisingly quiet except when the propane burners are firing," he said. "At times, you don't feel like you're moving much at all. It's a great feeling of floating, and the view is spectacular. It's something everyone should do at least once in their lifetime."

She sighed. "I hope I get the opportunity."

"I'm sure you will. Marta, I don't want to put a damper on your spirits because I'm having a great time with you, but—"

"You want to talk about the serious stuff that we haven't had the time, or the privacy, to discuss back at the camp?"

He nodded. "Yes, more or less."

"What do you want to know?" Removing her feet from the dashboard, she angled her body toward him, giving him her full attention.

"Have you ever dated anyone seriously?"

"If you consider being engaged seriously dating, yes." She dropped her gaze, embarrassed. "I met Liam in high school back in Kentucky when we were both juniors. I was a cheerleader and he was captain of our biggest rival basketball team. It was the typical high school romance. He went to the University of Kentucky his first year but then transferred to Baylor his sophomore year. Supposedly to be with me. We dated through the rest of college, breaking up a couple of times along the way."

She shrugged. "Getting married seemed the thing to do, and all of our friends were getting engaged and married. In September of our senior year, Liam asked me to marry him. The plan was to marry in June after we both graduated, and then he'd start law school the next fall semester. We got in a huge fight—I can't even remember what it was about now—and I broke if off."

Eliot seemed to visibly relax.

"But then we got back together again."

"Oh."

"Then he cheated on me. I was the one wronged, but he was the one who broke it off. The hardest part to take was that he married a pretty blonde law student within three months of breaking up with me. It was the final insult. They're still married and have several kids now, so I'm happy for them. But the disappointment lasted a long time."

"Liam was a colossal fool." When Eliot reached for her hand, Marta gave it to him.

"You're the prettiest nurse I've ever seen." Crossing his arms behind his head, Sam eyed Lexa. "Will you let me get up now and move around? It's not like I have to be confined in bed, is it?"

"No, you're not confined. You probably don't have to stay in the bed, either, but I don't want you out running around or doing any work. And I'm giving you strict instructions not to go over to the dining hall tonight. Dean and Sheila are on security duty this afternoon and evening, and he's cooking a special dinner for her. We don't want to interrupt their romantic dinner."

He chuckled. "I get your point considering how many emphatic *don'ts* you said in that speech." Sam quirked a brow. In the craziness of last night, he'd caught wind of Dean's plans tonight, but they hadn't really sunk into his scattered mind. Good for him. "What are we having for dinner?"

"I thought I'd take the Volvo and go pick up something for us and then bring it back here."

"Why don't we both go and enjoy a quiet dinner?" The way Lexa brightened at his suggestion revealed how much she needed a break. She deserved one. This mission had been full and rewarding, but also tiring.

"Are you sure you're up to it?"

"I think I'm over the sickness and only have a few leftover muscle aches. Thanks for putting up with me through the whole spider bite thing."

"Like you're so hard to put up with, Sam. And it's not like I had a choice. In sickness and in health, remember?" Lexa closed her book and set it on the table.

He wanted to tease her, see the pink rise in her cheeks. He darted a glance at the clock. "It's still the middle of the afternoon. I'm wide awake." Crossing his arms, Sam drummed his fingers on them. "Whatever could we do?"

Lifting out of the chair, Lexa began to pull her lightweight sweater over her head. She'd worn it with her skirt for church.

Sam swallowed. "Have mercy, Lexa."

She peeked out at him from beneath the hem of the sweater. "Something wrong?"

"No. Keep going. I'm enjoying the view."

She finished taking off her sweater and draped it over a chair. "You'd love that, wouldn't you?" Sidling over to the bed, she sat down on the edge of the mattress.

"The kids are at the Balloon Fiesta with my parents, right?"

"They are." She reached for her braid, playing with the ends, giving him a coy grin.

He tilted his head with a smile. "And the rest of our TeamWork crew is otherwise occupied?"

"Uh huh. As you said, whatever can we do?"

An hour later, Lexa sat back on the bed with a triumphant smile. "Yes! I can't believe I finally beat you at this game." Picking up the small drawstring bag, she dropped Scrabble tiles inside it, one at a time.

"Stop rubbing it in." Sam chuckled. "On second thought, go ahead and gloat away. My only excuse is that you distracted me with that nightgown. Totally worth it, though." She'd obliged him by trying on her new pink nightgown and she'd left it on while they played the game. "I never understood how I beat you at it, anyway. You're much better with words than me."

"Oh, no you don't. Don't you dare tell me you *let* me win."

"I won't, but I love playing games with you, Lexa. You're not a very good loser, but I love it when you win. You're irresistible. Come here."

"You also have a twitch in your eye today," she said, laughing after he gave her a quick kiss. She traced the outline of his lips with one light finger. "I think the Frisky Spider bit you."

"Could be. He's a brother spider to Corny and Grumpy." He caressed her soft shoulder and drew her close. "I'd suggest you stop doing that now if you don't want to—"

A man's shouts came from somewhere in the camp. Lexa blew out a breath and they stared at one another for a few seconds. There it was again.

"What now?" Lexa said. "Is it too much to ask for a little quiet for one day?"

Sam sat up slowly and swung his feet over the edge of the bed. "Better let me go. Sounded like it came from the dining hall area."

"I'm going with you." She quickly tugged on her jeans and a T-shirt, shoved her feet in tennis shoes, and followed him out the front door.

"Dean?" Sam called, stepping into the kitchen through the back door.

"In here!"

With Lexa beside him, Sam walked into the main portion of the dining hall. "We heard a shout. Everything okay?" A quick glance confirmed everything seemed in order.

In a crouched position, Dean had a dust pan in one hand and a broom in the other. Rising to his feet, he held up the dust pan, which held the remains of a spider. "May I present what I believe is the offending spider?"

"Eww!" Lexa clamped one hand over her mouth and turned away in disgust.

Sam shared an amused look with Dean. "Where'd you find it?"

"Out by the trash can. Mitch warned us it might be there. I managed to coerce it onto the dust pan but then either dropped it or the little bugger hopped onto the floor. If you'd been here a few minutes ago, I'm sure you would have gotten an eyeful. This little guy gave me a run for the money."

"I'm indebted," Sam said. "Let's just hope there's not an egg sac nearby."

Lexa shivered but kept her distance. "What a wonderful thought, but thank you, Dean. You're a brave man. We'll be praying for your dinner with Sheila tonight."

"I have a question to ask you. Hang on a second." Still holding the dust pan, Dean hesitated. "I'm not sure what to do with the spider."

"I vote we flush it down. I'll take care of it." Holding the dust pan at arm's length, Lexa walked out of the dining hall.

Dean chuckled. "Sam, do you know how long Sheila has stuttered?"

"Haven't a clue, but I'm guessing since birth. I know she's not close to her family, but somewhere along the way I heard that her grandmother stuttered. I believe it can run in families."

The other man nodded. "I did some research the other night, and that would go along with what I read. I don't want to upset her by asking her about it. She might be really sensitive."

"Take the cues from Sheila," Sam said. "I hope you two enjoy yourselves. Lexa and I are going out to get some dinner in a bit. Hold down the fort for us, but I expect it to be quiet."

Dean smiled. "I'm glad you're feeling better."

Lexa hung up the phone as Sam returned to their quarters. "Your mom and dad called. Everything's fine with the kids and they're having a great time. She asked how you were doing and made a suggestion if you wanted to get out and do something that's not too strenuous."

"She knows me well. What was her suggestion?"

"The Albuquerque Balloon Museum."

Sam's eyes lit. "That sounds good. Are they open today?"

"Until five." A smile spread across her face. "It'd be something fun to do so you wouldn't feel so cooped up, but it'd still be a quiet activity."

Sam laughed. "I'm not decrepit. Yet."

Chapter 35

~~♥~~

Angelina scooted closer to Felipe on the Sandia Peak Tramway. "How far up are we?"

"They said we're going up 4,000 feet in 15 minutes." He checked his watch. "We've been on here about half that time, so I'd say we're around 2,000 feet."

"I didn't really expect you to know the answer." She moved farther to the middle.

He followed her. "Angel, are you scared of heights?" His tone revealed his surprise.

"I might be, but I like roller coasters, so that makes no sense."

Felipe smiled. "That reminds me of your speech about airplanes and roller coasters that first night."

"That's right. And you admitted you were scared on the plane. And you aren't scared at all right now, are you?"

"Shh. Sometimes things don't make sense. If it makes you feel any better, The Tram is an engineering marvel. Here. Take my hand, Angel. I'll keep you safe. Promise. Nothing's going to happen."

Soothed by his words and comforted by his promise, Angelina gave him her hand. She didn't even have to think about it. "Ohhhh," she murmured, her heart beating faster the higher they climbed along the western face of the Sandia Mountains. It was rugged but beautiful with granite rock faces, cliffs and pinnacles, deep canyons, pines and aspens, oak, fir, and spruce trees.

"They say you can see 11,000 square miles of the Land of Enchantment from The Tram," he said.

"Look, Felipe! There's an eagle! Cassie and Amy, did you see the eagle?" From across The Tram, both ladies smiled.

"That's cool. I've never seen one so close." Felipe's expression was full of wonder. "It's almost like you can reach out and touch him."

"Hey there," Landon said, coming over to them. "There's a

construction engineer over by us, and he's been telling us some interesting things about The Tram."

"Like what?" Angelina said. Maybe listening to boring facts would help calm her down.

"The public was skeptical about it being built because of the steep, rocky terrain. A company from Switzerland was contracted to do the work, and even though they had a lot of experience, they admitted this was their most challenging project ever. The construction took two years and then they did 60 days of strenuous testing before the first riders boarded The Tram in 1966."

"Whoa. That's old," Felipe said.

Landon chuckled. "Right. When you think about it, it's amazing to think the cables are supported by only two towers between the terminals."

"I didn't need to know that." Angelina squeezed Felipe's hand a little bit tighter. It felt so natural that she'd forgotten they were still holding hands. At least Landon seemed cool about it. "I sure hope they have something to stop this thing if the cables snap."

"You need a little more optimism, Lambkin." She wasn't sure whether to laugh or swat his arm, but she wished he hadn't used an endearment with Landon right there.

"Never fear," Landon told them. "The engineer said there are track cable brakes that would close automatically and hold the car in place in an emergency or cable failure."

"That's comforting," Angelina said. "Thanks, Landon."

Putting his hands on her shoulders, Felipe turned her back to the window. She felt a little shaky and closed her eyes.

"No fair. Open your eyes," he said.

"Okay, I'll admit it. I'm scared."

"Landon told us that there are security measures in place. Nothing's going to happen. You're completely safe here." He kept his hold on her but didn't speak for a long moment. When she opened her eyes and turned back to look at him, Felipe was looking out the side window. A smile covered his face and he seemed so peaceful. He loved this. She couldn't spoil it for him by acting like a scaredy cat kid.

"You know, it *is* pretty cool to think that God made all this."

She snapped her gaze to his. "You're saying you believe it?"

"I've never denied the existence of God, Princess. I just haven't thought much about Him before. There's a difference."

"But…but you said you don't believe in Heaven or…the alternative."

"That was Wednesday. Today is Sunday."

A slow smile creased her lips. "I'd say it's been an eventful week. I'm glad you're open to thinking beyond the borders."

"Borders are confining. I've been confined too long, Angel. I'm thinking about spreading my wings a little. Soaring like that eagle out there."

She nodded. "I think that's a very good thing."

Two hours later, Lexa walked beside Sam as they exited the museum together. "That was great," she said. "We'll have to visit Pastor Chevy and Lila again in another year or two and bring the kids to the museum. They'd love it. The history and the multi-media technology exhibits were interesting." Lexa hooked her arm through his as they started toward the parking lot.

She could tell Sam was feeling better. Although she would have loved to have gone to the Balloon Fiesta, it would have been strenuous for him today. They'd hear all about it from the kids and Sam's parents later on that evening. They'd all be exhausted when they returned to the camp or else they'd be so excited that it'd take a while to calm them down. Although the twins and Joe could have gone with the others to the Balloon Fiesta, Lexa considered it providential that Sam Sr. and Sarah had shown up on this particular mission.

You always know, don't you, Lord?

"My dad and brothers would like the war exhibit." Sam gave her a grin. "I had no idea they used observation balloons back in the Civil War. Maybe Mom and Dad can stop at the museum on their way back to Houston."

"I'd love to hear Astronaut Will's take on hot air balloons," Lexa said. "I can just hear his speech now about how unsophisticated and primitive they are."

Sam frowned. "I don't think he'd say that at all. Are you saying Will's arrogant?"

"You said it, not me. Well," she relented, "not arrogant, but well…yes, I guess that describes him. I hate to say that, but he doesn't call to check on the kids the way your older sisters do. They live out on the West Coast, and yet I feel like we're in better contact and know them better than your younger brother who lives in a cul-de-sac in Houston!"

"I think you need to cut him a break, Lexa."

"If you start giving me the speech again about how he's still coasting on the fumes of being named as a shuttle commander, that excuse is starting to get old, Sam. As long as I've known him, Will's been very egocentric. My prayer for him as shuttle commander is that he'll be a great testimony for the Lord, but at the rate he's going, that's not going to happen."

She stopped. She'd said enough. True to his character, Sam didn't appear to want to pick a fight although she could tell her words had affected him. He'd told her about his mother's concerns for Will, so maybe he didn't need two women in his life getting on Will's case.

"He's a single guy, and Will's always been a geeky scientist. Conversational skills aren't his thing. Flying jets and going into space is all he's ever talked about since he was a kid."

"That's all good and well, but it's a little hard to cuddle up at night with a hunk of metal. Okay," she said, putting one hand on her brow, "I realize how that sounded. It did *not* come out the way I intended."

"Where's all this coming from?" Sam gave her a curious look as they reached the car.

Lexa stared at him for a long moment. "I honestly have no idea. Sorry. I think it's because I genuinely like Will, and I'm concerned about him. I love all your brothers and sisters, but Will's the one who makes it difficult to get to know him. He's closed himself off from the rest of the world in his pursuit of making world history."

"Will doesn't care about making history. Like I said, he just wants to do what he loves. If he happens to make history in the process, so be it." Sam tapped the top of the Volvo. "I happen to think it's awesome."

"It is. I'm not denying that point," she said. "Let's talk about where you're taking me for dinner."

"Up for spicy?"

"Not really. More importantly, let's not tempt anything,

especially considering what you've been through in the past 24 hours."

"You're all the spice I need," Sam said as they reached the station wagon in the parking lot.

Laughing, Lexa unlocked the car doors. "Just get in the car, Sam."

"Yes, boss."

Chapter 36

~~♥~~

Hearing noises outside, Dean stopped setting the table. Had some of the group come back to the camp earlier than expected? He'd wanted some time alone with Sheila. Was a romantic dinner alone with her in the camp too much to ask?

Darting to the door, he stepped outside, closing the screen door quietly so it didn't slam behind him. He heard angry voices. Men's voices. Alarm shot through him and heightened his senses. *Sheila!* She'd gone to the women's dorm to change. God help anyone if they'd entered the women's dorm and given Sheila as much as a hangnail. Fury surged through him as Dean stormed around the corner, following the sounds of the voices.

Lord, be with Sheila. Keep her safe.

"L-leave this p-property now!" Standing in front of the door to the women's dorm, Sheila's feet were planted apart. With an expression of fierce determination, she quickly lifted a bow and positioned an arrow in the direct path of three men standing about 30 yards away. "I s-said leave!"

Dean stared at Sheila and his mouth gaped. *This* fierce woman was his shy Sheila? She'd already changed into her dress and her hair was down around her shoulders. She looked gorgeous, soft and feminine. And fearless with a quiver full of arrows slung over one shoulder. What a woman! Then it hit him. She'd only stuttered a few times during that exchange. Although he was thrilled, it didn't make sense.

"Well, lookee here. It's Sacajawea come to protect her church camp. Be a good girl and step aside. Little wisp of a thing, ain't you? Pretty, too. Don't give us no trouble, and we won't hurt you." A paunchy, middle-aged man in dirty jeans and a stained, short-sleeved shirt sauntered in her direction.

"Leave her alone!" Dean growled. One fist was clenched and, in the other, he held a heavy flashlight, ready to take on all three men.

He might go down trying, and it was the only weapon at his disposal, but he had to do what he could to protect Sheila. Her eyes met his, and she gave him a slight nod.

"Move out of the way, Pocahontas." Another man, this one younger and leaner, moved toward her. He seemed more of a legitimate threat, a menace.

"I w-warned you!" Sheila stepped to the right and took careful aim before launching the arrow. Whizzing past the man's head, the arrow lifted a dark toupee off his head, revealing a shiny scalp.

Slapping one hand on his head, the man yelped and let out a loud curse. Stunned, he whirled around and motioned to the other two men. "We're out of here. This ain't over yet!" They hightailed it out of sight, stumbling as they ran. What a bunch of idiots.

Dean rushed over to Sheila. She'd lowered the bag to the ground along with the bow. Wrapping her in his arms, he kissed her forehead and then planted both hands on her shoulders. "Sweetheart, that was the most awesome thing I've ever seen in my life! I can't believe you knew how to do that. You were incredibly brave."

"Th-th-thanks, Dean." Lowering her gaze, a pretty flush invaded her cheeks. "It-it's b-b-been a-w-while s-s-since I-I've sh-shot a b-b-bow and a-ar-row. I w-w-was o-on a t-t-team."

In the near distance, they heard motorcycle engines revving and then roaring to life. Soon enough, the sounds faded as the men made their getaway.

"They might have looted the place and taken what they could if you hadn't stopped them. The guys have laptops and all kinds of expensive equipment and gadgets, especially Marc and Landon. And Mitch." He shook his head. "We all do. I hereby crown you the heroine of the TeamWork camp. Thank you on behalf of all of us."

"S-stop i-it, Dean. Y-you w-would h-have st-stop-ed th-them. I-I h-h-heard th-them c-c-coming, a-a-nd I-It w-w-was th-the f-f-first w-w-weapon I-I c-c-could f-f-find. I-I s-saw it i-in th-the s-s-storage r-r-room th-the oth-other d-d-day."

"Well, it sure did the job. I couldn't believe it when I saw the toupee go flying off that guy's head. That was crazy!" If she'd heard them, why hadn't he? His only excuse was that he'd been listening to music while getting everything ready for their dinner. Great security guard he'd turned out to be tonight.

"H-he c-c-called m-me S-Sac-ca-j-jaw-wea. S-S-She tr-trav-veled w-with L-Lewis a-and Cl-Clar-k, y-you k-know."

Dean hugged her to him again. "I'd say that's appropriate. Sheila, do you realize you hardly stuttered at all when you ordered those scumbags to leave?"

She nodded. "I-I d-d-don't st-stut-ter wh-when I-I'm r-r-riled up."

Good to know; he'd thought it would be the opposite. He was already learning that nothing about Sheila could be assumed or expected. "Dinner's almost ready if you're not too riled up—or shook up—to eat."

"I-I'm a l-l-little sh-shak-ken up, b-b-but I-I'll b-b-be f-f-fine." In spite of her reassurances, Sheila noticeably shivered as they walked into the dining hall.

Dean wished he had a jacket to put around her shoulders. Maybe a good meal and some conversation would ease her trepidation. "Let me run and get a jacket for you."

"N-n-no," she protested. "I-I c-c-could g-g-go g-get one i-if I-I r-r-really w-w-wanted."

He'd found a small round table, perfect for intimate dining for two, in one of the storage closets. When he helped Sheila scoot her chair closer to the table, she held up one corner of the tablecloth. "N-Noah's A-Ark?"

"It's the same fabric they used for the nursery curtains. I wouldn't be surprised if the ladies made play clothes for the kids out of the leftover fabric," he said, pleased when she laughed. "They're very creative."

"A-and h-h-helpful," Sheila said. "I-it a-all l-l-looks s-s-so l-l-lovely."

Dean lit a scented candle inside a glass jar and then extinguished the overhead fluorescent lights. Without their harsh, artificial glare, the dining hall was bathed in a soft glow. He had to admit, it was about as romantic as he could make the plain room.

Sheila seemed impressed when he brought his special chicken enchilada casserole to the table. "It's one of the few things I can make without a microwave," he said. "I'm not sure what it says about me that Felipe is a better cook." What a brilliant move to mention that someone else's cooking—much less a 15-year-old's—was better than his.

"R-r-really? Th-that's s-s-surp-p-r-ris-sing."

After Dean asked grace, he watched as Sheila took her first bite of the simple garden salad. "I hope ranch dressing is okay. It's what we had on hand here in the refrigerator."

"Dean, r-rel-lax. I-It's a-all g-g-g-ood." Taking a bite of the casserole, she gave him a thumbs-up.

"Felipe complained the food I made was lame and not very nutritious. He said I was either overcooking or undercooking everything and it offered no recognizable nutrients. My pride was offended, so I countered by bringing home take-out. After a while, Felipe rebelled against that. I challenged him to come up with a solution we could both stomach, and he did. And then some."

She smiled. "Wh-what d-d-does h-he m-m-make?"

"Some mighty tasty dishes. He went to the library and checked out some cookbooks. He said he was only following the directions, but there's more to it than that. Felipe's specialties are chicken and fish, and he's quite talented with spices and marinades."

As they ate, Dean asked more questions about her work since that seemed to be a safe topic. When he asked what she did during her free time, Dean learned Sheila taught a sign language class at a local community college. She liked to cook and Mexican dishes were her specialty. To relax, she worked on needlepoint and loved to rollerblade, of all things. When she asked if he'd like to go sometime, he grinned and agreed while his mind screamed *No!* He'd be flat on his backside in no time by participating in an activity that would do nothing for his masculinity or self-esteem. Not to mention his lower back. But, hey, if it meant he could spend time with Sheila back in San Antonio? Sure, he was game.

"Sheila, before we have dessert, would you like to dance?" All through their meal, he'd been working up the nerve to ask her. He was going crazy watching her every day, often working beside her. Dancing would give him a legitimate reason to put his arms around her. Hold her. Show Sheila he was serious about wanting to get to know her better. That he considered this a *real* date tonight, and not just a way to pass the time while on the mission.

"I ha-ha-ven't d-done th-that, b-b-but I-I'm w-w-willing t-to t-t-try."

"It's easy, and I'll show you. Something tells me you're a fast learner. We have a CD player here in the dining hall and"—he waved his hand toward the open area clear of tables—"a dance floor."

"Y-y-you've pl-plan-ned th-this v-v-very w-w-well."

"It's all for you, Sheila." When she glanced up at him, her eyes were bright. How was it possible another man hadn't stolen this woman's heart before now?

"We all went out dancing together in Montana, but I'm not sure the opportunity will present itself here," he told her. "This is what's called seizing the moment." He hoped everyone else would stay away for a little while longer. The sun was lowering on the horizon.

Sheila's laughter was feminine and throaty. "S-s-seize a-w-way."

"I have an idea. Do you want to go watch the sunset together? I know just the place where we can get a spectacular view."

"S-s-sounds l-l-like f-f-fun."

"It's on the edge of the camp, away from the line of trees, but we can still keep an eye on things here." He chuckled. "I doubt those guys will be returning to the camp after they saw how accurate your aim can be."

After running to his dorm and tugging his blanket off the bunk, he carried it under one arm and met Sheila outside the dining hall. "Shall we?"

With a shy smile, she nodded and curled her hand around his arm. "This is the spot," Dean said a couple of minutes later. Together they spread out the blanket and she asked him to tell her about his parents.

"Dad left us when I was nine. Mama Rose said he left *her*, not me, but she was trying to soften the blow and protect me, as always. He'd found another woman who apparently gave him something we couldn't. I never could understand what that something was, and he's gone now. He died five years ago."

"I-I'm s-s-sorry. D-d-did y-you r-r-rec-c-onc-c-ile b-bef-f-ore h-he d-died?"

"No, and it's one of the biggest regrets of my life. Our relationship had always been rocky. He wasn't a Christian, but my mother was born a Christian, or so she says. I still think that, even to this day, Mama Rose believes that my dad's abandonment was somehow God's curse on her for marrying a man who wasn't a Christian."

When Sheila lowered her gaze, Dean grasped her hand. "I'm sorry. Did I say something wrong?"

"N-no, b-b-but I-I c-c-can und-derst-st-stand wh-why sh-she m-m-might th-think that w-w-way."

"Sheila, surely you don't believe anything you've done brought God's curse on you. Please don't tell me you believe that."

"N-n-o, b-b-but m-my gr-grandm-moth-ther st-st-stuttered and m-m-my f-f-fath-ther t-t-told m-m-e sh-she br-brought sh-shame t-t-to th-the f-f-family. A-and s-s-so d-d-did I."

Curling one arm around Sheila's slender shoulders, Dean drew her close. "That's a lie, Sheila. You are wonderfully and fearfully made. You are perfect just as you are." His heart pumped harder when she kissed his cheek and then rested her head on his shoulder. Without speaking, they watched as the sun lowered on the horizon.

Standing, he gathered the blanket and then helped Sheila to her feet. "We still haven't had dessert. How about we have that and some coffee, if you're not too tired."

Giving him a small smile, she nodded but remained silent.

"Sorry I didn't make this," he told her, sectioning a piece of peach pie. "Sam's mom made it. Do you want me to zap it in the microwave to warm it up? I have vanilla ice cream, too."

"N-n-no i-ice cr-cream," she told him. "T-t-too m-m-many c-c-calories."

"You're right. Maybe I shouldn't have the ice cream either. I've got to start cutting back."

He told her more about growing up in San Antonio as they enjoyed their dessert. She laughed at some of his stories. Admittedly, he punched them up a bit to make them more lively and interesting. Not with untrue exaggeration, but by inflections and his delivery. If nothing else, he could tell a decent story.

After they finished their dessert, Dean switched on the CD player. Maybe he should have thought to play it quietly during their dinner. He smiled when Old Blue Eyes began to croon.

"Sheila, may I have the honor of this dance?"

"I-I'd l-l-love to." With her trusting gaze never leaving his face, Sheila placed her hand in Dean's and allowed him to lead her onto the dance floor. Her hand trembled a bit, cluing him in that he wasn't the only one who was nervous. Dean's heart was beating so hard he figured Sheila would be able to feel it pumping through the cotton of his shirt if he held her close enough. Would that be too close for her? Too much?

Felipe probably has more finesse with a female than I do.

"Hold that thought. I forgot one very important thing." Releasing her hand, Dean quickly walked across the room and flipped a switch. A disco ball in the center of the room began to rotate in all its sparkling, glittery tackiness. "Isn't it great?"

"I-I l-l-love it! Wh-where d-d-did y-y-you f-find it?"

"Eliot and I bought it when we went into town the other day. It's for the talent show. That's also when we went to the Christian bookstore."

Sheila looked surprised by that news.

"He bought the book for Angelina, the one she showed you. Then I bought a Bible and a cover for Felipe. The cover was made by Leather, and he seemed to get a kick out of that."

"Th-that's w-w-won-n-d-derf-f-ul, Dean. Y-y-you're d-d-doing a g-g-great j-j-job with-th h-h-him."

"I appreciate your saying that. I wasn't sure whether you felt that way," he said, easing her back in his arms. "I plan to do a better job once we go home." He began to sway gently with her. At least dancing was one skill he'd picked up easily, although he hadn't done much of it in recent years. Resting one hand around her waist, Dean drew Sheila closer, leaving what he considered an appropriate distance between them. He was determined not to do anything wrong tonight because under no circumstances did he want her running away from him.

"A-A-Ang-g-gel-lina and I-I t-t-talked l-last n-n-night. I th-th-ink F-F-F-el-l-lipe's g-good f-f-for h-h-her."

"Thank you," he said, touched by her words. "I know she's definitely been a good influence on him."

"H-h-how ex-act-tly is F-F-F-el-lipe re-re-rel-lated t-t-to y-you?"

"A few cousins removed on my mother's side. I've never even figured how far removed."

"I-I ad-adm-mire y-y-you f-for t-t-taking F-F-F-el-lipe int-to y-y-your h-home. I-I kn-know it c-c-can't b-b-be eas-sy."

The affection in Sheila's voice, mirrored in her eyes, touched him deeply. Lightly resting his jaw against her temple, he began to hum along to the tune of "The Way You Look Tonight." The song had long been one of his all-time favorite classics. "Sheila, I love the way *you* look tonight." Pretty corny line, but she seemed to like it. Shifting in his arms, she made a sweet murmur of contentment. The scent of her hair teased his senses. Slowly, he laced his fingers with hers, taking pleasure in the fact that she didn't resist him or pull away. This evening was going even better than he could have anticipated.

"You're very good at this."

"I-I h-h-have a v-v-very g-good inst-st-r-r-ruct-tor." Sheila leaned her head on his chest and he tightened his hold on her.

Nuzzling her hair, he pressed his lips to her forehead. "I'm sorry," he said, pulling back. "I don't mean to take advantage."

"Y-y-you're n-not." She gently tugged him closer again and he wrapped both arms around her, slow dancing like he hadn't done in years. He gloried in the closeness, the feel of her, the warmth of having her next to him. Dancing with other women had been nothing compared to how he felt dancing with Sheila now. The beginnings of desire stirred within him, and he moved his gaze from her eyes down to her nose, then to her lovely cheekbones, and finally to her lips.

"Kiss me, Dean," she whispered, as though reading his mind.

"You don't mind?" Why did it matter? *Kiss the woman, you fool.*

He leaned in close, but hesitated. Wait a minute. "The timing might be awkward to mention this, but you hardly stuttered just now. The same as when you were angry with Felipe and then again with those guys in the camp tonight."

She smiled. "I-I d-don't st-stut-t-er as much when I'm..." With a sweet blush, she leaned her forehead against his chest.

He skimmed his thumbs over her cheeks. "I don't want to make you mad, but I hope to make you feel..."—he brought his mouth close to hers—"romantic."

Still dancing, Dean moved them slowly together as he lowered his lips to hers. In that moment, he knew he was a goner. He was going to marry this woman, if she'd have him. He didn't know when, but he would. But, considering it was only their first kiss, he definitely shouldn't be making any proclamations of undying love and affection for a while yet. For now, he'd enjoy the moment, and it was a glorious one.

"D-d-d y-y-you s-s-see th-them, t-t-oo?" Her eyes skimmed over his face.

Dean chuckled. "If you mean the fireworks, yeah, I did." Sappy yes, but he'd take it.

Covering her hand with his, on top of his chest, he continued dancing with her for a very long time. "Sheila, I—"

"Shh," she said, stilling his words with one finger over his lips. "N-not n-now."

For now, he'd be content with whatever Sheila was willing to give, giving thanks all the while.

Chapter 37

~~♥~~

"Get enough to eat? Want some more dessert?" Eliot walked beside Marta on Vendor Row. This had to be one of the best days of his life.

She laughed. "I'm stuffed with Mexican sopapillas. I couldn't eat another thing."

"That's too bad because I have one more thing you must try. Did you know New Mexico is the first state to have its own official state cookie?" When she lifted a brow, Eliot took her by the hand to a nearby booth. "Two Bizcochitos, please." A second later he handed one to her.

Marta held up the fleur-de-lis shaped cookie, admiring it. "Here's to you," she said, toasting him and then sampling it. "It's really good." She chewed it and then bit off a bit more. "It's like a really thick sugar cookie flavored with anise, I think, and dusted with cinnamon sugar. I must warn you," she said, taking another bite, "if I spontaneously combust, it's all your fault. I'm glad you only got one for me because I. Can't. Stop. Eating. It."

Eliot laughed and they finished their cookies at the same time. "I promise I won't stuff more food in you unless you beg me."

Taking him by the hand, she pulled him behind a nearby tent, out of the way of most spectators. "I'm begging for a kiss. How's that? I'm storing up for the future." Locking her hands behind his head, she pulled his head down and their lips met for a sweet kiss. Very sweet. Perfection.

"Hmm," he said, licking his lips. "Cinnamon sugar." He dipped his head for one more round.

They walked around more booths and talked with some people, snapped photos of more balloons, and danced to lively jazz music on a small makeshift dance floor. Twirling her under his arm and then pulling Marta to him, Eliot wrapped her in his embrace. The sun was beginning its descent on the horizon. He never wanted this day, this moment, this time with Marta, to end.

"I'm never going to let you go," he whispered.

With her palms flat on his chest, she pushed back a little and looked up at him with big eyes. "What did you say?"

"Come with me." With his arm around her small waist, he led her over to a grouping of tables in a quiet area. "Let's talk." He waited while she sat on a bench and then sat beside her, close enough so that others wouldn't hear their words. "Marta, I can't go into this relationship without laying it all on the line, faults and all."

"Eliot, you're scaring me a little bit." She put her hand on the side of his face, and he leaned into it. "You're not an escaped convict are you? A runaway circus performer?"

"No, nothing like that," he said, shaking his head. "But I need to be serious. I need to say this."

"My flippancy is the way I react sometimes when I'm nervous. Forgive me."

"I'm the one who needs to ask forgiveness, Marta."

Something in her eyes dimmed when she met his gaze. "Tell me."

"Before I became a Christian, I did what I wanted. When I was growing up, the lifestyle was free, different. Sexual freedom was encouraged and almost expected. Not that it excuses anything. I'm not a perfect man in any sense of the word, and I have to constantly be on my guard. I wish I could change my past, but every experience has made me the man I am today."

He rested his hand on her cheek. "When I came to Jesus, my eyes were opened in so many ways. I stopped indulging in my own selfish pleasures. I realized how wrong it is and how it dishonors a woman. Not only that, but that kind of behavior grieves the Lord."

Marta had told him she'd been a Christian since her father led her to the Lord when she was seven years old, the year before he'd disappeared. Now it was his turn to tell her his story. "Let me tell you about a man named Juan." He told her about being in that Santiago church and how he'd never known Jesus as anything more than a name. "I'd heard of God, but not Jesus Christ. I'd never heard of the sacrifice, the blood, the redemption, and the grace," he told her. "The Bible I have here at the camp"—Eliot knew Marta had seen it since she'd found him studying it a few mornings in the dining hall—"is one that Juan gave me. That's why it's so old and falling apart."

He shifted on the bench. "Marta, we keep the things in our lives that are important, the people who are most precious. Juan's gone on to glory, but I carry him inside me. I never know where, when, or how people will impact my life, for good or bad. But, like I mentioned before, the Lord walks beside me. I couldn't do what I do without Him."

Marta swallowed hard but didn't look him in the eye.

He lowered his head in shame. "I've disappointed you." Like Liam. Like her father. "I'm sorry, Marta."

She grabbed hold of his hand. "No, Eliot. You haven't disappointed me at all. Everything you've told me only reinforces my feelings for you. But…" Her eyes filled and she lowered her gaze. "You're not the only one who sinned in the flesh, Eliot."

"You owe me no explanations, Marta. That's between you and the Lord."

"I *want* you to know. You weren't a Christian when you did those things, but I was. In my opinion, that makes it so much worse. I knew better. It was a classic case where I felt Liam was slipping away from me and thought I could keep him by giving into his constant pressure. Turns out, he took what he wanted, played me for a fool, and then ran into someone else's wide open arms."

"I'm sorry, Marta. Like I said, Liam was a colossal fool. Your past is just that—the past. You're precious to God, and you are precious to me. You are a woman to be cherished and you can trust me with your heart." He hated that she'd been with a man who'd taken her purity and then mistreated her by sinning with another woman. He hated that he couldn't come to her as a pure man, but life—and Jesus—would give them both a blank slate. Oh, that old blank slate.

Caressing her cheeks with his thumbs, he drew her close and kissed her with all the emotion, all the love, flowing through him for her. "I love you, Marta."

"I love you, too, Eliot. I don't know what's going to happen when we leave New Mexico, but like you said, we'll figure it out, right?" Her eyes were overly bright as she looked up at him.

"Yes," he said. "We will. He'll show us the way." He glanced at his watch. "It's time. I have another surprise for you, and then we'll head back to the camp."

"I'm not sure I ever want this day to end," she said as he helped her to her feet.

"I know the feeling."

A few minutes later, Marta stopped short and stared at him as he talked with the pilot. "Eliot, are we going up in a hot air balloon?"

He grinned. "That's the idea. At twilight, no less." He laughed when she squealed in delight.

"It's like floating on a cloud," she said ten minutes later as their balloon lifted into the sky. She looked over the edge of the basket and then gave him a smile that soared into his heart. "It's like we're the only two people in the universe."

"That would be great if it were true." Walking toward her, Eliot carefully lifted the baseball cap from her head, setting loose her mass of blonde curls. How he loved them.

She laughed and shook out the curls, running her fingers through them. "Know what I have to do now?"

"No," he said, mesmerized. She could stand on her head and recite Thomas Paine's *Common Sense* and he'd be a fool for love.

She began to sing a song. "Would you like to ride…" A light, sappy, bubblegum-type song. The type of corny love song she'd told him she loved. This one seemed to fit the bill, but her enthusiasm was irresistible.

"What are you singing?"

"Up, Up and Away!" She continued to sing in her slightly off-key voice. He must be in love because he found even that unbelievably charming. The song was perfect for an evening balloon ride. The lyrics mentioned a twilight canopy, a guiding star, the moon, sailing along the silver sky…and love waiting in a beautiful balloon. Indeed.

"The world's a nicer place…"

"In my beautiful balloon," he sang with her. He felt like an idiot, but he didn't care. Nothing mattered but being with Marta now and sharing her joy.

Laughing, she launched into his arms.

"Careful," the pilot cautioned. "The gondola's steady, but…"

"We'll be good, Mr. Pilot. Sorry."

"Not a problem, Miss. Carry on." The man winked at Eliot and saluted.

Marta's lashes fluttered and her cheeks were rosy, flushed with love. For him.

"The song talks about holding hands and chasing a dream across the sky. What's *your* dream, Eliot?"

"The rainbow was God's promise to Noah that never again would He destroy the world with floodwaters. Lavender is one of the colors of the rainbow, and I see it every time I look in your eyes, Marta. I see the promise of all we can become."

"Oh, Eliot," she said, leaning her head on his chest. "For a rough, tough, and tumble kind of guy, you say the sweetest things."

He chuckled and tightened his hold on her as the balloon floated through the night sky. The stars sparkled above them, and never had Eliot's heart felt so full. "God, you are amazing in your creation," he murmured.

Tell her. The urge inside him had grown more insistent. Drawing her close, he whispered in her ear. "I'm a Green Beret and work with special reconnaissance and foreign internal defense matters. I also work with the CIA in their Special Activities Division." Quickly and succinctly, Eliot gave her a brief overview of what his assignments could entail. He also told her he'd gone to Princeton and maintained dual citizenship with France and the United States. He could tell she had questions, but she listened quietly and did not interrupt him.

When he was done, Marta moved one hand over her chest, and she breathed heavily. "Why am I not surprised? It sounds very important and, of course, dangerous. But, in a weird way, exciting. I can't believe I'm saying that." She looked up at him with wide eyes.

"It is exciting, but there are days when it's mundane. Trust me. But mundane means things are quiet and at peace. And that's a great place to be. The best place."

"Yes, but again, you could get a call that could change all that in a heartbeat, right?"

He nodded. "Yes. Marta, it's imperative that you tell no one."

"Understood. Now I know why Sam called you in to find Mitch. You were the best man for the job."

Wrapping his arms around the woman with whom he wanted to sail into every tomorrow, Eliot smiled. No matter what tomorrow might bring, they'd always have this beautiful night.

Chapter 38

Day 8, Monday
~~♥~~

"It sure is nice of Lila and Pastor Chevy to offer the use of the church's new laundry facilities." Winnie worked beside Lexa to sort the small mountain of laundry. The washer and dryer had been installed in a side room off the kitchen a few days ago. "I don't know that many churches have a laundry room, of all things, but I imagine it comes in handy."

"We're inaugurating them." Finished sorting the whites, Lexa started a new pile of dark clothes. "I told Lila we could go to a laundromat, but she insisted we use the facilities here." Like everything else, they had a schedule for laundry. Amy and Natalie were coming later in the day. After breakfast, she and Winnie had run to the nearest grocery store to pick up detergents, fabric softeners, and stain remover—enough for their small army.

"The members of the One Nation Church are some of the most generous people I've ever met," Winnie observed. She cast a wary eye on the piles of laundry. "We might as well set up cots. We're going to be here a while."

Lexa nodded. "Agreed, on both counts. At least the washer and dryer are industrial size and can handle large loads. Don't tell anyone else I said this, but it's kind of nice to have some peace and quiet for a few hours." At least a spider bite wasn't contagious. The events of the past few days had made her tired before this new day had even begun.

As they worked, they chatted about the gifts the TeamWork men bought for their wives. Mitch bought a jeweled hair comb, supposedly to show his support for Cassie's shorter haircut, and Landon bought Amy a pair of sapphire earrings.

"Did you see what Kevin gave Beck?" Lexa said as she sorted more clothes. "Yep, we need extra stain remover on that one." She put one of Joe's shirts in a separate pile and picked up one of Sam's shirts. "Whew. Sam must have really worked hard when he wore this one."

Winnie laughed. "Same for this shirt of Josh's. And yes, Beck showed me the baby blankets. They're very sweet. Leave it to my thoughtful brother-in-law. Who knew baby blankets came in cashmere? Beck said Kevin wants to get them embroidered with the babies' names once they arrive." She shrugged. "If you can even embroider on cashmere. What do I know?"

"I couldn't be more thrilled for them," Lexa said. "Marc got Natalie a necklace similar to the one Sam got for me with the kids' birthstones, including the little girl in China and the new baby." She finished sorting and reached for the stain remover bottle. "Seems all our guys thought of jewelry."

"Works for me. That's not all Josh bought for me, though."

Lexa looked over at Winnie as she rubbed stain remover into a pesky stain on the knee of Joe's jeans. "I know. Sam and Josh went into that lingerie store together."

Winnie pushed one pile of clothes aside and started on another. "Josh got this beautiful, expensive, green satin nightgown for me. Then he made this whole beautiful speech about how he knew I felt less than desirable because I haven't lost the baby weight. How he loves every part of me—"

"And?" This was one of those times Lexa needed to keep her best friend focused.

Winnie met her gaze as they both continued to work. "Have you ever *worn* satin, Lexa? That fabric has absolutely no stretch or give. So, here's my loving, gorgeous husband giving me this lovely gift that I can't possibly begin to wear. Thank goodness we're not sleeping in the same quarters right now—believe me, I can't believe I'm saying that—but if we shared a bed, he would have expected me to put it on that night."

"And?" Lexa asked again, hoping Winnie didn't find her prompts obnoxious. She had a feeling where this story was going.

"I peeked at the tag. He thought he was buying it larger than my regular size, and it's two sizes too *small!* It was all I could do not to cry right then and there, but I managed to hold it together until Josh left. Then the kids came in. No time for tears when you're a mom, right?"

Reaching across the table, Lexa squeezed Winnie's arm. "You're a beautiful woman, Winnie, and your weight doesn't dictate who you are, or how treasured you are in the eyes of your husband. Sam said the sweetest thing to me the other night about how the Lord made him for me, and me for him. The same goes for you and Josh."

"I know, but I still feel like such a cow right now." Realizing she'd made a rhyme, Winnie laughed and wiped away a few quick tears. "I find it so ironically sweet that he thought he'd given me a nightgown that would make me feel pretty, and then it ended up having the opposite effect."

"Why don't we take a trip to the mall when we get back home?" Lexa suggested. "Let's see if we can exchange the nightgown for another size."

Winnie smiled at her through watery eyes. "I had the same thought," she said, heaving a deep sigh. "In my mind, I like to believe the guys are pining away for us while we're here. This is probably silly, but maybe Sam should add another marriage rule about going on a mission trip every now and then and sleeping in separate quarters."

Lexa nodded. "It's not silly at all, and I'll mention it to him."

Winnie picked up one of Luke's T-shirts and frowned. "How much stain remover did we buy? I'm going to use half the bottle on my son's clothes alone. What is it about camp that presents such unique laundry challenges?"

"There's a whole new world of opportunity here," Lexa said. "But I think Joe manages to get in just as much dirt back home."

"Josh said it was Sam's suggestion that the guys go to the mall. I think it was inspired."

"I have an idea why Sam suggested the men go shopping for us," Lexa said.

"Oh? What's that?" Picking up a pair of Luke's pants, Winnie shook her head.

"A woman at the board meeting openly admired Sam. It's not like I haven't seen other women eyeing my husband, Winnie, but this time it got to me."

Winnie stopped sorting her kids' clothes. "Did she say or do something to get Sam's attention?"

"She came over and greeted him at the meeting. She's the type of woman who commands attention. I think I was bothered because she acted so familiar with Sam. She'd paid a visit to the church earlier in the week and met my husband and Marc."

Winnie wiped the back of her hand over her brow. "Let me guess. She's tall, ridiculously thin, and beautiful."

"Pretty much. She didn't smile much but it was a business meeting, after all. I'll admit I felt frumpy by comparison, especially after the whole white hair episode recently. This woman seemed so put together and confident. You know the type. She exudes sensuality, and I know men are drawn to that whether they want to be or not. Sitting there with her in that meeting, the door was opened and my insecurities peeked out." Lexa frowned. "Insecurities that have been dormant until now, I guess."

Winnie giggled. "Did you say peed out?"

Lexa balled up a pair of shorts and aimed them at her friend. "You're silly."

"Did this woman act familiar with Josh and Eliot as well?" Although Winnie busied herself with her family's laundry again, Lexa sensed the underlying edge in her question. Seemed she wasn't the only one with a few lingering insecurities that surfaced every now and then.

"Not really. Sam introduced Josh, but she made it a point to meet Eliot. The guys were all great. Marta and I were the ones who didn't handle it so well."

Winnie glanced up at her again. "How did Marta react?"

"Marta and I discussed her. As I told her, it's been my experience that a woman who acts like that must be missing something in her own life. There's a void she's looking to fill. Then I told Marta we were giving her too much power. Not that it's a game."

"In a way, it kind of is. We can't be naïve, and we need to keep our eyes open. Men think they're the protectors, and they are. But sometimes we need to protect our men, too. You know?" With a frown, Winnie tossed one of Josh's shirts on the table. "Some women make it a game to try and tempt men, especially married ones. When Josh and I went to that marriage seminar last year, I could barely restrain my frustration when the woman told us how we needed to hold onto our husband because—guaranteed—there would always be another woman right around the corner who'd want him. As if I need to be reminded. Sorry, I got off track there."

"Turns out, you're on the right track," Lexa said. "You met the woman in question after the church service yesterday morning."

Winnie glanced up at her from where she was measuring detergent into the washer. "Wait a minute. Stephanie Colton?"

"None other. Turns out Sam had a package sent to her of TeamWork materials. She received it when she returned to her office on Friday afternoon after the City Council hearing."

"Well, that's interesting." Winnie began loading clothes into the washer. "Did you talk with Sam about her?" Finished with her task, Winnie came back to the table and began checking pockets in the next load to be washed.

"I think he has some kind of radar. He picked up on my feelings at the hearing and reassured me. Then he asked me the other day if we needed to discuss her, but I put him off. I told Sam that Stephanie showed up at the church service and what we'd discussed. So, after thinking that the City Council hearing might have been an exercise in futility, the way I see it now? If it ultimately might bring one more person to faith in Christ, it was all worth it. And if not? Well, I'm sure the Lord had a reason. He always does."

"Amen," Winnie said with finality, pulling a pen out of the pocket of Josh's shorts. "This could have caused some damage. That statement has nothing to do with my next question, but why do you think Sam sent that package to Stephanie?"

"Because that's my husband. He's planting more seeds. You know Sam. He had Bennie in the TeamWork office send her a Bible along with the TeamWork materials. He must have taken care of it right after he first met Stephanie out at the worksite. You ask me, it's another example of how God works. Instead of acting jealous or insecure, I need to pray for that woman. As Eliot would say, 'Everything according to His purpose.'"

When she looked over at Winnie, her friend held a business card in her hand. "I found this card in the pocket of Josh's jeans." Her blue eyes met Lexa's. "The same jeans he had on when they went to the mall on Saturday afternoon, if I'm not mistaken."

Lexa was almost afraid to ask the next question. Winnie's face had grown slightly pale. "Are you okay?"

"I'm not sure," Winnie said slowly, rotating the card between her fingers. "Why do you suppose Josh would have a card from a woman named Victoria Brighton?"

"Not a clue. Does it have a business listed?"

Winnie glanced at the card. "Says she's an image consultant. Lives here in Albuquerque." She sniffed the card. "Smells like it was spritzed with perfume like those sample cards they give out at the cosmetic counter at the department store. Smells…pretty. Tall. Thin."

"Please don't read anything into it, Winnie. Ask your husband." She didn't mean to sound harsh, but neither did she want Winnie's insecurities to escalate. "I'm sure Josh collects lots of cards from all kinds of people, both men and women. If you ask him, I'm sure he'll put your mind at ease."

Winnie tucked the card in the pocket of her shorts. "I hope so. I'll ask him tonight."

Lexa heard a knock on the outside door of their quarters. "Lexa, are you in here?"

"Come on in, Amy. Be forewarned that I might put you to work folding laundry." She'd sorted the clothing by family members but the piles were growing higher by the second. She hoped Sam would be up to giving her a back rub tonight because she could sure use one. Maybe even a combined back and foot rub, but that might be pushing it. He'd probably remind her he was still recovering although he felt well enough to work at the church again.

As Amy stepped inside, Lexa gave her a smile. "Feeling okay?" Ever since Beck's scare, she'd been extra mindful of the expectant TeamWork mothers.

"Other than cravings for salty and sweet foods and everything else fattening or bad for me, I'm fine. I almost made Landon go out and get me some potato chips in the middle of the night."

"I know you still need to go to the doctor to confirm your pregnancy, but do you have any idea when you might be due?"

"About the same time as Beck, I believe. I'll call you when I get home and have my appointment. May I?" Amy gestured to the edge of the bed. "Give me a stack to fold."

"Sit," Lexa said. "I'll never turn down good help. You can fold the girls' things, if you don't mind."

"Sounds good. Hand them over." Amy waited while Lexa sorted through some clothes and then transferred a pile to her. "I wanted to tell you about an interesting fiction proposal I received earlier this week."

Lexa lowered her gaze and picked up one of Sam's T-shirts. "Oh?"

"I wanted to run it by you and get your opinion. You read Christian romance, right?"

"Some, but not a lot. They relax me when I crawl into bed at the end of a long day. But it has to keep me entertained or I'm asleep in minutes."

"I understand. I feel the same way although I'm more prone to mysteries and Landon likes thrillers." Amy was proficient at folding and made quick work of her task. "As the acquisitions editor for LCJW Publishing, Landon gives me full authority to issue author contracts. As you know, up until now, we haven't contracted any fiction. We've focused on a certain marriage and family life author who's become extremely popular and is our bestselling author."

Lexa met Amy's gaze. "Sometimes I still can't believe Sam's had such success. Not that I don't believe in him, but I know what a competitive market it is. I know Landon's talking with Sam about another book tour when his new book comes out."

"That's right. I'd thought the book was going to be co-authored by you, Lexa. Not that I'm disappointed. Sam's new book is great, but you have so much to share as a mentor for the TeamWork ladies that I'd hoped to see your name on it, too."

"I'd love to co-author a book with him, but there have been so many other things to do." Lexa tucked the folded stack of Sam's T-shirts in one of the top dresser drawers.

"I'm sure. Let me tell you a little more about this manuscript query I received."

Lexa slowly exhaled. "Isn't that against some publishing rule? Should you really be telling me about it?"

"Between friends, in confidence, I wanted to get your opinion since you'd be in our target audience for a project like this."

"I see." Amy was teasing her and she'd make her point soon enough.

Shifting on the bed, Amy motioned to the stack of Joe's clothes. "Hand me some more. I can tackle them."

"I guess so. You're like the folding Nazi." Lexa managed a small smile even though her heart was beating overtime. Why was she nervous? She really had no reason. This day just kept getting more interesting by the hour.

"Get this. The name of this proposed book is *Alliance*, and the hero's name is Seth Lawson. Tall, dark, and handsome. He leads a missions group overseas and meets this petite, feisty, blonde woman named Leslie Carlson. He's a strong Christian but she's not. Leslie doesn't really understand what she signed up for, and Seth doesn't know what's hit him until she arrives. She challenges him, and they each discover God's purpose for their own lives as they forge a relationship together." Amy paused and looked over at her. "How am I doing so far?"

"Well, the author has to be careful to make Leslie sympathetic and not make—Seth, is it?—too perfect. And there should be humor to balance out the conflicts, of course. With that touch of fairytale whimsy. Goes without saying there should be lots of romance."

"Exactly," Amy said. "They fight their initial attraction but can't help flirting like crazy. He's been burned by love and is afraid to trust a woman again. She's been abandoned by men her whole life and is afraid every man will eventually leave her. They have all kinds of adventures in the Congo and almost get killed in the end. Want to guess what happens?"

"Oh, I don't know." Lexa paused in her work. This was fun in a nutty kind of way. "I'm guessing they don't die since you'll want a happily ever after ending in a romance. Maybe Seth goes off on a year-long mission trip and Leslie doesn't know if he'll return. He asks her to meet him a year later at the top of the Empire State Building, and if they both show up—"

Amy shook her head. "No. That's too cliché. That's already been done in *An Affair to Remember* and to a lesser extent in *Sleepless in Seattle*." Looking up at her, Amy held her gaze. "Not that it couldn't work given the right author and characters." Smart Amy. She never missed anything.

I've been found out.

"A year later, she's waiting for him at their agreed meeting place," Lexa said. "Will he be there? She hasn't heard from him, doesn't know if he's alive or dead. Cue the music." She grinned when Amy laughed. "Then the elevator doors open, and there's Seth. More handsome than ever. With a great tan, a few more silver hairs, and seems even taller than before. He has flowers for her, and maybe even has local children hand them to her as she waits, building the anticipation."

"Yellow roses might be nice." How Amy said that with a straight face was quite the feat.

"Sounds good to me," Lexa said. "Then Seth and Leslie pledge their undying love to one another, share a passionate kiss, and...fade to black. The end."

"Oh, that's not the end. They might even run off and get married that same night. Their adventures are only just beginning since it'll be a series, most likely."

Lexa met Amy's gaze. "It could be, yes."

Amy was really drawing this out. From the coy grin on her face, she was taking great amusement in their exchange. "I can tell this author has a fresh voice. Since I received the query, I've done some thinking and decided that a contemporary Christian romance line would be a very wise move for LCJW Publishing. Romances sell well, they're usually in high demand, and as I said, it has the potential to be a series. Readers love series, don't you agree?"

Lexa ran Joe's clothes into the adjacent room and then came back a few seconds later. "Personally? Yes, I like them, but I prefer it when there are different main characters in each book. The main characters can show up every now and then but not to the point of becoming annoying. But I have no idea what most readers like, Amy. That's just me. So, um, is Landon agreeable to publishing romances?"

"Done." Amy patted her hand on the stack of Joe's clothes.

"Thanks so much. You're a doll for helping me." Lexa grabbed the stack and darted back into the other room with them.

"I like to multitask," Amy said. "It helps me to be more productive in the long run. Now Landon? He's very logical, like most men. But he trusts my judgment implicitly. We both believe in building a solid reputation with consistent, reliable authors for LCJW Publishing. If this contemporary Christian romance manuscript is as fabulous as the query and the proposal, then I think this romance author might be a hidden treasure."

Amy rose from the bed. "I'd better get back to the kids. By the way, didn't you tell me you used to write stories?"

When had she said anything about that? "I did. Once upon a time, as they say."

"Written anything lately?"

Lexa glanced up from where she worked on the last of the laundry. Seeing Amy's smile, she relented. Might as well confess. "H.L. Joseph stands for Hannah, Leah, Joseph."

"I figured as much. Works for me. Send me the entire manuscript by e-mail as soon as you can."

"Thanks, Amy. I'll do that."

Chapter 39

~~♥~~

Sitting on the porch of their quarters shortly after the devotions, Sam finished the last of his peach. He wasn't planning on going back over to the church tonight. Pastor Chevy had called to tell him to give his troops a break and the late evening, post prayer circle work sessions were no longer needed.

Lost in thought, Sam looked up to see Angelina and Felipe walking slowly toward the building. They both looked scared to death. He had a feeling why they were here. He rolled the remains of the peach in a napkin and then wiped his mouth with the back of his hand.

"Mama told me you wanted to speak with us," Angelina said as they stepped onto the porch. More like Sheila asked him to talk to these two about the dangers of getting too close physically.

"That's right. Your mother, Dean, and I thought it might be good to talk about a few things."

Felipe shifted from one foot to the other and his expression was a study in aggravation. "Sam, I give you my word, we've done nothing we should be ashamed for. I haven't even kissed Angel much less anything else. I already told Mrs. Morris and Dean."

Sam nodded. "I'll take your word for it, son. Not that you haven't wanted to, I'm sure. On both your parts." His gaze encompassed them both, and—as he expected—they avoided looking at him.

"Let's go somewhere and talk privately. Lexa's giving the kids their baths inside. How about we take a walk?" He led the way and the young people walked silently on either side of him. "Let's check the dorms. I have no idea where everyone is tonight." The camp seemed unusually quiet. Suspiciously so.

"I think some of them are practicing or getting ready for the talent show tomorrow night," Angelina said.

"Ah, that makes sense." He needed to listen to the CD himself.

Later, he'd sneak over to the dining hall and quietly go over the two songs he planned to sing.

"Why don't we go over to the men's dorm and see if it's empty." A few seconds later, they reached the gray concrete structure that served as the quarters for the men. Opening the door, Sam thought he heard muffled sounds. "Hold on a minute," he said, stepping inside. As his eyes adjusted to the dim light, Sam's eyes widened and then he turned aside. *Marc and Natalie.* Quickly stepping back over the threshold, he closed the door quietly behind him and shook his head. "On second thought, let's try the women's dorm." He gestured for them to follow.

"Better let me go first," Sam muttered, opening the door and hearing it creak in protest. He heard a whole lot of scrambling before Sam spotted two more of his volunteers. *Landon and Amy.* "This isn't happening," Sam said under his breath, only praying Felipe and Angel hadn't gotten a peek. That wouldn't help his cause at the moment.

Back outside, Sam moved his hands to his hips. "Dining hall," he said, pointing and taking off in the opposite direction. No sooner had he opened the door than he heard a pan fall in the kitchen followed by muffled laughter. That was definitely Winnie's giggle. And Josh's laugh.

"I do believe I'm here with a bunch of uncontrolled primates," Sam groused, pushing the door back open and walking to the back of the dining hall toward the massive tree out back. Stopping about 50 yards out, he heard low murmurs and yet more laughter.

Groaning with frustration, Sam raked a hand through his hair. As he contemplated where else he could go other than the facilities— he only prayed no one was in there—Sam spied Kevin as he leaned around the tree trunk. Sam supposed he should thank the Lord he was clothed.

"Hey, Sam. If you need me, just give me a second." Sam heard Beck's laughter.

"And *he's* the quiet one!" Sam muttered. Felipe and Angelina both laughed like they were about to bust a gut. What fine examples his TeamWork crew proved to be tonight.

"You don't happen to know where Mitch and Cassie are, do you?"

"They're having their Bible study," Beck called from behind the tree. "Dean and Sheila are with them. They're out under one of the big trees on the far side of the camp."

"Good for the newlyweds in the group. At least some of my crew has a sense of propriety around here." Turning on his heel, Sam stomped back toward the teepee in the middle of the camp. "Anyone in here?" Eliot and Marta weren't accounted for yet. He lifted the corner of the flap. The teepee was lit with a few battery-operated lamps.

"Hey, Sam." Eliot gave him a bright smile. "Want to join us? We're working on some props for the talent show."

"Glad to see you're such a versatile guy."

"Winnie bribed us with some of her homemade brownies." Marta held up a large red paper heart for his approval. "Eliot's still on security duty, so we figured we might as well work out here."

Sam grunted. As much as anyone, Eliot could be counted on if something were to happen. "Carry on. You two have earned your homemade craft badges. Just leave the flap open, if you don't mind." What a weird sentence.

"Not a problem," Eliot said. He broke out in a wide smile and raised his hand when he spied the teenagers with him. "Hey, Angelina. Hey, Felipe." While they talked for a minute, Sam's mind whirled with ideas of where he could take the kids to have their little chat. What a situation, and one he never expected.

"Let's go back over to our quarters," he said. "Lexa should be finished giving the kids a bath." They probably should have stayed there in the first place.

Behind him, Sam heard Felipe mutter something about Mr. Lewis getting bit by the Grumpy Spider. That spider sure was getting a lot of credit.

Waiting until morning to address the issue of his crew's behavior wouldn't do. He needed to talk with them tonight. After Sam called an emergency meeting, Lexa enlisted Felipe and Angelina to supervise the kids in Winnie and Natalie's quarters.

Sam waited in the kitchen, leaning back against the sink while they filed in, two by two. How appropriate. Kevin and Beck refused to look at him. Landon and Amy gave him wide grins. Marc winked at him and Natalie avoided his gaze. When Josh and Winnie came in a couple of minutes later, they were ready to begin.

He moved his gaze from one offender to the next as they gathered around the preparation table in the kitchen. It didn't help that Lexa was clearly trying not to smile. While he understood her amusement to a point, his team needed to understand he considered their earlier amorous behavior very inappropriate.

"Okay, crew. I'm sure you know why I've called this meeting." Sam crossed his arms. "Imagine my consternation this evening when I was trying to find a place to counsel two teenagers about..."

"The facts of life? The birds and the bees?" Amy looked the other way and drummed her fingers on the steel table. Several of his crew made bird-like tweets while others of them made buzzing noises.

"You're not teenagers, but you sure are acting like it," Sam growled. "Have I taught you all nothing? I've heard things today, and seen a few things, that I really wish I hadn't." At that, the women hung their heads, but the men watched Sam with obvious amusement.

"We're here to work a mission, but it seems you're all more interested in other more...primal needs. I can't believe we need to have this discussion. Look," he said, raising his hands, "I know you're all married people and you're free to indulge your passion for your mates. However, for the duration of our time here in New Mexico, I'm asking you to please handle yourselves with more decorum."

"Come on, Sam," Marc said. "We're enjoying healthy relationships with our wives. We're all good friends here, and we were indulging in a natural expression of our love." He paused while some of the others snickered. "It's what you encourage all the time."

Sam ignored their laughter. "And you're an advertising man. I would have expected less cornball from you."

"I'm going out on a limb here, but you seem a little tense. I can suggest a remedy," Josh said.

"I can appreciate that, but there's a difference between relationships and relations, if you catch my drift."

"Oh, I think that we do," Josh said. "We miss our wives, Sam. It's as simple as that."

"We prefer to think you're pining away for us." Winnie laughed and Josh kissed her cheek.

"Can you not abstain for two weeks?" Sam said.

"Have you?"

Natalie swatted Marc's arm for asking that question. "Marc! That's none of our business." No wonder Gracie punched Joe. She'd learned by example.

Sam didn't dare look at Lexa. "Lexa and I have private quarters. What we do—"

"If I may point out, none of the kids were around and we were in private," Marc said. "Or at least we were until you came barging in the door."

"I didn't barge in, but why should I announce my arrival? Marc, it seems you're the self-appointed spokesperson for this group."

"They know I'm not embarrassed and will speak up for our rights as TeamWork volunteers."

"Your *rights?*" Sam frowned. "Never mind. Tell you what. If you can't control yourselves, I give you permission to go off to a hotel for a night." He shot a glance at Landon. "Or borrow the plane for a few hours. Just make sure you let me know."

"We'll be good, Sam." Kevin winked at Rebekah.

"I think that Frisky Spider made its way around the camp," Marc said, and they all laughed, including Lexa. Bunch of ingrates. Lexa must have said something to Natalie about that silly Frisky Spider nickname. Like it or not, what was done was done. Time to get on with it.

"Sam, your idea for the guys to give us gifts was great," Winnie said. "But I think it might have put other ideas in our heads. Not that we're pointing fingers or placing blame because that wouldn't be right. We got a little carried away, and we're sorry."

The others mumbled their assent with Winnie's statement.

"We didn't mean to add to your…consternation." Of course, that comment came from Marc.

"Unequivocally, completely, totally sorry, Sam," Landon said.

Sam waved his hand. "No, you're not." He couldn't help it and burst out laughing from the absurdity of it all. "Get out of here, all of you! Let's not have this discussion again."

"Try not to be too hard on them, Sam. None of them have been married as long as we have." Lexa walked beside him, hand in hand, on their way back to their quarters. The kids ran ahead of them and the front door slammed as they entered the building. "It's been a little tense with the uncertainty of the evil eye symbol, the City Council hearing, and then those guys coming into the camp. I think there's an air of uneasiness, as if we're all waiting to see what else might happen. We're hoping nothing will, but we're half expecting that it might."

"I know," Sam said, "but it's the principle of the thing."

Lexa tugged on his hand. Stopping, he turned to her. "If we didn't have private quarters, and if you knew we couldn't have any privacy tonight, would you want to kiss me right now?"

"That's not a valid question, Lexa. I always want to kiss you."

"Good answer, but how about an experiment?"

"Nothing doing."

"You didn't even listen to my idea."

"I can just imagine, and it's the most harebrained idea you've ever entertained. I think you've been bit by the Crazy Spider."

"Forget I'm even there tonight." Seemed his wife was determined to have her say.

Stubborn is as stubborn does. "Impossible," he growled. "In that case, why don't we switch places with one of our couples and offer them our bed for the night, and then we can go sleep in the dorms?" That last part came out more sarcastic than he intended, but Lexa appeared rather amused.

"I don't think that's necessary," she said, laughing.

"This isn't funny. I'm already disgruntled enough. I want you there with me. You know that." He blew out a sigh of frustration. If she persisted, he'd negotiate with her once they were inside and see if he could wear down her resistance.

Lexa began walking. "I didn't get a chance to ask how your talk went with Angelina and Felipe."

"As well as could be expected. I asked Felipe to work with me one-on-one at the church in the morning. Dean tells me he's good at doing touch-up painting, and we still need it in a few places. I'm going to see if he has any questions, ask him how things are going with Dean, and generally spend some quality time with him."

She nodded. "I think that's a great idea."

"Me too, baby." Lexa liked it when he called her baby, so hopefully that would give him some leverage.

Sam stood on the porch of his quarters, arms crossed on the

railing, as Dean rounded the corner on his way back to the men's dorm.

"Evening, Sam."

"How are you, Dean?"

"Very well, thanks. I just said good night to Sheila." Dean joined him at the railing. "She's a wonderful woman."

"Without a doubt."

Like Sam, Dean crossed his arms on the railing and stared out over the expanse of the camp. All was quiet except for an occasional rustling from a small animal or the wind in the trees. "Overall, I'd say the mission has gone well in terms of building the church and developing good relations between One Nation and TeamWork, wouldn't you?"

"It has," Sam said.

Dean glanced over at the other man. "Everything okay, Sam?" The TeamWork director was usually more jovial, but tonight he seemed unusually quiet.

"Nothing that tomorrow won't make better. Any update on the situation we talked about before the trip?"

"The case of the embezzling manager? Nope. Nothing since our last discussion. According to my high-priced lawyer, I've got to get some kind of evidence on the guy. Innocent until proven guilty or until he steals me blind, I guess." He frowned and ran a hand over his brow. "The guy's definitely moving money out of the company accounts into his own, but I need to find a way to prove it."

"Have you talked to a fraud or security expert?"

"That's next on my list once I get back home. Marc gave me a name of one of the best forensic accountants in the country."

Sam quirked a brow. "Marc hasn't had any similar problems in his agency, has he? He hasn't mentioned anything."

"No. Marc just knows a lot of people and has far-reaching contacts."

"True enough." Sam regarded him for a long moment. "Considering the circumstances, thanks for your commitment to TeamWork and coming here, Dean. I know your stores are your top priority, and we have to believe this situation will work out for the Lord's glory. Keep me posted on what's happening once you get back to San Antonio." Sam cracked a grin. "Pretty amazing about Sheila's skill with a bow and arrow. You can't make up a story like that."

"It was one of the most amazing things I've ever seen. Another interesting thing is that she didn't stutter much at all when she was confronting those guys. I thought the cause of stuttering was fear, but in Sheila's case, it seems to be the opposite. She became emboldened and fearless. I guess we never know how we'll react until faced with certain situations," Dean said.

"I take it the dinner went well?"

"I consider it a personal victory that Sheila took seconds. As far as the stuttering, you're right in that it runs in her family Sheila's been deeply wounded, but she's strong. In spite of the circumstances, she's risen above the obstacles and made a good life for her and Angelina. I admire her strength and resilience."

"Agreed. You're a good man, Dean."

"Coming from you, that's high praise."

"Coming from me?" Sam lowered his head, but Dean heard his quiet chuckle.

"Our leader, the head honcho, the big cheese."

"My kids would say I'm the big stinky cheese." They shared a grin. "There's an awful lot of people on the Leather payroll who would say the same about you, my friend," Sam said. "I'll be praying that you'll find a quick resolution for the embezzlement issue, and for your growing friendship with Sheila."

"I'm going to marry that woman, Sam."

Sam held his gaze and then slowly nodded. Somehow, he didn't seem surprised. "Feel like praying about it?"

"Sure. Sounds like the right thing to do." And so, with Sam beside him, Dean prayed.

Lexa yawned as she climbed into bed. Sam sat in a chair with a book opened on his lap. She could tell he was disgruntled by that ridiculous conversation they'd shared. So was she. "Tell me a bedtime story, Sam. Just don't be offended if I doze off somewhere in the middle."

He closed the book he was pretending to read. "Okay, since you asked. I did a little research the other day on the history of my favorite fruit."

For a moment, she stared at him. "All right."

"Daddy?" Leah and Hannah both stood in the doorway separating the two bedrooms.

Sam put aside his book. "What's wrong, girls? Can't sleep?" Leah scampered across the floor and Sam pulled her onto his lap while Hannah scooted over to the bed with her. "I was just about to tell your mother a bedtime story about peaches."

"I think the condensed version is best," Lexa suggested.

"The peach came to America by Spanish explorers in the 16th century," he said, tapping Leah on the nose. "And to England and France in the 17th century where it was a prized, but rare, treat."

"Treat!" Leah said, clapping her hands together.

"Daddy wants peaches?" Hannah asked, sliding down from the bed. That had to be a record for a bedtime story. If he'd continued much longer, she would have been asleep within the minute.

"Now?" Lexa frowned at Sam. "Didn't you have one after dinner?"

He shrugged. "Sounds like a great bedtime snack. A man can never have enough peaches."

She shook her head. "Only you." Climbing out of the bed, Lexa shrugged into her robe. "Okay, girls. Put on your house slippers and let's go over to the kitchen."

Five minutes later, she gave them cups of water and then the girls each selected a peach for their father. As they prepared to leave, Lexa felt a tug on her robe and leaned over so she was eye-level with her daughter. "Yes, Hannah Banana?"

Reaching for her, Hannah took hold of her face between her two little hands. "You're pretty, Mommy."

"Thank you, sweetie." She needed that compliment considering she wasn't feeling like the best wife at the moment.

Hannah giggled. "Daddy says you're the prettiest lady in the whole world. He loves you verrrry berrry much!" Lexa smiled, loving how her daughter liked to use that expression.

"Yep." Leah stretched her arms wide. "This big!"

"He does, huh?"

Both girls' heads bobbed up and down in tandem as quick tears filled Lexa's eyes. *These* were the moments of life.

"Well, I happen to think your daddy's the most handsome man in the whole world."

Giggling, the twins skipped out of the kitchen into the quiet of the night. "Come on!" Leah called to her. "Daddy needs his peaches."

"Coming." Turning off the lights, Lexa followed behind them.

"So, finish telling me the rest of your story," she said to Sam once the girls were settled in their beds again. He'd changed into his shorts and T-shirt, legs propped on the edge of the bed. He was eating a peach with an amused expression. He was waiting her out, waiting to see which one of them could outlast the other.

"Maybe I'll save it for another night." He took another bite of his peach. "Hmm. This one sure is succulent."

She smiled. "No, no. I'm waiting with bated breath to hear it tonight."

"Very well then. To recap, the peach was cultivated in China where it was the favorite fruit of the emperors. It was passed from the Persians to the Romans, brought to America by Spanish explorers in the 16th century, and then to England and France in the 17th century where it was a prized, but rare, treat." Sam laughed as he caught her expression.

"Not to mention it was reportedly brought to the United States from England by a horticulturist named George Minifie in the early 17th century who planted them on his Virginia estate. And finally," he said, "it was the American Indian tribes, don't you know, who are credited with spreading the peach tree across the country, spreading seeds as they traveled."

"Sam, I wasn't trying to tease or punish you."

"I know that. You were trying to make a point." Wiping his mouth with the back of his hand, he aimed and tossed the peach pit in the trash can. As usual, the man had precise aim. "You made it."

Giving him a smile, Lexa plucked a tissue from the box on the table and waved it.

Turning off the light, Sam grinned and slid in beside her, bringing the sheet up over both of them. "I thought you'd never ask."

Chapter 40
Day 9, Tuesday
~~ ♥ ~~

Sitting in the kitchen, sipping coffee, Lexa yawned. She needed to get moving but felt sluggish this morning. She glanced at the ancient wall clock. Five o'clock.

"Hey, partner." Winnie stepped inside the back door, closing it carefully so it didn't slam behind her.

"Morning. Let me get you some coffee." Lexa started to slide down from the stool.

"Stay put. I'll get it. How's Sam feeling this morning?"

"Much better, thanks. What a crazy few days, huh?"

"I'll say."

A minute later, Winnie settled on a stool across from her. She curled her hands around the coffee cup. "Based on our behavior last night, I'm sure it's obvious that Josh and I are fine. I asked him about the business card. As I suspected, he said Victoria was one of the women from his past. I can't explain it, Lexa, but I *knew*. I think the Lord gives wives intuition about things like that, don't you?"

"Perhaps." Lexa sipped more coffee.

"He said Sam saw her drop a business card into Josh's bag. I don't even want to think about how that card got into Josh's pocket without him knowing."

"I agree. Let's not speculate on that one."

Winnie took a tentative sip of her coffee and then blew on it a little. "I don't believe there are any chance meetings. There's a reason why Josh ran into Victoria in that mall. In the back of my mind, I always knew the day would come when he'd run smack into his past. I guess I just didn't expect it to be here."

As close as she was with Winnie, Lexa wasn't sure what to say.

"God doesn't discriminate, and I think He uses situations like this to teach us a lesson."

"I'm sure you're right," Lexa said.

Winnie eyed her curiously as she took a drink of her coffee. "You're being awfully cryptic this morning."

"Sorry. I'm just tired."

"You're not—?"

Lexa's eyes widened and she sputtered. "Of course not! Don't even go there. Your first clue should be the fact that I'm drinking coffee. Have you ever known me to drink caffeine when I'm expecting? Or even suspect I'm pregnant?"

"Good point." Taking another drink, Winnie shifted. "As far as Josh, he said that he witnessed to Victoria in the middle of the mall. You don't know how I would have loved to hear that conversation."

Lexa smiled. "Oh, I can imagine."

"We talked about it a little, and Josh said something that I found really interesting."

"Tell me, and then we'd better get started on the breakfast."

"He believes God uses something like this not so much to remind him of his past sins, but to remind him of his blessings now."

"I like that reasoning. Like Eliot's catchphrase of 'Everything according to His purpose.' I'm happy to know that everything's fine between you two." Reaching across the table, Lexa squeezed Winnie's hand.

"Couldn't be better. How about you and Sam?"

Lexa smiled as she finished her coffee and hopped down from the kitchen stool. "Let's just say he should be a lot less grumpy this morning."

"Angel told me you write books about family and stuff."

Felipe's comment made Sam smile. "You could say that."

"That's awesome, man. I didn't know that."

"You interested in writing?"

"Yeah." Felipe concentrated on painting the trim around the door frame of the church office.

That surprised him in a good way. "Does 'kinda' mean you've tried to write or you want to try it sometime?"

Felipe laughed. "Both. I've tried, but I stunk up the joint with it."

"I doubt that," Sam said. "You couldn't stink any more than I did when I first tried to write. It's like learning to walk or ride a bike or anything else. One foot in front of the other and you keep going until you can keep your balance, or—in the case of writing a book— until your words make sense. What kind of books are you interested in writing?"

"Something to give kids in bad situations hope that there's something out there that's better."

"If you've lived through some bad things, then you'd be well-qualified to write about them. Taking what we've learned from the not-so-good things in our lives to help others is an admirable thing. If it's a diatribe about everything that's gone wrong in your life and focuses on the blame game, then it's only self-serving."

Felipe stopped painting. "Sorry, Mr. Lewis, but you lost me. First off, what does diatribe mean?"

"Sorry." He hadn't worked with a lot of teenagers lately. "A diatribe is like a rant. It's something someone either says or writes that's angry and full of bitterness. If the purpose is to blame someone else for their problems, then it comes across as selfish."

"Why is it selfish?"

Felipe asked good questions. "Because it's not trying to help someone else. The way I see it, one of the best ways to help people is by uplifting them."

"You're talking about making them feel good about themselves, right?"

Sam nodded and dipped his paintbrush in the small can of white paint. "Right. In my case, I share insights about how God is working in my life, and the ways in which He accomplishes His purpose through different situations."

"Okay, then. I've got a big question for you."

"Sure. Lay it on me."

Felipe grinned but kept painting. "How come God gives some people good families and others…well, not so good?"

"It's not God's punishment if you don't have the best home situation, Felipe. Strong people don't allow the bad things in their lives to stifle them, and I can tell you're strong. I'm sorry life's handed you some curveballs, but you're better than those situations. Grow from them and rise above your circumstances. In other words, don't let them drag you down to their level. Take what you can learn from them, do the best you can, and then move forward."

The boy's shoulders slumped. "Kind of hard to do sometimes."

Sam put down his paintbrush and Felipe did the same. "I'm sure you have some feelings of resentment." When Felipe looked up at him in surprise, Sam put one hand on his shoulder and squeezed. "It's not wrong to feel that way, but in order to overcome them, you need to accept and forgive your parents. Do you think you can do that?"

"I don't know, man."

"I'm sure you don't want to end up like either one of them."

"You know the worst part isn't that my mom does drugs or that my dad's in jail."

"What's the worst part?" This kid had been through so much.

He could see Felipe swallowed hard. "They, uh, weren't there for me when I really needed them, even when I was little." His dark eyes were bright. Blinking hard, he stared at the wall. "You and Mrs. Lewis are always doing stuff with your kids. You play with them, you sit with them at dinner, you talk to them, and you listen when they ask you something. I'm sure you tuck them in bed at night and read them stories. And take care of them if they have a bad dream or need to go to the bathroom in the middle of the night."

Sam's heart swelled with compassion for this boy. "You never had any of that with your parents?"

"Nope. Maybe a few times."

"Felipe, who did those things for you?"

"There was an old neighbor lady, Mrs. King. She was pretty nice. But I learned real quick how to do things for myself." He finally moved his gaze to Sam's. "When your mother tells you that you were a mistake, you learn how to take care of yourself."

"I'm very sorry, son. You're even stronger than I thought." Sam cleared his throat. "I happen to think that Dean's a fine man. I'm thankful you're with him now."

"Why? Because he took me in when no one else would? I appreciate that, but he makes me feel like I'm always doing something wrong."

"You have to remember that Dean hasn't been a teenager for a few years. He's trying to understand you, but it's not exactly easy for him. From what he's said about you, I know he respects you a great deal, Felipe. He's a practical man, a logical man. Emotions and feelings are harder for a man like that sometimes. I think this work camp is good for him in being away from work. He's been stressed lately, and he's relaxing a little more and seeing there's other things in the world besides work."

"You mean like Mrs. Morris?" Shaking his head, Felipe laughed.

"Yes, now that you mention it."

"What do you mean about him being stressed at work? He hasn't said anything to me."

"That's because he keeps it inside. Let's just say there's someone who works for him who's hurting the business."

"Yeah, I think that manager in the San Antonio store is stealing from him."

Sam turned to Felipe. "Why do you say that?"

"I help him in the store on the weekends."

"That's good," Sam said. "I wasn't aware of that."

"I heard Paul—that's his name—on the phone. He was on the computer in the office and talking with somebody about transferring funds from the store's general account into some other account. Only thing was, the other account was in his own name. I figured Paul would get mad if he knew I was there, so I stayed until he left. He didn't leave until like three hours later. It was torture."

This might be evidence that could help Dean. It certainly couldn't hurt. The only question was, would Felipe tell Dean or would Sam need to tell him? "I hope you'll allow me to pray for you."

Felipe snapped up his head. "What? You mean right now?"

"Sure. Why not?"

"We don't have to hold hands or anything weird, do we?" The boy cast him a wary glance.

"No. You don't even have to bow your head or close your eyes. I spend a lot of time in prayer when I'm driving, when I'm lying in bed, and even when I'm in the shower."

"That last one's too much information, man." The tiniest hint of a grin creased Felipe's lips.

Sam chuckled. "Well, I'll tell you what. It helps keep me from stinking in more ways than one. My point being that God hears your prayers no matter when or where you pray."

"I don't even know how to pray." Felipe's words were spoken so quietly that Sam had to strain to hear them.

"Just talk to God like you're talking with me right now. Like you talk with Angel."

"You know, I think I might be ready to try that prayer thing now, but if you don't mind, I'd like to talk to Angel about it." He held up one hand. "No offense."

"None taken, trust me. Will you do me a big favor, Felipe? You've done a lot of great work here, but go now. I'd like you to think about telling Dean what you told me. You might be able to help him."

"Yeah? How's that?"

"He's ready to hire an expensive accountant to prove Paul is stealing from him. He needs evidence, and what you told me might be just what he needs."

"Hey, I could probably hang around and get some more goods on the scumbag, too."

"Could be. Go talk to Dean. Now."

"Is that an order?"

"Yes." When Sam grinned, Felipe did, too.

"Okay, but I'll come back and do more painting after lunch."

Sam nodded. "Fine. I'm proud of you, son."

Felipe turned away but not before Sam caught the overwhelming emotion in his expression.

"Is something wrong?"

"Nah." Felipe wiped beneath his eyes. "No one's ever called me son before. See ya, Mr. Lewis."

Marta sat across from Eliot at the lunch table as they finished their lunch. She found it endearing how the others left them alone these days. They knew how close they'd grown during the mission. They also understood that Eliot would be flying off to points unknown as soon as the mission was over. That thought pained her more than she would have expected. She wasn't ready to say good-bye to him. Wasn't ready to let him go.

"Let's go take a walk before you go back to the church," she said. "I'm taking the kids out to the spring one last time."

"How about I tag along? It sounds like fun. Although there's still work to do at the church, the majority of the big jobs are done. I'm not scheduled for security duty this afternoon. I'm sure I can arrange it. What do you say?"

"Sure, I'd like that," she said. His black eye was completely healed now, and she could sit and stare at him for the rest of the day and be completely happy. "Did you bring a swimsuit?"

"No, but I have shorts. That'll work fine. Did you bring one?" He lifted his eyebrows up and down, making her laugh.

"No, so don't get your hopes up. I have a tank top and shorts, but I hadn't actually planned on going in the water."

"I don't believe that for a second," he said. "You're a self-acknowledged fish. If there's a body of water, Marta Holcomb will be in it."

"You know me well."

"You know it. And I want to get to know you even better. Let's go." Shoving away from the table, Eliot gathered their trash and tossed them in the can.

"I wanted to tell you that I talked with my mom last night," she said as they walked toward the dorms. "And then Thom and Paine. I told them about you and about your offer to help find Dad."

"And?"

She looked up at him. "We're all in agreement. We'd like you to find him."

Eliot nodded. "What I need you to do is write his vital information on a piece of paper for me. I'll need his full name, place of birth, birthdate, social security number, names of parents, those types of things."

"I'll do it tonight." She sighed and looked past his shoulder. "I understand the answer might come easy, but the acceptance of what we find may never be easy. In my heart, I know what you'll find. It's just filling in the gaps, and knowing the details, that will help with closure for the family. If you can give us that, I'll be forever indebted."

"I don't want you to be indebted to me."

Her eyes searched his. "Then what do you want, Eliot?"

"To chase the dream across the sky. With you, Marta."

~~♥~~

Dean was surprised when Felipe sauntered into the men's dorm after lunch. "Everything okay?"

"Yeah. I was working with Mr. Lewis over at the church before lunch. I told him I was ready to pray. No offense, but I was looking for Angelina, but she's gone off to town with a couple of the ladies."

"Sorry I'm a second choice, but I'll be happy to pray with you."

"Aw, man, I didn't mean it like that."

An apology? He'd take it. "Tell me what's on your mind."

"Dean, you remember when I came home really late from the store that one Saturday night a month or so ago?"

"Yes." He'd grounded Felipe for a week. "You didn't come home until after two in the morning."

"There's a reason, and I guarantee it's nothing like what you probably thought."

Dean scooted over on his bunk and indicated for Felipe to have a seat. "Try me."

"Okay. Well, I was in the office and Paul was on the phone. He was talking about transferring funds from the store's general account. At first, I figured it was boring business stuff, but then he said a few things that seemed a little weird."

"Like what?" Dean's pulse picked up. Unwittingly, Felipe might have stumbled on the solid evidence he could use to prove Paul's embezzlement.

The more Felipe told him, the more he grew excited that this could, in fact, be a breakthrough. "Why didn't you tell me this before?" There was no sense in getting mad at Felipe. He'd told him now, and that was the main thing. Felipe couldn't have realized how important that information was to him.

Felipe shrugged. "I was mad at you. Like everything else, you were quick to jump down my throat and accuse me. Once a juvenile delinquent, always a juvie, right, Dean? Isn't that the way you operate?"

When he started up from the bed, Dean put a hand on his arm. "Wait. First of all, you might be able to help me save thousands of dollars. Are you willing to tell a police officer or detective the same things you just told me? They'd record or videotape the conversation."

"I guess so. You really think it could help?"

"I know it could. But I don't want you to feel that you need to prove anything to me. I'm sorry you feel that I treat you like that, Felipe. Maybe I do, but I assure you it's not intentional. I'm asking you to forgive me."

The teenager met his gaze and held it for a long moment. "Wait. You're apologizing to *me?*"

Dean nodded. "I can admit when I'm wrong, and I've been wrong about you. I'm sometimes quick to judge, and I've been a little on edge lately with the funds disappearing from the store. I talked with an attorney before I left San Antonio, and we have another big meeting coming up next week. I want you to come with me."

"Is it during the week? I'd have to miss school. My guardian probably wouldn't approve." From Felipe's tone, Dean could tell he was teasing.

"I'll get it arranged. Same as I did for his mission trip." Dean smiled. "I want to pray with you, but first I want to tell you a little story about me and Mama Rose."

As he suspected, that got Felipe's attention. He adored his mom, and Dean couldn't blame him. She was pretty awesome, and she'd done a better job getting to know Felipe than he had. He could learn a lot from her. When he returned to San Antonio, he'd have a long chat with her.

"Mama Rose makes the best cinnamon crown rolls in the world. Hot and fresh from the oven, you can't beat them."

"Yeah. I've had them, and they're awesome," Felipe said. "Thanks. Now I'm going to be craving them."

Dean chuckled. "You and me both. You probably know the rolls form a circle, and you peel them away from the outside. One day when I was six, I stole a candy bar from a store. It was the first time I'd ever done it, on a dare from a friend of mine. My cousin Luis saw me and ratted me out to my mom before I got home." He raised a finger. "But the important thing here is that I didn't know until later on that *she* already knew."

Felipe drew his knees up to his chest, and Dean could tell he had his full attention.

"About an hour after I came home from the store, I smelled the fresh cinnamon rolls and went into the kitchen. She casually invited me to sit at the table and have some of the delicious hot rolls with a glass of milk. Mama Rose, bless her heart, didn't scold me. She didn't say a word. Then she started talking about how it wounds Jesus every time we do something that goes against His teachings. She peeled away a roll and told me how every time we sin, it takes a part of our soul, and how it grieves God. Then she peeled away another roll and told me how if we don't confess our sins to the Lord, it rots away at our insides. And then she kept going on with things like that until I broke down and confessed my crime. I squealed like a squirmy little pig and told her I'd stolen that candy bar. On purpose. Not because I wanted to eat it, either, but because I wanted to see if I could get away with it."

"So, you stole something, too."

"Yes," Dean said. "No matter the motivation, it's the fact that I took something that wasn't mine without paying for it. You're never too young or too old to learn that lesson. I don't consider stealing a candy bar any less important than stealing a car. In God's eyes, big or little, it's still sin."

"Right." Felipe stared straight ahead, but he was listening.

"I became a Christian that same night, Felipe. It's easy to say the words to become a Christian, but you have to mean it in your heart. It doesn't mean you become a better person overnight. It doesn't mean you automatically know every Bible verse and have all the answers to life's problems. It's admitting that you're a sinner and need forgiveness. It's asking Jesus to come and live in your heart and acknowledging that He died for you."

"Will you pray with me, Dean? I'd like to tell Angel that I'm one of you before the end of this mission."

"You shouldn't do it to get Angelina to like you better, either. Or because you think she might date you or whatever."

Felipe frowned and Dean worried he'd stomp off in anger. *Please, Lord, don't let me have driven him away again.*

"I'm not. I've seen the way Sam and Lexa and everybody here treat other people. They're the best people I've ever met in my life. They want to help and they give to others not because they want something out of the deal, but because that's what makes them happy. There's a difference when you have Jesus in your life, and I'd like to have that, too."

Sitting on the bunk with him, Felipe prayed and asked Jesus to become the Lord of his life. When they finished, he smiled. "I don't feel any different."

"You're changed inside," Dean said. "You've got the Holy Spirit in there now."

"You'd better explain that one to me. Later." With a wave, Felipe departed. A changed man.

Chapter 41

~~♥~~

"Welcome to the first annual TeamWork Talent Show. I'm Joshua Alexander Grant, your Master of Ceremonies for the evening." Lexa laughed at the way Josh spoke in a deeper, radio announcer worthy voice into a small, handheld microphone. Winnie had managed to convince her husband to wear the ugliest tuxedo Lexa had ever seen—maroon and garish with a stiff-looking white shirt featuring ruffles trimmed with black piping. His hair was slicked back with enough gel for three men, making Josh appear tacky and completely ridiculous. Still, he managed to look handsome. Winnie must be so proud.

Lexa clapped and smiled while some of the others assembled in the dining hall whistled, stomped, and cheered. Josh was going to ham it up to the hilt, and it promised to be a fun evening. Their crew *needed* this. For coming up with the idea, Winnie, Marta and Gayle deserved the flowers they'd be presented with at the end of the show.

"First," Josh announced, "we want to thank the One Nation Church for providing the security detail tonight so we can all be here. They've done a great job to help watch over our camp during the mission and we thank the Lord for the friendships that we've developed as we've worked together over at the church. Secondly, it's time for me introduce you to my two lovely assistants. It's my honor to present Miss Marta Holcomb and Miss Gayle Ferrari. Put your hands together and give it up for them, ladies and gentlemen!"

The kitchen door started to open and whispers could be heard behind it. That door hadn't been closed the entire trip, but now it served to separate the main dining hall from what Winnie termed the "staging area." No wonder Winnie had been a chief costumer and worked on set design for high school plays. Mother Hen would prove very adept at keeping everyone in line tonight, just as she did with the catering business.

"I think our ladies need a little encouragement. I guarantee they're going to knock your socks off, if you're wearing them," Josh said, darting a quick glance around the room. He signaled to Dean who raised an APPLAUSE sign in the air and then to Eliot, who raised a sign that said MAKE SOME NOISE.

Marta appeared first from behind the door. Wearing the same lavender gown she'd worn to the TeamWork banquet where they'd honored Sam, she was gorgeous. Her hair was freshly styled and she wore a hint of makeup to highlight her naturally radiant skin and features. Lexa moved her gaze to where Eliot sat beside Dean and Sheila. As expected, he stared at Marta, slack-jawed with unabashed admiration. Recovering quickly, he stuck his fingers in his mouth and let out an ear-piercing whistle.

And Gayle? She looked nothing short of spectacular in a green satin gown. Lovely enough to make Lexa wish another single TeamWork guy were on this mission trip. She'd been praying for a man to come into Gayle's life, but Gayle was a whole lot more patient than either she or Winnie in that regard. Her career as a portrait artist was taking off, and it was only a matter of time until Gayle left Doyle-Clarke Catering.

In God's will and His timing, Lexa.

Marta's cheeks colored pink while she and Gayle waved like beauty pageant contestants and then stepped to the side of Josh. Trading amused glances, both ladies focused on the Master of Ceremonies.

"Next, we have a little surprise," Josh said. "We've—meaning me and Sam—have decided we'd like to present a few prizes at the end of the evening. To help us do that, would you please give a rousing TeamWork welcome to the lovely Miss Angelina Morris and my own Miss Chloe Grant." He motioned to where they stood to one side of the room. Chloe giggled and Angelina smiled as she darted a glance in Felipe's direction.

"What do you say, let's get started," Josh said. "For our first act, we have Kevin and Rebekah Moore. Kevin will be singing, *I've Got a Crush on You*, and Rebekah, my twin sister, don't you know, will be sitting on a chair looking extremely pretty, a talent unto itself."

Lexa's eyes misted as she listened to the sweet song. Kevin exaggerated the lyrics and made comical facial expressions while Rebekah batted her eyelashes and gazed adoringly at her husband. Beck had been taking it easy—at everyone's insistence—but she'd watched over the kids and helped to make the curtains and other items for the Sunday school rooms. The few times she'd tried to help in the kitchen, she'd become a little queasy.

"Okay, enough of this sap," Josh teased as they finished. "This next act is definitely one for the guys and you'll only see it here, folks. I got a sneak peek, and you're in for a real treat, let me tell you. Marc Thompson, Mitch Jacobsen, and Landon Warnick, come on out! They'll be performing a Three Stooges routine. Ladies, if you didn't like the Stooges before, I think you'll change your mind as you watch these buffoons…uh, stooges."

Lexa laughed along with everyone else as the three men chased each other from behind the door and around the dining hall. Landon's dark hair was combed flat against his head and his bangs were brushed straight down on his forehead. He must be Moe. Chasing Marc, he carried a heavy a frying pan in one hand. She knew a few things about the Three Stooges since her dad had watched old reruns on Saturday afternoons when he was off work.

With his hair parted down the middle and styled wildly so that it stuck out from his head in all directions, Mitch must be Larry. Marc's blond waves were somehow stuffed beneath a skull cap, and by process of elimination, he must be Curly. He also looked the most absurd. All three wore short pants and suspenders with short-sleeved shirts and played off one another as they heartily got into the spirit of their scripted routine. They were actually good and had the sounds and mannerisms down pat. The men, in particular, laughed at their antics and pratfalls while the women shook their heads and traded glances.

"Okay, we concede that was probably more for the men," Josh said. His eyes widened when Landon came up behind him and tapped his head with the frying pan. "Who let you out of the kitchen, Moe? Get back in there." He waited as everyone laughed and the guys headed back into the kitchen. Josh's gaze zeroed in on Lexa. "Don't you worry, ladies. We definitely have something for you coming up later on. Let's just say it's of royal proportions."

Josh grunted. "Moving on now to our next act. Ladies, get out those tissues, and men, pull out your hankies if you carry one of those disgusting things. TeamWork Productions—yeah, I just made that up—is very proud to present Miss Chloe and Miss Gracie, doing a dance for us. They've both studied dance this past year and are ready to wow you with their skill and grace. Of course, that goes without saying. But wait," he said, raising one hand in the air as everyone applauded, "they are joined by two special little ladies who are making their professional ballet debut tonight. Would you please welcome, this time with reverence, Miss Hannah and Miss Leah. Not to be outdone by my baby girl, Miss Emily, who is presiding over the dance." Josh waved to Gayle who carried Emily in her arms. "Next time, Emily. I promise."

After Josh nodded to Marta, she pushed the button on the CD player. Lexa sat up straighter and her eyes misted as she watched her daughters dance to a song she recognized from *Swan Lake*. Gracie and Chloe took their hands and guided them in twirls and ballet moves. The twins stood still and watched the older girls at times and then imitated them. Chloe and Gracie wore black tutus and tights and the younger girls wore pink tutus and shoes. Winnie and Amy found them at a thrift store they'd visited while she'd gone with Angelina, Cassie, and Felipe to the hair salon.

Lexa glanced around the room, gratified to see that Marc had come back into the room to watch. The other Stooges had also come out of the kitchen, and all three were still in their costumes. She hated that Sam wasn't beside her to see the girls, but she saw the kitchen door cracked open enough that she could see that her husband wasn't missing this performance. Sam Sr. and Sarah sat nearby, with smiles. Sam Sr. caught Lexa's eye and winked. She saw a tear roll down Sarah's cheek.

Gayle had been taking photos, and she moved about the room now, snapping away. The applause was thunderous as the girls finished their dance and took low bows. Everyone rose to their feet and gave them a standing ovation.

"For our next act, we'll ask Larry over there to contain himself"—Josh nodded to Mitch—"but hold onto your hair for Cassie Jacobsen. I heard her rehearse, and let me tell you, this girl's talent is amazing. Gayle, get that camera ready." He nodded to Marta and she pushed the button on the CD player. As the music began to play, Cassie emerged from behind the kitchen door.

Lexa drew in a breath. In a platinum blonde wig, Cassie hugged the door frame in a silver, sequined gown. Someone handed her a fake white mink stole, and she draped it around her shoulders as she made her way into the dining hall one slow step at a time. She batted her baby blues and began to sing "Diamonds Are A Girl's Best Friend" in a breathy, soft voice.

"Oh, Marilyn." Cupping his hands around his mouth, Mitch whistled. "Sing to me, baby!" Cassie smiled but stayed in perfect character as she slowly moved among the audience. She smoothed her hand over Marc's skull cap, making both Marc and Natalie laugh. Pausing in front of Sam Sr., she lifted a brow. Beside him, Sarah shook her head and gestured for Marilyn to move along.

Cassie walked across the room to Eliot and, standing behind him, leaned down and trailed her fingers along his shoulder. Marta waltzed over to Cassie and wagged her finger in her face. Laughing, Cassie moved to Dean. When Sheila pretended to shoot an arrow at her, Cassie backed away and then set her sights on her husband. She ended the song in his lap and gave Mitch a quick kiss before hopping up and hurrying back into the kitchen with flushed cheeks.

"See what marrying Mitch and moving to New York has done to our formerly shy, sweet Alabama girl?" Josh wiped his brow with a handkerchief that Gayle handed to him. "Mitch, I know you're not ashamed of yourself, but how's your blood pressure? Doing okay there?"

"Not sure." Mitch fanned himself with one hand, and thanked Natalie when she gave him a paper fan.

"Speaking of corruption," Josh said, "Amy Warnick is up next, but she's going to redeem the Jacobsen family reputation with this performance. My beautiful wife, Winifred Grant, will be joining my favorite journalist-turned-publishing whiz to sing that old favorite of yours and mine, 'Sisters.' They will be joined at the hip—I mean at the end—by two lovely surprise guests." Holding his microphone, Josh opened his arms in a wide arc. "A collective *Aww*, if you please."

The audience complied and the two women positioned themselves, back-to-back, and they sang with Kevin accompanying them on the guitar. Considering these two were as close as sisters in so many ways, Lexa reached for a tissue and dabbed at her eyes from the sentimentality and sweetness of it all. Near the end, Lexa darted out of her chair and Natalie did the same as they pretended to come between Amy and Winnie. Then the four ladies performed a short skit that Lexa had written for them, a good reminder of the close friendships they cherished.

"We have a few more acts and then we'll hand out our prizes,"

Josh told them as Lexa returned to her seat. "Sheila Morris has a unique talent, ladies and gentlemen. You need to see this one to believe it, and she's going to demonstrate it for us now." Sheila stepped forward, and Marta handed her a tall glass of ice cold milk.

"You see, Sheila has the ability and stomach capacity, apparently, to drain this very large glass of milk you see before you now in only five seconds. Can it be done? Let's see, shall we? Gayle, start the timer, please." In her hands, Gayle held up a large, oversized alarm clock with a second hand for all to see. Like a game show model, she smiled and waved one hand over the clock with a pasted-on smile. Everyone turned their attention to Sheila as Gayle started the clock.

"Five, four, three, two, one," Josh counted. Lexa sat back, amazed. She did it! Sheila drained the glass of milk in record time.

"Where she puts it, I'll never know," Josh said. "Check the floor and make sure some of it didn't slosh down there. Very unusual and wonderful talent there, Sheila. Let's hear it again, everyone!" he said, prompting shouts and claps. "Think you could repeat it?" he challenged. Sheila raised her hands in protest, laughing as she took her seat.

"Well, at least we know she got her calcium intake for the day. Next up is Dean Costas demonstrating a talent I don't believe any of us knew he possessed. Trust me on that. He's going to perform the familiar classic 'Ode to Joy'—the final movement in Beethoven's Ninth Symphony—using various body parts. Let's just say I'll never use the word *armpits* again without thinking twice."

Alternately using his hands, knees, tongue, mouth, elbows, and even his armpits, Dean also hummed and whistled. Lexa smiled when she recognized the tune. She wouldn't have thought it possible and shook her head.

"Words fail me, man," Josh said as Dean finished to wild applause. When Dean reached out to shake his hand, Josh shook his head. "I know where that hand's been. Go wash your hands, man." They all laughed hysterically at that comment. Refastening the top few buttons of his shirt, Dean laughed and acknowledged the applause. Lexa enjoyed the gleam in Sheila's eyes as Dean headed into the kitchen.

"Seriously, people, I never knew body parts could sound like that." Josh's enthusiasm was infectious and everyone erupted into laughter again.

"Actually, as a little history lesson," Eliot told them. "'Ode to Joy' was composed by the German poet, Friedrich Schiller, and celebrates the unity and brotherhood of mankind. My friend, Dean, thought it would be appropriate for TeamWork and our mission here in New Mexico."

"Right he is. Amazing talent. The man might be quiet, but he thinks deep." Josh nodded to Eliot. "Thanks for the history lesson in the absence of our history-loving, insanely tall TeamWork director. Never fear, folks, Sam is nearby." Again, Josh seemed to zero in on Lexa, making her wonder what Sam planned to do for the Talent Show. From all the hints Winnie and Amy had dropped, it promised to be quite memorable.

"Okay, listen up," Josh told them next. "We're all in for a truly unusual treat now. Miss Angelina Morris will be doing something uniquely different for all of us here tonight. I guarantee you it's probably nothing you've ever seen before. No, it's not death defying, but it *is* a demonstration of uncommonly great skill as you'll see in a minute if I ever finish this introduction."

After Josh nodded to Marta, she started to bring an easel forward. Jumping up from his chair, Eliot lifted it for her and then positioned it beside Angelina.

"While Angelina does her thing, Felipe Hernandez and his friends—Amitola and Avonaco from the One Nation Church—will serenade her with a little rap ditty." Stopping, Josh tilted his head with a silly expression. "I think I might have just come up with a whole new music genre. You heard it here first, folks. Give it up for Felipe and the Triple As!"

Lexa giggled as Felipe and the young couple performed a song acapella about getting to know one another and the differences between the TeamWork group and the One Nation Church members. No doubt Felipe had written the lyrics and they all danced around each another and had a great time with it, play acting a bit as they performed the song.

While they sang, Angelina used her pen and worked on something on the easel. She'd make a few strokes and then flip to another page and then begin again, nodding her head as she performed a dance move with the others every now and then. Moving over to her, Felipe peeked over her shoulder and gave a thumbs-up to the audience with a wide grin.

The song ended with lyrics highlighting their similarities in spite of the cultural differences and then tying it all together with the bond of Christ. As if on perfect cue, Angelina put down her pen and smiled.

As they finished, everyone rose to their feet again and clapped with enthusiasm.

"I don't know if you noticed," Josh said, "but Angelina was using her time wisely in these past few minutes while the trio entertained you. If my assistants would be so kind as to come and help." Gayle, Marta, Chloe, Gracie, and the twins moved over to stand by the easel.

Silence filled the room as, one by one, the helpers took a paper from Angelina and held them up for all to see. Angelina had drawn caricatures of Josh, Dean, Natalie, Cassie, Eliot, and Sarah. The resemblance to her subjects was uncanny, and it had only taken a few skillful strokes for Angelina to create the drawings. Everyone in the room clapped wildly.

"I can safely say this will be an impossible act to follow, Angelina," Josh said. "Absolutely fantastic. Let's hear it again, ladies and gentlemen!" Smiling, and with great poise, Angelina instructed her helpers to deliver the caricatures to their subjects. As each one accepted their drawings, they mouthed their thanks to the lovely teenager.

Angelina caught Lexa's eye. As Lexa returned the teenager's smile, she couldn't help but wonder what on earth Sam planned to do. She had the feeling she'd find out soon enough.

Chapter 42

~~♥~~

After everyone calmed down, Josh addressed them again. "We have two more acts and then we'll ask you to vote. Eliot will make balloon animals for the kids while the results are tabulated for our Grand Prize winner tonight. Joe Lewis and Luke Grant, will you please come on out here and take the stage!"

Lexa motioned for Gayle to take some photos. Glancing at the kitchen door, Lexa could tell Sam was positioned there again to watch his son. Likewise, Josh watched from the front, deep emotion in his face as he prepared to listen to his son, named for Josh and Beck's late father.

Taking a deep breath, without musical accompaniment, Joe began to sing "What A Friend We Have In Jesus." Luke joined in as best he could, and both boys carried the tune well. Joe's gaze found his mother's and centered on Lexa as he sang. Toward the end of four stanzas, Joe darted a glance at the kitchen door, which opened a bit more. When the boys finished their song, Joe gave a short bow and then took off to the kitchen, presumably to his father. Luke followed suit and ran over to Josh.

"Now, drum roll please, Felipe!" With one arm around Luke, Josh nodded to the teenager. Felipe beat his hands on the top of a table.

Josh laughed. "All right then. Is everyone finally ready for our fearless leader—who refused to be felled by a spider—as he comes to serenade his lovely bride tonight? Lexa, we need you to come up here to the front, please."

Lexa sank lower in her chair. Goodness, what was coming? "Is that necessary?"

"Yes, it is. Trust me, Sam will thank you for it. Thank you very much."

Josh turned to the audience. "I said, are you ready? Let me hear you!" Eliot and Dean held up their signs again and they all went wild.

Rising to her feet, Lexa made her way to the front and seated herself in the chair.

"I'm ready." The deep drawl was Sam's, and it came from the kitchen. Marta changed the CD and then clicked on the player. At the first few strains, Lexa's eyes widened. The kitchen door opened and Sam appeared. He stood in the doorway for a moment, probably for effect.

Oh my word. Her husband wore a white jumpsuit. With rhinestones. His hair was brushed up in a pompadour and he wore dark sunglasses. *Thanks, Winnie.*

Tuning out everyone else around her, Lexa focused on Sam as he began to sing "Are You Lonesome Tonight?" and walked slowly into the room. Tapping her on the shoulder, he slid down to one knee beside her, taking her hand in his. Lexa felt a bit heady and gave him a nervous smile. She was glad he didn't make the speech about a lying lover that Elvis did in the original song—she'd always found it quite sad—but simply sang the song.

Ending the song, Sam offered his hand to her and helped Lexa to her feet. She thought they were done, but oh no, he wasn't quite done yet.

"Shake those hips, Elvis!" Marc whooped and several of the other men joined him.

"Ohhh, it's the King!" Winnie stood outside the kitchen and gave her a wink as she, Amy, Gayle, and Marta all pretended to swoon. They ran over to them and circled Sam, acting like they were fawning over the music superstar of days gone by. As the music started again, they blew kisses and took off again.

"Please tell me you're not going to swivel your pelvis," Lexa whispered as Sam took her in his arms.

He leaned close, his lips pressed against her cheek. "Only in private for you, Lexa."

"Then you won't mind if I do this," she said, zipping up the jumpsuit another inch. "Much better." She patted his chest and felt his low chuckle beneath her hand.

Sam began to croon "Love Me Tender," removing the dark glasses and gazing into her eyes as he did so. The room was strangely quiet. She'd always heard about times when the room stood still, but in that moment, Lexa experienced it. In that moment, it was Lexa Lewis and Elvis Presley. Make that Sam Lewis.

"Thank you, thank you very much." Laughing, Sam shot an apologetic glance at the group. "Your wife made me do it!" he said, pointing to Josh.

"Then take this!" Josh tossed him a bouquet of a dozen, long stemmed yellow roses.

"Love me tender, love me always," Sam whispered for Lexa's ears only as he put the flowers in her arms.

She gave him a saucy wink. "Later, Elvis."

He laughed and—was that a hint of a swivel?—strolled back to the kitchen, blowing kisses to his adoring audience as they clapped and cheered some more.

"I honestly don't know how to top that. And yes, I do believe Elvis has now left the building."

The men all groaned at that one. "Hey, you try doing this!" he protested. "Eliot, come on down! If I can have the kids come up here with Mr. Eliot, he's going to make balloon animals. It seems his talents extend to more than just paper napkins. Let's see if you can stump him. Name your favorite animal."

"How about an armadillo?" Lexa called out, and everyone laughed.

"You've already got your roses," Natalie teased. "Be happy with what you have, Mrs. Lewis."

"Oh, I am." Lexa inhaled the fresh scent of the roses and smiled. As Marta played more music, and Gayle snapped more photos, she rose to her feet and started to hand out the roses to the ladies, starting with Sam's mom. Leah and Hannah followed her, and they'd been given the task of passing out small pieces of paper for everyone to vote.

"Josh, we need to change the prize," Sam said in low tones. "Come outside with me a moment."

"Excuse me," Josh told Winnie. "Elvis needs me. We're leaving the building now."

Winnie laughed. "Don't let the door hit you on the way out."

"What's on your mind, E.P.?" Josh asked as soon as they were outside.

Sam shook his head. "What Winnie must do with you

sometimes."

"Do you really want an answer to that? Sorry," Josh said, laughing. "It's been a fun evening."

"Angelina won the prize fair and square. She certainly deserved it. Considering the talent that girl has in her little finger, I'd like us to gift her with more than a certificate."

Josh grinned. "I follow what you're getting at, and I like it. I take it you're talking about a cash prize."

"Exactly, but it'll be safer if it's a check. I'm going to walk over to my office and make one out now. Hold off on the presentations until I get back."

"Sure thing. You know I'm good for whatever you want to do. I'm sure Marc, Landon and Mitch will be happy to contribute, and no doubt the others, as well."

Sam paused and looked back at Josh. "Thanks. It's called an investment in the future."

When Sam returned a few minutes later, Josh rose from his seat and moved to the front of the dining hall. "Okay, it's time for the announcement of the honorable mentions for tonight's TeamWork Talent Show. Not that you aren't all winners, but we thought we'd honor a few of the acts."

Within minutes, the little ballerinas as well as Joe and Luke were honored for their talent. Beaming with pride, they stood at the front of the room. Eliot offered to make more balloons for them, and that seemed to be all the prizes they needed.

"Our Grand Prize winner was a unanimous decision. Miss Angelina Morris, would you please come up here. Sheila, come on up with her."

Felipe stood on a chair and pumped his fists in the air. "Way to go, Angel! That's my girl!"

Sam chuckled as Felipe put his fingers in his mouth and whistled. Dean clamped one hand on his shoulder, laughing. It was good to see the boy so enthusiastic and happy for someone else's success.

"Angelina, we were all privileged to witness a demonstration of your immense, God-given artistic abilities here tonight. In honor of your talent, we'd like to present this to you with the hope you'll be able to use what's inside to further that talent."

After Josh handed her the envelope, Angelina pulled out what looked to be a certificate. She clamped a hand over her mouth. Stepping closer, Sheila took it from her and her eyes opened wide.

"Let me say a prayer and then we'll have pie and ice cream." Bowing his head, Sam thanked the Lord for the great time of fellowship and fun they'd enjoyed together. He prayed for the safety of his team and the continued growth of the One Nation Church.

As soon as the prayer ended, Sheila ran over to him. "Sam, th-this is t-t-too m-m-much."

"Consider it TeamWork's contribution to furthering Angelina's artistic career. She's extremely talented, and we want to see it continue. I had no idea your daughter could draw like that, Sheila."

"Sh-she's b-b-been t-t-taking ar-art l-les-s-ons, and h-h-her t-t-teachers t-t-tell m-m-me sh-she h-h-has an eye f-f-for d-d-depth and d-d-detail. J-j-just kn-know th-the p-p-prize m-m-money w-w-will p-pay f-f-for m-m-more l-l-lessons."

"As it's intended."

"As we enjoy our dessert, we have another special treat to end the evening," Josh announced. "Would you please give a warm TeamWork welcome to U.S. Air Force Captain, Samuel J. Lewis, Sr., and his lovely bride, Sarah."

Lexa nudged Sam in the chair next to her. Surprisingly, he still wore the Elvis costume, and neither had the others changed out of their costumes. "Did you know they were going to do this?"

"No, although I knew they wanted to stay through tonight so they could be here for the Talent Show."

Hand in hand, Sam Sr. and Sarah appeared as those in the dining hall clapped with a certain reverence. Tall and handsome, Sam Sr. wore his full dress service uniform, complete with his hat, from all those years ago. Lexa knew he'd worn it the day he proposed to Sarah in the diner where she worked.

"Does your dad carry that uniform around with him wherever he goes?" Lexa whispered.

Sam chuckled. "There's an Air Force Base here, and they had some kind of event. Mom had him put it in the car just in case."

"Ah. He still looks great in it," Lexa said, settling back in her chair to watch.

Raising one hand to his and placing the other on his shoulder as he pulled her close, Sarah was lovely in what looked like a vintage or replica dress from the early 1960s when these two first courted in their tiny hometown of Rockbridge, Texas.

Lexa's eyes filled with sentimental tears as she recognized the beginning strains of "Some Enchanted Evening" from *South Pacific*, one of her Nana's all-time favorite movies. The others quieted down quickly, as if making noise was irreverent and disrespectful. Sam reached for her, wrapping his hand around hers and caressing it with his thumb. Darting a quick glance at him, Lexa could tell he was every bit as affected as she was by this tender moment shared between his mother and father, and maybe even more so.

Mitch had dimmed the lights in the dining hall and miniature twinkling lights had been installed around the perimeter of the room, adding a romantic and whimsical touch. Sam Sr. and Sarah moved together as one, a testimony of lives well-lived. They'd glorified the Lord as a couple and modeled a godly marriage as parents to their six children. A shiver ran through her, and Lexa nestled closer into the warmth of her husband.

When Sarah moved her hand over her husband's jaw, caressing him, her expression was one of a wife who'd been well-loved, treasured, and cherished through the years. Reaching for a tissue in her pocket, Lexa wiped away the tears that fell onto her cheeks. Of course, Sam noticed and moved closer. Draping his arm around the back of her chair, he kissed her temple.

As the song ended, Sam Sr. lowered his lips to Sarah's for a tender kiss.

"That's the most romantic thing I've ever seen," Winnie said, sniffling.

"I'd say so," Lexa heard Marta say from farther down the table. "Better than any movie." Several of the ladies murmured their assent, and the men nodded.

"Come on," Sam said, gently tugging on her hand and helping Lexa to her feet. "Time to dance, everyone. Mitch, please spin that Elvis CD again."

Lexa's heart caught in her throat as she spied her TeamWork children—as she liked to call them—pairing off.

"I have a request, please," Sarah called to Mitch. "Can't Help Falling in Love."

Mitch nodded. "Coming right up, Mrs. Lewis."

"That song was playing in the diner the day I arrived home in Texas after my tour of duty ended," Sam Sr. told them. "April 24, 1962."

"Your birthday?" Lexa said as Sam easily pulled her into his arms and they began to dance. "I didn't know you were born four years to the date after your dad returned stateside. Tell me, was this song also playing on the Volvo's radio the day you picked me up at the Greyhound station in San Antonio?"

Sam's smile reached his blue eyes and his smile lines surfaced. "No, but it would have been appropriate."

"Seems there's always something new to learn about you," she murmured.

"I hope we'll always discover something new about one another, Lexa." Tipping her chin, he lowered his lips to hers. After they parted, Lexa rested her head against his chest, swaying slowly to the music, bodies in perfect rhythm. How she loved moments like this. Falling in love with her husband all over again. That's what marriage was all about. The disagreements they'd had through the years faded into the background, replaced by how *right* it was to be in Sam's arms.

Dancing closest to them, Marc held Natalie close. Same with Josh and Winnie on the other side of them. The sight of all the children dancing near their parents made Lexa smile. Cassie danced nearby with Mitch. Next to them were Rebekah and Kevin. While Lexa watched, Kevin moved one hand over his wife's belly. Her breath caught when Lexa spied Joe son dancing with Leah and Hannah. Amy and Landon only had eyes for one another, as usual.

"Sam, go dance with Gayle," Lexa urged, keeping her tone low. He'd done the same for Amy when she felt the odd-woman-out at Rebekah and Kevin's wedding.

"Sure. Hold my place. I'll be back." With her heart full, Lexa watched her tall, handsome husband bow before their pretty red-haired friend. After Gayle darted a questioning glance her way, Lexa nodded and moved to the side of the room. She smiled at the tender way Dean held Sheila in his arms and stifled a smile when Felipe attempted to inch Angelina closer. How that boy had grown spiritually since he'd been with them on this mission. Matured. Allowed the Lord to work in his life.

Lord, you are so good to us. Thank you.

Some thought she and Sam were perfect people. Far from it. Sometimes when she snapped at Sam or the kids, or when she grumbled about someone or something that irritated her, she felt so far from perfect that only divine intervention could make her whole again. But she was valued by God and by the man holding her in his arms. She was a wife, a mother, a business partner, a sister in Christ, a child of God. For all these reasons, and the joy her various roles brought, and how they enriched her life, she was truly blessed beyond measure.

Coming back to claim her and sweeping her into his embrace, Sam whispered "Amen" against her hair.

"How do you always seem to know what I'm thinking?" Lexa moved her hand over his chest and smiled when he covered her hand with his own.

"Because I'm made for you, and you for me." He tugged gently on her braid, one of her favorite, private ways Sam told her that he loved her.

"I love you, too, Sam. Always."

"Want to dance, Plum Pudding?"

Feeling suddenly shy, Angelina put her hand in Felipe's. She darted a glance at Mama, but she was in her own world with Dean. Following her gaze, Felipe smiled. "Don't worry. They're not going to stop us."

"I'm not worried, but it's like a reflex. What can I say?" She wasn't sure what to do and lowered her gaze. She'd gotten to know Felipe pretty well on this mission, and as crazy as it seemed, it was almost as though he was her best friend now. Sure, she had friends back home, but she'd never had deep conversations with them like those she'd shared with Felipe. Meaningful conversations. Discussions that reinforced her faith and hopefully stirred his curiosity. He'd been asking more questions and seemed less resistant to the things of the Lord.

"You've never danced before, Angel?"

"No. Sorry it's so obvious." She was ticklish, and a nervous giggle escaped when he rested one hand lightly on her waist and then began to slowly sway with her. Why did she have to act so silly? Why couldn't she be full of grace and act like a grown-up? Her gaze traveled to where Amitola and Avonaco danced across the room. Lost in one another, they looked so happy, and she could tell they'd have a great marriage.

"Don't be sorry," he whispered. "It looks great in here, doesn't it? I like those little twinkly lights they've strung up all around the place."

"Yes, it's…romantic." She giggled and averted her gaze. "Don't get any ideas."

He laughed quietly. "You can't stop a guy from hoping or getting ideas, but I'll be good. Promise." Angelina was thankful he didn't pull her too close but kept a respectful distance. She'd heard the speech about dancing from Mama several times. It was a miracle she'd even let her go to a few dances at school.

"I've been asked to dance, but until now, there wasn't a boy I wanted to say yes to," she said. She felt her cheeks warm. "You know what I mean."

"I do. Listen," he said, moving them over to a more quiet corner of the dining hall, "I thought maybe you'd like to see some of my stories tomorrow."

She looked up at him in surprise. "Really? I'd love to see them." She'd begun to think he'd changed his mind. He was telling her that he trusted her because she'd come to understand those stories were intensely personal to Felipe. His escape from reality. She needed to encourage him so that he'd continue pursuing interests like writing instead of other things that could get him in trouble.

"Would you look at us?" He laughed under his breath. "The juvenile delinquent and his Angel are dancing together. I doubt anyone would have guessed this would ever happen after I first got here."

"You're no juvenile delinquent." Angelina put one hand on his chest. "You've just done a few things you shouldn't. We've all done that." She liked the way he'd called her *his* Angel. Something about that made her feel protected.

"I confessed them to God, Angel." He slowed their dancing.

"What do you mean? You confessed what?" Her pulse accelerated. Did he mean what she thought he meant?

"I talked with Mr. Lewis yesterday morning. It was good. He wanted me to go talk to Dean. Turns out I might be able to help my guardian with something going on in the San Antonio store. I work there on the weekends, and I happened to see and hear some things."

"Wow. That's good, right?"

"Yeah, I'd say so." The song changed, but Angelina was thankful it was another slow ballad. No big surprise there with the TeamWork crew. "He asked me if I was willing to tell my story. With my record, I hope they'll believe me. But they can get proof on the computers if that guy hasn't done anything with it." He shrugged. "Guess we'll find out when we get back to San Antonio."

"Let me know what happens."

A wide grin spread across his face. "Are you saying you want to keep in contact with me when we get home?"

She smiled. "Yes, that's exactly what I'm saying. But, wait a minute. Get back to the part about confessing."

"Dean prayed with me to ask Jesus into my heart, and well… I'm a Christian now, Angel."

Angelina couldn't help it. She cried out with joy. Throwing her arms around Felipe, she kissed his cheek. Realizing what she'd done, she put her hands over her mouth and backed away from him. When she noticed several of the others staring at them, she laughed. "Felipe accepted the Lord, and I'm so proud of him. So happy!"

Truly, her soul was happy.

Thank you, Jesus.

Dancing in Eliot's arms felt as natural as swimming. Memories of a middle school dance—standing by herself along the wall, staring longingly at Trey Parker—filled her mind. Only Eliot had asked her to dance but Trey never had. She hadn't danced much in her life, only danced *around* someone. Skirting around relationships, afraid to get too close, reveal or give too much of herself. Until she'd gotten close with Liam, and then felt the sting of rejection, the loss of a part of herself she could never recover. She'd learned from it, but she'd also erected walls. Seemed she'd been erecting walls her entire life.

Soon she'd need to say good-bye to Eliot. Again. Only the Lord knew for how long, and all Marta wanted was to dive in head-first and immerse herself in her newly awakened love for the man holding her in his arms. At the beginning of this mission, she'd wondered if what she felt for him was love or merely infatuation. She'd admired him from afar for so long. He was one of the strongest and bravest men she'd ever known, one of the most giving and loving. What she felt for him was unlike the feelings she'd had for any other man, even what she'd believed she felt for Liam.

Loving this man meant letting him go to places unknown, facing danger on an almost daily basis. Was her love for him strong enough to withstand the separation, the not knowing, the doubts, the insecurities? For his part, Eliot had made it clear that he had no doubts.

"Will you let me in?" Eliot whispered.

Marta met his gaze. "Eliot," she said, swallowing hard. "I'm—"

Something dimmed in his eyes. She needed to reassure him.

She heard a commotion from outside the front door of the dining hall. Two men from the One Nation Church burst through the door, their expressions worried, and they were both talking at the same time. Seeing them, Avonaco and Amitola came over to find out what was happening. Behind them were Sam, Josh, and Marc.

"We've got trouble," one of the men told them. "A group of locals claiming to be from that Extant group is over at the church. They're threatening to torch it."

Marta's heart slid down to her toes. *Oh, dear Lord. Please be with us.*

Eliot released her.

And then he was gone.

Chapter 43

~~♥~~

Sam waved his arms. "Men, we're needed over at the church. No time to waste. Let's roll!"

They all took off at a run. Perhaps foolishly, Sam had thought this kind of trouble was behind them. He'd been praying, and he'd continue to pray, for the safety of the church and the One Nation congregation. They'd accomplished what they'd come to do in spite of the odds they'd faced.

When they reached the church, Sam could tell there was a standoff in progress. Five of the One Nation men, including Pastor Chevy and four of the leaders in the church, stood on to one side, and the Extant group—ten of them by his quick head count—faced them. A bridge of about ten feet separated the battle lines.

Sam walked over to speak with Cheveyo. "What's going on?"

"Hey, Elvis! Bring your stooges with you?" The men from the local group called out other derogatory comments, laced with profanity, which Sam ignored. He glanced at several of the guys in his crew, silently warning them not to make any false moves, and they all nodded.

"Just having a Talent Show with our group."

"Well, ain't that sweet."

Cheveyo stepped close. "We can handle this, Sam. Maybe you should take your men and go back to the camp. I don't want any trouble, and I can't have anyone hurt on my watch."

"We're in agreement on that, but we're not leaving," Sam said. "We've come this far, and we're not going to back down now. Have you asked them what they want?"

"Kind of hard to do when they keep flicking lighters and threaten to torch the church. This is one of those times I wish I still carried my gun when I'm off-duty."

"Do you recognize any of these men?" Sam said. "Think one or more might have a grudge against you or any of the men here who are police officers?"

"Not to my knowledge."

"Is it okay if I talk with them?"

Sam could tell the other man was waging a mental debate. Finally, Cheveyo blew out a breath. "You can try," he relented. "I'll be right beside you."

Walking toward the group of men with Cheveyo beside him, Sam halted a few feet away, facing them. "I'm Sam Lewis with TeamWork, and—"

"We know who you are. All of you," one of the men said, his gaze moving down the row of his TeamWork men. Standing in the middle of the group, he was the man who'd spoken before. The men on either side of him remained silent, but they stared at Sam and Cheveyo with contempt written in their expressions.

"Why did you violate the TeamWork camp and file the complaints against the church?" Cheveyo demanded.

"Because we can," one of the men sneered, his voice full of contempt. "How about that? It's our right as citizens, and it's still a free country last time we checked."

"TeamWork has as much right to be here as you do," Sam said.

"Is that right? We got a problem with you helpin' this group of Indians. They don't belong here."

"They've done everything properly and legally, and their rights are fully protected under the law," Sam said.

"They're no good," another man said. "They lie, they steal, and they'll molest your women. I wouldn't trust no Indian as far as I could see him."

Inside, Sam seethed, but he forced calm into his voice. These guys might not listen to the voice of reason, but he needed to try. "That's a very broad and overly generalized statement. The color of a man's skin, his race or nationality—none of those things determine the measure of a man. Neither are they an indicator of intelligence or a level of tolerance, or intolerance, it would seem."

The spokesman snorted. "Listen to the rich man talk! I don't even know what you said, man. Why don't you get off that high and mighty pedestal you're sittin' on and talk in plain English. We been watchin' your group. You got some mighty fine women over there." The other man's dark eyes bore into his, making Sam flinch at the pure hatred reflected in them.

"Real pretty ladies. I bet they'd like real men for a change."

"Yeah," another man said, the fire in his eyes begging for a fight. "I bet they'd be real sweet—"

"Enough!" Sam took one step closer to the opposite line of men.

"Let us at them, Sam." Marc came to stand beside him with Josh right behind him.

Sam nodded to the spokesman. "If you say another word like that, you *will* have a fight on your hands. Is that what you want? Is that why you came, to fight us, to try to get some kind of satisfaction for your shortcomings by acting no better than common street thugs?"

"Shortcomings, eh?" The spokesman laughed, a bitter, harsh sound. He nodded to the guy standing on the end. Pulling a lighter out of his pocket, the man walked in the direction of the gazebo. Another man reached behind him and then took off with something in his hand. A gas can. Sam stiffened and the muscles in his jaws hardened.

"Stop! No!" Shouting, Landon and Mitch started running after the men.

"Let them go," Kevin said, his voice resonant in the quiet night. With his mouth set in a firm line, he stared straight ahead. "The gazebo can be rebuilt. Better and stronger."

Sam watched with deep sorrow as the men doused the gazebo with gasoline and then set it on fire. The pungent smell of burning wood filled his nostrils, turning his stomach.

"Go get the fire extinguishers," Cheveyo ordered one of his men.

"Are you happy now? Proud of yourselves?" Marc stepped forward. Sam prayed they could somehow resolve this confrontation without any physical contact. Maybe torching the gazebo would satisfy them and they'd leave. That seemed unlikely, but the men who'd come into their camp on Sunday afternoon had fled when Sheila pulled out her bow and arrow. If needed, they'd have a fist fight or an old-fashioned brawl.

"Please leave the premises. You're welcome to return if you need a place to worship the Lord," Cheveyo told them. "And if you come in a spirit of peace and unity."

"Yeah, right. That's not gonna happen anytime soon," another man said, and several of them laughed.

The ringleader of the group stepped forward, and several of his men did the same. "Don't you get it? What we're sayin' is we don't want your kind around here," he said to Cheveyo. "Never did. Never will." He tossed a derisive glance at Sam and his men. "Yours either."

"This property legally belongs to the One Nation Church," Sam said. "As such, you're considered trespassers if you damage property and harm anyone on the premises."

"I say let's torch the church," one man sneered. "Laugh and spit on it as it burns all the way down to the ground."

"There will be nothing left of your precious church," another said. "We'll be dancing on the ashes."

"It's what we should have done in the first place," the spokesman said. "Shouldn't have bothered with this group of—"

"Do as you wish, but the spirit of God will remain," Cheveyo said. "The church is nothing more than a shell, a place to gather for worship."

Sam stepped forward. "You can tear down the building, but the spirit of the Lord lives in the hearts of its people. Their spirit will not be broken."

Cheveyo stepped beside Sam. "You will not steal our joy."

Several of the men stepped forward with threatening expressions. A number raised their fists.

Sam linked arms with Cheveyo, the One Nation men, and his TeamWork men. Together, they formed a stalwart wall of faith. A wall that would not be broken by taunts, lies, threats. And prejudice.

"'By transgression an evil man is ensnared,'" Sam said, "'but the righteous sings and rejoices.'"

"'Scorners set a city aflame, but wise men turn away anger,'" Cheveyo quoted. Then, from one man to the next, moving down the line and speaking in loud, clear voices, they each quoted a verse from Proverbs 29. Not a one faltered, not a one doubted.

"'When the wicked increase, transgression increases; but the righteous will see their fall.'"

"'An angry man stirs up strife, and a hot-tempered man abounds in transgression.'"

"'A man's pride will bring him low, but a humble spirit will obtain honor.'"

"'The fear of man brings a snare, but he who trusts in the Lord will be exalted.'"

"'An unjust man is abominable to the righteous, and he who is upright in the way is abominable to the wicked.'"

The leader stared through Sam. "We could have done a lot more damage to you. We just wanted to warn you, but you don't listen very well, do you? Maybe we should have come after your children. Maybe that would have gotten your attention. Your God can't always protect you."

"'A fool always loses his temper, but a wise man holds it back,'" Marc said, his voice elevated. "No one ever said I was a wise man. Let's go, guys!" He led the charge.

Putting his arm across Cheveyo's chest, Sam backed off. Then he saw his father. Sam Sr. stood nearby, poised to join the fight. *No, no, no, no! Go back to the camp, Dad,* he silently willed. *Dear God, please keep Dad safe.* He gestured wildly with his arms, pointing in the direction of the camp. Relief filled him when his dad departed a few seconds later.

The fire at the gazebo had been extinguished, and lingering sparks drifted upward in the dark sky. The charred scent filled Sam's nostrils, a scent he'd never forget.

Fists were flying fast and hard between the Extant men, several of them big and burly, and the TeamWork men.

Landon handily took care of one man, sending him to the ground. "We're havin' some fun now," he called out as his fist landed in another guy's stomach, knocking him to the dirt.

"Careful, bro," Mitch hollered. "Don't get full of bravado and be caught unaware."

"Got it!" Landon turned around and took a punch to the gut. Dean intervened and clipped the jaw of Landon's attacker. Eliot handily and expertly dispensed of two of the men singlehandedly, at the same time. Josh and Marc were holding their own. Kevin had another man in a chokehold, and stood off to one side. Sam winced as one of the men slammed into Josh's shoulder. That had to hurt.

If left on his own, Eliot could handle every one of these men. Something caught Sam's eye—a flash of silver in the hand of a man headed straight for Mitch. At the same time, one of Cheveyo's men raised his pistol in the air and fired. At the sound, most of the men took off running.

"Mitch, left shoulder!" Sam rushed forward and shoved Mitch

out of the man's path. With a glint in his eye, the man raised the knife in his hand as he moved closer.

"Oh no, you don't," Marc shouted from behind him, pushing Sam to the side with such force that he stumbled forward and fell to his knees on the ground. Not to be deterred, the man whirled around in a circle, keeping the other men at bay by slashing through the air with the knife.

As if in slow motion, the attacker headed toward him again, focused on him. Seemed *he* was the man's sole target. Rising to his feet, facing his attacker, Sam felt a hand on his shoulder as Eliot moved in front of him, directly into the man's path—a human shield, and his protector. With a loud cry, the man plunged the knife into Eliot's chest. Backing away, his eyes widened, and then he took off at a fast run.

Staggering forward, Eliot glanced down at his chest before slumping to the ground.

"Eliot," Sam rasped, his eyes widening in horror.

Josh reached his side first, dropping to the ground. "Mitch, what do we do?"

"Leave the knife in his chest!" Mitch said. "The knife will actually help stem the blood flow. Talk to him. Keep him awake and calm. Someone call 9-1-1 now!"

"Got it!" Pulling out his phone, Landon started to pace. "Pastor Chevy, I need the physical church address." Cheveyo hurried over to join him.

"Eliot," Sam said, kneeling by Eliot's head with Marc and Josh on either side of him. "Hang in there, buddy. We're calling for help now." One of the One Nation men handed Sam a jacket and Mitch told him to put it beneath Eliot's head.

"Leave...leave the knife where it is," Eliot said, his breathing somewhat labored. "Needs to be...stabilized."

Mitch tugged down the suspenders of his costume and ripped the shirt from his chest, bunching it around the knife in Eliot's chest. "Get 'em off, guys. Put them around the knife."

Landon and Marc followed suit, as did Kevin. Kneeling by Eliot's feet, Kevin began to pray, and Dean joined him, as they all laid their hands on Eliot.

Mitch spoke to Sam in low tones. "In the interest of time, we can drive Eliot to the hospital." In the far-off distance, they heard the sounds of a siren. "Thank the Lord," he said. "He's showing signs of going into shock. We need to get him to the hospital and this is the fastest way."

Sam grew alarmed by the coolness and clamminess of his skin. Leaning closer, he noted Eliot's uneven and somewhat labored breathing.

"Mitch, what's happening?"

"He's going into shock from the internal bleeding. The blood might be building up around his lung, putting pressure on it, making it collapse. If air enters the pleural cavity, that could also make it collapse." Sam watched as Mitch applied pressure around the wound site.

Within minutes, the ambulance arrived. Working quickly, the EMTs assessed the situation and Eliot was lifted onto a stretcher and into the ambulance. "I'll go with him," Sam said to Josh and Marc. "Tell Lexa. And pray."

After he climbed into the back of the ambulance, Sam clasped Eliot's hand, being careful not to squeeze too hard. "God be with you, Stephen Polaris."

Bowing his head, Sam prayed. Sometimes it was the only thing he had. Always, it was the best thing.

Chapter 44

~~♥~~

An hour later, Josh walked over to Sam in the hospital emergency waiting room and put a hand on his shoulder. "Here." He put another cup of coffee in his hands. "Drink something."

"All this coffee is dehydrating me," Sam said quietly. "I should drink water."

"I'll get it. Be right back," Mitch told him. He'd been monitoring the situation and periodically talked with any of the medical personnel he could find in the area.

"How's the shoulder?" Sam asked. "You took a pretty hard blow."

Josh rotated it a bit. "Just sore. Don't think anything's dislocated."

Sam shook his head. "This night will do nothing for my reputation as a TeamWork director."

"Nonsense," Josh said. "No one could predict something like that happening."

"Does Marta know?"

"She does. You know Marta. She's calm, but I can tell she's frightened." Josh rubbed a hand over his brow and sat down across from him. "Lexa's bringing Marta over here along with a change of clothes for you, Mr. Presley. They should be here within the hour." He chuckled when Sam smirked. "I heard you talking with the nurse. Stephen Polaris?"

Sam nodded. "Yep. Trust me, it's necessary, Josh." Taking a sip of the coffee, he winced from the bitterness.

"I know you well, my friend. You wouldn't go along with something that's unethical, illegal, or immoral." Josh shook his head. "Have to tell you, though. It makes me wonder even more about our man Eliot. Do you know if Marta's been privy to his 'other life,' for lack of knowing what else to call it?"

Sam nodded slowly. "Yes. Eliot told her when they were at the

Balloon Fiesta. Telling someone in a hot air balloon is one of the most secure places, I should think."

"Unless she decided to deck him and sent him over the edge. Glad that didn't happen. Sorry, Sam. I'm feeling a little punchy, being the middle of the night and all."

Sam stretched out his legs and blew out a breath. "First thing I want to do when I get back to Houston is sleep for a day non-stop. I know it won't happen, but it's what my body's craving right about now. As far as Marta, I don't think she was all that surprised to hear about Eliot's…work." Sam glanced over at Josh. "She's not going anywhere. The Lord knows, as always, and she's the right woman for him."

Leaning back against the chair, Josh crossed his arms. "After this, do you think he might retire?"

"That's a good possibility, but not because of this incident. He's been wounded several times in the past, but he's never had anyone else to consider until now. He told me he's booked with assignments here and there until sometime in the spring."

"Then he can retire."

"Let's hope so," Sam said. "He's going to have to start turning down assignments or else quit cold turkey. Don't mind saying I'd like to see that happen. I've put in extra prayer time for that guy since he's been a member of my TeamWork crew."

Josh nodded, and a slight frown creased his forehead. "Like you did for me a few years ago, I'm sure."

"Yes, but for different reasons."

"We meet again, Mr. Lewis."

Sam rose to his feet and held out his hand. "Hello, Dr. Robinson."

"I'm glad to see you've recovered well from your spider bite." Dr. Robinson shook his hand, and then did the same when Sam introduced him to Josh. "Now I know my nurses weren't drinking or smoking anything funny on the job, as I'd suspected when they told me Elvis was in my ER waiting room. You have certainly livened up their evening."

"How is my friend doing?"

Mitch returned and greeted the doctor before handing water bottles to Josh and Sam.

"You can be grateful your friend Mr. Polaris is in such great physical shape. The knife was a five-inch, fixed, straight knife used mostly for hunting, and the wound measured 2.5 centimeters. The knife nicked an artery, and he suffered a Class II Hemorrhage, with a 25% to 30% blood volume loss."

"Will he need a blood transfusion?" Josh asked.

"No. A body can lose up to 1.5 liters of blood before a transfusion would be needed. A strong, healthy young man like Mr. Polaris should be able to naturally replenish his blood count quickly. We're giving him IV fluids now. He had bleeding around the lungs, called a hemothorax. The thoracic surgeon on duty performed a chest tube thoracostomy. You've probably heard it referred to as a chest tube, and it's a hollow plastic tube that's inserted between the ribs and into the chest to drain fluid or air from around the lungs. The tube will remain in his chest until all or most of the air or fluid has drained out, usually a few days."

The doctor turned to go. "I'll check on him again later. Obviously, he won't be able to do any more physical labor for the rest of your time here in Albuquerque."

"Not a problem," Sam assured the doctor. "Thank you, Dr. Robinson."

A slight grin upturned the corners of the physician's mouth. "As wonderful as your group is, Mr. Lewis, I hope I won't be seeing any more of your TeamWork crew here in the hospital."

Sam nodded. "I'll do my best to make sure that doesn't happen."

Chapter 45
Day 10, Wednesday
~~♥~~

Dawn peeked through the drawn blinds in Eliot's hospital room. "Am I dead?" His gaze settled on Sam dozing in a nearby chair. "Guess not." His mentor looked ragged, but at least he'd changed out of the Elvis costume. Laughing a little, Eliot groaned with the effort.

Sam startled and lifted out of the chair. "I heard that. You're going to be around a long time, buddy." He put his hand on Eliot's arm and gave him a light squeeze. "How do you feel?"

"Like someone put a knife in my chest." He lifted the sheet and looked down at the hospital gown covering his chest. "Good riddance to that thing. How long was it, anyway?"

"I think Dr. Robinson said it was five inches."

Eliot whistled under his breath. "Not bad. I see I've got a tube. How long will I be wearing this fashion statement?"

Sam chuckled. "A few days. The main thing is that you're going to be fine, my friend. I'm not sure how to thank you for taking that knife for me. I owe you a debt of gratitude. Lexa, my mom and Dad, my kids, and I all thank you. I realize that guy was headed straight for me."

"Yeah, well, as I recall, Marc jumped in the way first."

"Then you pushed Marc out of the way. I'm a grateful man to have such loyal friends. Not many would take a knife and put his life in danger, even for a brother. Speaking of friends, it seems you have some friends in high places."

Eliot leaned his head back on the pillow. "What do you mean?"

"Seems the members of the Extant group were rounded up this morning by some guys who swooped in and hauled them into Pastor Chevy's precinct and then disappeared." Sam's eyes met his. "Now, the lot of them are sitting in the county jail and confessing all, from what I hear. We need to discuss the legal ramifications with Josh and any action we want to take. But, from what Pastor Chevy told me, the men are going to plead guilty. He's already given them Bibles and sent the jail chaplain in to see them."

"Nothing like beating them over the head with it. Don't make me laugh, buddy." Grimacing, Eliot shifted in the bed.

"Eliot, I'm thankful to you. More than you know."

He grunted. "You're getting sappy on me again, Sam."

Sam tapped the bed rail with one hand. "In that case, there's a young lady waiting outside to see you. Marta was here through most of the night. She just returned a few minutes ago with Lexa. I'll say good-bye for now and give you two some privacy."

"Thanks, Sam."

He could hear Marta talking in the corridor outside his room. The sound of her voice made his heart jump. A moment later, she stood by the side of his bed. "Eliot Marchand, if you weren't a wounded warrior, I'd punch you." Her eyes filled with tears and she smoothed hair away from his forehead.

"I'm sorry you're not seeing me at my best. And yeah, no punching the wounded dude, please."

"Eliot, I don't know what I would have done if I'd lost you." Tears streamed down her cheeks as Marta gingerly sat on the edge of his hospital bed.

"You don't need to worry about it. I'm still here."

She laughed and sniffled. "You know what I mean. I thought we'd have a quiet two weeks, finish getting a church building ready, not all the crazy stuff that's happened."

"We had some fun times in the midst of everything," he said. "The Balloon Fiesta was an awesome day. Do me a big favor and grab the controller. I want to see you when I kiss you. Although"— Eliot put his hand over his mouth and breathed into it—"I seriously need to brush my teeth. We're talking breath that's more gross than caffeine here."

"Like I care." After helping him adjust the bed, Marta grabbed his face between her hands and kissed him. Lingeringly. Longingly. Lovingly. Her kiss was full of passion and the promise of dreams fulfilled. "I'd tell you not to scare me like that again but a lot of good it would do me."

"About that."

Her eyes widened. "Go on."

"I have some commitments I need to keep, but maybe it's time to think about hanging up the James Bond gadgets and gizmos and settling down in one place."

"Can you keep the Hummer?"

He grinned. "I can keep the Hummer."

"And could you give up the woman in every port?"

"Honey, you *are* my port."

She sputtered and laughed, wiping away tears at the same time. "I'm glad you told me who you are, Eliot. *Really* are." She glanced around the room. "I mean Stephen. Stephen Polaris," she said.

"There's more."

"What do you mean?" She gripped the bed rail. "Should I sit down again for this one?"

"I don't think it's necessary. Let's just say my family's not just any family in France."

"What are you, like a mob family? Serial killers? Tightrope walkers? Reality TV stars?"

"Why would you assume something like that?" He laughed and then groaned. "It's not good to make me laugh right now."

"Why didn't you tell me this before?"

"I wasn't sure you'd want to have it all loaded on you at once. I'll admit…it's a lot."

"Tell me. I'm ready." She squared her shoulders and looked so beautiful that all he wanted to do was hold and kiss her for the rest of the day. The rest of his *life*. Since he was in a hospital bed, that wasn't the best idea.

"I'm a direct descendant of Henri II, Prince de Condé, Premier Prince du Sang, born in 1588 and died in 1646. House of Bourbon-Condé and Bourbon-Conti, part of the Monarchy in France. Honestly, in today's society, it's nothing more than a title, and in some circles, our family lineage is considered more or less the black sheep, but there are some privileges and a rarely used title that come with it. Your history lesson for today is this: the son of the last Condé, the duc d'Enghien, was kidnapped at night in German territory by a French platoon, judged in Paris, and executed the same night in Vincennes by order of Napoléon Bonaparte."

"The name Napoléon rings a vague bell," she teased. "So, what does all this mean?"

"It means that I get invited to some pretty swanky parties in

France, but there are some who target me because they seem to think I'm important to my home country in the grand scheme of things."

Shaking her head, Marta tucked a pretty blonde curl behind one ear. He needed to kiss her again. "Are you saying you're not important? Or that you are?"

"I'm saying I only want to be important to the most beautiful woman I've ever known. Marry me, Marta. No one else fills me with joy and hope like you do."

She looked at him as if in a daze. "I also drive you crazy sometimes. And irritate you, and infuriate you, and maybe even anger you—"

He put two fingers over her lips, quieting her. "I'll make you happy. We'll have a nice home, a pretty sweet tank to drive, Barney and maybe Brute, lots of kids and…" Beckoning her close, he whispered in her ear. As he expected, her cheeks immediately flushed a pretty pink.

She stared at him. "You really mean it, don't you? You're saying we should get married?"

"I think I just did."

Putting one hand on his forehead, she frowned. "Are you delirious? What is it about you TeamWork guys getting bit by a spider or being stabbed that makes you start flirting, spouting show tunes, and making proposals of marriage?"

"I haven't sung any show tunes. Was 'Up, Up and Away' in a movie?" Eliot refused to laugh. It'd hurt too much. "I love you, and I want to marry you, Marta Holcomb. If you'll have me."

"You're completely serious, aren't you?"

"Last time I checked. I'm still alive, still breathing, but you're right. I'm pretty certain I stink right now, and this isn't the best place for a proposal. Then there's—"

Marta silenced him with a deep kiss that had him thinking he'd died and gone to Heaven. "In case you didn't get my point, that's a yes. I'll marry you, Eliot. You could stand to brush your teeth, but you're still the most handsome man I've ever known. And brave. And selfless. And I know you can be romantic when you want. When are you thinking? Shouldn't we go back to Houston and date a little?"

"Why?" He smiled at her startled expression. "I know everything I'd ever need to know about you. Enough to know I want to spend every day I can with you for the rest of my life. I don't need to do the dance, Marta. I'm ready. I don't know how to be a boyfriend, but I want to be your husband."

She inhaled a quick breath as she apparently grasped his meaning. "Here? Are you saying you want Sam to marry us here in Albuquerque?"

His smile grew wider. "I think I just did. As I recall, you're the one who said we're not—"

"Like most people. I know." She ran a hand over her curls and he could almost see the wheels in her mind already turning. "We're like an old married couple already, finishing our sentences. Oh, my. We need to ask Sam."

"I'm not eavesdropping, but I heard," Sam called from the hallway.

Eliot glanced up to find Sam lounging against the doorframe.

"I repeat, do you two need an ordained man to marry you?"

Smiling at Sam, they both said, "I do."

Chapter 46
Day 12, Friday
~~♥~~

Her father was gone.

Marta knew it as soon as she looked in Eliot's eyes and glimpsed the sadness. She imagined it was much like hearing your loved one had died after they'd battled cancer for years. Although it was expected, and everyone knew it was coming, when it happens, you're still in shock. Then the grieving can begin. Or end.

They gathered in Pastor Chevy's office at the One Nation Church, chairs arranged in a circle. Marta knew she'd either remember every detail of this meeting or else she'd remember very little except the basic facts. The human mind could be strange like that. Likewise the human heart.

Her mother, Brenda, sat in the chair beside her, holding her hand. Thom and Paine sat opposite them. Eliot sat in a wing chair in the middle of the group. He was still sore from his injury, and it would take time to heal. But he was here, and he was otherwise healthy and strong, and that's all that mattered.

Sam and Pastor Chevy told them to take as much time as they needed, but that they were available for the family, if needed. If that wasn't an indicator of the news to come, nothing was.

How strange that her family had met her fiancé only hours before. They'd flown into Albuquerque from Louisville earlier that morning. Marta thought her brothers would never stop going on about the Hummer. After arriving at the hospital, she'd introduced them to Eliot as he was released into her care. Her mother was quiet and, although she sensed no disapproval, Marta understood she had questions. It didn't help that the female nurses all watched Eliot leave with dreamy-eyed expressions and kept calling him "Stephen" or "Mr. Polaris." Yes, she'd need to do some explaining and hope her family would know she wasn't going out of her mind.

She was in love.

And Eliot was the man of God's choosing for her.

Eliot started by giving them the basic facts. They'd all asked him not to sugarcoat the truth, but to give it to them straight. Although Marta could tell he was conflicted in doing that, he did so with an air of sad resignation. Her father, Christopher Michael Holcomb, had died within days of leaving their home in Louisville when she'd been eight years old. He'd been on a business trip for his pharmaceutical firm, but instead of reaching his intended destination of San Francisco, his flight had been rerouted to Sacramento because of inclement weather.

"From what we can tell, he went to dinner in a restaurant in a good area but then he was attacked and murdered by a group of thugs who stole his wallet," Eliot told them. "They dumped his body in a shallow grave on the outskirts of town, but when the remains were discovered several years later, there were no teeth to pull dental records and positively identify him."

Swallowing hard, Marta squeezed her mom's hand. This was the closure they'd needed.

"For years, his case was considered cold in California." The way Eliot's broad shoulders slumped, Marta could see how difficult this news was to deliver. She wouldn't ask him until much later how he was able to find him. He might not even be able to divulge that information.

"Thank you, Eliot," Brenda said. She'd wiped her eyes a few times during the report, and so had Marta. "It's good to finally know the truth."

Her brothers hadn't moved, had barely twitched or shifted in their chairs. Stunned, they said nothing, their expressions devoid of emotion.

"If you'd like, I'll arrange to have him flown to Louisville for a proper burial," Eliot said. "Just let me know what you'd like."

"I think that would be good."

"Mom, after hearing this news, maybe it's best that Eliot and I not get married tomorrow." Marta ignored the look in Eliot's eye at that statement.

"Your father would want you to follow through with your plans. Eliot's brought us closure, and I thank the Lord he was able to give that to us." Wiping her eyes and tucking her tissue in her handbag, Brenda sat up straighter and gave them a smile. Forced, but it was there. "This is a time to celebrate life, not mourn the dead. Your father was a Christian man," she said, including all three of her children in her glance. "He would not want us to be sad, but to be happy that he's been with the Lord for many years now. It sounds as though his death was quick, and for that, I suppose we can be thankful."

"My deepest sympathies to all of you," Eliot said.

"Eliot, are you parents coming to the wedding?" Brenda said. "I realize France is a long way off."

"No, they can't come at such short notice, but I'm hoping Marta would like to fly with me to France next week to meet them."

Marta's jaw gaped. "Next week? Fly to France? Meet your parents?"

Her reaction brought much-needed smiles to her brothers' faces.

"I'd like to bring Sam and Pastor Chevy in for a time of prayer," Eliot told them. "For the news you've learned today and for our marriage tomorrow morning." Rising to his feet, Eliot walked across to where Marta sat and held out his hand.

Placing her hand in his, Marta allowed him to pull her to her feet.

After sweetly kissing her, he faced her family. "I promise you that I'll watch over Marta all the days of my life. I love her dearly, and I want nothing more than to make her happy. I realize this marriage has come as a shock to you." He turned and gave her a wink. "It has to us, too, but Marta and I have known each other for a few years now. We just needed time to be together one-on-one, and this mission to Albuquerque with TeamWork has given us that time. I know I've grown as a man, as a Christian, and as a friend to her, and I trust she feels the same way."

"I do," Marta said. "Well, not as a man, but...all the rest."

"As long as you say 'I do' tomorrow when Sam asks the question," Thom said. She loved hearing that from her oldest brother. They liked Eliot, and she felt sure they'd get along well.

"I think I'll remember," Marta murmured. "Now, let's invite Sam and Pastor Chevy to come join us, and then Mom and I have some shopping to do."

~~♥~~

Felipe worked with Angelina in the sanctuary of the One Nation Church later that afternoon. Winnie, Lexa, and the other ladies were all running around like chickens trying to get ready for Marta and Eliot's wedding, the first wedding in this church. Sam and Pastor Chevy would be co-officiating.

She and Felipe had been given the job of counting communion cups since the couple wanted their guests to take communion with them. That seemed like a neat thing to do at a wedding. The thought struck her that Felipe would also be taking communion for the first time. That made her smile. A lot of firsts on this trip.

"Angel, I hope you'll want to see me again when we get back to San Antonio."

She stopped counting cups. "I'm not allowed to date yet, if that's what you're talking about."

"Well, how about we get Dean and your mom to take us places? They can go smooch or whatever and then we can be together. To smooch…or whatever."

"Don't go getting any big ideas."

"Oh, I've got all kinds of ideas for you and me, Angel."

"I'm sure you do."

Felipe took one step closer. "Would you like that, Angel? Spending time with me? I hope you're not tired of me."

She shook her head, confused. "Why would I be tired of you?"

"Just checking. I plan on being around a long time, like it or not, so you might as well get used to me."

"You could try coming with me to my church youth group. I think you'd like the kids and the leaders, Felipe. They're nice and I'm sure they'd love you."

"Yeah? Love? That's a pretty strong word."

When he leaned close, she put one hand on his chest, keeping him at bay. "Someone's feeling romantic or whatever because of all this wedding hoopla. Here," she said, handing him a stack of cups. "Finish counting this stack."

He did as she asked and, when they were finished, they headed in the direction of the church nursery. They'd volunteered to help watch the kids so the ladies could go to into town and pick up whatever supplies were needed. Marta was out with her mom shopping for a wedding dress and Eliot had gone with some of the men to pick out a tux—to buy one, he'd said, and not rent one. She'd caught wind of a honeymoon in Paris, France. She couldn't even imagine. What exciting lives her TeamWork friends led.

Dropping into a chair, Felipe played peekaboo with Emily. Then he played cowboys and Indians—make that Native Americans or whatever—with Joe and Luke. Joe was so cute with his little swagger. Was that something else they taught little boys to do, especially in Texas? She read a story to Leah and Hannah, and then played Candy Land with Gracie and Chloe. Those two asked her all kinds of questions about Marta and Eliot getting married.

"I'm not going to get married for a long time," Chloe announced. "I want to marry a man like my daddy. Mommy says a man like that will be hard to find."

"I want to get married, but not until I'm older." Gracie darted a glance at Joe as she said it, and Angelina bit her lower lip not to laugh.

"What's on your mind?" Felipe worked beside her to help pick up the toys scattered about the room after Amy and Beck took the kids back to the camp. They'd been pretty good about cleaning up, but they'd still left a few things sitting around. Plus, Angelina could tell that Felipe wanted to spend as much time with her as he could before they left the camp tomorrow. She understood the feeling and felt the same way.

"I'm thinking about having to go pack up everything. Not that there's much to pack," she said. "A big group is going into Albuquerque for dinner tonight. Are you going?"

"I hadn't thought much about it." He put a game on the shelf and turned to look at her, their gazes locking.

"Want to put some sandwiches together and go have a picnic under our tree?" she said. "You could bring your notebook. I've made some sketches. We could talk about your books."

A broad grin spread across his handsome face, warming her heart. "That sounds really good, Angel."

"Felipe," she said as they walked side-by-side on the path back to the camp, "You know that note you gave to me with the Christian romance novel? I think you could be my hero one day. I'm not promising anything, but I'm saying it's possible."

Tugging on her hand, Felipe pulled her close, and kissed her cheek.

"What was that for?" She moved one hand to her cheek.

"It's my promise to you, Angel. I plan on being in your life for a long time."

"Whoa! Hold up there." Lexa laughed as Sam reached for her and pulled her into his arms. "You've been going 100 miles an hour. I need a kiss from my wife."

"This is the best way to end the TeamWork mission that I can imagine, Sam." She slipped her hands around his neck. With a playful grin, she tugged off the Stetson and perched it on her head. "Who could have guessed? Not me, that's for sure." Seeing the look in his eye, she tugged him into a Sunday School room and gave him the kind of kiss he wouldn't soon forget. Neither would she.

Goodness, the man's kisses only got better with age. She smoothed a hand over her hair and tried to focus. "Did you see the new gazebo? Kevin and the guys are almost done, and it'll be beautiful for Eliot and Marta's wedding photos." Her eyes widened. "Did you check the weather forecast?"

"There's a chance for light showers, but then the sun will come out, and it will be gorgeous. No worries. Cheveyo and I have the service all planned out—he'll do the welcome, opening, and prayer, and I'll handle the charge and the vows. Then together we'll announce them as husband and wife."

"I love how Marta and Eliot want the entire TeamWork crew to stand up with them," she said. "We'll fill the entire front of the sanctuary. Let's make sure to get lots of photos."

Sam laughed. "I'm sure we will. Lexa, everyone is leaving tomorrow, but I'd like to stay an extra day so I can attend the service here in the One Nation Church. You don't have any pressing catering events for the next few days, do you?"

"Nothing that can't be handled without me. I think that's a terrific idea. The camp will be quiet with everyone else gone, but I think I might enjoy the peace."

He offered his hand. "Ready to head back to the camp?"

"Yes." They walked out of the church and started down the path. "I'm glad we're going out to dinner tonight, and it's so nice of Lila and the ladies to provide the refreshments tomorrow. Wait a minute! Have the guys decorated the Hummer yet? I've got lots of tin cans, and we have some string in the dining hall."

"Everything's under control, beautiful girl." He wrapped his hand around hers. "On to the next adventure the Lord has planned for us."

She put her hand in his. "Always."

Dean smiled at his group of friends sitting around the massive dinner table at the Albuquerque restaurant. The men toasted Eliot and then the women took turns teasing Marta. He couldn't believe the turn of events, but he also couldn't be happier for his friends. They were ready for marriage.

Dean stole a glance at Sheila, sitting to his right. *He* was ready, but she wasn't. Giving him a small smile, she slipped her hand in his.

He leaned close, for her ears only. "I think you know I want to see you once we get back home to San Antonio. I want to take you on dates and treat you right, like you deserve. Wine you and dine you. Buy you pretty things and kiss you silly. Show you my stores and learn how to cook something other than chicken enchilada casserole. Please tell me you'd like that."

She gave him the smile he'd learned was reserved only for him. "I-I h-h-have o-one q-q-question," she said.

"What's that?"

"C-c-can I-I-I m-m-meet M-M-Mama R-R-Rose?"

Giving her a quick kiss, Dean slipped his arm around her shoulders. "That I can do."

Chapter 47
Day 13, Saturday
~~ ♥ ~~

Eliot couldn't believe he was marrying the most beautiful woman in the world. He was a groom, waiting for his bride. In a few short minutes, he would be a husband, and Marta his wife.

And there she was, coming down the aisle. Smiling into his heart, forever in his soul.

He wore his new black tux, and it'd been worth it to see the light in Marta's eyes when she'd started down the aisle with her brothers on either side of her.

She looked almost ethereal in her long gown—off-the-shoulder the way he'd secretly hoped it would be—with little sparkly things that caught the light as she moved. Gayle had made a simple bouquet for her with a variety of sunny yellow flowers since they were Marta's favorite. He'd already shelved away that information for future use, as well as everything else she'd told him.

As calm and regal as a princess, she walked toward him—so confident, so calm, so sure of him and of their future together. He'd give her a good life, and together they'd work to give God the glory for bringing them together in the most marvelous of ways—in *His* time, not theirs. He'd spent a lot of time in prayer last night, thanking the Lord for this mission. In spite of its frustrations, in spite of getting stabbed—an odd thought, to be sure—and all the challenges they'd faced, they'd come away stronger. TeamWork at its best.

As he and Marta stood at the front of the church with their friends, his mind wandered to the future, both near and distant. He'd scheduled a meeting with his superiors in Washington and would be tendering his resignation as soon as he finished his current assignments. He was important to them, but Marta was more important. He loved his job, but he loved her more. Life was about setting priorities and making the decisions that were the best for his ultimate, long-term goals.

Getting a nice house in the suburbs and settling down with his bride was uppermost in his mind. Living a normal life. A safe life, as much as that was possible. Marta had said they weren't like other people. That was true enough, but then again, he yearned for normal. He'd tasted life and what it had to offer. And discovered the best place to be was where he found the deepest contentment his soul had ever known—in Marta's heart, from now and until he drew his last breath.

He had enough savings to take his time in starting his agency, but he'd begin to lay the foundation toward it becoming a reality. He looked forward to the possibilities. If Marta became a weekend weather anchor, he'd support her. If she continued working with Doyle-Clarke Catering, he'd chow down on her blueberry muffins and tell her they were the best he'd ever eaten, even if they were horrible. He'd mow the yard, take out the trash, leave his socks on the floor, and watch weekend sports. She'd try to learn to cook, and he'd bring home takeout whenever needed. He'd push Barney off the bed at night, and get a puppy companion for Barney and name him Brute.

They'd love well, love often, and laugh always. Have 2.5 children, maybe more, and buy them one of those backyard swing sets with a fort. They'd have a little boy with dark hair and rough and tumble ways. Then a little girl with blonde curls, sass, and a smile to melt her daddy's heart. They'd teach them to swim, to read, to play nicely with their friends, and most importantly, to love Jesus with all their heart and soul.

Their wedding ceremony was poignant, based on all the ladies soaking their tissues. Sam honored his request by reading from his tattered Bible. That old Bible, practically falling apart at the seams. Sam had to be careful that the pages didn't fall out. But Sam understood his reasons for wanting that Bible included in the ceremony. He loved how the TeamWork crew cheered when Sam and Pastor Chevy jointly announced them as husband and wife.

"Eliot, look! Isn't it incredible?" Stepping outside the church, Marta pulled him by the hand and pointed to the sky. Fresh rain coated the sidewalk. Go figure. It barely rained in Albuquerque and yet it had rained during their ceremony. Now the clouds had given way to the sunshine.

Following her gaze, he spied the most glorious rainbow in a high arc directly above the church. "It is." Wrapping his arms around her from behind, Eliot pulled her close. "Did you know the colors of the rainbow are always in the same order?"

"No," she said. "Starting from the outside, top arc, there's red, then orange, then yellow closer to the center."

"Then green, blue, indigo and last, but definitely not least," he said, turning her around in his arms, "violet. The last color in the rainbow, always at the inside, closest to the earth, closest to the *heart*, is violet. The same exact color I see in your eyes. I love you, Marta."

"Everything according to His purpose," she murmured, raising her chin and inviting his kiss in the way he adored. "I love you, too, Eliot." This kiss, their second as husband and wife, touched him to his core. Full of simmering passion, yet reverent with a gentleness that promised sweet blessings to come.

Their guests formed a receiving line and it seemed like a thousand photos, if not more, were snapped. Kevin and a group of men from both TeamWork and the One Nation Church had finished building the new gazebo, and although the fresh white paint had barely dried, it made another great backdrop for more wedding photos. They took fun ones, silly ones, and the ones Marta would show all her friends—the romantic ones. He didn't care. Whatever she wanted.

Preparing to depart, Eliot glanced at their gathered guests, thankful for all of them, and especially his TeamWork friends. The one he sought in particular shouldn't be difficult to spot. And there he was, with Lexa beside him. As if sensing his gaze, Sam looked his way. With a deep smile, he tipped his black Stetson.

With the woman he loved at his side, Eliot knew he was the most blessed man in the world.

Amen, Lord.

THE END

About the Author
~~♥~~

In addition to *Enchantment*, JoAnn Durgin is the author of the prior adventures in The Lewis Legacy Series: *Awakening, Second Time Around, Twin Hearts, Daydreams,* and *Moonbeams,* as well as *Prelude,* the prequel to The Lewis Legacy Series. Her standalone novels include *Catching Serenity* and *Heart's Design,* as well as novellas and short novels including *Perchance to Dream, Love So Amazing* (The Wondrous Love Series, Book 1), *Echoes of Edinburgh,* and the popular Starlight Christmas Series: *Meet Me Under the Mistletoe, Starlight, Star Bright, Sleigh Ride Together with You,* and *Starlight in Her Eyes.*

A former estate administration paralegal, JoAnn now writes full-time and lives with her husband, Jim, their three children, and new grandbaby Amelia Grace, in her native southern Indiana.

JoAnn loves to hear from her readers! Please feel free to contact her:

WEBSITE:
www.joanndurgin.com

FACEBOOK:
www.facebook.com/authorjoanndurgin

Awakening
The Lewis Legacy Series, Book 1

A God-fearing man. A God-seeking woman. For Sam Lewis and Lexa Clarke, it proves a combustible combination.

Lexa Clarke signs up for a TeamWork Missions summer assignment expecting adventure in a far-off, exotic country. Instead, she's sent to sweltering San Antonio to help rebuild homes destroyed by sudden flooding. She survives the four-hour bus trip from Houston, dust in the lungs, a flat tire, a tool-throwing incident and a spitting goat—not to mention an inquisition from a distractingly handsome cowboy—all before reaching the work camp.

TeamWork director Sam Lewis isn't sure what to think of his newest volunteer. She's feisty, witty, and incredibly pretty, but looks more prepared to board a cruise ship than build houses. Burned by a past betrayal, he's got a job to do, a reputation to uphold. Sam can't afford to be distracted by a woman who attracts animals, defies his rules, finds trouble at every turn and questions God's purpose. But when she tumbles from the top beam of one of the houses into his arms, Sam suspects his life will never be the same. During their weeks together in the TeamWork camp, Sam and Lexa learn the power of forgiveness and healing.

Enduring a chain of incidents which challenge their faith, trust and growing relationship, they look to the Lord for guidance as together they discover a love greater than either could ever imagine. At the end of the eight-week work camp, Sam is committed to a year-long, dangerous overseas mission for TeamWork. Can Lexa trust the Lord enough to let him go? Will Sam safely return and keep his promise to meet her at the Alamo? You'll keep turning the pages of this sweeping romantic adventure.

With great characters, plenty of humor, enough emotion to make you shed a tear or two, and an ending that'll have you cheering, Awakening will leave you breathless. Hold on tight. The adventures of Lewis and Clarke have only just begun!

Second Time Around
The Lewis Legacy Series, Book 2

Marc Thompson is on top of the world—a newlywed with a beautiful wife, the owner of a thriving Boston sports advertising agency, and a century-old home they're renovating in the suburbs. Then the unthinkable happens. Two months after the wedding, Marc sits in a hospital emergency waiting room after Natalie suffers a horrible fall. One shock follows another. Not only does his wife remember nothing of their life together, but now he has a personal timeline to reconnect with her—seven months.

Marc's gold wedding band mocks him, a glaring reminder of a promise broken by a rotting basement stair and his own negligence. His renowned psychologist advises him to court his wife again—a daunting task the first time around. Then Marc's pastor suggests he call Sam and Lexa Lewis of TeamWork Missions, a ministry dear to Natalie's heart. Determined to help her reclaim her life, the young groom makes great strides until a ghost from the past surfaces, opening fresh wounds and threatening to destroy it all.

With Natalie's trust shattered and Marc's faith wavering, they head to Milestone Ranch outside Helena, Montana, with TeamWork for a two-week work camp. But instead of romancing his wife in the freezing November temperatures with warm fires and shared sweet moments, he's out in the cold and back at square one. Even if Natalie recovers her lost memories, will she forgive him? If not, can Marc come to terms with his deepest fear—the failure of his marriage?

You'll root for Marc and Natalie as they fight against the odds and discover that surrendering all at the throne of grace doesn't mean failure. It's simply called faith. And it might be the only way to finding their way back to one another…the second time around.

Twin Hearts
The Lewis Legacy Series, Book 3

Joshua Grant is a man redeemed. He's worked hard to put the past behind him. A mergers and acquisitions attorney in a prestigious Baton Rouge law firm, he pours his energies into his career, hurricane relief efforts, and numerous civic and charitable causes. A near-fatal event in the life of a fellow TeamWork Missions volunteer prompts him to make some apologies, starting with his friend and mentor, Sam Lewis, Domestic Missions Director for TeamWork in Houston. It's been more than four years since the fateful events in San Antonio when Sam threw him out of the missions camp, and he's still haunted by the bittersweet memory of his final meeting with another TeamWork volunteer. When he also seeks her forgiveness, Josh gets the shock of his life. Could turning his deepest sin into his greatest blessing be God's answer for his hurting heart?

Rebekah Grant, Josh's twin sister, is torn between two men. Adam, a dashing British aristocrat, offers her a world of exotic travel, socializing with royalty, fabulous couture and the life of leisure. Then there's sweet Kevin, the strong, intelligent, faithful TeamWork member. Will the shy Louisiana lumber man ever take the step of faith to move their relationship to the next level? What Kevin lacks in terms of Adam's style and panache, he more than makes up for with heart-stirring kisses and soul-searching conversation. When Rebekah suspects Adam is planning to propose a second time, she knows it's time to make her decision. Juggling both suitors is wrong for so many reasons, but what's a girl to do if she wants to marry and have children in her lifetime?

When family tragedy strikes, Josh and Rebekah learn the true meaning and value of love, loyalty and what's most important in life. Leaning on the encouragement and support from Sam and Lexa Lewis and their TeamWork friends, both twins look to the Lord for His divine guidance. It's up to them to stake their claim on love before it slips beyond their reach, which means it's also time for a road trip from Louisiana to the peace to be found in seeking and finding the sweetest desires of the heart.

Daydreams
The Lewis Legacy Series, Book 4

It's early December 2002, and Amy Jacobsen is living the dream: a job she loves with a trendy New York City magazine, a Manhattan walk-up inherited from her grandfather, and a busy social life *without* the unwanted complication of a steady boyfriend. During dinner one evening with her Wall Street financier brother, Mitch, she spies Landon Warnick at the next table. He's one of the most influential, successful and youngest magazine publishers in the country—not to mention one of New York's most eligible bachelors.

After Mitch wrangles a meeting between the two, Landon wastes little time asking her to dinner. Usually wary of smooth men and romantic entanglements, Amy questions her sanity when they share a cozy carriage ride in Central Park and she comes *this* close to kissing him. Is it the joy and wonder of the Christmas season that's put stars in her eyes or the enigmatic, intelligent, challenging and incredibly handsome man?

The following weekend, she travels to Louisiana to be a bridesmaid in a wedding and a reunion with Sam and Lexa Lewis and some of her dearest friends and fellow volunteers in TeamWork Missions. Headed down the aisle at the wedding, Amy's steps falter. Standing at the front is a groomsman who flew into town only an hour before . . . She does a double take. What's Landon Warnick doing in *her* world, with *her* friends? Perhaps more important, why does he suddenly have a Texas drawl and a crescent-shaped scar on his forehead? Sharing a romantic dance at the wedding reception, she casts aside her better judgment and kisses him. She's lost her mind, and her heart might not be far behind, it seems.

Let the adventure begin! Is the Lord showing her the "right" man for her heart or is Amy in *way* over her head?

Moonbeams
The Lewis Legacy Series, Book 5

Mitch Jacobsen's younger sister, Amy Warnick, has tried to pair him off with her fellow TeamWork Missions volunteer, Cassie, for over a year. Why can't Amy understand that the harder she pushes, the faster he'll run? Dating a woman who lives 1,600 miles away—no matter how gorgeous and compassionate—isn't on his radar.

Cassandra Thorenson wants nothing to do with a man who works with money and contributes to corporate greed. Dating a Wall Street broker—no matter how handsome and funny—is the last thing she needs.

Surely, the Almighty must have a better plan.

When these two meet during a TeamWork mini-reunion in Houston over Valentine's Day weekend, Mitch and Cassie discover they have a lot more in common than they'd ever imagined. Their plan to resist one another quickly derails and then an unexpected event sends them all reeling.

Let the sparks and the tempers fly!

Prelude
Prequel to The Lewis Legacy Series

What's a guy to do when he comes home to stay and the girl he wants can't wait to leave town?

On April 24, 1962, U.S. Air Force Captain Samuel J. Lewis returns home to small Rockbridge, Texas. Six years older, Sam is the boy who moved four houses down when Sarah Jordan was ten. A teenager who nicknamed her Tomboy and teased her like an older brother. That boy is now a handsome military man who makes her heart race, but what does she know of love or life?

After his years away, Sam finds himself drawn to Sarah. The sassy, funny girl he used to tease has grown up into a beautiful charmer with wit and intelligence who challenges him like no other woman. Sarah's frequent reminders that she's leaving Rockbridge to attend nursing school, along with her encouragement to date other girls in town, unsettle him.

During the eventful summer of 1962, their friendship grows deeper and blossoms into love. Sam knows he can't hold Sarah back from achieving her dreams. When an unexpected financial gift gives her the needed funds to enter nursing school, they face saying good-bye earlier than expected. Are Sam and Sarah destined to be together or go their separate ways?

The prequel to the popular contemporary Christian romance series, **The Lewis Legacy Series**, *Prelude* is the love story of Samuel J. Lewis and Sarah Jordan, parents to the core character of the series. *Prelude* lends insights into the Lewis family history in this heartfelt story of family, friendship, and love. A story of never letting go of our dreams, and how faith, sacrifice, and trusting our lives to the Lord's guidance will always triumph over our human fears and temptations.